The Fire in the Rock
A Novel of the Exodus

By

Charles Henderson Norman

For my wife, Lynell Moses Norman.

She believes in Him — and in me.

Thank you, Lynell.

"The Torah is true —
and some of it may even have happened."

— Rabbi William Gershon

Book One: Midyan

1

I am old now, old beyond counting. The One has taken my eyes, and my strength, and the skill of my hands, but my mind is as sharp and clear as it was when I was a girl of ten years. Why I have been allowed to live so long, I cannot say; perhaps to tell this story, for I am the only one left who can tell it. All the rest — all who were there and saw these things — all are gone now. All but me.

Some who grow old are cursed with forgetting what has gone before; but my curse is different.

I remember everything.

2

I live in a little house that my sons built for me, here at the foot of Mount Nevo. Few people live nearby, and those who do, do not disturb me. They know who I am, and they fear me.

It is said among them, I am told, that heavy curses will fall on those who trouble me; and so no one does. But it is also said that blessings will come to those who help me, so I am never in want of the things I need. On many mornings, I find food, or firewood, or fruit or clothing or even wine on the bench beside my door. My neighbors leave me gifts, but they never knock nor speak.

With my own well nearby, I had all that I needed and more, I thought. I had cared for myself for many years, and though it had grown more difficult as I grew older and lost my sight, I still managed. I expected to live in that way, alone, until the day came when I would follow Kisil up the mountain.

I was comfortable enough. But I bore a burden, and it troubled me.

In times past, pilgrims would come to gather at my feet and hear my stories — many, and often. I told them much, though I told no one everything. Even so, it warmed my heart to speak of those times, of my husband, and of what we did and saw. I felt that I was carrying on with his work, in a small way — his work of teaching and guiding and imparting his wisdom.

But the storytellers' tales of those times, passed down from generation to generation, soon diverged from my own. They became more grand and glorious, and then more grand and glorious still. As happens with such tales, the miracles and wonders in them grew with each telling — and the people began to prefer those tales to my own. Peace to those who tell them and hear them; they do no harm, I think. But they are only tales, for all that they are beloved of both the young and the old. They are very entertaining, without a doubt, but they are now very far from the truth.

The pilgrims still came, but fewer and fewer. My tales were not grand enough. People began to say that I was old, and addled, and did not truly remember —though they never said that to my face. As time went on, fewer and fewer came to listen, and finally there was a day when no one came at all. And so it remained for long years; I sat beside my little house, blind, alone and silent.

This was my burden. I knew the truth, but I bore it in silence. There was no longer anyone to tell, and no one to believe me if I had. And, too, there were some truths that no one had ever heard, nor ever would.

It troubled my nights as well as my days. In my dreams, I saw and did things again that I had seen and done long ago. I often prayed to The One to lift this weight of memory from my shoulders. At first, I meant that I wished Him to let me forget. As I grew older, I meant that I wished for Him to allow me to follow Kisil up the mountain, to let me rest.

But He sent Zev instead.

It was early on a winter morning when Zev came. The day was still cool, though it would grow warmer as the sun climbed into the sky. I was returning from my privy pit, where I had emptied the earthenware vessel that held my night soil. I was holding the pot in one hand, and with my other I was brushing the ground before me with my stick.

I knew the way, but I always used my stick. Some of my visitors had not the courage to come all the way to my door when they left their gifts, and I would often find an offering on the path — kindly meant, but unthinking. If I had not used my stick, a jug of wine or a bundle of wood left on my path could have caused me to fall, and old bones break easily.

I understood their fear. I had known it all my life. People feared my eyes when I was a girl, and they still do, even though my eyes no longer see.

As I carried the jar back to my house, I heard someone approaching. One person, alone, a man by the heaviness of his tread. For a single bright moment, my heart was filled with wonder; the sound of his walk was like the sound of my Kisil's. The scuff of his sandals, the slower, subtler ring and rasp of his staff striking the ground at every second step, and the soft liquid sound of a half-filled waterskin. I could almost see my husband's twisted smile, the smile that I so loved.

Then I scowled and shook my head at my own folly. "Who is there?" I called.

"My name is Zev," came a man's voice. A young man, by the tone of it. By his way of speaking, from a place far away.

"Mine is Tzipporah. What brings you to my house?"

He did not speak for a few heartbeats, and I could hear that he stood still. "I have traveled far to see you," he finally said, with wonder in his voice. "To see you, for myself. To see if what I heard was true. That you still live."

"I do. If that is all you came for, then we are done. Good day to you." I turned back to my path and continued on it, feeling my way with my stick.

"Wait," he said. I stopped, but did not turn back. "Are you not the widow of Moses?"

I resumed walking. "My husband's name was Kisil," I said, a bit scornfully.

"Oh." There was a deep well of disappointment in that single word.

I heard it, and relented. "They do call him Moses now. That was his Egyptian name. But his birth name was Yekusiel, and I and all who loved him — we called him Kisil." I had not stopped walking and swinging my stick before me.

I heard him move closer. "Oh," he said again, in a very different tone. Then, "May I carry that for you?"

"It stinks," I said, but I held out the vessel. "Do you not fear the Evil Eye?"

"What is the Evil Eye?" he asked as he took the pot from my hand.

He is from very far away, I thought. Then a memory came to me. I knew where he was from. I suppressed a smile.

"Here, take my arm," he offered politely.

"I need it not." I made my way back to my little house without his help. Ungracious it was, but I did not know him then.

My stick struck the threshold, and I stepped up into the one room. "Come in," I said. Then I pointed with my stick. "Cover the pot and put it beside the bed, at the head. The cover is there."

I heard him do as I told him. When he was done, I stood facing him. "Thank you. What do you want?"

His sandals shuffled on the hard wooden floor, a luxury provided by my sons. "I want to know the truth of what happened."

I waved at him in dismissal and turned toward my chair. "You have heard the stories. Go away and leave an old woman in peace."

"I do not believe them."

I sat down, and I looked up at him. Turned my face toward him, I should say, toward the sound of his words. "No?"

"No."

I found that I was beginning to like this young man. He did not speak more than was necessary, and I had known another man like that.

I pointed my stick at the other chair in my room, which was not often occupied. "Sit down and tell me why you do not believe." He sat. I snorted, and pointed again. "Zev. Put down your waterbag and your staff. Make yourself comfortable."

"How did you —"

"I am blind. I am not deaf." He laughed a little then, and I heard him get up and lean his staff in the corner, then set his waterskin and another bag beside it. When he was settled again, I said, "Tell me."

He hesitated, one heartbeat, two. Then, "How old *are* you?" he asked.

I shrugged — and heard and felt my shoulder joint make a small sound of protest. I wondered how long it had been since I last shrugged. "I cannot say. Kisil went up this mountain many years ago, long before you were born, or even your father — and I was a very old woman, even then. I am — very old. Tell me why you do not believe the storytellers' tales."

He shifted in his chair. "They are..." He hesitated. "They are impossible. Wonder tales, stories for children. Plagues, darkness, the Parting of the Sea... Such things... cannot happen...?"

I heard the question in his voice. He was asking, not telling.

I smiled, I hope gently. I had not smiled for a long time. "And if I were to tell you that those things did happen? What then, Zev?"

There was another silence. "I still would not believe. I am sorry, but I must tell the truth."

I felt my smile grow broader, and I felt myself nodding. I did like this young man.

"Those things did happen, Zev... But not in the way of the tales." I stood. "Come, help me build a fire, and we shall have food."

He did not rise. "Will you tell me?"

This young man did not know what he was asking. Still, I felt that it was right. The time had come.

I nodded, then nodded again. "Yes. Yes, I will."

He built the fire, and for that I was grateful. Of all my tasks, I hated fire-making the most.

And Zev stayed.

3

At first, Zev camped nearby, in a tent or shelter of some kind. He said it was just for a phase of the Moon or two. But I fell one day, inside my house, and Zev found me that next morning, lying helpless on the floor beside my bed.

I was very angry, and I cursed at him when first he tried to lift me. I was not accustomed to needing help, and I resented it. But Zev waited patiently for me to calm down and think sensibly, and before the sun was high I let him pick me up and place me gently on the bed, though I still grumbled. Then — I blush to say it — he touched me all over, through my clothing, to be sure I had taken no great hurt. I cursed him again, but he ignored me, and there was little I could do to stop him.

He was right to do it. I was not hurt, but if I had been, I have no doubt that I would have lied and said I was not.

I smile at that as I speak. Zev dresses me now, and bathes me, and cares for me in many ways. It is good to be clean again, and warm, and not alone.

Since that day, Zev has lived here with me. To care for me and keep me safe, he says, and I do not doubt him; but I suspect, too, that like my Kisil a lifetime before, he has nowhere else to go. He has never told me this, but he never left my side again to say farewell to anyone.

Zev has become my dearest friend, closer and more trusted than even my sons. I tell him things that I have told no one — about Kisil, about myself, and about the times that Kisil and I lived through together. And from the beginning, from the time he first heard me speak, Zev has insisted that I allow him to write this book. He told me that I must make a record of it, all of it, to open my heart at last and tell the whole of what I know. I thought little of it — until one day he told me a thing I did not know.

"You must let me write this down, Grandmother." So he calls me. "There are many who do not believe the other tales, the —" He stopped to think of a word. "The fabulous ones, the fantastic ones."

"No?"

"No. There are many like me, who cannot believe in the miracles and wonders. They should know the truth, Grandmother. They should know that even without the wonders, there is still something there to believe in — something worth believing."

I had never thought of that, but Zev was right. After all, I myself believed — and I knew the truth.

And there was another thing. There was little time. I must tell this story before I follow Kisil up the mountain, and that day will be soon. I have been saying that, and hoping for it, for a long, long time, but I feel it now more than ever.

So Zev lives with me here, in my little house at the foot of Mount Nevo, and he cares for me — and he writes as I tell him.

I will tell, soon enough, of the day my husband led the Avru out of Egypt, of the day we walked through the sea on dry land, and of the day that the people heard the Lord God Himself speak to them from the Mountain. I will tell the truth of all those things, and of how they came to be.

But I will tell, too, of my Kisil, my friend, my love, my lover, my husband and the father of my sons. I will tell what he was — and what he was not. I will tell of what we had, and of what we lost, and of what we did that changed the world. All of these things I will tell, in due time.

But first, I must tell you of my life before Kisil, and of my people, and of the land where we lived.

4

My name, Tzipporah, means "bird." I liked my name when I was young, and I still do; but I was never a gentle dove or a graceful crane. I was compared, more often, to a hawk. When I was young and my eyes bright and clear, they were a pale gray color, like the eyes of a bird of prey. My father, Yisro, liked to say that I had "falcon's eyes." Not all who saw them liked them, though.

I remember a day when I went to a village marketplace with my father. He went to that village from time to time on market days, to trade wool and hides and even dried bones for things that we needed. I was a child. I must have had five or six years then, but no more.

There were many things I had never seen before — bright fabrics and pottery, people shouting and singing the praises of their wares, rich people richly dressed, poor people barely dressed at all, musicians and dancers and so much more — and as I stared at them all, people stared at me. I wondered why. I remember seeing a ragged man with a bald head point at me with his fore and little fingers extended.

"Father, why did that man do that?" I asked. The man's eyes went wide, and he did it again. I was angry. I did not understand what the gesture meant, but I did not like the way the bald man, or the other people who were staring, were looking at me, and I scowled back at them, furious. I was so angry, tears came to my eyes.

Father gave a disgusted snort and waved the man away. "Do not frighten her, you fool," he growled. "She is only a child." Then he glared at the others who were watching. The man retreated with a backward glance, and the others turned away and went back to what they were doing. Father lifted me up in his arms and kissed me.

"That was a sign to protect against —" He paused — "against bad luck, Tzipporah. It is a silly belief of silly people."

"I am *not* b-bad luck! I am *not!"* My nose was running, my cheeks wet.

He smiled then. "Of course you are not, little bird. Come, let us sit down." He carried me to a low, broken wall which had once been part of a house. He set me down there, and then sat beside me and wiped my face.

"Have you noticed that most people's eyes are dark?" he asked. I wiped my face and nodded. I looked at his eyes, which were as black as burnt wood. "You have the eyes of your mother, Tzipporah. Your eyes are light-colored, like hers. They are not like the eyes of others. People fear things that are strange to them."

I looked around, my eyes going to those of the people around me, and I thought. I was thinking, and no longer crying. It was a trick Father would use on me often as I was growing up.

He touched my mouth. "Your voice, too, is deeper than the voices of most children, and even those of many women. They fear that, too." He pulled me toward him and hugged me, and whispered, "It is *good* to be different, little bird. Be glad you are yourself."

And before long, I was. When I was still very young, I learned how to use my eyes and my voice to my advantage — and when not to.

Father had said "bad luck," but it would not be long before I heard the words that would follow me throughout my life: the Evil Eye. I could frighten people when I chose, and that power fascinated me; I played with it as if it were a toy. But I learned, too, that there are always times when it is better not to frighten. I soon knew when to lower my eyes and speak softly.

My voice is old and raspy now, and my eyes are even paler; they are white with blindness. Even so, they still say that my eyes pierce men to their souls. That makes me laugh, just as it did when I was a girl. My eyes are only my eyes; people feel and think what they will. It has more to do with what is in their own hearts than with my eyes, I think. I am only me.

I smile as I speak, again. I remember another who spoke those words.

5

The land where we lived is called Midyan. It is a dry land, a place of rock and plain and mountain where it rains only once or twice in a year. It is bare and bleak, but even so, it has a stark beauty all its own. It is not a desolate land; people and animals live there, and there is grass, though it is sparse and dry. It is not truly a desert, though many people, and even I, often call it so.

It is a harsh land, though, and it teaches the people who live there to know the difference between what is important and what is not, between what is real and what is mirage. It teaches us to go at life directly, without illusions, and to leave wishes and dreams aside. Wishes and dreams feed no sheep and find no water.

We did not go to village markets often. We were shepherds and nomads, and we lived in tents and wandered with our flocks. Sheep crop the grass closely, so we moved our camp often. From wadi to well in summer, from well to stream in winter, we wandered.

Other people like us, who herded sheep or goats or cattle, most often wandered in groups, sometimes very large ones; but my family was different. We lived apart and alone, separate from other camps and villages — but we always stayed near the Mountain.

It had no name that I knew then, though some call it Horev today, or Shinai. It was isolated, far from the other mountains in Midyan, and for a great distance around it the land was a flat and featureless plain. The grass was more plentiful there at most times of the year, but people avoided it, even so. It was a fire-mountain, and dangerous, but there was another reason as well.

My father's name was Yisro. He was the head of our clan. Some say now that he was a great chief, a *shaykh*, but he was chief only of our family. It became a large family, later, but it was never a tribe, nor even a village.

Yisro was tall and slender, but strong. He had a scar down one side of his face, the left, and his left eye did not quite follow his right. It was from some battle he had fought long before I was born. He was ugly to the eyes of others, but he was a good and wise man, and I loved him.

We all loved him. I was the eldest of seven daughters; my father had no sons.

I was the eldest by more than five years. Perhaps that was one reason why I grew up with a profound sense of being — *alone*. Not lonely — I was close to my parents, and later to my sisters — but I was aware, from earliest childhood, that no one could ever share what was in my mind and my heart, not entirely. No one could ever know, as I knew, what I thought and felt within myself, nor could I ever truly know what lay within the mind and soul of another. We are all alone in that way, of course, but few seem as troubled by it as I was. All my life, until Kisil came, I felt as if I stood two steps back from behind my eyes, watching. Even when I was crying or laughing, I was watching — detached, silent, alone.

6

I remember another time when I went to the *sooq,* the open market, with Father to trade hides for grain and other foods. I had perhaps eight years by then, or a little more. I loved going to the villages on market days; there was so much to see and to do, not like life in our camp, where every day was much the same as the next.

As we walked among the stalls and tents, my eye fell on a group of village girls my own age or a little older. They were playing a handclapping game that I had never seen. The girls were laughing, teasing each other when they missed, nodding in delight when they did not. I stood and watched them, fascinated, till Father called to me to catch up.

All the way back to our camp, I was silent. Father noticed, I think, but said nothing at the time. It was my part to lead our donkey, laden with supplies, and I pretended to be occupied with that simple task as I thought. Again, I was thinking, but this time, I was feeling anger as I thought, and my anger grew.

I had never played that handclapping game. Indeed, I had never even seen it. I had no friends my own age, as those village girls did, or any friends at all. My sisters were too young to fill that role — the twins, Malkah and Tharah, nearest me in years, were no more than three at that time. They were more my charges than my friends, more responsibility than company.

For the first time, I began to reflect on the fact that our clan lived alone, isolated from others, and on what that meant — to me. I felt cheated. I knew only work and sleep, I thought. I did not know what *play* even meant.

That was not entirely so, of course. There were times when I would play games with my mothers, and even with Father. But that was not the same. It was true that I had no friends my own age or outside of my family, and in my self-pitying mood I thought only of that — and I brooded on it, and resented it. All the way home, I chewed on my aloneness, and on the unfairness of it.

After a few days of this, days when I was uncharacteristically silent and even surly, my mothers called me to them not long after sunset. Their names were Sabah and Qamra. Neither was my birth mother; her name had been Oma, and she had died giving birth to me. Perhaps that, too, had to do with my feeling alone.

"What troubles you, child?" asked Sabah. Sabah had tightly curled hair, like mine, and was always smiling and laughing. She was short and plump, as her daughters would be — the twins, and later Basimah, who was then not yet born. She was the wife Father had taken next after Oma, and was her sister.

I shook my head and frowned. "Nothing," I said, and made to go back to the fire, where I was preparing fresh fuel for the evening.

"Tzipporah." I stopped. This was Qamra, my other mother. She was neither short nor plump; she was tall, like Father, though not as thin as he. She had long, black hair that had a hint of a wave to it — not curly, but not straight. Father had taken her to wife not long after I was born. Though she was second in rank to Sabah, she seemed to be more in charge of our household than she, and Sabah did not mind. Qamra was better at such things, and liked doing them. Sabah was better at caring for the children and the domestic details of the camp.

Qamra was very different from Sabah in other ways as well. She seemed very solemn and serious about everything. When I was very small, I was a little afraid of her.

Her dark eyes bored into mine. "You are angry about something, child. That is as plain as if you were shouting it. What is it?"

I looked at them both for a heartbeat, and then it burst out of me: "I have no friends! There are no other children here! Only you, and the babies, and the stupid *sheep*!"

It all came out then, as my mothers sat open-mouthed and listened: The game in the marketplace, my bitterness at knowing nothing of it or any other games, or of laughter or play with other girls. My eyes stung with tears, and I shook them away angrily. "It is not *fair!*" I finally said. "Why can I not have friends, too? Why do we have to live out here all alone?"

Sabah and Qamra looked up, and I turned. My father was standing there, listening.

I was very afraid that he would be angry. I had never spoken with such bitterness and resentment before. But he came close to me, and knelt, and to my surprise, he hugged me. When he let me go, I saw that his eyes too were wet.

"Come, little bird," he said. That was his nickname for me, always. "Let us sit by the fire and talk. There are things you should know."

That night was the beginning of the end of my childhood.

7

The sun had set, and the sky in the East beyond the Mountain was already growing dark. The Moon was barely past new, a sliver like the paring of a nail, low in the sky. Father took my trembling hand in his, and we walked the few steps to the fire at the center of our camp, between our two tents — one for Father, and a larger one for my mothers and sisters and me.

There was a cool breeze in our faces from the desert beyond, and I wiped my eyes. We lived at the edge of the world, in a way; to the east and southeast of the Mountain was nothing — only the great desert. It is called the Empty Land, then and now, and empty it was. Nothing lived there. The breeze carried no scent, of beast or man. That only brought home to me, again, our isolation. I bit my lip. I was still angry.

It was a cool night, in the fall, I think. The sandy ground was still warm from the sun through my sandals, so it could not have been winter. The fire was banked low, as we kept it during the day, and Father bent to take some of the fuel I had gathered — sticks and dried sheep's droppings — and built it up again.

I wondered if he was about to lecture me or punish me. I was determined to stand my ground, even so. I was a bit obstinate, I suppose, even then.

I remember how my father's dear, scarred face looked when he sat down to talk to me. The firelight was in his eyes as he spoke, his right eye looking at me, the other looking a little to my right as it always did. His hair was only lightly streaked with gray then, and it shone in the dimness. I remember it all, as if it had happened last night.

"Once, little bird," he began, "long before you or your sisters were born, we — your mother Oma and I — lived in a village." He pointed to the west, where low hills rose on the horizon, a deeper blue against the darkening sky. "It is not far from here, three or four days' journey. I was what my people called a 'holy man.'"

This surprised me. It was not at all what I expected to hear, and I could not see what it had to do with my feelings of anger and loneliness. I wondered if he were using his trick again, of making me think to distract me from my feelings. If he was, it worked — a little. "A holy man? What does that mean?"

He smiled. "I was a *priest*, Tzipporah. I wore the robes of a god that I shall not name, and I lived with the other priests in a special house that we called a 'temple,' in the center of our village. We slaughtered sheep and goats before an idol — a statue made of wood — and we chanted and prayed before it, and pronounced blessings and curses, and led the people in our rituals and rites. Most of all, we pretended to know things that we did not know."

This puzzled me, but I did not know how to ask about it. Finally I asked, "Why were you a priest, Father?" And then, more forcefully: "Why do we not still live in a village? There would be other children there. I could have friends."

He gave me a rueful smile. "I was born into a priestly family and I was raised in that life. I knew no other. As for why we live alone — that is what I am telling you, little bird. Listen a bit longer."

I was impatient, like all children, but I was — usually — obedient. "Yes, Father."

My mothers were busying themselves preparing our evening meal, and went back and forth from the tents to the fire before us, but without speaking or looking at us. I was kicking my sandals against the donkey-saddle on which I sat, still angry and wondering what all this had to do with my loneliness. "Why are you not a priest now?"

His smile disappeared, his bushy eyebrows drew together, and suddenly he looked very solemn. "One night, I gave up that life and walked away. I could do it no longer. I left not only the priests, but all our people. That is why our clan lives alone."

I stopped kicking and waited, listening. I was growing more interested.

"I was standing outside of the temple, the house of the priests where we — put on our performances." His eyes were distant. "On a night like this one, with a narrow moon." He pointed again, and I looked at it. "It was after our evening ceremonies, and I was tired from the chanting and the rituals. I was watching the people, and they were watching their children as they all went back to their homes..."

He paused and smiled at me. "And I wondered who was watching me." He pointed, and we looked up into the night sky together. "Look at them." His voice was soft. "Look at them, Tzipporah."

It grows dark quickly in that part of the world, and the sky was filled with stars, so bright, so close — it seemed that I could lift my hand and touch them. So many. The Sheaf, with the three bright stars binding its stalks; the Net, with its catch of bright stars clustered close together; the Serpent, writhing across the sky; and so many more, with the broad River sweeping among them all. My mothers, overhearing, stopped for a heartbeat and looked up as well.

"How many are there?" he asked, still looking upward.

I knew that he expected no answer. I watched him and waited. A night-bird called, and another answered. I wiped my eyes again.

"No one knows," he went on. "Or why they are there, or even what they are." He looked at me again. "We pretended to know, we priests." He was nodding wisely, but with a wry expression. "We pretended to know many things. And we took what we needed from the people, and what we wanted, and we pretended to teach them the things we pretended to know."

He shook his head, and then looked up at the stars again. "But that night — I looked up, and I understood. And I could do it no more." His face was serious again. "I could no longer be a priest, and pretend, and fool the people."

He fell silent, and his arm went round my shoulders and squeezed me gently. My father was always gentle with me. "What did you understand, Father?"

He gave me a half-smile, one eyebrow raised. "That there was One who did know."

"Ael Shadu?"

"Yes, little bird. The One. *Ael Shadu."* God of the Mountain. That was what the words meant.

We looked at the mighty peak that loomed above us. "He is everywhere, Tzipporah, but this Mountain —" He inclined his head toward the peak, dark against the starry heavens — "this is His special place."

"Is that why it rumbles and shakes the ground and we see the fire in it?"

He shook his head. "No. There are other fire-mountains. But this one —" He fell silent. As we watched, there came a low murmur from the Mountain, a rolling grumble that we felt through the earth, and a glow of red from its summit. It was there, and then it was gone.

"You see? He speaks. But not in words."

"He — speaks?" I did not understand, not then.

My father nodded, gazing at the place where the fire had been. "Yes, Tzipporah. But that is all He ever says, just as you heard it, just now. *'I am here. And I know you.'"* Then my father squeezed me again. "And that, little bird, is enough. The rest is up to us."

I still did not understand. I looked at the Mountain, and felt it murmur again. The fire in its heart glowed again, subsided again — and then the Mountain was dark and silent. My father and I sat and watched it for a long time. I would like to say that I felt reverent or awed, but the thought in my mind, still, was — *I have no friends.*

"But why do we no longer live in the village?"

"I left the priests' temple, Tzipporah. And that meant we had to leave the village, your mother and I." I opened my mouth to protest, but he lifted a hand to stop me. "When the other priests asked why, I told them. I told them that their god was no god, but only a — *thing*, a thing that men had made. A thing carved of wood, a toy. A nothing, a trick, a dream. A lie. A way for the priests to grow fat on the people's fears." He paused. "And they hated me for it."

He laughed then, and his teeth gleamed a little in the starlight. "Oh, how they hated me! They cursed me with mighty curses, Tzipporah, but I laughed at their words, and they hated me all the more. Some even threw stones at me as I left, but none struck me. They were fat, lazy men, and they threw like women."

I wondered if that night had been when my father's face was scarred, and I was beginning to understand why we lived apart; but my attention was on something else at the time. I was a little offended. "I throw straight!" I protested. He laughed again.

"That you do, little bird. And you can use a sling, as well. But you are not like most girls and most women. You and your sisters will have to learn the skills of boys, and of men."

"Because you have no sons," I said innocently.

He blinked, looking at me with what I now know was sadness in his eyes; and then he smiled and hugged me closer. "Yes, Tzipporah. Because I have no sons. But I have you and your sisters and your mothers to help me." He pulled back, smiling even more broadly. "And I *will* have sons one day. Your husband, and your sister's husbands. And then I will have grandsons, too," he added, leaning close and grinning broadly.

I frowned. "But how will I find a husband when we see no one else, Father? There are no children here. Only me and my sisters."

His grin vanished. "Ael Shadu will send you a husband when the time is right. You will see."

He had said such things before. I was not moved. I did not ask, *When?* because I knew what he would say. *When the time is right.*

I thought of something else. "But, Father — do not women leave their families to live with their husbands'?" I had heard this from my mothers, who had done this themselves.

He sat upright and nodded solemnly. "That is true. But I think that for you and your sisters, it will be different."

In my stubborn mood, I did not understand that either, not then; but I did later. Any man who would marry a daughter of the renegade priest Yisro would have already abandoned his own people. And so it proved to be.

He went on: "I left the priests' temple that night, and I left our village and our tribe. That is why we live alone, and why we live by the Mountain." He looked up at it again. "And that is why the others leave us alone. Their fear keeps them away."

"They fear the Mountain?" I asked.

"Yes, little bird. The Mountain — and the One Who lives there."

"They fear Ael Shadu?"

"Oh, yes. And well they should."

He saw my questioning look. "Part of the reason men make their own gods, Tzipporah, is so they can control them. Make them safe, put them in a box, in a temple, and call them when they want them, and close the door when they are done with them, and not worry or wonder. But Ael Shadu —" He looked up at the Mountain again. "He is beyond their control. He does not come when called, nor does He answer their cries."

I was still thinking about the friends I did not have, but some of this did not make sense to me. "Do none of them believe in the gods they serve, the priests?" I had never seen a priest, nor an idol.

He shrugged. "Some do, perhaps. At least, I think they do. Perhaps they have pretended for so long, they fool themselves that they do believe. Or perhaps they only believe as they were taught, and have never thought for themselves, or wondered why they bow down to things made by men's hands."

He lifted a hand and waved it, as if shooing a fly. "But I think that many of them know better, and go on pretending." He grinned and shrugged again. "After all, little bird, it is a good living, and an easy life. Priests herd no sheep. They thresh no grain, carve no wood, weave no cloth. They live by the work of other men's hands. Even the gods they worship were made by other men." He laughed. "All they do is — talk!"

Then my father turned fully toward me, leaned forward, and took both of my hands in his. "If we still lived in the village, Tzipporah, you would still have no friends. Other children would shun you, call you names, even throw stones at you and hurt you. I know this is hard for you to understand, but it is better here."

It was as if he could read my thoughts. I hated to admit that I did understand, and that my father was right. But I thought I knew, even then, what he was about to say. "I see, Father. I am sorry I was angry today, and rude to my mothers." I saw them from the corner of my eye, listening as they pretended not to.

He surprised me again. "You have a right to be angry, little bird," he said. "It is a sorrow to me that you have no friends, that you cannot live like other children. But this is the life that we have chosen. That *we* have chosen," he said again. I knew what he meant; he and my mothers, that they had joined him in exile willingly. I nodded.

"Your sisters will soon be old enough to play with you," he said then. "And sisters are better than friends. You will see."

"Yes, Father." I doubted this, but accepted it.

His eyes were locked on mine. "The priests lie to themselves, my daughter. We — you and I, and all our clan — we must never do that. Not even to have friends, or to have others like us. You must always tell yourself the truth, because Ael Shadu knows your mind, and He knows you. There is no use in pretending. Tell the truth to yourself, always, and follow it, and fear nothing."

"And tell the truth to others." I nodded firmly.

His hands were still holding mine. He smiled indulgently and shook his head, just a little. "Most of the time. But there are reasons not to. Take care that they are good reasons." He laughed again. "Life is simple, Tzipporah, and not simple, too."

He squeezed my hands, then dropped them and straightened. "Come, little bird. We will talk more, as you get older." He made to get up, but I was full of questions and spoke up. "Wait, Father. What is Ael Shadu like? Is He like a man, only bigger?"

He settled back in his place and shook his head emphatically. "Oh, no, Tzipporah. No, no. He is not like us. He is not like a man, or a beast, or — or anything else of this earth."

"Then what *is* He like?"

He shook his head again, but more slowly this time. "No one knows that, little bird. No one." He looked at the sky again. "We are not meant to know what He is like. And we do not need to know. We need only to know that He *is*."

Once again, I was puzzled. I opened my mouth again to ask more, then closed it. I was not sure what to ask.

Father went to make sure the sheep were settled for the night as my mothers prepared the evening meal. The sky had grown dark, the fire bright. I sat alone before the flames and thought about all these things, perhaps for the first time. I still wished that I had friends to play with, but I thought perhaps that there were things more important than playing and having friends.

I did not understand all that he told me. Not then, and not for many years. But I remembered it. I am old now, and I remember it still.

I was proud of my father that night, and I still am. The fathers of Kisil's people — Avram, Yitzhak, Yaacov, Yusuf and the rest — they knew of The One long before my father did, and taught their children and grandchildren; but Yisro was not of their line. He knew of The One without being taught, and he taught us.

When our two peoples met, our traditions became one. I think they were always one, in a way. We both knew Ael Shadu in our own fashion. And when those teachings, those two ways of knowledge, fused and became one — they became one in Kisil, and in me.

8

I was a good child, an obedient child, for the most part; but there was one thing I did for which I would certainly have been punished severely, had Father or my mothers ever found out.

The Mountain was forbidden ground. We were taught never to set foot upon it, that it was dangerous. It was said that no one who had ever climbed the Mountain had returned, and that to walk on its slopes was death. But I had seen a wild goat high up among its peaks, and I thought, *if a goat can climb the Mountain and live, why not a girl?*

So one day I climbed it. It was not long after my talk with Father, and I was very curious about the mysterious Mountain. The twins were hardly old enough to walk, and another child had been born; Charah, Qamra's first. My mothers were very busy with the three of them, and me, to care for. I chose a morning when Father was away with the sheep and they were both working at weaving and sewing — tasks I had not yet mastered — and I told them I wanted to look for fuel for our fire farther from the camp. We needed it, and they gave their permission.

I took my staff, cut for my height, and an old skin bag, and set off. I did not walk directly toward the Mountain, but at an angle to it, and when I was behind a slight rise in the ground, I began approaching its slopes. I knew that they were gentler on that side.

I stood at the foot of the Mountain and looked up. The great mass of earth and stone seemed to look down upon me, but I sensed no danger, no forbidding Presence, no aura of warning; only a gentle slope that gradually grew steeper, with scattered tufts of desert grass and a few spindly shrubs here and there. Just a mountain. As if to confirm my resolve, there was that goat again, looking down on me from some ledge or outcropping farther up. After hesitating for a few breaths, I began to climb.

My heart was pounding, but I was determined, and as I climbed farther and farther up the slopes and no harm came to me, I began to feel calmer. The slope grew steeper, but it was still manageable, especially with the help of my staff. Before long, I reached a kind of shelf, a level place where the smooth slope of the Mountain was broken. Above me, the terrain grew more varied — broken rock, fissures and cracks between ridges of stone, some almost vertical. The place where I stood was a sort of wide ledge, a place where the ground was level, with a ridge of higher rock at its outer rim. I saw droppings; this was the place where the goat had been standing.

I followed the goat's path. It was worn deep into the gritty stone. There must have been many generations of goats who had followed it. I followed it as well, around toward the side from which I had come, but I moved cautiously. There were gaps in the rocky rampart, but I would not be seen from the camp if I was careful.

On my right, there was the steep, broken ground I had noticed before; great creases and outcrops of stone, blind passages open to the sky that ended abruptly, and even an overhang or two that appeared to be caves, but that did not penetrate into the Mountain more than a few steps. I explored a few, but saw nothing of much interest. There were scrubby bushes and spindly trees here and there, and I wondered at this. There must be water beneath the surface, I thought, but I did not see how this could be.

I crept around a broad outcropping of stone — the ledge had grown narrow there — and saw the mouth of a cavern. It was a big one, an opening perhaps five times as tall as a tall man. The mouth of the cave sloped back from the ledge, and the passage turned sharply to the right as it did so. It could only be seen as a cave from where I stood, or nearby. It faced our camp, but in all the years we had lived there, none of us had ever seen it.

I could not resist exploring the cavern. I crept into the opening with some nervousness; it was a very large cave, and I felt very small. I expected it to turn out to be nothing more than a hollow in the surface of the Mountain again, as the others had been, but I saw, when I followed the curving passage around to the right, that it went on deep into the mountain. It was strangely round, as circular as the inside of a cooking-pot. As I walked farther, it turned and turned again. Soon the light of the day was hidden by the turns, and it grew too dark to continue. The passage went on farther than I could see, the interior disappearing into the darkness.

I ran back to the entrance and tugged one of the scrubby trees from the slope. My firestones were always with me, hidden in a pouch in my tunic, and after a few tries I got the oily wood to light. I ran back into the cavern with my crude torch and explored further.

The cave went on and on, deeper into the Mountain, and I noticed that though the passage had begun to grow smaller, it remained perfectly round. I wondered what could make such a peculiar cave, then shrugged. Some formation of the rocks had made it so. I could see that the walls had never seen the mark of a tool, and the randomly curving track of the passage could have no human purpose that I could see. It seemed as natural as the path of a wadi in the earth, wandering as it chose.

My torch began to sputter, and though I could see that the cave had much farther to go, I decided that it would be wiser to return. When I reached the entrance, I saw that the sun was high. I had better get back to the camp, I thought.

Besides the living plants, I had seen many broken sticks and dead shrubs on the slopes of the Mountain as I ascended. Remembering my supposed mission, I gathered some and put them in my bag, leaving more for my next visit — for I knew I would come back again. I wanted to see where that strange cavern led.

I hurried down the Mountain, though I was careful to climb prudently —- it would not do to fall and hurt myself in that place — and I took the same roundabout way back to the camp that I had taken when I left. I gathered some dry goat droppings on my way, as well as those from our sheep.

My mothers were pleased with the fuel I had found, and I knew that they would be quick to give me permission to leave the camp again. I was pleased with my adventure as well, and though I was smug about climbing the forbidden Mountain and returning unharmed, I spoke of it to no one.

9

Over the next few years, I returned to the great cavern again and again. It required several more explorations before I found the end of that strange passage, and I learned to prepare four or even five torches for my journey in and back. The cave passage wound back and forth, round and round, doubling back on itself again and then again. It sloped downward, then up, but always deeper and deeper into the Mountain.

My torch would gutter low, and I would light another. The cavern grew gradually smaller, but all the way, it remained perfectly round. Back and forth, up and down, round and round. I could not guess its length, but it seemed very long indeed.

Finally, during perhaps my fifth or sixth visit, I came to a long, straight passage, and at last I could see the end of the cavern. The tunnel was now much smaller, only as tall as a tall man, though still perfectly round, but at the end of it there was a chamber where the cavern expanded to twice a man's height again. That space was round too, as round as a ripe fig. I was still a child, but even if I had been a full-grown woman, there would be no need to stoop.

It was a wonderful place to my child's mind. My own secret place, deep in the Mountain, far away from anyone, protected by the legends. I knew that no one would come here. The place was forbidden, said to be death to anyone who trod upon it — but I knew better. I remember giggling in that strange round chamber, and being shocked at how the sound echoed. After that, I took care to be silent.

I went to my secret cavern many times, but as I grew older, I went less and less often. It was a wonderful place, but after all, there was nothing to do there and no one with whom I could share it. It also took a very long time to reach it, and many torches. Still, I went back from time to time to savor my secret knowledge.

Never when the Mountain was awake, though. When it rumbled, and the earth shook all around it, and when we could see the red fire in its peaks — at those times, I stayed away. It might indeed have been death to climb the Mountain then, I thought, when Ael Shadu was in residence — when He was speaking. I wondered what it was like in my secret place then, at the far end of that long, mysterious passage.

I hugged myself and smiled at my secret knowledge. I had been in a place that no one had ever seen, that no one else even knew existed. I never shared that knowledge with anyone, not even my sisters. The cavern was my secret, and mine alone.

10

The years passed, and I and my half-sisters — the girls born to my other mothers — grew. I rarely went to my secret place after the twins were old enough to be curious when I was away from the camp, and I had even fewer chances as the others grew older. By the time I was grown, I had not gone up the Mountain for some years, and I hardly ever thought of it.

As the other girls grew, I no longer felt so isolated; but I was never as close to my sisters as they were to each other, perhaps because I was so much older than they. I helped raise them, and was as much a mother as a sister to them in many ways. I often settled arguments and disputes among them. Indeed, they would often come to me before they went to our parents.

I suppose I should have felt honored that they all thought me impartial and fair. But then, at times, they seemed to unite against me. I suppose it was easier for them to rebel against my authority than Father's, or our mothers'.

One day — I had perhaps fourteen years by then — I was stung by a scorpion. It was because of my own carelessness; I had reached down to pick up some kindling from our store of fuel, and had failed to look at it closely. I cried out, and the twins, Malkah and Tharah, ran to help. Malkah happened to be holding a clay cup when it happened, and she captured the scorpion beneath it while I ran to Father. I thought nothing of it then.

Father examined my hand while I stood whimpering before him, then applied a paste he made from crushed herbs and earth. My hand soon felt better, though it still hurt, and my whole arm ached for days.

I went back to tending the fire. The days were hot in our land, but nights could be cold, even in summer, and there was always a fire. It was there to keep us warm, to cook our meals, and to keep the wild beasts away — and it is always easier to build up a fire than to start one. I hated fire-building, even then.

The sun rose higher in the sky, and the mirages appeared as they always did — the illusion of shining water, shimmering on the ground, close enough to reach with only a short walk. I often wondered what it was that made them appear when the day was hottest, and never in the morning or the evening.

I noticed that all the girls had left their work and were kneeling around something — and giggling. I went to look, and found that they had broken off the scorpion's tail and had formed a circle around it, tormenting the ugly thing with burning sticks. They were scorching it, making it scramble this way and that, and laughing at its struggles.

I stepped into the middle of their circle and stamped on the scorpion, grinding it into the gravel with my sandal.

The girls were puzzled — and furious. "Why did you do that, Tzipporah?" Malkah asked angrily.

"We were just having fun!" put in Nazirah, who had no more than seven years then, but was already the most defiant of my sisters.

I tried to sound calm and grown-up. "That was wrong. You should have killed the thing, not tortured it."

"But it stung you!" cried Tharah.

"It was a *scorpion*," I said — reasonably enough, I thought. "That is what scorpions do. It is wrong to make anything suffer, even a scorpion."

"Did Father say so?" This was Nazirah again, who was both quick and suspicious.

I nodded firmly. "Yes, he did. Now get back to your tasks. Nazirah, you and Charah were to look for sticks and dried dung, for fuel. Tharah, Malkah — the water is still in the wadi, and not in our waterskins!" They scowled and went back to work. Basimah and Rivkah had already gone, to help our mothers with grinding grain.

Later that evening, after we had eaten, my sisters went to Father. They stood in a half-circle round him, and Malkah asked, "Father, did you teach Tzipporah that it is wrong to make *anything* suffer — even a scorpion or a jackal?"

We had not mentioned jackals, but Malkah was clever to add them. That is the animal that herding people despise the most.

I watched and listened from the other side of the fire and tried not to look nervous. Father had, in truth, never taught me this, though it had seemed right to me.

His eyes never so much as flicked in my direction. He looked up from the sandal he was mending and said, "Why, yes, I did. Have I not taught that to you?"

The girls all shook their heads. "You taught us that it is wrong to kill without a reason," said Malkah. "But that it is *good* to kill scorpions. They can hurt us."

"And that is true."

Charah's long curls bounced as she cocked her head sidewise. She was confused, as were all my sisters. "But if it is not wrong to *kill* a scorpion, why is it wrong to *hurt* one?"

Father put the sandal aside. "Why are you asking me these things, my daughters?" By this time, our mothers had come to listen, so I went to their side of the fire and sat down beside them. Sabah was munching on a handful of dates, and offered me some. I took a few.

Tharah told Father what I had done, and he nodded judiciously. "Tzipporah was right," he said. "Better to simply kill the scorpion than hurt it beyond what is necessary. There is enough pain in the world without adding to it."

Red-haired Rivkah, the youngest of my sisters, stamped a small foot and protested, "But sco'pions —" she could not quite manage the word — "hurt *us!*"

Father nodded. "Yes, they do. But scorpions do not sting because they enjoy it. The sting is what Ael Shadu gave to the scorpion to defend itself. The creature probably thought Tzipporah was attacking it when she reached into its nest." He pointed at my sisters. "But *you* were making a game of hurting it, for nothing more than idle pleasure. And that is *always* wrong, my children, even when your victim is a scorpion — or a jackal. You may kill them, because they are a danger to us; but if you torment them, you become worse than they."

He lifted a finger again to emphasize his words, as was his way. "It is good to question what you are taught. You have done well, children." Only then did he look at me, and he smiled and nodded. "And so has Tzipporah. It is not only your mothers' and my task to teach you. It is also the part of your eldest sister. Remember that."

He picked up the sandal again, and resumed mending it. "Let me tell you a story..."

The girls all sat down to listen, and Father told us one of his many tales as he worked. This one was about a scorpion who wished to cross a stream. I have heard it since.

11

After the others had gone to sleep, I peeked out of our tent to see if Father still sat alone by the fire, as he often did. He was there, and I crept out to speak to him. The gritty earth was still warm beneath my bare feet, though the wind was growing cold, as it did at that time of year after the sun set. I heard the soft sounds of the sheep as they stirred in the night, and saw the light of a lamp beneath the tentflap where my mothers slept with the youngest girls. Somewhere a night-bird called.

My father's mismatched eyes shone in the firelight. "I thought you might want to see me, little bird," he said.

"Father, you did not really teach me — what I said," I began, but before I could go farther, he interrupted me.

"No, I did not. Why did you tell your sisters that I had?" He looked at me sharply.

"I thought it was wrong, what they were doing. And — and —"

"And they would not have listened if it had been *your* word alone," he finished for me.

"Yes." I sighed in relief. That had been my thought exactly, though I had not found the words for it. "Did I do wrong?"

He smiled and shook his head, back and forth, very slowly. "No, my daughter. You showed that you have learned the truths that lie *behind* the things that I have taught you." He tossed his head back, toward the Mountain. "The One gave us heads to think with, little bird. And you have used yours as it was meant to be used."

"But I *said* that you taught me that, and that was not true," I protested.

His good eye was fixed on my face. "From where do these laws of right and wrong come, little bird? What have I told you?"

"They come from The One," I said, very conscious of the Mountain looming behind him.

"And has The One told me these things? Has He spoken to me, in words?"

I blinked. I had never thought about it. But Father had always said that Ael Shadu did not speak, not in words.

"No?" I ventured.

He shook his head again. "No," he said, smiling. "But I think they are true nevertheless. All I have from Him is a sense that the truth is important. I worked out those ideas for myself, just as you did from what I taught you. You have done no more than I have done myself. Do you understand?"

"I think so," I said, though I was not sure of that at all.

He grinned then, and pulled me toward him and embraced me. "You did not lie, Tzipporah," he said into my hair. "I *did* teach you that, in a way. You knew that tormenting the scorpion was wrong — and who taught you right and wrong?" He released me and his eyes looked into mine. Or, to speak truly, one of his eyes.

"You did," I said, frowning. "But —"

"And you have learned it well, and what you taught your sisters was wisdom. I am proud of you, little bird." He smiled, and then his face grew serious once again. "What is the one highest law, Tzipporah?"

I knew the answer, and gave it: "Never to do anything to anyone else that you would not want done to you."'

Father said nothing. He only watched me with the hint of a smile on his lips, half-concealed by his beard. I knew what that meant, what he expected. That smile meant, *And...?*

I thought — and then I went on. "And that law is about other creatures too, not just people... Is that right?"

He nodded deeply, then lifted a hand, as was his way when he wished to indicate that what he was about to say was important. "Yes, little bird. You see? The laws of right and wrong are not only the things you have been taught. They include the things you work out for yourself." He smiled. "What I said to your sisters was true, Tzipporah, and I say again to you. It is not only my part to teach your sisters; it is your part as well. I need you, my daughter. I need you to be there for them, to speak for me when I am not there to speak. You did not do wrong to speak with my authority. You knew that what you taught them was true, did you not?"

I thought, and then I nodded. "Then it would have been wrong *not* to say it." He touched my frizzy hair. "Go back to your tent now and sleep. There is much to do in the morning."

I did, and I slept, though it was long before sleep came to me.

12

The day after I killed the scorpion, I rose early, as we all did. The girls were more respectful than the day before, and did what I told them; but Father had taught me never to give them orders for the pleasure of making them run. We worked and laughed and complained together as we always did, and it was as if nothing had happened. My sisters truly were my friends, and we loved each other, even though we fought and complained and could even be jealous and petty, as all sisters can be.

Our days were long. Little could be done in the heat of the day, so we were up and working before the dawn, and rested when the sun was high. We worked again when the sun was low — till dark, most days, and if there was a moon, till long after.

That day was New Moon, as it happened, and New Moon was a special holiday for our family. It was too dark to work after the evening meal, so we would gather round our fire and celebrate. We would sing and tell stories — Father knew many stories — and we would laugh, for many of his stories were funny. Not all, though; he also told us about the tribes around us and how they lived, about the history of our people, and why we lived as we did.

And he told us about Ael Shadu — The One, the God of the Mountain — though he never told us much. We had no ceremonies and no rituals. I did not know those words, or that there even were such things till much later. And we had no *beliefs*, exactly; nothing that we had to think, or to pretend to know, as Father put it. We had guesses, and questions, and hopes. That was all, and that was enough.

Every New Moon was different, but we always looked forward to them. Celebration in the night, and a lazy day to follow. That night would prove to be one of our best.

"Tzipporah, would you play your flute for us?" asked Tharah that evening as we sat around the fire. The Moon had set with the sun, so our work was done for the day. The other girls were smiling and nodding. I thought the request was by way of apology for doubting me the day before, though I knew that they did like to hear me play.

My hand, where the scorpion had stung me, was still stiff, and it ached. I must have looked reluctant. But then little Rivkah looked at me with her bright blue eyes and said, "Please, Zipp'ah?" I laughed and said I would.

I went to our tent for my flute, and found my mother Qamra there, holding it out to me. When I took it, I realized that she had not taken out her own. I asked, "Mother, will you not play with me tonight?"

She smiled and shook her head. "No, Tzipporah. Your sisters want to hear *you* play."

"But —"

"Thank you for asking me, my daughter, but no. Your skill has long since surpassed my own." We left the tent together. "Yisro, come!" she called. "Tzipporah is about to play for us!"

I blushed as Father hurried to the fire, then waited as he settled himself on the cushions that were reserved for him. Sabah brought him his cup of ewe's-milk beer, then sat on his right on her own special cushion.

Qamra took her place on Father's left. I loved both of my mothers, but as I grew older, it was Qamra with whom I felt the greater kinship. We found it in music; she had been the one who taught me to play.

Everyone was waiting for me to begin, and that night I was very conscious of their attention. I looked at the fire for a few breaths, then closed my eyes and brought the flute to my lips. I think I was as interested as my family in what we would hear. I never knew till I began.

As the sounds rose up and flowed from me, I thought of how I first came to play, and love, the flute. The sound of Qamra playing for me, to help me sleep, was among my first memories. I think that must have been to comfort me because Oma, my birth mother, had died.

I opened my eyes. My sisters were sitting crosslegged, swaying back and forth in time to my music. I closed them again, and I played as it came to me, as I always did. I thought of Oma, and the melody was both sweet and sad.

They say she was pretty, with a silvery laugh and eyes of pale gray, like mine; but her eyes danced and sparkled, while mine did not. I was a somber child, and so I suppose I took after Qamra in that way too. I was happy enough, but I did not laugh often. My laughter was in my music.

I loved the sound of Qamra's flute, and when I was still very young, she taught me to play. I remember sitting in her lap with her arms around me, her grown-up hands on my small ones, showing me how to place my fingers. I remember being surprised that my child's fingers could reach all the holes — and I especially remember the delight I felt at discovering that I could vary the pitch and the tone. In only a few weeks I was playing on my own as Qamra watched. "Yes, Tzipporah," she would whisper. "Like that..." And she closed her dark eyes and listened, and smiled.

As she was doing now. My father's eyes were closed too, and so were those of my sisters who were not watching me, entranced, lost in the melody I was making.

It was that night, I think, that I first realized how well I played. When I was younger, it never occurred to me to take pride in my playing. I knew only that I loved it. My sisters could not play at all, and I wondered at that; for me, it was easy and natural as walking and running. When I was feeling good, or happy, or even when I was angry or sad, it was easier for me to speak with my music than with words. The music seemed to come from me without my having to think about it. That night I played till the fire burned low and Rivkah and Basimah, the two youngest, were sleeping.

That was our celebration, that New Moon; listening to me playing my flute by the fire. That made me feel good. I felt loved, and valued, and most of all I felt — unique. I possessed a skill that was a kind of magic, better, in its way, than spinning, or sewing, or weaving. I suppose I was proud of my skill, but I do not think that was wrong. My pride came from something I could give, not from something that I could keep to myself.

I can still play, a little, though slowly; my fingers are no longer agile. But now I play for no one but myself, and perhaps for Zev if he is listening. I play, and I remember.

Those were good years. Our lives were hard; but I loved my hard life, and I loved the hard land, for the desert has blessings of its own. I learned to love the important things, the real things, about life on the Earth. Life, and freedom, and the love of family.

It would be more than ten turns of the stars before I met Kisil; but I was being prepared to be his mate, even then, just as he was being prepared for what he would become and do.

13

It was long ago, a lifetime ago and more, but still I remember the day that Kisil came.

That day began in an ordinary way, with me waking my three youngest sisters. I entered their tent quietly and approached the oldest of the three. I reached for her shoulder. "Nazirah, wake up —"

She opened her eyes at the first touch of my hand, and was fully awake and alert before I finished speaking. I turned to the others, but before I could touch them, Nazirah snapped at me. "Why are you smiling?"

I laughed. "I wish I could wake up as quickly as you," I said.

She blinked. "Oh. All right, then." Always ready for a fight, my sister.

As Nazirah dressed, I turned to the two younger ones. "Basimah. Rivkah. Wake up." I shook one's shoulder, then the other's. "We must go soon."

"Go where...?" asked Basimah. She blinked at me, still half-asleep.

"It is still dark," whined Rivkah as she rolled over and settled herself back on her pallet.

Nazirah laughed and lightly kicked Basimah's bare foot with her own, then Rivkah's. "We are driving the sheep to the far pasture today, lazy ones," she laughed. "Did you forget?"

The younger girls groaned and rose, fumbling for their woolen day tunics as they shed the light linen ones we wore for sleep. "We are filling the waterskins at the well on our way back, too," I said. "Bring an extra shawl to pad your shoulders." They groaned again, but did as I asked.

We were all grown women by then. Rivkah, the youngest of us, had sixteen or seventeen years. The three of them brushed their hair — always an ordeal for me, with my thick, tight curls. I had already done it in the tent I shared with our mothers, so I helped Basimah brush hers, which was much the same as my own.

"Ouch!"

"Hush. I did not pull that hard."

"Tender Basimah, who squeals at a grain of sand in her sandal," simpered Nazirah. At least she's smiling, I thought.

The girls slipped on their sandals and covered their hair, and we left the tent. It was still dark.

Father was already awake and working, as always. I cannot remember a single time when I rose before him. He was gathering the family's waterskins for our journey. "We have dry bread and cheese and some dates for breakfast, my daughters," he said cheerfully.

The girls grunted and sat down in the light of the fire to eat as my other sisters came from their tent and joined us. They would be staying with our parents that day, helping our mothers move our camp to another site nearer the Mountain. They would be working hard, too — striking the tents, filling in the privy pit, packing our donkeys with tents and ropes and bedding and the wood and bags of dried dung for our fire. It would take more than one trip, as it had the last time we moved; but we were not going far.

The sky grew gray in the east as we ate our breakfast, but it was still long before dawn. When we were finished, the four of us chose our staffs and crooks, took the empty waterskins, and we were ready. On an impulse, I ran back to our tent for my flute. I did not like to go far without it at any time.

When I picked it up, I was seized with an overwhelming feeling that something was about to happen, something important. I just stood there, frozen, looking at my flute in my hand.

Nazirah came in for her sling and a pouch of sharp stones that she kept by her pallet. She saw me standing there holding my flute and gazing at it. "What is it?"

I shook my head to clear it. "Nothing," I said. "Just a feeling. Something — is coming," I said.

She cocked her head and regarded me curiously. "I believe you."

I blinked at her. "You do?"

She nodded soberly. "When you have feelings, Tzipporah — they mean something. We have all noticed."

"You have?" I asked foolishly. This was the first I had heard of this.

She nodded. "It is Father's blood. It runs strong in you. If you say something is coming — then something is."

I did not know what to say. "I — I just came back for my flute," I finally managed. I thrust it into my sash.

She held up her sling. "You can play while I hunt," she said with a grin.

I shook off the feeling and laughed. "You may not wish to carry your kill back to the new camp. We will be burdened enough with the waterskins."

She shrugged. "A few coneys will not burden me much. Besides, I have not yet killed them!"

By this time our family had acquired a dog to help us herd the sheep. I whistled for him when we left the tent, and he came bounding up happily, tail flapping, eager for whatever the day would bring. Father had named him Kadin, because he was a faithful companion and stayed close to whomever he was with. He was black, with white on his face, paws and belly, a ruff around his neck, and an oddly long-haired tail that he waved like a flag when he was happy. He was not a large dog, but he was very skilled with the sheep, and very protective of us.

The four of us, and Kadin, set about gathering our scattered sheep into a flock. With the dog helping, it did not take long. Azzan, our big ram, took his place at the front, to the west, as if he knew where we were going. We waved to our parents and sisters, clicked our tongues and cried "Ai! Ai!" to the sheep to get them moving, and the journey began.

We settled into an easy rhythm, the empty waterskins swinging from our sashes. It was not long before the horizon behind us, beyond the Empty Land, began to grow light. Day was coming.

"At least we will not be walking into the sun," said Basimah. The rest of us murmured agreement, between our whistles and cries to encourage the sheep. I used my crook to nudge a lamb nearer its mother, and Kadin yipped at another stray to send it back to the flock. We and the sheep were moving at a steady pace. That feeling, of something approaching, was still with me, but it was no longer uppermost in my mind. I tried to think about my sisters, the sheep, and our journey.

It was hard, hot work, but that was the shape of our lives, and we had all grown up with it. Shepherding was the most essential skill of our people, and we had all learned it as soon as we had learned to walk.

Our whole lives revolved around our flocks. Everything we had came from our sheep; our tents and our clothes were made from their coarse brown wool, our meals were made from their meat and milk and cheese, our tools from their bones, and our sandals and waterskins and parchment and much more were made from their hides.

We even used the horns of the rams to signal each other, to give the alarm, and in celebration. My father had a large one, very long and with a curious twist, that sounded a note all its own. I learned to blow that horn when I was very small, and as with the flute, I was very good at it. When I grew older, no one, not even my father, could blow it as loudly as I.

The sun touched the horizon, and suddenly we all cast long shadows that stretched before us in the direction we were going. The day was already hot. There was no wind at all, and our robes hung heavily on us as we walked. Some wonder why we wore long robes of heavy wool, but those who wonder never lived in Midyan. The fabric protected us from sun, wind and sand, and we were accustomed to it.

Kadin ran back and forth, keeping the flock together, and we all kept them moving. Azzan set the pace, and we made sure it was a brisk one. We did not want to be all day at this.

The land and the sky were the same color, yellow-white, and both were empty. Other than a few sprigs of dry grass and our sheep, there was nothing living to be seen. The ground was gritty; not sandy, but hard and unyielding, and it would soon be hotter than the air.

We trudged along, and time seemed to pass very slowly. I remember wishing for a breeze, but none ever came. The dust raised by the passage of our flock seemed to hang in the air as if it refused to fall to the baking earth. The mountains to the west and north, dim gray shapes, hardly seemed real. I had never been that far from home; for all I knew, they were mirages too, only shadows.

"I wish I was at my loom," said Charah.

"And I at my spindle." That was Malkah.

"I'm sure you do," I said, "And I wish I were playing my flute to entertain you as you worked. But without sheep there will be no wool to spin or weave, and with no grass or water there will be no sheep."

"We were just wishing," grumbled one of them. I was not sure which.

"Wish all you like, but remember what we are about."

"How can we forget with you to remind us?" asked Charah lightly, but with an edge to her words.

"Oh, hush," said Nazirah. "She's the oldest. That's her job."

We looked at each other. I saw her smile, and let it go.

14

Herding and guiding the sheep was something we all knew how to do, but as we had grown older, we had all found different talents, our own ways to contribute to the family's life. As one might expect, most still had to do with sheep and wool.

Basimah could cut the wool from a sheep so fast you could hardly follow her hands with your eyes, and comb it faster than any of us. Malkah was best at spinning; her thread was fine and even. From it, Charah, the most skilled among us at weaving, made the best cloth. Tharah, Malkah's twin, could cut and sew the cloth better than any of us. She wasted little of the wool, and her garments always fit well.

I was adequate at all of those things, but in none did I surpass my sisters. My skill was in playing my flute, and I would often play while they worked.

But that day, we were using none of those skills. We were driving the sheep, the first we had learned.

I smile again. I had another skill, as well as playing the flute. I was as good at leading and directing my sisters as I was at herding the sheep, and that day I was doing both. Nazirah had been right. That was my job.

The day grew warmer. "What an oven this is," complained Rivkah. "Why are we not doing this at night?" This trip was harder on her than on the rest of us. She had just completed her first time, the time that marked her as a grown woman. It had been difficult for her, as the first time often is. She pulled out the neck of her tunic to allow the air to flow beneath.

For once Nazirah did not mock her. She knew how hard Rivkah's time had been, for her first had been the same. "You will feel better when you have some water, baby sister." We were all thirsty. We had brought little water with us, so our father and sisters would have enough to last till we returned. There was water in the wadi near our camp, but not much.

I smiled at Nazirah, to acknowledge her kindness. It was not rare, but she was more likely to tease than comfort at any time.

The sun was still low, only a handsbreadth above the horizon. I pointed at it. "Father said we should go today, before the sun is high. There was no water in the wadi yesterday, and only a little this morning — and the sheep need fresh grass. We will stop at the well on the way there for a little water for ourselves — it is not far, Rivkah — then we will stop again to fill our skins on the way back."

"Well, we should have gone last night," Basimah whined. "It would have been cooler." She was already puffing a bit. She tended to plumpness, like Sabah, her birth mother.

"But just as far," I said. "And it would have been black dark. The moon is one day past new, and it set after the Sun did. You might have tripped over Azzan and fallen on your face." The girls laughed, even Basimah, and our mood was lightened.

"Look there," Nazirah hissed. There was a jackal watching us from the top of a rocky rise, perhaps a hundred paces to the left of our path. *Better stay away, beast,* I thought to myself. I was not afraid, not with Nazirah among us. We watched it carefully as we moved the sheep along, but Nazirah began to edge toward it. I saw her fishing in her pouch for a stone.

Of all my sisters, I was least close to Nazirah when we were young. I loved her, but she had a hurtful streak. Perhaps that was why she had mastered the sling. She, alone among us, could do little good with wool; but using the sling is as useful a skill for herders. She was the best of us at hunting, and when we ate meat other than mutton, it was Nazirah who provided it.

But she was always the one to tease, to mock, always the one with the sharp tongue and the ready retort, and sometimes she would speak, as far as I could see, only to wound.

As for Rivkah — well, Rivkah was always the prettiest, with her bright red hair and brighter blue eyes, and she could sing like an angel. She was a good cook, too, but then we were all good at that. Nazirah would often make fun of her, since Rivkah had no skill like the rest of us, and sometimes she would even make the poor girl cry. She had to be taught to stop tormenting her — and since she never did it in front of our parents, that task fell to me.

It took some time, but Nazirah learned. It was not my superior wisdom that convinced her. I was older and bigger and had harder knuckles. Once or twice was enough.

We were older now, grown women, and all that was far behind us — or most of it. Today, Nazirah had a different target. The jackal was moving closer to us, even as she moved closer to it.

Suddenly, long before I thought it would happen, Nazirah's sling whipped the air, and the animal fell as if clubbed. It was at least forty paces away.

Rivkah gasped. "Nazirah! You have killed it!"

She grinned and shook her head, her eyes still fixed on the beast. "Only stunned it, I think. But it will be dead soon anyway. Look."

Two more jackals were sniffing at the beast, and one began tearing at its throat as we watched. "They eat their own. Our sheep are safe now — they have other meat."

"You struck its head," I said. "That was a good shot." She shrugged, but I could see that she was pleased by my praise. We were troubled with no more animals that day — of the four-legged kind, at least.

The girls continued to talk, sometimes complaining, sometimes joking. In the past I had often joined in, but that day I did not. I was occupied with watching the horizon. I was watching for more beasts, for the end of our journey, and for men.

As it happened, I was thinking about men that day, perhaps because of Rivkah. I was thinking of how long I, myself, had been a woman — and wondering if I would ever have a man. I was not sad, only wondering. As I looked at the dry land ahead of us and clicked my parched tongue to drive the sheep along, I was thinking of what lay ahead — for me.

I had perhaps a score of years and five by then, and was already considered a spinster, as were all of my sisters but the two youngest. Women who were not married by sixteen or eighteen, among our people, were not likely ever to marry at all.

Even so, there was a man who sometimes came to our camp to see Malkah, and another who seemed friendly with Charah when we went to his village to trade — and you can believe that when we went there, she made sure to go. Both, we knew, would have to leave their own tribes and live with us if they wanted to marry my sisters. Our clan was despised and even hated, but I thought that at least one of those men, and perhaps both, were thinking about it. For me, though, there was no one.

I was content, even so. If I were to end my life unmarried, but still among my family — perhaps caring for a sister's children at times, and having them for company nearby, even with none of my own — well, that would be all right, I thought. I would not worship some pretend-god of stone or wood to have a husband, that I knew.

One of the lambs was straying again, but before I could pursue it, Kadin ran to chase it back to the flock before its mother strayed as well. A few soft yips, and the lamb — almost as big as Kadin himself — was hurrying back.

We walked on, and soon my sisters were speaking less often. It had grown even hotter, and we were crossing a narrow band of black, stony ground. The heat rose from the earth as if from a banked fire, and it burned our feet through our sandals. There was still no wind.

My sisters had been making more noise than the sheep — the poor things were too thirsty to bleat, even as they hurried over the hot black rocks — but by then the girls' dry mouths kept them silent as well.

Soon we left the black stones behind, and were on softer ground that did not burn so. Not long after, we were glad to see the tops of the palms that marked the well on the horizon. We were all tired, especially Rivkah and Basimah, and we hurried the sheep along. Azzan smelled the water, and he began to trot, the bell at his throat clanking dully. We did not hear it often; Azzan was a lazy thing, and rarely hurried.

There would be more work when we reached the well. It was not deep, but the water would still have to be brought to the surface before we or the sheep could drink it. We hurried on, and soon we topped a low ridge and saw our flock below us, gathered around the ancient brickwork that surrounded the well. They were bleating and bumping the troughs and the wooden post that held the well-sweep, making it shudder.

Before we caught up to the sheep, Nazirah — always the most vigilant among us — hissed again and pointed. There was a man there, sitting on some rocks perhaps thirty paces from the well with a staff in his hand. There was a low ridge there, a natural curve of stone that seemed placed to shield the well from the wind.

"Say nothing," I said in a low tone. "He looks harmless enough, and he is alone. If he does not bother us, we shall not bother him."

The man was Kisil. I did not know it then, but my life was about to change.

15

The man was a foreigner, by his clothes and hair. An Egyptian, I thought, or perhaps a Greek. His clothing was wrong for the desert; he wore a short tunic with a leather belt, and there was nothing on his head, which was especially unusual in our part of the world. Most men, and all women, wore something to shade their heads from the sun — a hat, or a hood, or a turban. His hair was cut very short, as well, curly and dusted with gray at the temples, and his face was lined and rugged. He was much older than I, perhaps even as old as my father, but it was hard to tell his age. He had no beard, which was especially strange to me. I had never seen a grown man without a beard.

He carried only his staff, a waterskin, and a worn, shapeless bag. He was not tall, but he was powerfully built, with broad shoulders and a deep chest. His skin was dark, but from the sun only. He was not a Kushite.

Other than his clothes and hair, he seemed an ordinary man. Perhaps I only looked at him closely because I had been thinking about ever having a man, and he was the first man, other than my father, that I had seen for a long while.

I could not have told you, even then, why I thought this; but he looked *lost*, as if he did not know where he was nor where he was going. He was staring at the dusty ground, as if there might be an answer for him there.

He turned his head and looked at us, but for no more than a heartbeat. He seemed to take us in at a glance — four women, our sheep, our dog. His eyes were quick, and I had the feeling that he saw much in that glance. Then his eyes focused on me, and just for an instant, our eyes met. Then he turned away and seemed to take no further notice of us.

Kadin showed no interest in him, and that, too, proved that he was harmless. The dog was good at sensing intentions, whether good or ill.

"Do not stare, sisters," I said quietly. "We have work to do." Since the man did not bother us nor speak, we ignored him and set about filling the troughs for the sheep. Basimah and Nazirah worked the well-sweep, and Rivkah and I poured as the sheep crowded each other to get to the water.

We were all watchful and alert, looking around nervously as we worked. We did not like to use that well. When we did, the people who lived nearby often grew angry and drove us away. They worshiped some desert god or other, perhaps even the same one that our father had abandoned, and they despised him and all our clan because we did not.

There was usually no trouble, even so. Father had taught us to wait, to say nothing, and to let them sneer and jeer. The water would still be there, and there was always time, he said. The well would not be dry, and sheep never hurry.

But no one troubled us, not then. We watered the sheep without difficulty, then filled one skin for the day. I left the rest empty, so we would not have to carry them farther than necessary. We would fill them all on our way back. I made sure that Kadin got his share of fresh water, too.

Before long, we moved on, refreshed and prepared to drive the flock to the distant pasture, which was not so distant now. We clicked our tongues and cried "Ai!" to the sheep again, and they began to move. I looked back at the man as we left, but he was still sitting on his rock, looking at the ground and ignoring us.

We drove the flock over one hill, and then another, and then we found the field that we sought in a kind of broad, low valley beyond. "Look at it!" cried Rivkah, who had never been there before. "Why is it so green?"

"The place may collect more water when it rains," I said, "and hold it somehow. Look how rocky the hills are, all around here."

"More likely it is closer to the water beneath the ground," said Basimah. "This is a low place. That well was not as deep as I expected." Basimah did not often give her opinion on anything, though when she did she showed a remarkable intelligence.

For whatever reason, the little valley was all we had hoped. The grass there was still thin and sparse by the standards of others, perhaps, but in our dry land, it seemed rich and green. The sheep set about grazing with a will, and we sat down to watch them. Basimah began taking the bits of food we had brought from a skin bag, and we passed them around — dry bread, some tough smoked meat, a little cheese, some olives and some dates. We talked only a little as we ate — the day was too hot — but what we talked about was the stranger.

Rivkah was the first to speak. "I wonder where he comes from. He does not dress like us." There was no need to wonder who she meant.

Nazirah was quick with her joke, gesturing with a piece of brown bread. "Of course not, silly. He is a man."

Rivkah, her mouth full, made a face at her. Basimah laughed. I spoke my own thoughts. "He might be an Egyptian. Or perhaps a Greek. They dress similarly."

Nazirah frowned. "He looked tired. I would wager that he will be there on our way back, too. Pass me some of those dates."

I handed them to her and shrugged, and we spoke of other things.

I made a little shelter for us, using a shawl and our staffs, mostly to give Rivkah some shade. At her request, I took out my flute and played. Her bright blue eyes were still hard to resist, though she was no longer the sweet child who could not pronounce my name.

Soon, she slept. Basimah did too, and I played a little longer while Nazirah and I watched our sisters and the sheep.

"I hope Rivkah feels better," she whispered when I stopped. "I think her first time was worse than mine."

"I hope so too." I scratched behind Kadin's ears, then sat thinking. He had lain down beside me; he was tired and hot too, and the sheep hardly needed watching. They were not likely to stray far with good grass to eat.

The afternoon passed in a kind of silent, dreamy haze. I took a drink of water and played a little more, till Nazirah was also dozing.

I put down my flute and thought about the stranger, about men, and about the future, and I stroked Kadin's ruff. He grinned at me, his long tongue comically hanging out of the side of his mouth as he panted in the heat. "What will happen to us, funny dog?" I asked softly. "What does the future hold for us?"

He cocked his head as if to say, "Do you not know?"

16

The sun began to move toward the horizon. I woke my sisters, and we gathered our things and our sheep and set off to return. It was more difficult to get the sheep started than when we had left. The sheep liked the grass and did not want to leave. It took some time to form them into a flock and get them moving, but at last we were on our way. A few tried to break away and go back, but all of us worked to keep the flock together, and with Kadin helping, we were soon making good progress, though at a more leisurely pace. On our way to that grazing-land, the sheep had been moving quickly, eager for fresh grass after being watered, but now they had full bellies and moved more slowly.

The stranger was still at the well when my sisters and I arrived there, as Nazirah had predicted. He was still sitting on the stone and looking at the ground, as if he had not moved. This time he did not even look up as we approached. As before, we ignored him as he ignored us.

No one else was in sight, so we thought we could water the sheep again and fill our skins without being bothered. But before we had well begun, I saw Kadin bare his teeth and heard a deep growl from far down in his chest. The hair on his spine was rising as he stared toward the north.

I looked. A group of men was coming toward us, driving a few scruffy goats before them. Their robes were filthy, and we could see even at a distance that they were filthy themselves. They were Melikites, and that tribe did not love us. They were approaching confidently, laughing, grinning with their brown teeth, and staring. This will be bad, I thought.

They drove our flocks away from the well and made them scatter. Kadin did what he could, barking wildly, snarling and snapping; but when he attacked a man who was coming close to me, the ruffian struck him with his staff. Kadin ran away yelping, tail tucked between his legs, holding a hind leg high.

I cried out for our dog. The Melikites laughed — and then they began to look at us in a way we did not like at all. Four women, all young, and no man with us. To them, we must have looked like — *prey*. Nazirah was fumbling with her sling, but it was too late. They were too close for her to use it.

The stranger did not intervene. He only watched — and even that, he did sidewise, pretending he saw nothing. We will get no help from him, I thought. But when the goatherds began to gather close around us, grinning, he grew more alert, watching openly. Still, he made no move and spoke no word.

Three of the Melikites gathered around Rivkah. They began to reach out with their grimy hands and play with her red hair and touch her cheeks. She was frightened, near tears, and they laughed at her fear. Two others were grinning at Nazirah, laughing at her fierce expression and mocking her balled fists, and another, a tall man with an ugly smile, was whispering something to Basimah that made her eyes go wide and wild. They began to talk openly about what they were going to do to us, taunting us, laughing and rubbing their bodies through their foul, ill-fitting robes. I was facing them and could not see the foreigner, but I did not expect him to do anything. There were six of the Melikites, all younger than he, and he was alone.

One man, whose teeth were either missing or brown, drew near to me. He reached for my face. He stank, a thick, sour smell of goat and unwashed Melikite. I felt his rough hand with its black-rimmed fingernails on my cheek. I shuddered, and he grinned. Then his eyes widened and went past me, though his grin remained —

And suddenly he fell to the ground, holding his arm and howling. I whirled to look behind me.

The stranger was there, crouching and holding his staff sidewise in both hands. His face was grim and determined, but his eyes were empty of anything but watchfulness. There may have been anger there, but if so, it was a cold anger. The other Melikites left off tormenting my sisters and came at him, shouting. He glanced at me and pointed behind him. I moved there.

He did not move as the Melikites ran toward him. He waited, then lunged at them when they drew near, his staff whipping and thrusting. In less time than it takes to draw a breath, he had struck at them so many times that I could not count them. He moved with a speed and a skill I had never seen before in any man.

He whirled and turned and twisted and struck with his staff, slashing and jabbing with it more quickly than my eyes could follow. His face was as still and solemn as it had been when he was sitting alone, and though he seemed detached, he moved with a control and precision that was devastating in its effect. One of the Melikites managed to get close enough to grab at him — but the foreigner grasped his hand and twisted it somehow, and I heard the bone snap. The goatherd cried out and backed away.

The man moved like a dancer, but a dangerous one; his staff struck a man in the mouth, breaking teeth and drawing blood, and in the next instant the butt of it speared into another's ribs. The stick moved so fast, it was a blur. I saw it whip around to strike a grimy arm as he kicked hard at the side of another Melikite's knee, making its owner cry out and fall. The stranger's lightning-quick staff shot out and struck deep into the tall man's groin, and then smashed into another's face without a pause as his elbow struck one more. He whipped the staff again, one-handed, at a Melikite's shins and knocked him to the ground. His other hand pulled another's robe tight around his throat, jerked, and then spun him away to fall on his face beside the first. The staff whirled around and was back in both his hands again, and in an eyeblink had struck twice, three times, four times more.

I had never seen anything like it. The stranger fought like a whirlwind, his staff and his feet and his fists everywhere at once. And through it all, his face remained impassive — his mouth was grimly set, but his eyes were empty, watching only, as if he were outside the fight and not at the heart of it.

I was watching for a chance to help with my crook, perhaps to trip one of the Melikites or pull his feet from under him, but there was no time. It was over very quickly. In the space of a few heartbeats, three of the goatherds were on the ground, groaning or crying out, and the other three were falling back, then retreating, staggering and stunned. I watched them backing away, then looked back at the foreigner.

The man was standing there with his feet wide apart, still holding his staff in both hands. Both ends of it dripped blood, and there were more smears of it here and there along its length. He was watching the Melikites, his eyes flicking from one of them to another. Then he set the foot of his staff back on the ground and stood still, as calm and cold-eyed as when he began. The Melikites who were still standing helped the injured ones up, and they all backed away, watching him. I saw drops and smears of their blood on the ground. So did they.

My sisters were cowering by the well, eyes wide, looking from the stranger to the Melikites and back. I remember Nazirah's face especially; it bore a delighted, admiring grin, and she was biting her lip in excitement. I also noticed that she had her sling in her hand with a sharp stone ready in it. If the Melikites tried again, they would get yet another wound.

I realized then that all of these filthy beasts had curved knives in their sashes, but the stranger had given them no time to draw them. I remember thinking that it would not have mattered if they had. Any hand that had drawn a knife would have been empty and broken, and very quickly.

The man had gone from explosive motion as fast as lightning to complete and utter stillness in an eyeblink. He watched the Melikites silently as they stumbled away, cursing and looking back at him with wide eyes.

The strangely dressed man remained watchful, but was still detached and distant. He was not even breathing hard. I was.

I looked at him more closely. The stranger's mouth bore no hint of a smile. He was all alertness, all attention, nothing moving but his eyes and some drops of perspiration running down his face to his clean-shaven jaw. I think if one of the Melikites had even thought of attacking again, he would have known it.

They must have sensed that as well, because they stopped cursing us and began to hurry away, cursing at their goats instead as they drove them. One of the men was holding a bruised and probably broken arm, another a broken wrist, two more had swollen eyes and bleeding mouths. All but one of them limped, and two could barely stand. The stranger had done a lot of damage in that short span of time.

As the goatherds stumbled away, the foreign man seemed to relax, just a bit. He looked down at his blood-smeared staff, and for a moment, there was an expression on his face, where there had been none before. He seemed to be — surprised. His eyebrows moved up, then down, and he looked up at the retreating Melikites again, as if wondering what they were doing.

Then he turned and looked at me.

17

The stranger said nothing. Indeed, he never spoke a word, not before the fight, not during it, and not after. Nor did he smile, exactly, not then. His expression was still cold and distant. He nodded, and that only.

Not at the other girls. Not even at Rivkah, the pretty one. Only me.

He only looked at me for a heartbeat, that second time, but it was not like the first. This time, I did feel something. I looked back, and boldly. This was not done among my people, not with strangers, but I looked him in the face, unafraid.

I will never forget his eyes. I had never seen eyes like his before, nor have I since. They were gray, like my own, but darker; and they were sad, and bleak, but knowing somehow. Sad, but wise.

Then, abruptly, he turned away and began looking around, searching. I realized that he was seeking our dog, Kadin. Soon we saw him, huddled next to a clump of bushes not far from the well. He was whimpering, his tail still curled beneath him, and his leg was bent in an unnatural way.

The man looked to make sure the Melikites were still moving away, and then he laid down his staff and approached the hurt animal, very slowly, hands out, palms toward the earth. I realized that Kadin would have been frightened by his staff, or by a sudden movement or an upraised hand, and that the stranger knew this and was being careful not to alarm him.

He knelt and let the dog sniff his hands. Then he began, very gently, to examine the leg. Kadin whimpered softly, but allowed it.

The man said nothing, but he rose and looked around again. Then he shook his head and drew his own knife. I and my sisters gasped, but he ignored us and began working to cut off a branch of the little bush under which Kadin was hiding. I had no idea what he was doing; none of us did. His knife was not curved, as knives in our part of the world normally were; it was straight, with a leaf-shaped blade, double-edged. Those edges glittered brightly, the bronze well and freshly sharpened. It was a Greek dagger, I learned later.

When he had cut the stick free, he stripped off the twigs and dry leaves and laid it on the ground. Then he cut another, about the same size, and stripped it as well. When he had finished that, he thrust the knife back into the sheath that hung from his belt and tore a strip from the hem of his tunic. We watched in fascination, but he never looked at us while he was doing all this, not once.

Working carefully, he bound Kadin's leg between the branches, gently, but firmly. He petted the dog, soothing him — and then, before any of us could react, he took Kadin's leg in his two hands and jerked it, hard, as if he were trying to pull it apart, but he did it with a kind of precision. I had never seen anything quite like it before, and had no idea what he was trying to do.

Kadin yelped once, loudly, then snarled and snapped at the man's hands — but then he stopped. The stranger waited till the dog seemed calmer, and then, as Kadin watched his hands warily, the man tied the leg again, around the middle this time and more tightly. He bound the leg between the two sticks so it could not move. Then he petted the dog's head.

When Kadin licked his hand, he smiled a little and rose. That was the first time I ever saw him smile.

Then he smiled at me — and gestured at the dog with a petting gesture. I understood what he meant. Kadin would be all right.

I came closer, knelt, and examined what he had done. Our dog's leg was straight. It was swollen, but the unnatural bend in it was gone. His tail flapped uncertainly, and he licked my hand too.

I looked the stranger in the face again — and nodded, twice. My intent was to thank him. I wondered if he could speak our tongue.

He nodded again, his smile fading. It had never reached his eyes. He was looking at me, again ignoring the others. He gave a small shrug, then went back to his place and sat on the stone. He bent down and took a handful of earth, then began to clean the blood from his staff. He gave us no further attention. When he was finished, he resumed staring at nothing, in the same defeated posture as before.

Once more, I thought he looked like a man lost, without home or destination. *Haunted*, I thought at the time — and then I wondered, how could I know such a thing? And what could that even mean? I shook my head in confusion.

Among our clan, women spoke when they liked; the only man among us was Father, and he encouraged us to be forthright and open. He did not mind when we addressed him first, or even when we interrupted him. But we knew that among other people in our land, a woman who spoke to a man without his speaking to her first, especially a man she did not know, was — well, she was either a very rude little girl, or not a good woman.

The foreign man had not spoken, so we smiled our thanks only, but I do not think he even saw that. After we had gathered our flocks again, and calmed them and watered them, and filled all our waterskins, we left him there, sitting and gazing at the ground as he had been before.

It did not feel right to leave him there, but we did.

We clicked our tongues and cried out and kicked at the sheep to get them moving, since our staffs and crooks were on our shoulders holding the waterskins. It was harder, and we walked more slowly. The waterskins were heavy, and each of us bore two or three on either side. Kadin hopped along beside us, and though he whimpered a little from time to time, he seemed all right. I noticed that the man had bound his leg so his foot could not touch the ground; only the sticks did, and in a way that put no pressure on his leg.

I marveled at this. I had never seen anyone take such care to treat an animal's injuries. We treated our sheep's small wounds and scratches, but if one of them broke a leg, it would be roasting on the fire that night. I wondered where the man had learned to do that.

Time and again, I thought of going back. It was wrong to leave the man there, after what he had done for us. But I did not know what he would think if I returned and spoke to him, so we went on.

The day was still hot, and there was still no breeze. Even so, it seemed less oppressive somehow, even with the weight of the water I was carrying. The land seemed less bleak and bare, and I noticed more life than I remembered seeing on the way to the well. Insects and lizards, mostly, scrubby plants and dry growth, a bird or two — but still, it was life. The day seemed softer, though the sun was as bright and hot as it had been.

We walked in silence till the sun was low and we were near our tents. We could spare little energy or attention for talking. The waterskins were heavy, and we had to take care to keep them balanced as well as keeping our sheep together and moving. I was sure that my sisters were still thinking of the ordeal we had escaped — rape, certainly, and murder likely — but I had already forgotten all that. I was thinking of the stranger.

He was older than I, very much so, though he had certainly not moved like an old man. His eyes, especially, were different. Somehow both old and young at once. They were like the eyes of a child in an older man's face, I decided. He saw everything as if for the first time, but he understood what he saw, perhaps better than anyone.

How I knew these things, I could not tell you.

18

It was not a long way back to the Mountain, but it seemed long that day. The four of us hardly spoke at first. That was not like us; normally we chattered like birds, and after something like what we had just seen, one would think we would all be eager to share what we thought — but it seemed we had little to say. We were all grateful for our escape, but I soon found out that the foreign man had impressed my sisters, too.

After a time, we stopped to put down the waterskins and rest for a moment. As we rubbed our shoulders, Basimah spoke: "Why do you think that man — did that?"

Rivkah stretched and bent. "I guess he liked us."

I blurted out, "No. That is not why." Before I could stop myself, I went on: "I think he thought it was wrong. What they were doing, what they were about to do."

"Why would it concern him?" asked Basimah.

"He thought it did." Then I added, "I think that to him, to stand by and do nothing would have been as bad as joining them."

"But when we first saw him, he looked like he cared about nothing." This was Nazirah.

"That is true." I said thoughtfully. I remembered how he had looked.

"And it was six against one, too," said Rivkah.

I remember I laughed at that. "That did not help them much."

We all laughed then, and Nazirah lifted a fist and shook it. "He was amazing. I wish I knew how to fight like that."

"Me, too." This came from Rivkah, which surprised all of us.

The sheep were still moving. Even with his injury, Kadin was still working them, running back and forth to keep them together. We shouldered our burdens again and hurried to catch up.

The sun behind us was a handsbreadth from setting, and the Mountain loomed large, glowing red in its light as we approached it. I saw our new camp in the distance, closer to its slopes, not far from another wadi that sometimes held water. We had camped there when I was small. It was a good place, with shade in the morning. We were all looking forward to washing our feet, having something to eat, and then resting by the fire.

We walked on in silence again for a while. The sheep had been bleating more on the way back, I noticed. I suppose their throats were less dry. I remember that I kept shifting the staff bearing the waterskins on my shoulders.

Rivkah looked down at our dog as he hopped beside us. "Did you see how he fixed Kadin's leg? I have never seen anything like that."

"Nor I," said Basimah. "I wonder where he learned it."

Nazirah snorted. "I wonder *why* he did it. Kadin is only a dog."

We all thought on that. Kadin was more than only a dog, to us — but why would the stranger care?

When we reached our camp and told Father of what had happened, he was furious.

"Why did you not invite the man to come back with you and join us in our meal?" he asked angrily. "You owe him much! Perhaps your very lives!"

Qamra and Sabah were helping us with the waterskins. I set the last of mine down. "He did not speak, Father —" I began, but he stopped me.

"Perhaps he was unable to speak!" He pointed back at the way we had come. "Tzipporah, take these foolish girls back to the well and ask that man to come back with you!"

The other girls groaned. It was not a long way, but it was hot and they were tired. I must have reacted differently somehow; Father looked at me quickly, and though his face was still set in a stern scowl, before he turned away I saw a smile beginning.

Kadin would have gone too, but Father restrained him. Rivkah, who was exhausted, was excused as well. As we left, I saw Father studying what the man had done to Kadin's leg. I wondered what he was thinking.

Nazirah and I hardly spoke on our way back to the well. She was angry. Basimah had been excused as well — to be fair, she too was very tired — and it was only the two of us. The lowering sun was in our eyes, which did not help her temper.

When we were younger, I was Nazirah's disciplinarian as often as Father or our mothers, and she always resented my authority as the oldest. We had been growing more affectionate — or perhaps only more tolerant — toward one another as we grew older, but I thought even then that we would never be close. Our walk back to the well was made in silence for the most part.

There was one exchange of words, and it was unusual, for us. As we crossed the stretch of black rock, still blazing-hot from the sun, Nazirah spoke with an edge to her voice. "Father was right. We should have invited the man to come back with us. You are the oldest of us — why did you not do that?"

Nazirah was trying to pick a fight. It was not the first time, and on any other day I might have snapped back at her. I would have told her, as I did Father, that the man did not speak, and it was unseemly for an unmarried woman — or even a married one— to invite a man she had just met to come home with her. But I knew how the argument would go, and I saw no reason to have it just then. There was something else I wanted to think about.

Besides, she was right; so I told her that. "You are right, Nazirah. And so was Father. I should have extended our hospitality to the man. You are right."

She opened her mouth — then closed it again. I smiled inwardly. She had expected argument, not agreement.

What I wanted to think about, of course, was the stranger at the well.

The foreign man was the first man ever to look at me without either fear or hatred, or — as the Melikites did on that day at the well — as a potential victim.

But he certainly had no fear of me, and he had done something for me — for all of us — without asking or expecting return or reward. It was a new experience, meeting him, even with no words passing between us.

I guessed that he had about fifty years when I met him, and I thought perhaps even a few more, but that was of no importance. It was common among my people for an older man to marry a young girl, and many girls preferred an older husband. Older men were much more settled and mature than boys our own age, and likelier to have established a home and a livelihood. Most such men had several wives already, as my father did; but a woman like me would be lucky to find a husband at all, even as a third or fourth wife. On that day, of course, it was silly to even think about all this, and I knew it. I did not even know his name. He was only the oddly-dressed stranger that we had met at the well.

But still, my heart leaped at the thought of seeing him again.

When we finally reached the well, the sun was touching the horizon. I wondered if the man would be gone, but he was still there, sitting on the same stone, still looking at the ground. *He has not moved at all*, I thought.

I approached him with the universal gesture of welcome — arms wide, hands open, palms up. My stomach was fluttering, and my hands quivered. I realized, again, that I did not even know if he spoke our language. He was not looking at me, but at the ground, so I spoke. My voice came out in a dry croak. I cleared my throat, my face burning, and started again.

"We are grateful for what you have done for us. Would you — would you come back to our camp with us, and let us thank you properly by sharing our meal?"

The man looked up, and then at me, for a long, long time — or what seemed a long time. *He is not deaf*, I thought. His gray eyes were bleak and blank. Then he blinked, and he seemed to see me for the first time.

He frowned, seemed to think for a moment — then shook his head and looked back at the ground.

Nazirah and I looked at each other. She lifted her hands; what can we do? the gesture said.

I turned back to the stranger. I did not think about giving up for an instant. I felt compelled to try again, and afraid that he still would not come. "*Please* come with us. Our father was very angry that we did not offer our hospitality after you — after you saved us from the Melikites. I was wrong not to have invited you back with us then. Please share our meal, at least. Will you not accept our thanks?"

He looked up again, still frowning. He seemed to be examining my face, as if he were searching for something. He opened his mouth, as if to speak, then closed it again.

"Please do not shame us," I pleaded. I had a sick, hollow feeling; *he is not going to come*, I thought. I remember that even at that time, I wondered why this was so important to me — but I knew beyond doubt that it was.

The stranger was still looking up at me, watching my face. I wondered what he saw there. Finally, he nodded, then gave a little shrug and nodded again.

He stood up slowly — not wearily, but without hurry. He hitched up his bag and settled it and his waterskin on his shoulder, and then he picked up his staff, looked at us, nodded again, and lifted a hand: *after you*, the gesture said. He did not speak.

We started back as the sun was setting behind us. The Mountain, in the distance, glowed a duller red in the fading light. As we trudged along, I stole glances at the man. I tried not to stare, but I suppose I did, a little. I saw my sister smirking, but she said nothing.

He had a tattered fabric bag slung over one shoulder, a well-worn waterskin beside it, his staff, and that seemed to be all. He looked so foreign to our eyes; besides his being clean-shaven, his hair was cropped close to his scalp, and was the shortest we had ever beheld on man or woman. Everything about him was different. Even his sandals were of an unfamiliar design. He was not from any place or people that we knew.

We asked him no questions, since it was clear enough that he did not wish to talk. I watched his face, and he seemed less distracted, less preoccupied, though there was, once again, no smile there.

I suppose I spent more time looking at him than I should have. I could not call him "handsome," but his face was strong, and there was a kind of gentleness as well as sadness beneath the strength. I thought his nose had been broken, but that only gave him a rugged aspect. As we walked along, his eyes were always on the horizon, searching, seeking, looking for something that I could not see. He seemed contained within himself, thoughtful and reflective. Haunted, perhaps, as I had thought before, as if he were listening for something he never quite heard. I could not have seen all that on that first evening, I know, but that is how I remember it.

I remember this, especially: Watching his sandals move along the ground as he walked, his staff striking the ground beside them at every second step. I distinctly remember having the feeling that I would see that again — and again, and again.

It was not, I thought, as if I were seeing into my future. It seemed more that my future was somehow looking back at me.

I had no idea where these thoughts were coming from. I was beginning to wonder what was happening to my mind, if I were losing it somehow.

I looked around, and at the path before us. This was my home, familiar, the place where I had always lived. But it seemed changed. The whole world seemed different that day, as I walked beside the stranger back to our tents. These were only the first of many strange thoughts and feelings I had after meeting Kisil.

My sister watched us, and she seemed less amused than before. After a time, she leaned toward me and whispered, "Sister, I think the thing that you felt was coming—has come."

I blinked at her. With all that had happened, I had forgotten our conversation in the tent that morning.

19

It was almost full dark when we saw our tents and the glow of our fire in the distance. We got back barely in time; the moon was two nights past new, and still only a narrow sliver, low in the western sky. Before much more time had passed, there would have been nothing but starlight to see by.

We were still far away when Kadin began to bark, and my father looked up; when he saw us coming, he rose and watched us approach, holding Kadin back and scratching behind his ear. When we finally came into the light of the fire, Father moved toward us, approaching the man with his arms extended in that same gesture of greeting that I had used. Kadin came up to the man eagerly, almost leaping in excitement in spite of his injured leg.

“Welcome, my friend!" Father had a broad smile on his battered face. "I am Yisro, father and chief of this clan. I thank you for what you have done for my daughters. And for our dog,” he added with a grin. The man nodded and smiled again, almost shyly, I thought, but still, he said nothing. My father looked at me, and I shrugged a little and shook my head.

“What may we call you?” Father was still smiling, but he was as baffled as we at the man’s silence. The stranger looked at the ground. He seemed to be thinking, but that made little sense. Who has to think to remember his own name? We blinked at each other, even more puzzled.

Then the man looked up and spoke, and the mystery of his silence, at least, was solved.

“My name is Yekusiel. I wish to be called — Kisil.”

His voice was deep and resonant, but he spoke thickly, with a heavy lisp. His name came out "Kithil." I was touched, and thought it endearing.

In the light of the fire, I saw that his lips were subtly scarred. I had not noticed it till then. He had suffered some injury to his mouth long before, though I could not guess how. He knelt to pet Kadin, and the dog licked his hand. Kisil ruffled the fur on his head, and the dog made a small whuffing sound of contentment.

"Yekusiel — so, Kisil." My father spoke thoughtfully. "Yes. I have a distant cousin by that name." He watched the man petting our dog, then shook his head, as if to clear it. The stranger seemed to be affecting him too, somehow.

"Come, wash your feet and join us!" Sabah was filling a large basin from one of the waterskins we had brought. After a journey, it was good to rinse the dust and grit from feet and sandals, and of course to offer the basin for washing was an ancient gesture of hospitality and welcome. After Kisil, who as guest had the privilege of going first, we all took our turns at it.

Father indicated a place to sit by the fire. "Rivkah, bring our friend a cup of ewe's-milk beer." She ran to fetch it as Father went on: "Would you like something to eat, Kisil? We have roast meat, and some pottage of lentils and onions, and dates. Also some bread, still fresh."

"Thank you." The stranger — Kisil — sat down. He had set his waterskin, bag and staff down nearby. "Yes. I am hungry." Kadin settled beside him, as if it were an old habit. From that day on, Kadin was Kisil's dog, not ours, but we did not know that then.

Kisil looked up at me, and, to my surprise, he smiled — and this time, the smile seemed to reach his eyes.

I knew that I was staring at him, and that my stare made men flinch. But Kisil did not flinch, nor even blink. He smiled at me, so openly and in such a kind way, that I felt he knew me somehow, knew my own shyness, and how I covered it with an appearance of boldness.

I will not say that I knew then, on that first night, that he would be my husband. That would not be true. But I did sense that he was different, and that there was — something, some bond, some connection — between us. I stared terribly, but he did not seem to mind. He only smiled, and I wondered if he felt it too.

We spoke little as we ate that night. My sisters and I had not eaten, either, and we had some meat and pottage and bread along with Kisil. My father had a cup of beer himself, and settled himself between my two mothers, who were smiling and trying not to stare — at me.

Kisil spoke only the bare few words necessary not to be regarded as impolite: "Thank you." "Yes, please." "It is very good." "No, I have had enough."

Soon we were done, but I noticed that Kisil seemed to be enjoying the dates, so I offered him some more. After some hesitation, he took, to my surprise, a whole handful.

He gave a wry smile at my open mouth. He cocked his head and said, "I have not tasted dates in a very long time." It sounded as if he were speaking around something in his mouth, or against some sort of resistance. I sensed the effort it cost him to make his words clear.

I laughed and urged him to take more. He grinned and did. He had good teeth for a man his age. I remember noticing that.

My father asked, "Where are you from, Kisil? Who are your people?"

Kisil looked up. The question seemed to surprise him. After another of those long pauses that seemed to us unnecessary, he spoke again. "I have no people, Yisro. Not any more." His voice was deep, and sad.

Father nodded. We all understood; the man did not wish to speak of his past, and it would be rude to press him.

"Are you married?" asked one of my sisters. Father frowned, and some of the younger girls giggled. My mother Sabah put her hand over her mouth, and Qamra snorted — whether with disapproval or suppressed laughter I could not tell.

Kisil did not answer in words, but smiled indulgently at the girls — and shook his head with a kind of sidewise shrug that indicated he thought the question silly, even funny. I was watching him the whole time, very closely, and my sisters were watching me and trying to stifle their giggles. I am very sure that I blushed.

Father turned to me with no hint of a smile on his face. "Play for us, Tzipporah," he said, a little gruffly. "Let our new friend hear the song of your flute." We all knew, all but Kisil, that his gruffness meant he was trying not to laugh.

He had been watching me watching the man, and I think he wished to give me something to do other than stare. It did not come to me till later that he wanted Kisil to hear my special skill as well.

It has only occurred to me now, so many years later, that my mother Qamra did not join in that night, nor did Basimah or Rivkah, to sing with me or keep the rhythm. I think they were all hoping that Kisil would be interested in me. I had never thought of that before, not in all these long years. It makes me smile now — and miss them. My sisters are all gone now, and have been for a very long time.

I took out my flute and played, and Kisil listened; and before long, his face filled with wonder. Soon he closed his eyes to hear me better.

By then I was used to people listening to me with their eyes shut. I knew that there was a power in my playing, the power to bring peace and calm to troubled hearts. I could see that this man, this Kisil, was troubled by something. I wanted to give him that peace, and I played my best for him.

I played till the fire burned low, and he listened, with eyes closed and a hint of a smile on his weathered face. My family listened and watched.

Kisil and I did not speak that night, only smiled at each other; but my father sensed something as well. When I went to our tent that night, where I slept with my mothers, Father grinned and winked at me, his mismatched eyes bright, before I went in. He knew before I did, before Kisil did. I heard his words in my mind, from so long before: "When the time is right."

Looking back, I know now that my father Yisro was not like other men, though I never thought about that at the time. I had known so very few other men. He was always just my father. I thought all fathers just — *knew* things, like he did. They say now that he was a prophet. Perhaps he was — and perhaps I did carry his gift, as well as his blood.

20

That night was still and quiet, and Kisil slept under the stars, near the fire. He was wrapped in a thin cloak he had taken from his bag. Kadin was snuggled against him, and he threw one arm over the dog as he slept. I blush to say that I know this because I peeked out of the tentflap once or twice to see.

The next morning, Kisil made no move to leave. He sat by the fire for a while, thinking. We all left him alone — well, all except me. I brought him some bread and a cup of milk, and another handful of dates. He looked up in surprise, then gave me another of those rare smiles.

"Stay with us," I said abruptly. "You have nowhere else to go. Stay with us." I realized as I spoke that it was not my place to say such things, but I said them even so.

His eyes searched my face again, and I blushed as the silence stretched out. "I am a wanderer, Tzipporah," he finally said, and I noted again the effort that it cost him to speak. "I have no home and no people, and I have never stayed anywhere for long."

I smiled. "Stay for a while only, then. Rest with us before you wander on. You will be welcome here for as long as you care to stay." He took another date and chewed it thoughtfully.

I did not want to press him more, so I left him then. He returned to his thinking as he ate, and I busied myself with other things, watching him sidewise.

He finally stood and picked up his bag and his staff. I held my breath — but then he set them down again and left them lying where he had slept, and walked away, out into the desert. I stopped pretending not to watch him.

He stooped to pick something up, once, twice, then again. He was looking around, searching. Then he stooped again.

He was gathering sticks and sheep dung for our fire. I felt a deep warmth spreading through me. He was going to stay.

After he had stacked the fuel he found with the rest, Kisil approached my father, who was tending the sheep near the wadi. I do not know what was said, but Kisil remained at our camp all day, finding ways to make himself useful. He examined a few of our sheep with minor hurts, and pointed out a young ram who had injured a hoof. He bound it, then spliced a tent rope that was wearing thin. He rarely spoke, but smiled at me from time to time.

As the sun sank lower, I caught his eye and lifted my eyebrows in a silent question — and he cocked his head and nodded, with a crooked smile that I would grow to love.

That night, my father told us that Kisil would be staying with us for a time. Kisil sat by and said nothing, drinking his milk beer as if he were somewhere else, ignoring our inquiring looks.

My father did not tell us directly, but we all knew. It was as I had said: Kisil had nowhere else to go. He would work alongside us to earn his keep. We were all pleased. It would be good to have another man around. And I, of course, was especially pleased.

21

Kisil spoke little at first. He was not ashamed of his way of speaking, I think, but only reluctant to subject others to the difficulty of understanding him. He was never rude or obstinate in his silence, but he spoke only when it was necessary — and even then, he used as few words as he could manage. As he got to know us, he spoke more. Especially to me.

It seemed very natural to have him there, even at the very first. I got the feeling that he could fit in and make friends anywhere, and had done so, many times and in many places. He was unfailingly pleasant and friendly, and had a way of really listening when someone else spoke, as if he were very interested in whatever that person had to say. I think he was. I know that he never forgot a single thing I ever told him.

He was always ready with a compliment or a kind word, but more often, only a silent smile. His laughter was especially precious to me, because it was so rare.

I was not the only one with whom Kisil was friendly. He won over all of my sisters, though I did not think he would, at least at first.

One day — a windy day, with much dust in the air — he was in my sisters' tent, watching Charah at the loom. They were not alone, of course; that would not have been proper. I was there, and I think Basimah too, or perhaps Rivkah. Though Charah was making something of a point of ignoring him, Kisil seemed very interested in what she was doing and was watching her very closely.

I did not quite have time to become jealous. After only a short time he stepped forward and, without speaking, showed her something. He lifted a finger, as if to say, "Watch"; and then he leaned forward and had her observe him as he made a few passes with the shuttle.

Though she seemed annoyed at first, her eyes grew wide as she watched his hands. He exaggerated his movements and moved the threads slowly, so she could see, and she nodded excitedly and gestured for him to do it again. He did, then he watched her for a while as she worked the loom herself. She looked back at him hopefully, and, as was his way, he said nothing, but smiled and nodded. Charah beamed and returned to her work with renewed enthusiasm as the wind whipped the tentflap back and forth.

I was never good at weaving and did not understand, but Charah was delighted at whatever technique it was that he showed her. After that day, her fabric had a tighter texture, and seemed thicker somehow, even though it was in truth a little lighter than it had been. After that day, Charah was no longer sullen and reserved around Kisil. They had become friends with hardly a word passing between them.

Nor was Charah the only one affected by Kisil's charm. Nazirah had been openly disdainful of him at first; when he smiled at her, she tossed her head and turned away with a sniff, and made more than one cutting remark behind his back — "tongue-tied vagabond" was one phrase that I remember. But after a few days, when he showed her a trick with the sling — a way to sling two or even three or four stones in quick succession, again without speaking a word — she grew respectful, and even laughed with him. Before long, they were practicing together, and Nazirah showed him a few things, too. It was not long before they, too, became friends.

The same happened with all my sisters, and with my mothers as well. Kisil would teach them something — or they would teach him — and soon we all enjoyed his smiling, though largely silent, presence.

He showed Malkah how to use a bit of tallow on her fingers when she was spinning, to make the thread dense and hard. He showed Tharah new kinds of clothing, new designs, which he had seen in other lands. He showed my mothers some tricks with tentmaking, and knots, and fire-building, and he even showed Father a thing or two about the use of letters and numbers. Father had insisted that we all learn to read and write and do tallying, even though that was not common among women in our land.

Most of Kisil's instruction was given in silence. He showed us, rather than told us, what to do, speaking only at need. When he did speak, I was struck, again, by the depth and resonance of his voice in spite of its being so impaired. Still, it was a long time before he began to speak more than a few words at a time.

Especially touching to me was what he did for Rivkah. One day she came to me with her bright blue eyes sparkling to show me how Kisil had taught her a new way to weave baskets. Rivkah, the youngest of my sisters, had no practical talents like the rest of us; but from that day she became our basket-maker. It made her proud, and even Nazirah admired and praised her skill. I tried to thank Kisil for what he had done for her, but he waved my thanks away.

He knew much, and shared it freely, but never in a condescending way. Besides teaching us all new things about the skills we already had, he taught us things of which we knew nothing at all. He taught us how to fight with the staff, for instance, and with the knife — and some tricks for fighting without either as well.

It was at about that time that he began to speak more often. I think it was because he wanted to teach us how to avoid fights as well as win them, and that took words. He also taught us much that we did not know about the plants in our land; how some that we thought were useless were good for cooking or for healing, and how others, that we did know, could be used in new and different ways. He showed us one, which we had always thought only a weed, that could be dried and beaten into fibers that made a strong rope. All this took words as well.

After he began to speak, he spoke more and more, and he got better at it. I wondered how much of his impairment was simply from his habitual silence, from his never having spoken much.

Kisil taught me, too. I learned much about herding sheep and the use of the staff and crook — and most of all, how to train Kadin to help.

Even with his splinted leg, Kadin picked up on the new training quickly — and after the splint was gone, he was twice the dog he had been, even though that leg was always a little stiff. Kisil trained him to respond to gestures and signals more than to words. This was not because of his own reluctance to speak, as I had guessed: "It is safer," Kisil said. "In a storm, or a high wind, he might not hear you, but he can still see you. Dogs want to help, and they want to understand what we want. They *want* to be trained, Tzipporah." Then he grinned. "In that way, they are not like people." That was perhaps the longest speech he had made by that time, and I was glad of it. I already cherished the sound of his deep, careful voice.

Teaching me about herding the sheep, and how to work with Kadin, gave us much time away from the others. It was not by chance that he chose me for those lessons, I knew. We all herded the sheep; but these things he taught to me only.

22

Kisil and I began to spend much time together, especially in the evening. Sometimes I would play for him as he listened. Sometimes we walked out away from the camp and looked at the moon, or the Mountain, or the sheep, or the stars. We did not speak much, though he spoke more to me than to anyone. He seemed to enjoy my company, and even though those evenings were often silent, I enjoyed his company as well.

I remember a night when I tried to teach him to play the flute. It was a night with a big moon, though not a full one, and there was a gentle breeze off the Empty Land beyond the Mountain. He tried his best with the flute, but had no ear for it, and his fingers — so agile on the loom and with the sling and with animals — were clumsy and slow. He finally laughed and handed the pipe back to me, shaking his head. He made a circling gesture with his hand, and I knew what it meant; play for me. So I did, and he listened. His back was to the fire, and I could see my sisters, or their shadows, as they rose to join us — and my father's shadow as he gestured for them to sit back down.

It was hard to play the flute when I was smiling, so I shut my eyes.

One morning I rose early. What woke me I do not know, but I dressed, left my mothers' tent, and went outside to look round. I felt I was searching for something, though I knew not what. I walked around the tents, then aimlessly out into the plain. And there, in the dimness of the early morning, I saw Kisil. He was standing alone some distance away; still, arms at his sides, looking at the Mountain.

I approached him quietly. I sensed that it was important not to disturb him. I walked around him, and I saw his face.

Kisil's eyes were distant, far away, as they were so often; but this time, they were sharply focused. His mouth was set in concentration, grim and determined.

I spoke, but quietly. "Kisil?"

He did not look at me. I began to speak his name again, but he lifted a hand — gently, I thought, though quickly and firmly. The meaning was clear: *Not now*.

I touched his uplifted hand with my own, then went back to the tents. He did not mention the incident later, and I saw him in that same posture, with that same expression, many times thereafter. He was always looking into the distance — sometimes at the Mountain, but often not. I knew better than to bring it up. He knew that I had seen him so, and if he wanted to speak of it, he would.

By this time, Kisil no longer wore his short tunic, but dressed as one of us. He wore a robe that had belonged to my father, and later a robe that I made for him myself, the first of many. He let his hair grow, and his beard. He wore the same folded cloth bound with a cord on his head and shoulders as the other men in our land. I once saw him looking at himself, at his reflection, in a pool of water. He frowned at the sight, but he never told me why.

We often left the flocks in Kisil's charge by this time, and he was a good shepherd. He was as skilled as any of us at herding, and as quick and accurate as Nazirah with a sling. The jackals soon learned to run when he stooped for a stone.

We learned much from Kisil, but we taught him some things, too. He learned to cut the wool from the sheep — and even though he was a man, he insisted on learning how to prepare food for meals, and how to cook it, and how to grind grain and bake bread. A cook, he told us, was one thing he had never been. My mothers were pleased that he was so respectful and eager to learn from them.

He had become one of us.

23

I remember the first time that Kisil spoke out of something more than bare necessity. We were sitting by the fire, and it happened that we were alone. I think the others conspired to leave us alone often, and I think we both knew it.

"Tzipporah." No one else ever pronounced my name in quite the way he did. I remember the sound of it still.

His tone was different from any that I had ever heard from him before; it was thoughtful, abstracted. I turned to face him. "Yes, Kisil?"

"Do you ever wonder... Why we are here?" He was still looking at the fire, not at me.

It was such an odd question, and so uncharacteristic of him, that I could not think what to say. He looked at the fire, and I understood somehow that even if I answered not at all, it would be all right.

Finally, I said, "No. I do not wonder." I thought about his question. "I have always lived day to day, doing what I must do to care for my sisters, my mothers, my father, and the sheep. One day, then the next. That is enough for me, I suppose."

He was stroking Kadin's back. The dog was lying next to him, as he often did. I looked back at the fire too. I wanted him to know that it was all right if he said no more, and for a long time he was indeed silent.

The moon rose. It was a half-moon, bright and golden, like the firelight. Kisil looked up at it. "I have always been alone. No one to care for. Perhaps that is why I wonder."

He spoke carefully, trying hard to make his words clear. "But what about your peop—" I stopped.

He knew what I had been about to say. A shadow came over his face, though he did not speak.

A little later, he asked, "Have your people always lived apart?" I think he asked to make me feel better, to show me that I had not offended him. That was one of the things I loved most about Kisil — no matter what was in his own heart, he wanted to make sure that he never wounded that of another.

I told him a little of what I knew — about my father, about his being an outcast, and why. He listened carefully, nodding often, but saying nothing. When I was done, he looked at the Moon again. "You have given me much to think about."

On impulse, I spoke again. "I think you have always had much to think about, Kisil." At his surprised expression, I added, "I think that perhaps you think too much." And then, "Perhaps you need someone to care for like the rest of us."

At that, he laughed lightly — and then he grew serious again, even solemn. There was that burden he carried again; I sensed it, there on his mind, in his heart. I wondered what it was, what was in his thoughts.

I knew better than to ask. He would share his thoughts with me when he was ready — or he would not.

Kisil and I began to speak more and more, but never of his life before he came to us, not at first. That came later. Then, in those early days, we talked of other things when we talked at all.

He never behaved improperly in any way, and he never touched me; but we would sit close together and watch the sheep as the sun went down behind the Mountain. It became our routine, every night when the work was done. I hardly thought about it at the time. It had simply become our way.

I have heard, and seen, that love can come like a lightning bolt, sudden and overwhelming, and hot and intense; but it can slip into your heart quietly as well. You can begin to love someone and not notice the depth and power of it till later. That was how it was for me. I loved Kisil from very early on, but I did not realize it, not in the front of my mind, not till it had become deep and powerful.

Very often, we did not talk at all. We were together, that only, without speaking, without having to speak. There is a quiet comfort you see in old couples, people who have been together for many years. They have no need to talk, but can sit in warm silence and feel the closeness, the trust, without words. Kisil and I had that from the beginning. I trusted him, and he trusted me, and we were comfortable together. It was good between us from the very start.

24

I wanted to know Kisil better. We talked more now, and enjoyed being alone, and we both felt the closeness; but I wanted to be closer still. To know what was behind those soft, gentle eyes, what had happened to him before we met, where he had been, what he had done, who he was. What was on his mind at those times when he stared at the horizon, or when his brow clouded over like a gathering storm. What he thought about then, and what burden he carried.

One cool night, I tried to find out.

"That time at the well, when I first saw you..." I began one evening. It seemed like a good way to work back to his life before, by talking about the time when we had first met.

We were out at some rocks where Father and I had talked so often, farther away from our camp now but still within sight of it. Kadin was with us, as he usually was. The night was cool, though there was no wind. The sky was filled with stars. There would be a moon, but not till much later.

After I spoke, Kisil looked up, but as was his way, he was silent. He did not have to say, "What?" to me; I saw it in his face.

"You seemed so — so lost, Kisil. Sitting there by the well. You looked like — like you had nowhere to go, nothing to live for."

He stared at the ground, as he had that day, but this time with his hand on Kadin's neck instead of his staff. "I remember," he said softly. "And I remember what you said to me after I came back to your camp." Then he lifted his head and added, very quietly, "What you said was true. That was how I felt. Nowhere to go." It was still hard to understand him at times. His voice grew more indistinct when he spoke softly.

"But why?"

It took him a long time, but by then, I understood those pauses. He was choosing the right words. The only sound was Kadin's panting.

He took a deep breath, then another. And then came a short, puffing breath, as if he were clearing dust or the like from his mouth, and his head came up.

I sensed it, as surely as if he had told me. Some wall, some barrier, came down inside him at that moment. Something broke open, or some wound began to heal. I could almost feel him relax, and then he gazed at me with love and something like gratitude in his eyes.

Still, he was silent a little longer, gathering his thoughts now that he had decided to open his heart to me. When he finally did speak, he spoke longer than he ever had before. Even Kadin seemed to be listening closely.

"I was old, Tzipporah. I was old, and alone. I had done many things, and gone many places, but I had never really had a home." He was speaking carefully now, making his words distinct. "No one knew me, no one —" he paused — "loved me, no one even knew I existed." He looked out at the dark horizon. "I saw the darkness coming, and I knew that I would leave no trace. No children. No family. No friends. It was all for nothing."

Kadin sniffed the air. A faint breeze had come up, a dry wind out of the Empty Land — dry, but clean. Even dogs could smell nothing from that barren quarter.

Kisil went on. "I was no one, from nowhere, going nowhere." His expression was bleak, as if he were back at that well. "I was ready to die, Tzipporah. Then. That day."

It was overwhelming. He had never spoken for so long, and had never told me so much. I searched for a response, to keep him talking. It was not hard to find one. "You did not seem sad to me. You seemed — lost."

He nodded again. "I was not sad, not exactly. It was the way things were." He smiled then, though bleakly. "I have no fear of death, Tzipporah. It comes to us all. I only wished that there would be someone to remember me. That

I could have meant something to someone, left something behind to mark my time here, before the darkness came. I felt — empty. Alone..." His words trailed off.

We sat in silence for a time, but a warm silence, not an awkward one. We looked up at the River which flowed across the sky, a band of mysterious light. As I often did, I wondered what it truly was.

Something occurred to me. "How long had you been there? At that well?"

He reflected, his eyes on the horizon, his brows creased. "A day. Perhaps two." He paused. "I had a little dried meat, and some figs and olives. I had eaten them that morning. It was not worth the trouble to find more." He shrugged and fell silent.

I could think of nothing to say. Even Kadin had stopped panting, and seemed to be watching Kisil just as I was.

After a time, he went on: "Nothing I did mattered, or would matter. There was no reason to do anything So I decided to — wait. Wait for whatever happened. For the end, if that was what came." He looked at the ground again, and so did I. The wind ruffled his hair, which was longer by then.

I remember gazing at a stone that night, a little square-shaped rock. I wish now that I had picked it up as a memento. Before then, I had never heard him speak more than three or four sentences together, and that not often. I was delighted, in a way, even though his words made me feel sad for him.

I did not want that conversation to end. He was opening up to me, at last, and I had not realized till that moment how very much I had wanted that.

But, even as I felt gratitude at his opening his heart, what he said bewildered as well as saddened me, because of what had happened later that day. "But then we came, and the Melikites — those goatherds —"

"Yes." He nodded, remembering. "Yes. Yes, suddenly there was something for me to do. Something that mattered." He took a breath. "So I did it."

I thought back to that time. "You looked — surprised, after."

"I was." I saw that he was still surprised, even as he remembered it. "I had never done anything like that before

—" He paused. "Except once. And there were five of them..."

"Six." He turned quickly toward me, his eyes opening wide.

"Six?"

"Yes. Were you not afraid? Afraid that they would hurt you, or kill you? They would have if they could."

He blinked again. His eyes grew distant, and even more puzzled. "I never thought about that. If I had, I suppose I would not have cared. I knew I had to stop them, or try to. So I did." His eyebrows moved up and down, once, as they had that day. "And there were six of them, you say..."

"You fought them like a whirlwind, Kisil. I have never seen anything like what you did with that staff of yours."

He twisted where he sat, a little uncomfortable now at the memory of it. "I was taught how to fight, when I was a soldier. Long ago, in a land very far from here. We were trained in the use of the staff, and other weapons, and we practiced with them every day, for years. I suppose it all came back to me." He shook his head and went on. "But it was not hard. They were moving so slowly..."

I blinked at him. "Kisil, they did not move slowly. *You* moved like — like a striking snake, like fire from the sky. I have never seen anyone move so fast."

He stared at me, then his eyes grew distant again, remembering. "But — it seemed to take forever. I hit one, than another. There was no hurry. It was like they were waiting their turns..." He shook his head again, confused. "Then we were done, and they were going away." His words were hard to make out, his mind in another place, but I had found that I could understand him more easily now. I was growing accustomed to his way of speaking.

"It took — three heartbeats," I said. He blinked at me, surprised again. "Or four. No more. You were not even out of breath."

"Hm." His eyebrows went up and down again. I could tell that he believed me, but did not know what to make of it. We sat in silence again for a while.

He was different, this man. He had a kind of strength, a power — and not only a physical power, I knew even then — but he did not seem aware of it.

I wanted to keep him talking. "And then you fixed Kadin's leg. None of us had seen anything like that before."

"He is a good dog. I knew how, so I helped him." He grinned down at Kadin and scratched him behind his ear, and the dog grinned back, his tongue lolling out comically. Kisil chuckled.

"But where did you learn that?"

"In another place far away. I was a physician's apprentice for a while, in Greece." I did not comprehend the word at first; it sounded different in his mouth. Then I nodded my understanding, and he went on. "We learned how to set broken bones by using animals. Kadin's break was a clean one. It was easy." He ruffled the dog's fur, and Kadin snuffled contentedly and laid his head down beside Kisil's leg.

"Afterward, you —" I hesitated. "You sat down again. As if nothing had happened."

"I remember that too." He smiled, though ruefully. "I felt alive, for a while. Then it was over, and there I was. Still at the end of my path."

He sighed. "Everything was still the same. Nothing had changed. I was still — waiting." We sat and gazed at the little square stone, and Kisil's fingers moved in Kadin's ruff. He sighed again, and then the dog sighed, as if to echo him. We both smiled at that. Kisil looked at me then, back in the present again.

"It happened," he went on, "and then it was over. I was glad you and your sisters were all right — but you did not know me. You did not even know my name." After a few heartbeats, he added, "I did not know my name myself. Not then. I still wonder what it truly is, at times." That puzzled me, but I said nothing.

He took his hand from Kadin's fur, then picked up and tossed the stone as he sighed again. The dog looked up, alert; but Kisil was back at the well again, remembering. "I only sat, after that. I thought nothing at all. Not till you came back."

Then he looked at me, into my eyes. His hand touched mine, and then he took it. "Tzipporah —" He was speaking slowly and carefully again. "I think my life began that night. A new life, a real one. When I met you. Not when I beat the Melikites." He waved a hand dismissively, as if that meant nothing. "When you came back. There is something different about you. Something I have never seen before."

He was speaking my own thoughts at the well. "You are different too, Kisil. You are —" I hesitated. "Different," I finally finished. I was confused and suddenly shy, which was not like me. I looked at him mutely, and he smiled with some sort of secret in his eyes.

Then I remembered. "I had to push you a little, to get you to come back with us, with Nazirah and me."

He blinked, then nodded. "Yes. I did not want to go. I just wanted to wait, to see what happened." He blinked again. "I have always done that. I do not like to — to try to change things. I go where the wind blows me, I suppose."

"I'm glad it brought you here."

He grinned then. "Not the wind, Tzipporah. You. You brought me here. You insisted."

I blushed. "Yes."

"You pushed me — but I needed pushing. And you pushed me again, later, to stay."

"I am sorry —" I began.

He squeezed me. "Do not be sorry. Look what has happened." He kissed my head. "I am happy, my wild bird. I am happier than I have ever been." That was the first time he ever called me that, and I liked it.

I had no more words, so I hugged him. It was the first time for that, too.

He held me. Into my hair, he murmured thickly, "I was not waiting to die that day, as I thought, Tzipporah." He nuzzled my head with his chin. "I was waiting for you."

We sat like that for a long time, and then noticed Kadin watching us. The dog looked puzzled, and when we looked at him, he cocked his head as if to ask, "What is happening here?" We laughed, and then we talked a bit more.

He told me a little of his past that night. He had wandered for years, he said, but he did not say exactly where, then or ever. He did tell me that he was born in Egypt, and that he had left when he was barely grown.

I thought little of that at the time.

25

We talked much more in the following days, and then more still. It was as if, now that his wall of silence was broken, his words flowed out like water from a spring. I was grateful, and moved, and warmed, and I bathed in them.

He told me more and more about his life, and about himself. He had done many things. Besides being a soldier and a physician's apprentice, he had been a sailor, a merchant, a camel driver, a teacher, and a laborer at many trades. A weaver, of course, but also a smith, a wagon maker, a charioteer, and much more. It was true that there seemed to be few things he did not know how to do, or know something about. Sometimes I told him he knew everything, and that always made him laugh. "I am only me," he would say. "I am only Kisil."

I did not care who he was, or where he had been. His life had been aimless and lived at random, it seemed. He had nothing of ambition about him, no desire for power or wealth. But even so, I knew that he was, above all, a *good* man. I admired him, and more than that, I *trusted* him. I trusted him like no one I had ever known, not even my father. He knew me — and he seemed to think well of me, too. That was the sweetest thing of all, that Kisil could care for me as he did.

And then, one night, he told me — well, I remember his words, every one of them, as if I had only heard them this morning. I can still hear them, spoken as only he could speak them, in his soft and clumsy voice:

"I have never been so close to anyone, Tzipporah. Not even to my own mother or sister or brother. I have never had anyone know me so well, or even anyone who was there to do it. I have never had anyone to care about." Then he smiled. He had begun to smile more often by then. "Now I do."

We never spoke the word "love," not then, nor do I think we knew that that was what we were feeling. We were friends first, and that seemed more important. We had both been alone, each in our own way, for a very long time; but Kisil had been very much more alone than I, and for much longer.

It happened gradually. Kisil began to take my hand now and then as we sat in the evening. Then he began to take my hand every time. Soon we began to walk that way, hand in hand. I think we had been doing that for a long time before either of us were even aware of it. Nothing was said, but I saw the affection in his eyes and knew that there was something like it in my own. We found ourselves sitting closer, and his arm — or his arms — were often around me, my shoulders, my waist.

Did I not say? Of course I did, but I will say it again. Kisil's eyes were gray, soft and gray. They could grow steely and as hard as flint, I knew; but I rarely saw them like that. When he looked at me, his eyes were always soft. They were still sad eyes — but only a little, now. Now, his eyes seemed to smile more.

I remember him gazing into my own eyes one night, without speaking, and how his hand came up and stroked my hair. My hair is white now, and straight, but then it was black, and tightly curled, like my mother's. I hated my hair. It was impossible to comb, and I struggled with it often. "My hair is awful," I said as he touched it.

He shook his head. "It is a glorious cloud." And then, to his surprise as much as my own, I think, he kissed me. His lips were scarred, but soft.

After, there was no questioning look, no doubt or shyness — Was that all right? We both knew that it was.

We smiled. And then we laughed. It was revelation, recognition.

Then he put his arms around me, and for a time we did not speak. Not at all. Not in words.

He was such a gentle man. I remember thinking, many times, how hard it was to believe that he had fought six men, all at once, and defeated them all. Even after seeing that, I could not imagine him angry, not then. I saw his anger again, later, and it was terrible, like a thunderstorm, like fire from Heaven, like the fire in the Mountain. But that time had not yet come.

And so it began. Kisil and I began to acknowledge our feelings for one another. He would hold me in the evening, and we kissed. Often.

But not always. We talked often too, and spoke of how much we meant to each other. We were both grateful for what we had found. For different reasons and in different ways, perhaps, but we both knew that our love had brought a profound change in our lives, and a great blessing. It will surprise those who know only the legends, but Kisil and I would sometimes run and play and laugh and chase each other like children. Kadin would join in the game, and we would make my father and mothers laugh. Sometimes my sisters would join in, too. Those were happy times.

One day, when we were minding the sheep together, watching the sun set beyond the Mountain, we heard its voice. We felt it rumbling through the earth. The Mountain had not spoken for a very long time, but it was waking up again.

I was used to it, but Kisil looked up. "What is that? It sounds like thunder, but different. And there are no clouds. And I feel it through the ground..."

"That was the Voice of The One." I pointed. "This is His Mountain."

"Whose?"

"The One. Ael Shadu."

Kisil understood the words, that it was not a name. "Ah. Your god."

"We do not use that word for Him, but yes. He is The One. He is more than a god. He is above all gods." I pointed at the Mountain again. "He is everywhere," I said. "But this Mountain is His Mountain. It is His special place, and it is holy."

Kisil cocked his head curiously. I shrugged. "I know. I do not understand it myself. But that is what my father taught us." The Sun was setting, and we could see the red glow at the Mountain's fiery heart. It gave me a warm feeling. I had not seen it since before Kisil came.

Kisil looked at the light. "I have heard this kind of mountain called a 'fire mountain.' I have seen them before. There are many like this."

"I know. There is another, not far from here, and perhaps more. But not like this one."

He watched the light for a while. "Is that why no one else lives near us? Only your father Yisro and his clan?"

I smiled. The way he said my father's name — it always came out "Yithro." He knew why I smiled, but said nothing, only cocked his head and smiled his crooked smile in return.

"Yes. People fear the Mountain, Kisil. No one goes there, no one climbs it. It is forbidden — and it is dangerous." I said nothing of my own explorations. "Sometimes death comes from its summit, and those around it are found dead in the morning."

"Then why do you stay here?"

I shrugged. "My father says..." I stopped. The old superstition — speak of something, and it can happen.

"What does your father say?"

"He says that — that The One can take us at any time, anywhere. Father wants to be close to Him even so."

"But if The One is everywhere...?"

I looked up at Kisil's face, and I could see that he was not really wondering. He knew. "This place is special, somehow, Kisil. Can you not feel it?"

He shook his head and looked at the Mountain again. "No. I cannot." He frowned. "I never feel such things."

"What do you mean?"

"I have been to shrines and sacred groves and temples and holy places in many lands, Tzipporah. I have never seen nor felt anything." He shook his head. "They are only places. Many times I prayed that — " he stopped.

"What, Kisil?" I asked. "What did you pray?"

"That my voice would —" He stopped again and pressed his lips together, eyes closed. After a moment, he began again. "That I could speak properly. That my mouth would work." He shook his head, then pointed at his lips. "You hear my words. My prayers were never answered. I felt nothing, and nothing happened. No one was listening."

I watched his face. There was something there, something else he asked to have lifted from him besides his lisp. Something else lay behind his soft, hesitant words, but what, I did not know. Not then.

After a time, I asked, "Do you worship a god, Kisil?"

He shook his head slowly, back and forth, still staring at the Mountain. He said nothing, but I knew there was more, and that he would tell me; so I remained silent as well, and waited.

As I knew he would, he spoke again. "I know of a God like yours, with no name and no face. Perhaps He is the same one. But I do not know Him, and I do not worship Him." He was silent again for a while. "I think He is more dream than real. Either way —" He tossed a stone again. "He does not need my worship. If He is there, what He cares about is —" He stopped and looked at the ground.

I thought of that day at the well, when we met. "Right and wrong," I said softly.

"Yes." He looked at me and nodded, and said the word again. "Yes." Then he turned and gazed at me thoughtfully. "Does Ael Shadu care about those things?"

Of all that we had talked about, we had never spoken of The One. I thought for a fleeting moment of how strange that was. "Yes. Very much. More than anything, I think. Perhaps you should talk to my father."

He nodded thoughtfully. "I will." He looked up at the Mountain. "I will, Tzipporah."

26

He did speak with my father after that, and often. We heard their voices, from the rocks where Kisil and I talked and where Father had told me of his days as a priest, or from inside his tent, or Kisil's. Their voices were not always quiet; sometimes they shouted, though they did not sound truly angry.

Father was teaching Kisil of The One, sharing what he knew, what he guessed, what he hoped. Sometimes I joined them. Kisil would ask questions, and sometimes he would echo my father's words, but in a different way; and more than once, I saw my father sit back, surprised or gratified at one of Kisil's questions or remarks.

One night the three of us were talking in Kisil's tent. It was smaller than the rest — Kisil said he needed little space, and truly, it was all but empty, since he had few possessions. It was lit by the light of a single lamp. We could hear the wind outside, and the tent's fabric flapping and popping as it blew.

"It is not that He tells us anything," my father said. "We *know*, and when we think of Him, we know that we know."

Kisil considered that. "What to do, you mean. Not what He is." I noticed, once again, how deep and resonant Kisil's voice was, behind the clumsiness of his speech.

I remembered what Father had told me so long ago, and I smiled in anticipation. "Yes! Yes!" my father said. "No one knows what He is, or even what He is *like*. No one *can* know those things, any more than we can know what is beyond the sky or what happens after we die. It is what we *do* that matters to Him. He will not tell us. He does not have to. We know what is right. If we are honest. If we tell the truth. To ourselves."

"And if we do not know…?" Kisil asked, his brow furrowed, his eyes full of doubt. "Sometimes we do not know what to do. Sometimes... It is harder."

There was a certain edge in his words. No one else could have heard it, I think, but I did. This meant something to Kisil, something more than talk and speculation.

My father lifted a hand. "Sometimes it is not so plain, yes. It most often is, but sometimes not. When that happens…" Father's hand became a fist. "We are to think harder. We are to talk with each other, with those we know to be wise. We try to find out together."

"And if there is no one to ask?" Kisil's eyes were on the ground again. He was thinking of something, I knew. Later, I found out what that something was; but at that time, I could not guess.

Father watched him, his own face troubled. He saw it now, too. There was something about Kisil's manner that touched him.

He shook his head. "I do not know, Kisil. We must think as hard as we can, I suppose, if there is no one to talk to." Then he smiled. "But we have each other, here, do we not?"

Kisil shook off his troubled manner — I could almost see him physically push it away — and he nodded amiably. "Yes. Yes, we do. And I see what you mean. We, we men —" He looked at me and grinned. "And women — what we do, why we do it — that is in our hands. Not His. Ours. *We* have to determine what is right and wrong — because no one else can."

"Yes." Father lifted his hands. "Who else will tell us?"

Kisil frowned. "So The One does not speak..."

My father laughed. "Of course He does! He speaks — but through *us!* The One needs us as much as we need Him. Perhaps more."

We thought on that, and then Father went on: "Perhaps He inspires us, places the thoughts in our minds. Perhaps it is only that He gave us the ability to think and understand, as He thinks and understands."

"But how are we to *know* what He would have us do? Truly *know?"*

I spoke up for the first time. "Kisil."

They both turned to me. "You knew how to fix Kadin's leg, did you not?"

"Yesss..." He nodded, listening.

"Did The One tell you that? Did He give you that knowledge?"

He shook his head, frowning. "No, of course not. I told you — I learned that in Greece, from a priest of a god named Apollo." My father's eyes went wide.

"Would that knowledge be any more true and good if The One had given it?"

He blinked, twice, and then he sat back, smiling and nodding.

My father's mouth fell open, and then he smiled too. "Very good, my daughter," he breathed. "Very, very good. Do you see what she means, Kisil?'

Kisil's eyes were on mine. "Yes, I do. I do. Truth is truth. The good is — the good. And the true and the good —" He smiled even more broadly — "are always His."

"Always," I said. "And when we speak the truth, we speak for Him."

"You are fortunate, Tzipporah," said Kisil. My father cocked a bushy eyebrow at him.

"Why?" he asked.

He waved an arm expansively at the horizon. "I have traveled much, and seen many lands and many peoples. Few of them allow women to speak so freely."

My father laughed. "Nor do the people here," he said. "But I am surrounded by women, Kisil. Did they not speak as they choose, our camp would be silent." Then he grinned. "My wives and daughters would not take kindly to being silenced were I to try to silence them. They outnumber me, and they know it."

We all laughed at that. "We are fortunate too," said Kisil. "Their wisdom is not lost to us, as it is in other places. If God does not speak, it is good that women do. They can speak for him as well as men, I think. Perhaps better." My father nodded, looking at me with pride.

Kisil's eyes grew distant — and then, suddenly, were sharply focused again. "Wait." he lifted a hand and looked at me directly, then back at my father, his brows knitted again.

"*Can* The One speak? Can He make promises to men? Does He?" There was something different in his tone, something that neither Father nor I had heard before. His gray eyes went from one of us to the other.

My father frowned. "Who would expect such a thing?"

Kisil persisted. "Does He ever speak directly to men? In His own voice, with His own words?"

My father blinked at him. "Who can say?" He shook his head. "I do not know that He cannot. But I have never heard of it..." He looked beyond us both. "I cannot even imagine what that would be like. He has never spoken to me. But I suppose that it is... possible."

Kisil frowned and sat silent, thinking.

My father looked at him curiously. "Has He ever spoken to you, Kisil?" He was met with surprise.

"Me? No! I do not think He speaks to anyone. It seems to me that He might only be a sign, a story. A dream. A hope. I only know of tales. There are some who claim that He has spoken, in His own voice. Some seem to believe those tales."

"Do you believe them?" I asked.

Kisil turned to me and cocked his head, his eyes on mine. Once again, we were sharing something without a name.

"I do not," he finally said. "But those tales seem to give those who hear them — strength. Courage. Something. Perhaps that is enough."

"What tales?" I asked.

Kisil looked at me, then at my father. There was an awkward silence, and then he laughed lightly and shook his head. "Another time." He waved a hand dismissively. "I have heard many tales in my travels. But those are for the campfire, not for our talks here."

This felt wrong to me. Kisil was an honest man, but he was hiding something. There was something there, something that was important to him — not only the "many tales" he spoke of. I knew it. I opened my mouth to speak again, but my father's eye warned me. I kept silent.

Later, Father told me, "Tzipporah, I think that all this has to do with Kisil's past, and why he wanders. Give him time. He will tell us when he wishes to — if he ever does."

And my father was right. That time would come.

27

"Why do you not believe in Him?" I asked one night when we were watching the stars.

It was New Moon, and it was late. The family celebration had long since ended, and Kisil and I were in a place far from the camp where we liked to sit and talk. The Mountain loomed dark against the backdrop of the spangled sky, and a dry wind cooled us as it blew from the desert. The day had been hot.

Kisil knew what I meant: The One, Ael Shadu. "Are you so sure that I do not believe?" he asked. Then he grinned easily, and shrugged. "I do not know that I do not believe, my sweet bird," he said. "I told you — I have no knowledge of gods, and never have. I believe in right and wrong. But hearing the teachings of your father about this Ael Shadu, and thinking on the tales I have heard — I am not so certain. Some days I begin to believe, in a way, and some days — I have doubts." He shrugged. "And some days, I believe in nothing."

"I do not understand."

He started again, speaking slowly and very clearly. "I said, I am not certain —"

"No, no," I said with a laugh. "I understood your *words*, Kisil. I do not understand what you *mean*."

He grinned and lifted his hands helplessly, and we both laughed. Then his face grew solemn. "I mean I have no way to *know*, my bird. Whether or not He even *is*. And..." He paused. "And *if* He is, I am not certain that He is *good*. And to *worship* One who is no better than we, and perhaps worse —" He shook his head. "That makes no sense. At least, that is what I think."

I waited, saying nothing. I knew there would be more.

"Most of all," he went on, "I am not sure that it *matters*, what one believes — or even whether or not one believes at all." He paused. A jackal coughed and snarled in the distance. It was an evil sound. "Whether He is, or He is not — what can we do about that? What would change, in the world, in our lives, either way?"

I could only listen and think, trying to understand. He went on: "But what we *do* — *that* matters. *That* can change things. That, *we* can change." He stood and looked out at the stars on the dark horizon. "I cannot pretend to know things that I do not know. Is that not what it means, to *believe?* To say I know things that I do not truly know?"

I was struck by his words, so similar to things my father had told me when I was a child. How alike they are, I thought.

"What *do* you believe in, Kisil?"

"I believe in *truth*. I have to tell myself the truth, always, because without truth, we have nothing."

Like Father again, I thought. "My father taught us the same thing," I said, "when we were little. Except that he said that we must tell ourselves the truth because He, The One, knows what we are thinking. There is no fooling Him. There is no pretending. Father, too, said that he could not pretend to know things he did not."

Kisil considered that. He looked back at the Mountain, thinking. "Your father is a very wise man. I have learned much from him, even though I am not sure of this Ael Shadu." I said nothing.

After a pause, he asked, "What do you know of The One, Tzipporah? What did Yisro teach you, when you were small?"

"He taught us that no one knows Him. That He has no face, no form, answers to no one. That he is Sovereign. Unknown, and yet knowing all. We do not even know His Name." I lifted my hand to the blanket of stars above us, swept it to include the desert around us. "He made all this. Everything. He is the Creator, the Source of all."

"How did He make it?"

I shook my head. "That, also, no one knows."

There was another pause.

"Is He *good*?"

I could feel his gray eyes on me, searching.

I tried to speak truthfully. "I know that that is what you most want to know, Kisil, but that is hard to answer. When we look at the world, we see great beauty..." I waved at the sky again. "But there is great ugliness as well." I tossed my head toward where we had heard the ugly sound of a jackal, only a moment before. "Have you ever seen jackals ripping a lamb apart and devouring it while it still lived?"

"No." He frowned. "But I, too, have seen much that is evil. And the most savage creature of all is Man." Even in his soft, lisping voice, the words sounded harsh. He bent, picked up a pebble, and tossed it, a gesture of anger, and somehow of despair as well.

"That is true." I thought. "But what is it, in you, that knows that? What makes that judgment? Is it not an awareness of what is good?"

He laughed. "The knowledge of good and evil..."

"Why are you laughing?"

He shook his head. "Something I heard a long time ago."

I blinked at him, then went on. "That knowledge comes from The One too. It is as Father said, Kisil. He gave us the power to think and to know, and a sense of right and wrong. Inside us, all of us."

Kisil stared at the horizon, thinking. "And perhaps that was all He ever gave us," he said. "All the guidance that we shall ever get from Him. And perhaps that is enough..." He paused. "But what happens if you lie, inside yourself, Tzipporah? Men call good evil, and evil good, sometimes. Perhaps they even believe it. Perhaps we even do it ourselves. Is He angry then?"

I tried to remember what Father had said, then shook the thought away. *Think for yourself, Tzipporah*, I thought. Kisil watched me and waited.

Finally, I said, "I do not know, Kisil. Perhaps when we do it knowingly, for evil reasons. But no one knows the mind of the One."

"What is an evil reason?"

I thought. "Selfishness. Laziness. A cold heart. There are many."

"Is there a *good* reason to lie?"

Now it was my turn to laugh. "Oh, yes," I said. "Father taught us that. To tell the truth when it is hurtful, and when there is no good reason to hurt — that is wrong, and a good reason to lie. To tell Nazirah —" I stopped.

He smiled gently. "What you truly think of her," he said softly.

"Yes. No. Well, yes. I love her, but —"

"She can be hurtful herself."

"Yes. And I think she likes to hurt, at times. But she is not always like that. And what good would it do? That would only put more anger into her. It would not help to show her my own hurtful side."

"You have spoken of this with Yisro."

"Of course."

"And what does he tell you? Is Nazirah bad?"

"Oh, no. Father says —" I looked at Kisil suddenly, to make sure he was not teasing or mocking me; but his eyes were steady, his mouth still. "Father says that there is a desire to do good in all of us — and a desire to do evil. We are to follow the first —"

"And fight the second." He nodded thoughtfully.

"No, more than that." He looked up at me quickly and blinked

"More?"

"Yes. We are to turn the wish to do evil into a reason to do something good."

He touched his lips for a moment. When his hand came away, he was frowning. "How can that be?"

I thought. "Take Nazirah. She wanted to be better than the rest of us at something, and she likes to hurt things; so she worked hard to be the best with a sling." I shrugged. "And so she is. I have seen her kill — not hurt, but *kill* — a full-grown wolf at thirty paces with a single stone. And killing a wolf is a good thing, for people who herd sheep." I gestured, mimicking her throw. "She stunned a jackal, at a distance greater than that, on the day we first met you."

"I shall have to be sure never to anger her," he said with his crooked smile, but then he nodded. "I see what you mean." His face was thoughtful. "He gives us the power to choose, as well."

"Of course. That is what makes us humans, and not animals."

Kisil nodded his agreement, but he did not appear satisfied. "I understand, and that all makes sense. I do not know about this — One, though. If He is there, why does He not —" He stopped.

I wanted to ask, *Why does he not — what?* But something prevented me.

We were silent for a little while.

Then, "What DO you know?" I asked suddenly.

He looked at me as if he had never seen me before. "Why do you ask that?"

"Because I want to find out. What do you *know*, Kisil? What do you know, for certain?"

He looked at the Mountain, then back at me. "Let me think about that for a while, Tzipporah." He looked at the Mountain again. "That has been on my mind, that very question. Let me think about that a little longer."

I held his hand and we looked at the stars in silence as they turned slowly above us. It must have been in the fall of the year; I remember studying the wooly stars that bind the Sheaf.

After a time, I spoke softly, unsure what I was about to say. "Kisil..." I said, and found I could say no more.

He heard it in my voice, and said it for me as he squeezed my hand. "I love you, my wild bird." His voice was soft, his lisp thick. I still found it endearing. "I think I always have." Then his eyes were on mine. "I know *that*. I know *that*, for certain."

Neither of us had ever spoken the word before.

"I love you, too, Kisil." The words felt right in my mouth. I snuggled closer and said them again.

28

One night, instead of walking away from the camp with me, Kisil went in to talk to my father. He had done this before, but this time was different.

I waited by the fire. My sisters joined me, all of them. We giggled and whispered like little girls, and even Kadin seemed excited. We all knew what was happening in Father's tent, and they teased me about it. We even played a handclapping game that we had not played since childhood — the same one I had seen in the village so long ago. I would be the first to marry, and that night was somehow special for all of us.

I did not speak of it, but I was worried. I knew that Kisil had nothing but what we had given him, nothing with which to pay a bride-price. He had come to us with nothing but his clothes and his staff and an old water-skin. I wondered what kind of bargain he and my father were making.

When they finally came out, all I saw was Kisil's smile. I ran to him, and as was his way, he said nothing, but he took me in his arms and kissed me, right there in front of everyone. My father looked on, and he smiled too.

When I looked up at my father, questioning, he only grinned. "Kisil will work for me for seven years. A man he has heard of did that once, for his bride." He saw my stricken expression and laughed. "Oh, you will not have to wait that long, little bird. The wedding will be at the full moon." He called me by the name he had used when I was a child.

I looked up, though I knew what the moon looked like; when you are a shepherd, you always know. It was a little past new, so we would be married in ten or twelve days.

I laughed. So did Kisil, and he swung me around like a child as everyone joined in the laughter.

That night, we sang and danced and celebrated, and we stayed up late to talk and feast on things my mothers had prepared. There was even wine.

Even Kisil danced. He danced in ways that none of us had ever seen, stamping rhythmically and swinging his outstretched arms in wide circles. It was wonderful to see, and there were only a few times that I ever saw it again.

They had known, my mothers and sisters, thus the feast. Perhaps my father had told them to get it ready. That that night was coming had been no secret to anyone but me. That it would come had not crossed my mind, not really. I was too busy loving Kisil.

He could have come to my tent that night, if he wanted; we were betrothed now. But we chose not to. I am not sure why, but it seemed right. I needed to prepare my mind, and maybe he did too. It only seemed natural to wait. There was no hurry. The next day my mothers and sisters and I began to plan and prepare for the wedding — and the real feast.

It was during those days, before our wedding, that Kisil finally began to tell me of his past. Not where he had wandered, exactly — he never told me that — but of where he had come from, what he had done, who he was. I had a right to know, he told me.

We walked out to our favorite place. Not the rocks, but a different place, a place that was ours alone. It was marked by a barren date palm, far from the camp. It was nearer the Mountain, on the bank of a deep wadi. If I had my eyes, I could find the place, even today.

We reached the place and sat down, our legs hanging over the edge and our back against a tall hump of smooth rock behind us. I saw Kisil gathering himself to begin. Finally, he turned to me. "What do you want to know?"

My mouth dropped open. "How can you ask? Who are you, Kisil? Where do you come from? Who are your people? Or — who were they?" I added quickly, seeing the familiar shadow cross his brow.

He looked out at the dry wadi, then picked up a pebble and tossed it as he so often did. He did not speak, for a long, long time. I knew he was not ignoring me — that would have been unlike him. Kisil would never have been so discourteous. No, just as at other times, he was gathering his thoughts, choosing his words. He had brought me here for this, and he was working himself up to it.

He tossed another pebble, then another. I looked out at the night, felt the breeze on my face, and waited. We had left Kadin at the camp, or I would have petted him. We heard the cry of some distant bird, eerily clear in the silence.

Finally, he took a deep breath and began.

"I was born to a people called the Avru."

I looked at him blankly. "The Avru?"

"Yes. Do you know of them?" I shook my head. I had never heard the word. "That is not surprising. There are not many of them."

I noticed that he said "them," and not "us."

"They are all descended from one man, and his son and grandson. His name was Avram. Some call them Avramites."

"Avramites... The Avru." I repeated, feeling the words in my mouth.

"Yes. Avram had a son when he was very old. He named him Yitzhak; and Yitzhak had a son named Yaacov. And Yaacov had twelve sons."

I blinked. "Twelve? And they all lived?"

He nodded. "He may have had others. But there were twelve who lived. And a daughter, I think."

"How many wives did he have?" Any woman would ask.

"Four. The twelve sons — well, the Avru are all descended from them. They call themselves the Twelve Families. I was born into the family of Levi."

"Levi was one of the twelve sons? Which one?"

He frowned. "The third, I think. The twelve sons lived a very long time ago."

I waited, but Kisil said nothing more. Finally, I asked, "Well, what happened? Why are you no longer among them?"

He turned slightly toward me, but he did not look at my face. He was gazing beyond me, behind me, to the east. I could see that this was hard for him. I wondered how long it had been since he had spoken of it, or if he had ever spoken of it at all.

He did not answer my question then. He went on: "The Avru worship one God, Tzipporah, like your clan does. Perhaps it is the same God. Your people know little of Ael Shadu, and the Avru seem to know little about their God. They make no images of Him, and He has no name at all. Avram was the first to worship Him. I do not know what he, or his son or grandson, knew about Him. But —"

He fell silent. "What is it?" I did not see what any of this had to do with Kisil's own history, but it was plain that he did. "But — what?"

"He spoke to them, they say, this God."

"Ah." I remembered his question to my father. Now I knew where it had come from.

"They say that this nameless God made an agreement — a covenant, they call it — with the Avru. With Avram, then with his son Yitzhak, and then with his grandson Yaacov too, and with all *his* sons, so that all their descendants share in it. He is their God, and they are His people." He shook his head. "A covenant. With a God who has no name."

"And He spoke to them? How? What did He say? What did He sound like?"

Kisil looked at the Mountain. "I do not know. I wonder about that too. Perhaps it was something they felt. Like the way you feel things, and I cannot." He shrugged. "I do not know. I was not there. But I sometimes wonder what it was like, for Avram..." Then he looked up, startled. "Could it have been like it is for your father, for Yisro? Perhaps he came up with these things himself, somehow."

"Perhaps. But Father never taught us that Ael Shadu speaks — in words, I mean — or any other such things. Ael Shadu cares about the way we live, about right and wrong —"

"But you work those things out for yourselves. Yes."

"Yes." I shrugged. "Ael Shadu — only *is*."

"Perhaps Avram did the same." We sat and thought for a little while, and then Kisil went on.

"I know a little about their history, the Avru. Their stories. Of how the world was made, of the first man and woman. Of the twelve sons. I told your father how Yaacov worked for seven years for his wife Rakhel. Stories like that. But I know little more than what I have just told you. I know the story of how some of them came to Egypt — and a few of the customs they keep."

He looked down at his lap then. I know why, now, but at the time I barely noticed it. I was too busy listening carefully, trying to understand Kisil's clumsy speech. It was better, but he was growing tired. It still cost him much effort to speak clearly.

"What do the Avru teach about their God?"

He shook his head. "They do not often speak of Him directly. I know very little. I never knew my people, Tzipporah. I have no memory of living among them. I have told you most of what I know, and I learned none of it from my mother — my foster mother, I mean. Basia was her name."

"You cannot remember your real parents?" We were finally getting to why Kisil no longer lived among his people. I let him take his time about it.

"Only a little." He took a deep breath, and I wondered what was coming.

Then it came. "I was raised in the palace of the king of Egypt, Tzipporah. Basia was the king's daughter — and when he died, the new king's sister."

That set me back. "The king's daughter? She was a princess?"

"Yes. I was raised as a prince." His face was dark, his brows drawn downward.

I almost felt dizzy. This, I had not expected, nor anything like it. "How — how did that happen?"

He would not look at me then. "My people are slaves, Tzipporah." His voice was low and soft. "I have not told you that part. A group of them came down to Egypt from their own land, they say, many generations ago. For a while, they prospered."

He sighed. "But then a new king came to the throne, and they were enslaved. Most of them make bricks for the king's palaces and temples, stamping the wet clay in the brick pits, slopping the mud into the molds, setting them in the sun to dry. They drag them on sledges for the brick masons, then go back for more. The Egyptians whip them like animals." He paused, his eyes closed. "Their lives are bitter. And short." He snorted. "They have a legend, though, that a Deliverer will come one day and they will return to their land as free people. It gives them hope. They have little."

His voice had grown very thick, more from emotion than from his lisp, I thought. "You said most of them. What about the rest?"

He shrugged again. "Some are servants. Maids, wagon drivers, cooks, grooms, swineherds. Singers, dancers. Other things. Their lives are easier, though they are still slaves.

"But I was spared their fate — and when I learned what I was, I abandoned them."

"How — what —" I was confused; I could not even think of what to ask.

He paused. "My mother — my real mother — did not want that life for me. She made a basket, and put me in it, and set me adrift in the river where she knew the king's daughter and her women were bathing." He looked at me then.

"She had a plan. Everyone, even the slaves, knew that Basia could not have a child, even though she desperately wanted one." He shrugged. "The princess found me, and raised me as her own, as my mother hoped she would." He frowned. "But Basia never told me where I came from till I was grown. I found out then that everyone knew." He rubbed at his eyes. "That is the reason I say I have no people... One of the reasons."

We sat silent again for a time. Then I asked, "Why did the basket not sink?"

He laughed, a small snort of derision. "It was covered inside and out with pitch. I must have been a mess."

He leaned back against the palm and cocked up one knee, then clasped it with his hands. We looked toward where the sheep were grazing nearby. On impulse, I moved closer and snuggled against his side.

He looked down in surprise, then let the knee go and put his arm around me. "I wish I could have seen you as a baby." I leaned against his chest. "You must have been beautiful."

He smiled and gave me a squeeze. "I suppose Basia thought so. She knew what I was, but she kept me even so." He smiled. "She was young, barely grown. How the physicians knew she would be barren, I do not know.

But so she was. I was her only child." We sat in silence for a time.

Kisil spoke again. "She gave me an Egyptian name."

"What name?"

He opened his mouth, then closed it and shook his head. "It does not matter. My name is Kisil now. That was my birth name."

I leaned against him, thinking, for a while. It was a lot to find out, all at once, Kisil's story.

I suppose he thought so too. "Enough for now. Let us go to our tents and sleep. I shall tell you more when I am — when I am ready. Oh, yes, Tzipporah," he said at my expression. "There is more."

We walked back to the tents in silence, but it was a warm silence. I could feel that Kisil bore less of a burden now that I shared it. And I knew that we would talk again.

I wondered how much more there could be.

29

We did not speak the next day. There was no time for it. Besides the preparations for our wedding, it was sheep-shearing season, and by that evening, all of us were covered with sweat, dirt, and wool lint, and we were exhausted. Indeed, it was two days more before we spoke again of Kisil's past.

I think he hoped that he could put it off even longer, but I was persistent. "Come, Kisil." I patted his hand we were settled out at the palm tree once more. "You promised to tell me the rest."

I knew this was hard for him, but I wanted to know more. "What else do you want to know?" he asked, as I knew he would.

I took his hand, then impulsively leaned in and kissed him. "How did you come to be with us, Kisil?" I asked when our lips parted. "Why did you leave Egypt? If you were a prince..."

He sighed. I saw that he was resigned to going on, to telling me the whole tale, but he did not relish doing it. "Very well. But first give me that waterskin."

He took a drink, then settled back to think. I was patient; I knew he would speak when he was ready.

He was silent for a long time. I snuggled into his arms and whispered, "It is all right, Kisil. You can tell me anything."

He held me close, then I felt him relax. "I ran away."

"Why?" I whispered.

He spoke in short phrases with much space between them. "I was young. I had twenty years, perhaps. Perhaps less. I had only then learned where I came from. Who I was. It was my mother — my stepmother, Basia — who finally told me. I went out to see my people, the Avru, and..."

He stopped, a longer pause this time. "...and I saw them. The mud. The bricks. The whipping. The people more dead than alive.

"I sought out my real parents. I stayed with them. A few days. They taught me about my people — the things I have told you. And a little more."

His face was bleak. "I felt like a foreigner. They looked at me as if I were — a stranger. An enemy. A traitor. Even my father..." He closed his eyes.

After a few heartbeats, he said, "I met my older brother. His name was Aron. There was such hatred in his eyes... My own brother."

I made a small sound — a small cry of sympathy, I suppose. I sat up and took his hand in both of my own.

His face worked, his anguish visible. "I did not know!" he finally burst out. "How could I have known?"

I kissed his hand. "You could not have known. You did nothing wrong, Kisil."

"Of course I did." His words were bitter. He took his hand from mine and rubbed his face with both of his own, then dropped them and looked at the horizon again. "Their slavery, their misery, their pain and labor — I had escaped all that. That was wrong, even though I had not planned it, had not done it myself. But that is not what I mean."

"Then what do you mean?"

"I did not know that *I* was Avru, but I knew about *them*. I knew about their slavery, their suffering, when I was growing up. I had seen it all my life. But I thought I was an Egyptian! And like all the other Egyptians, I did not care. Not till I knew that they were my own people." His head sank, and he looked at the earth. "I was one of their enemies, Tzipporah. I was one of their oppressors."

I began to understand why he looked haunted, troubled.

"Yes. I see." There was nothing else to say.

We sat in silence for a while. I felt him relaxing, letting go, finally able to tell someone. As hard as it was to hear these things, it was a warm and loving feeling for me, helping Kisil to bear his burden, and I think it was a comfort for him too. I knew he was telling me things he had never told anyone else.

It was some time before he could go on. "I stayed with my family — my real family — for only a few days. It was so hard, the way they lived was so different —" He shook his head. "I had to leave. I had to get away and think. I was so confused..." His eyes went to the horizon again, and now I knew where his mind went when his eyes sought it out.

He sighed. "I was trying to decide what to do. I knew I could not stay in the palace, living like a king's son while my people suffered in the brick pits." He lifted his hands, gesturing, questioning, even now, so many years later. "Nor did I want to live as a slave. I could not do either. What I should do..." He shook his head. "I did not know."

He was silent for a time, but then he finally looked directly at me — and, to my surprise, he smiled, and warmly.

"But I do now."

I did not ask; my face asked for me. *What do you mean?*

I knew, but I wanted to hear him say it in his dear, clumsy voice, the voice I had grown to love so much.

"You are my life, Tzipporah. I love you. I want to stay here with you. I finally have a home — a real home, where I belong. A family that is really my own family." He looked down, then back into my eyes. "I have found peace."

I hugged him, and for a little while there was no need to speak with words. Our lips and arms spoke for us.

He held me, and I nuzzled his chest. "I have never spoken of this before..."

"I am here," I murmured.

He froze.

I knew there was something about what I had said that gave him pause, but it would be a long time before I learned what it was. Then he took a breath — I remember feeling his chest rise and fall under my cheek — and he went on.

"I walked back to the stable where I had left my chariot and horses." He was fighting his lisp, trying to make his words clear. "I did not know what to think. My mother — Basia, the king's sister, not my real mother, I understood that, but she was the only mother I ever knew before that time — she knew where I had gone, but no one else did.

"What was I going to do? I was trying to think, and I could not.

"I thought of the palace, of the trays of fruit and sweets that were always prepared for me, the scented bath that waited for me, my soft, clean bed, the servants who waited on me....

"And then I thought of my family — the rags they wore, the dirty straw they slept on, their labor from dark to dark again, with never a day to rest...

"I knew I could not go back to the palace. My people — my people — had seen me as a stranger, an enemy, and if I went back there, I would prove them right. But I could not go back to the slave camp. I did not know how to live that way.

"I did not know who I was, Tzipporah." He paused. "I still do not know. I did the only thing I could see to do. I ran away. I told no one. I took my chariot and I fled." He took the waterskin back and held it up. "I did not stop for water or a change of clothes. I drove the horses till one picked up a stone in its hoof and went lame, then I left them and walked."

He glanced down at me. "Do not be concerned, Tzipporah. I left the horses within sight of a village. They were treasured and well cared for there, I am sure. Poor people do not often get horses, especially fine, well-bred horses, for nothing. The chariot, they probably broke up for firewood. It was an ordinary chariot, not one of the king's. But they were very fine horses."

Kisil knew my thoughts as well as I did. I had, indeed, been thinking about the poor horses. *No wonder I no longer feel alone*, I thought. *He IS inside my head, and behind my eyes.*

He squeezed my shoulders and went on. "I walked for a long way. I had a little gold with me, and I bought a waterskin and some fresh sandals in some village, and I walked. I have been walking ever since."

He was silent again.

"For how long?" I finally asked.

"For many years, Tzipporah. Ten, twelve, fifteen. Twenty. More. I do not know." His face was empty, and sad, and he looked old. That was the first time I ever thought that, I remember.

"I ran away, Tzipporah. And I have been running ever since. I had no people, no family — at least, none that would claim me, or whose lives I wanted to share. I was — a stranger, wherever I went, as I was to you when you met me."

I remembered how I had thought of him: *the stranger.* But I said, "You are not a stranger any more." He smiled.

We sat silent for a while. Then, "You see, Tzipporah, that is what I regret. I ran away. I abandoned my people."

"But what else could you have done, Kisil?"

"I do not know. I could not have helped them — but I could have shared their misery. What good that would have done, I do not know. But I could have done that. I owed them that."

"But —" I found I had nothing to say. Neither did he. We sat in silence.

I watched his face. His eyes were distant again, on the horizon. "Where did you go?" I finally asked.

He shrugged. "North. East. West. Even south. I saw many nations, many peoples, very different from ours — yours, and mine. I did many things, learned many things, saw many things." He tossed a stone. "I was a soldier once, a commander, and had a fine house in a walled city, far to the south, where the people have dark skin and hair like black wool and live very differently. Still, I was respected there. I could have stayed..." He was lost in thought for a heartbeat or two, and then he went on. "But even there, I did not feel at home. I was restless still. I returned to my wandering.

"And finally I wandered here. I felt drawn to this place, for some reason. And then there I was, at that well. I had had enough of wandering, and I could think of nothing else to do, nowhere else to go. I felt that I was at the end of my road. I have told you of that day. And that is where you found me."

"And I am so glad I did." I snuggled closer.

He held me. Tightly. "So am I, my wild bird. I think now that what drew me here — was you." And he kissed me.

We took a different way back to our camp that night, perhaps just to put off our return to our separate tents and be together a little longer. As we walked together, hand in hand, we passed a place where there was a broad, circular depression in the earth, like an enormous, shallow bowl. The earth in the center was flattened and smooth, as if it had been shaped so. I had known the place from childhood, and avoided it.

We stopped, and Kisil looked down at the smooth, round center of the bowl. "This looks like a good place to camp. The center is smooth and even, and the steep sides would protect our tents from the wind. Why does your family not pitch their tents here?"

I shuddered. "It is cursed. Father told me. When his father was a boy, long ago — very long ago — something terrible happened here."

"Something terrible? What?"

"He never told me. But we never even walk down there." I paused. "I think someone did something horrible here. Something ugly. But that is only my guess. Father would never tell us, but he always told us to stay away from this place."

Kisil studied the shape of it. "That is a shame. I have seem similar places, in Greece, where the people gather on the slopes around and watch performances — of music, plays, even athletic contests. They call it a *theater*." He pointed. "Look at the shape of it. Everyone gathered around can see what is happening in the center, even up on the higher slopes."

I saw what he meant. The people in the back would be higher than those in front, and everyone could see. "What is a *play*?" I asked.

"A story, but acted out instead of told. A Greek invention. They can be very good." He pointed. "See, the center is flat and even, as if it were made for it."

"Yes, I see. A place like this would be good, for that." Then I shivered. "But not — not this place, Kisil. Not this place. I have feared it since I was a child."

"In the cities, such things are purpose-built, and made of stone. There are a few, I think, even in Egypt." He examined the slopes. "Are you sure that men did not make this?"

"Father never said so, but perhaps they did. Perhaps that has something to do with whatever it was that was done here." I waved my hand, brushing it away. "Let us speak of something else. I do not like it here. It feels — unclean."

We walked on, and perhaps to take my mind off my disquiet, Kisil told me a little more about Greece. He said that the athletes in these contests competed naked.

I gaped at him, shocked and amazed. "Of course, women are not allowed to attend," he added with a twinkle. "Even in the plays, the women's parts are played by small men, and boys."

I laughed. "Are the women allowed to see those, at least?"

"In some cities. Not all."

"What do they eat there, Kisil?" I was suddenly curious.

"Many of the same things we eat here," he said. "Olives, and lamb, and figs, and bread. But they eat much fish, and many other things. They have fruits that we do not have, called apples. They make a kind of flat bread..."

We walked on, and he told me of dishes he had eaten, and of sights he had seen, that I could not imagine. Once again, I wondered how far his wanderings had taken him.

Reflecting on what he had told me, of his fleeing Egypt and his travels since, I felt that I was beginning to understand what haunted him. I understood the silences, the distant look when his eyes were on the horizon. He still wondered what to do, and who he truly was.

Well, I would show him, I thought. He was a good man, and he would be a good husband and a good father. What else was there?

He had a people now, a family. Our people, our family. He had a home. And when he squeezed me again, I thought, *he knows that too.*

I wondered then if his past would ever be truly behind him. But now, so many years later, I understand that it was not his past that drove him.

It was what still lay in his future — our future.

30

Preparations for our wedding continued, and the discussions — and sometimes arguments — with my father went on as well. One night, the three of us were sitting at the rocks near the Mountain and talking. I was hemming a section of cloth for a new tent, one that was intended for Kisil and me. I watched and listened as they spoke.

There would only be a half-moon that night, and it would rise late. That was all right, because I sewed more by feel than by sight; but much more important, it meant that our marriage would take place in only another week. We women were busy, indeed consumed, with preparations for the feast.

I had left the woman's tent on the excuse of needing space for hemming the large section of cloth, but what I really wanted was to escape their frantic activity and chattering for a while. It was the first wedding among us, but it still seemed to me that the women in my family were making far too much of what was, at bottom, a simple thing. I saw Kisil and my father sitting by the fire, and decided to join them.

I had to smile as I walked toward them with the rolled cloth over my shoulder. The lives of men and women are so different, I thought. I suppose they still are, and will always be. The women were scurrying around the camp preparing for the wedding, but the groom and the father of the bride were still absorbed in talking about The One. They hardly noticed when I sat down and unrolled the fabric.

"But there are rules that must be kept," Kisil was saying, pounding a fist on the rock. "Things that are absolutes. Rules that must not be broken — except perhaps to save a life." He was fighting his lisp, spitting out the words emphatically.

My father nodded quickly, but added more: "Yes, but men must work out those rules for themselves!" The argument had apparently been going on for some time.

"But then other men can disagree with them, and violate them, and change them! Ignore them, even! Make new rules for themselves, for convenience, for greed, for pleasure! If rules come from men, men can change them!" My husband-to-be's voice rose.

My father's voice rose to match Kisil's. "And so they should! Few rules are immutable. Times change, and so should the laws of men!"

"*Some* rules are for always!" cried Kisil. "Do not murder, do not steal!"

I had already forgotten my sewing, and watched my father as he answered. He nodded, conceding the point in a calmer tone. "Yes, certainly. You are right in that." He frowned. "What else?"

Kisil blinked. "What do you mean?"

"What other rules can never change? What laws are for all times and all places? Do not murder, do not steal... What else?"

"Do not lie without a good reason," I said. Both men laughed, and I bristled. "What is funny?"

"Forgive me, Tzipporah," said Kisil, still laughing. "But can you not see the arguments that will follow? What is a good reason?"

My father smiled, nodding. "They would be endless."

I sat back. They were correct in that. "All right. Then... Perhaps, do not lie about a matter of — of importance? No, I see. That would lead to arguments too."

"No. No, you have something there," said Kisil. "On a matter before a judge, or concerning — life or death, or property..."

"Yes! Yes! Before a judge! 'Do not speak as a false witness.' That is essential!"

"Do not betray your spouse — or your parents," I said.

"Good!" they said together, and laughed again. Then my father lifted a finger, as was his way. His voice grew deep and solemn. "Do not worship as a god a thing that men have made."

"Idols," said Kisil. "Yes, that is wrong. Do not worship *things.*"

I thought of something else. "Perhaps a day of — not working. Like our New Moon."

Kisil and my father frowned. "Mmm — that would be hard," said my husband-to-be.

My father scratched his head. "The same day? For everyone?"

We talked long into the night. The waxing moon rose. My father looked at it and said, "How late it is! Moonrise! Come, we should all sleep. He made as if to rise.

"Wait," said Kisil. "From where will these rules come? What authority lies behind them?"

My father shrugged. "Are they not self-evident?"

Kisil shook his head. "No. Not to everyone. Greedy and petty men will deny them for their own purposes. There must be some absolute, some foundation that cannot be shaken. The only —"

I interrupted Kisil, I think for the first time. "The rules must come from God."

They both stared at me. My father frowned. "God does not speak."

Kisil's eyes were on mine, and never left them as he spoke the words I felt forming on my own lips: "Then we must speak for Him."

I looked at my father. "Yes. As you did for us, Father, my sisters and me, when we were small."

"That was different. I was teaching children."

Kisil smiled. "And are not we all, all of us, children when it comes to wanting our own way?"

Kisil was right, but that was not my point. "You taught us that, Father. And me especially. All truth comes from Ael Shadu, whether He speaks the words or not."

Father opened his mouth to speak, then closed it again. He looked at the rising moon. "Yes. Yes, I did say that."

"And it is true," I whispered.

Kisil nodded thoughtfully. "Your daughter is right, Yisro. Someone must speak for Him."

My father was shaking his head. "But —" he began. Kisil lifted a hand, and he stopped.

"What matters more, Yisro? That these laws truly come from The One directly — which no one can command — or that men do what is right?"

My father opened his mouth again, then closed it again. His face clouded. He was thinking.

Kisil pressed him. "Was there nothing that you taught, when you were a priest of — whatever god you served — that was true?"

Father made a face. "Of course. But those were things we had from our fathers, or had worked out for ourselves, or were —" He stopped and shrugged. "Like the things we spoke of tonight, and others. Things that were true. But when we needed more incense, or more food for ourselves, we told the people that Ba— " He coughed. "That the god commanded it. But we were lying!" he burst out. "Would you have men lie, and teach that Ael Shadu says things that He has not said?"

"But Father — I once said that you had taught me things, when you had not. Do you remember?"

"The scorpion. Yes, I remember. But —"

"Wait. What did you tell the people that was *not* a lie, Yisro?" asked Kisil.

"Do not murder, do not steal, all those things," he said. "But even those —"

"The god did not command them. No. But they were still true, were they not?"

Father lifted his hands in surrender. "Yes, of course. And even though it was a false god we worshipped, those laws were good and right." He shook his head. "I do not completely understand what you are trying to say, Kisil."

"Nor do I," he said. "Not yet. But there must be an answer. Not everyone cares enough to think deeply, Yisro. Not everyone is *able* to think deeply. And not everyone will accept the authority of other men, as you say."

He paused. "So The One must speak. And if He will not, that means that someone must find a way to speak for Him."

"But that is —" began my father. He fell silent then, and looked thoughtful.

"Who else will?" Kisil asked again. "It is a riddle, but it must have an answer. No one can speak for Him, no one has that right; but even though He will not speak, someone must. It is as you taught Tzipporah. If The One speaks, it must be with our own voices. He has no other."

My father was watching Kisil with narrowed eyes. "One who spoke for God would have to be very sure of his words. Very sure indeed."

"Yes. Yes, indeed." Kisil nodded for emphasis. "But on some things, one can be as sure as that." He lifted his hand as if grasping at something and made a fist. I found that I understood the gesture; certainty. "That are things that one can be that sure of — things that God would command, if He did speak. Do you not think so?"

Very slowly, my father nodded, too. "Yes. The same things we taught in our village temple. Do not murder, do not steal. Do not betray your wife or your parents. Some things are simple and clearly true. But beyond that — if a man dared to speak for God —"

"Yes. Beyond that..."

My father's brows drew together. "Such a man would have to know when he had stopped speaking for The One and began speaking for himself."

"To know when he stopped speaking the truth," Kisil corrected him. "Yes."

Kisil sat back, and his eyes seemed to turn inward. "He must be rigorously honest about that, and have no illusions. He must not speak for himself... But only the truth..."

My father and I watched him as he spoke, as if to himself. "And other laws will come from them... And there must still remain a way for those laws to be changed, because no law is perfect for all eternity..."

"Some are." That was my own voice.

Kisil waved a hand. "Yes, of course. We have established that. The laws that lie at the core of all laws. But not the ones that grow from them. Those must change as times change..." He had not looked at me.

We sat and watched the fire, listening to the crackling of the oily wood. After a time, Kisil added, softly: "But when the man is sure — he *must* speak..."

My father and I looked at each other. Then we looked back at Kisil.

We listened to the fire, and let him think.

I remember saying to my father later that night, "Father — Kisil does not believe in The One, not — not really. How can he —"

"That does not matter, little bird." He shook his head, his eyes soft. One looked at me, the other away, and I thought how right that was; he saw me, but he saw beyond me as well. "That does not matter. Kisil serves Him, even so."

"What do you mean?" I was confused. I felt like a child again.

"I am not certain what will happen. But Ael Shadu —" he looked toward Kisil's tent. "The One — He has His hand on Kisil. Kisil does not know this, not yet. Perhaps he never will. But neither does that matter. That Kisil does not truly believe — that may even be something that must be, so that Kisil can do whatever it is he must do."

His voice trailed off. The fire had burned down to red coals, and we gazed at them in silence.

31

The days seemed to fly by and to drag at the same time. Before long, the day came, and Kisil and I were married. My father performed the rite, which was short and simple. The feast was longer and more elaborate, with much song and much dancing, much laughter and very much food and wine.

A few guests from the surrounding villages even came, people we traded with and who were not afraid to call us their friends. The young men who seemed interested in my sisters were there, too, and a few of their friends. The girls were delighted, wearing their best finery and sandals, with their hair freshly oiled and combed.

Finally, Kisil and I went back to our tent, which I had prepared for us. And there, in the light of a single lamp, we became one in body as well as in mind and heart.

There had been a connection between us from the day we met. But that night, there was a bond forged between us, one that never dimmed, not till Kisil went up this mountain and left me here — and sometimes I feel it still. I have no words to tell of that bond, nor would I if I had them; that mystery was ours alone, and for no others to know. But it brought us closer than we were already, and that was no small thing.

I can, and I will, speak a little of our passion that night, for that was the least of it. His hands were calloused, but gentle, not the hands of a shepherd or a workman. They were insistent, too, and so knowing. He could excite me with the lightest touch, and he did. I felt his love for me in every caress. I could tell that it was not the first time for him, but that was all right. He was much older than I, after all.

I will say a little more, because it will be important later. Kisil looked different, down there. I had seen my father, and boy-children from other clans, and Kisil was different. He told me that when the sons of his people are eight days old, they cut away their foreskins. It is a sign of the Covenant with their nameless God, he said. Whatever the reason, I liked him that way. He seemed cleaner, somehow.

There was little pain when he entered me, and that only for an instant. I have heard women complain of love, and say they hated it. I cannot understand this. For Kisil and me, it was a way to tell each other what we felt without words. It was wonderful.

Our lovemaking was sweet, but it was, in a way, only more of the same, more of what we had from the beginning. It was more profound, more intimate, more deeply felt. But it was not a surprise, not in the way it brought us closer.

What was a surprise was the ecstasy. I have never felt anything like the way Kisil made me feel. Today he is remembered as Moses, the Deliverer, the Teacher, the Lawgiver. And so he was. But he was a man for all that, and a good man, and a gentle man. Before he was all of those great things, he was my lifemate, a sweet and skilled lover, and a faithful one. Before he was the Lawgiver, he was my husband, and I loved him, and he loved me. I will tell you little of our intimate times together, but I will tell you this: he made me melt, my Kisil did, and I was liquid in his arms. And before he made me melt, he made me burn, and the fire did not consume me.

Yes, I am smiling. Because I made him burn too, and melt, and we burned together and melted into each other and kept each other warm for many, many years, more than you might believe. The old can burn too, my children. The flame may not burn as high or last as long, but it warms as deeply as it ever did.

My sisters said I glowed, on that first morning. I suppose I did, and for many days thereafter. Many years, perhaps. Perhaps I still do.

I have said this already, and more than once: from the time I was very small, I always felt apart, somehow, alone, even among my family, my sisters.

But with Kisil — I was no longer alone. He knew my mind, somehow. That was true even before we were married. In some ways, it was true from the afternoon when we met. He told me that, later, and I knew that I had been right. He *had* felt that link between us, as real and solid as a chain of gold, just as I did. Not from the first time he looked into my eyes on that day at the well, but from the second. And from our wedding night, I think he could look out of my eyes, know what was in my mind, my heart, as intimately as I.

For my part, I knew much of what was in his mind; but not all. To the very end, there was a mystery there. It had to do with what lay between Kisil and The One — but no one, I think, could ever know that, not even his wife.

32

After the wedding, our life continued much as it had, except that we shared a tent of our own. We kept the sheep, we moved our camp from place to place, we traded our cloth and wool and hides for the other things that we needed, and we spoke of The One and the ways of men.

Those were good years for Kisil and me. Seven years, he worked for my father, but that was only living with us and caring for our sheep, and we continued to do that even after the seven years were up and a son had been born to us.

We named our son Gershom. Kisil told me that the name had to do with his, Kisil's, being a stranger in this place, and of his being so welcomed by us and finding a home here. I liked the name. It was a strong name, and the boy was strong too. He was curiously silent much of the time, and cried little. Gershom learned to speak late, and like his father, spoke little and only at need.

Kisil and I shared a tent, and a bed, and our lives, and it was good. I wondered, sometimes, if he ever thought of taking Gershom and me and moving away from our clan and going to live somewhere else, a different kind of life in a different place; but he told me that he had had enough of wandering. We lived a quiet life, and a happy one.

Gershom was a fortunate boy. He had two fathers — Kisil, who doted on him, and his grandfather, my father, who had never had a boy-child in his tents and doted on him even more. The two of them seemed to think that teaching Gershom how to be a man was their most important task.

They took turns at it, and by his sixth summer, Gershom could herd the sheep, saddle and ride a donkey, sling a stone, and — this was my own teaching — play a flute, and very well for a child his age. He was even learning his letters, both the Egyptian style and the style of Midyan, and his father and grandfather were very proud of him. So was I.

And Gershom did not only have two fathers — he had nine mothers! If it had not been for me and Kisil, the boy would have been spoiled till he stank, with my mothers and sisters fawning over him. He was a smart boy, and played them as well as he played his flute, or better. Even Nazirah spoiled him, teaching him to use the sling and taking him hunting. They stalked the wild coneys and showed the jackals and even the lions why they should stay away from our flocks.

And the food! My mothers outdid themselves, feeding my husband and my son as if every day were a feast day. We had more sweets at our meals — made with honey, dates, and a sweet plant that Kisil had shown us — than I ever remembered eating before. When Malkah finally married, and I was expecting another child, I wondered how much more wonderful it could be in our camp.

Kisil loved me, and he loved our son, and he loved all our family, and we all loved him. I thought it would never change, and I was happy at that thought. Growing old with my husband, keeping our sheep, raising our children, living near the Mountain — it was a sweet thought.

I remember one night especially, a night that I still think of today, so many years later. It was the dark of the moon, when we gathered around our fire to celebrate life, the sweetness of it, and a time of rest. Father had told some stories, and Kisil had told a few of his own. Gershom and I and my mother Qamra had played our flutes, with two of my sisters joining in and singing, and the others keeping the time. Later, all of us women sang as our men listened and beat the ground in time with their hands. We had feasted, earlier, on a fresh-killed lamb, fresh-baked bread, figs, dates, ewe's-milk beer, and other delicacies that we had put by for the feast. It was the first New Moon of the spring, and a special time.

Later in the evening, a sweet silence came as we all looked at the fire in contentment. We were full, satisfied, and feeling the joy and peace that comes with being surrounded by loved ones. I remember their faces in the firelight. Even Nazirah's face seemed serene and deeply joyful. I remember leaning on Kisil's chest and thinking how happy I was. I will remember that night till I no longer draw breath, I am sure of it.

I think that night, and others like it, were the happiest times of my life. They happened before the world changed, and before Kisil became — what he became. I have often wondered what our lives would have been like if we could have lived them out in Midyan, there in our camp by the Mountain.

He told me this once, and I shall always remember his dear, clumsy voice as he spoke the words: "This life is so different for me, my sweet bird. I have spent so many years wandering, without a home, without knowing who I was or for what I was made. Everything in my life is different now. Now I have a home. Here, with you. I know who I am: Your husband. I know what I have to do: Love you. Care for our sheep. Raise our sons." His eyes held my own, and then he held me close. "My long journey is finally over."

33

But somehow, still, Kisil seemed haunted, troubled. I knew this, even if he tried not to know it himself. I saw him, often, staring into the fire or into the sunset — looking west — and I knew he was thinking of his people.

And I knew Kisil, and I knew that one day he would have to face his own discontent, his own yearnings. He would have to tell the truth to himself, as my father had said, as Kisil himself had said. I saw it in his eyes, in the set of his mouth, in his posture. While we herded our sheep, while we sang by the fire, while we watched our sons grow — both Gershom, and his brother still in my belly. I did not know what would happen when Kisil finally faced his burdens, but I knew that he was haunted by them still.

His people sweated in the brick pits, and bled from pulling the sledges. They saw their own children, and their children's children, condemned to lives of toil, and misery, and death. How bleak a future — one of slavery, of labor unrewarded, from generation to generation.

How different from what we had, he and I.

He seldom spoke of it, but I saw it in him, often enough that I knew what was on his mind. The only time it ever left him, I think, was when we — became one, in body as well as in our hearts. At those times, there was nothing and no one in the world but we two, and he always slept more peacefully afterward. Those nights were sweet, together in our tent.

And that remained for us, even through all that came later. The world moved around us, but the bond between us remained till the end. And perhaps beyond.

Kisil spoke of his people to my father sometimes, but my father had little to say.

"The Avru are few, and weak, and weakened further by servitude," he told us once. We were sitting near the fire, at the end of a long day of shearing the sheep and settling them down again afterward. "I know they cannot rise up and free themselves. But if The One is God — *their* God — why does He not set them free, as they say He promised them?"

My father lifted a hand. "Because that task is not for Him to do. Men must do what is right because they choose to, or the right will not be done."

"Then where is justice?" asked Kisil angrily, fighting his impaired mouth as always, struggling to speak clearly. "Why does He stand by and allow this?" He frowned blackly and shook his head. "That is why I do not believe there is such a God. If there is, He is unfaithful and a liar. A poor God indeed."

My father lifted both his hands. "The One controls everything — except what men do. The Egyptians may know that they act wrongly, or they may never think on it; but no one else can think for them. No one can change them, only they themselves."

"What can men do, then? If The One will not intervene, what can men — what can any man — do? If there is no Ael Shadu to soften the hearts of men, or if He will not, how can a man do it?"

I realized something then. Even though Kisil said that he was not sure he believed in The One, it seemed clear to me that he did — but was angry at Him. I wondered if he knew that himself.

My father shook his head sadly. "Perhaps nothing. But a man is still obligated to try, to try to do right, to set the wrong right."

Kisil's face was as earnest as a child's. "But how?"

"That I cannot tell you. I do not think that even The One could tell you. That, a man must find out for himself."

Kisil looked up at the Mountain. "The Avru say that He calls men at times. Even calls them by name. I have heard the tales." Kisil shrugged. "I do not know if I believe them."

"I think that even if Ael Shadu called him, a man would still have to choose to answer. And he would still have to find his own way. The will of man — of any man — is not determined by the will of Ael Shadu."

"*Can* He command?"

My father shrugged lightly. "He could, of course. But if he were to compel us, what then would a man be? Each man is responsible for what he does, he and he alone. And what he does not do, as well. And he must bear the consequences for both."

Kisil nodded again — but his eyes grew darker and even more troubled. I wondered why.

34

One night — it was a night in the spring, with a half moon — I felt restless and troubled. I was straightening our tent, Gershom was dozing on his pallet, and Kisil was out watching the flocks. Everything was quiet and peaceful — but something was wrong, or unfinished, or hanging over us. I felt it. I could not put my finger on it — but it bothered me just the same.

I was still with child then, with Eliezer. I was barely showing, but I was far enough along to make me clumsy and careful, so I thought little of my feelings. Women with child often feel restless and troubled. I had been very moody with Gershom, but not so much this time. Still, I felt unsettled and obscurely worried. I tried to dismiss it, but the feeling would not go away.

We had long since settled into our life with my father's clan. Kisil had truly become one of us, a true Midyanite. My sister Malkah had married her husband Yusuf, and as my father had predicted, he had come to live with us; and Charah had married the young man who admired her as well. Walid was his name, and he lived with us too.

Both young men were outcasts themselves in a way, disliked and unappreciated by their own tribes. I always suspected that it was because they, too, doubted the priests and the pretend-gods that their people worshipped. It did not help them, of course, when it became known that they often visited the camp of Yisro. After their marriages, they were much happier with us.

Malkah had given birth to a daughter, and Charah was expecting her first — and there were other young men interested in my other sisters as well. Our clan was growing.

We had thought, Kisil and I, that we would live out our lives as ordinary people, shepherds and nomads, wandering with our flocks. That our time would be quiet, uneventful, and not worthy of campfire tales. My expecting another child only added to that feeling. We were both quietly content, and Kisil seemed to have left his unease behind — most of the time.

But that unsettled feeling, of something coming, something out of place, had been growing in me, and I was not alone. Kisil had been troubled for days, obscurely oppressed and withdrawn. He spent his days in silence, thinking, brooding. He was short with me and with little Gershom, which was unlike him. He was not even talking to my father much, as he sometimes did when this mood came upon him. I noticed him looking up at the Mountain often — almost as if he were angry at it.

But that night, the mood had come on me too. I felt somehow oppressed. Not fearful, but as if there were something I had forgotten to do, or something that I needed to do.

I remember one thing especially. I was folding a blanket, stroking it and thinking about it. I had made it myself, from raw fibers to hand-spun thread to woven fabric, from the wool of sheep that I had tended from their births. That blanket was me, my life, in a way. I was holding it against my swollen belly — and I remember looking up suddenly and speaking aloud. "Something is about to happen."

"What is it, Mamma?" I had awakened Gershom, or else he had not really been asleep. He blinked and looked up at me curiously.

I blinked back at him. The words had come out of my mouth almost unbidden. It seemed at the time that I had spoken an instant before I heard the words in my mind. That was the first time I had ever that feeling, but it would not be the last time, not even the last time that night.

And then I laughed. Of course something was going to happen! "I am going to have a baby, Gershom!" He blinked at me, puzzled and a little disgusted.

"Well, I know that, Mamma." He rolled over to go back to sleep. I laughed again. "Your mother is silly tonight. I am sorry I woke you, darling."

He murmured something indistinct, as children do, and wriggled restlessly. I took out my flute and played for a bit, and before long my son was still and breathing deeply. I kissed him gently, put away my flute, and went out of the tent to watch for Kisil. I was still thinking of what I had said, smiling at my own foolishness.

We were camped very near the Mountain, the rocky lowest slopes of it only a short distance from our tents. It loomed above me in the darkness, huge and silent. When I looked up at it, I stopped laughing.

It seemed to be watching, as if it were aware of me, so far below it, so tiny, so weak. I felt its mass, its enormous weight, above me. It was more than a feature of the land, more than a mere mass of stone and earth. It was a Presence. I was still smiling, but the feeling of something coming toward me returned, stronger than ever. I remembered the feeling that I had the day I met Kisil. Something was approaching, something important.

And then the Mountain spoke. Very softly, but I felt it; a movement of the earth, very like the ones we had known so many times before, the deep thunder in the ground that could be felt and not heard — but this time, soft, small, a whisper and not a deep growl.

My father had always told us that the Mountain was a special place, His special place. The place of The One. That night, I felt it. He — Ael Shadu, the God of the Mountain — was very near.

I walked away from the tents, toward the great dark mass, and stood there gazing up at it. "What is it that you want?" I whispered.

I saw Kisil approaching, coming toward me from among the sheep, swinging his staff at every second step. Our dog accompanied him; Kadin's pup, that we had named Awwa because he howled. The flocks were settling down for the night, scattered across the lower slopes in twos and threes and fours. The air was still. It seemed the whole world was still.

I still remember every detail of the way Kisil looked that night, as if it were a painting or a carving. It remains frozen in time in my mind. He had his staff in his hand and his half-filled water-skin hanging from one shoulder. His face, from where I stood, was just at the line between the Mountain and the stars. He seemed to be etched in a special clarity, very vivid, very real and present. I have never forgotten the sight of him, or how much I loved him at that moment — or how that feeling of something approaching us, something very big, very important, grew even stronger as I watched him moving toward me.

I was filled to overflowing with love for him. This man was my life, and I would be devoted to him whatever came to us. Something was coming, but whatever it was, we would still be together.

I looked around, trying to find something out of place. I saw nothing. The flock was quiet where Kisil had left them, and as I was looking around — at the desert, at our tents behind me, at the sky — my eye was drawn to a light behind Kisil, high up, far above the sheep.

When I first caught a glimpse of it, from the corner of my eye, I thought it was a bright star, but when I looked at it directly I saw that it was not. It was something else, something on the Mountain and not in the sky.

I pointed. "Kisil. Look."

He turned and looked. High on the slope, far above us, there was a light, a spark of brilliance. Small, but sharp, and of no color I had ever seen before. It seemed to vary in intensity, but it did not flicker. It was not a fire. Nor was it anything else I knew.

Kisil's mouth fell open. "What is that?"

That soft, small whisper of thunder through the earth came once more. Kisil looked at me and blinked in surprise, and I looked back at him, as surprised as he. "I do not know."

It was not late, but it happened that there was no one near us. My sisters and their husbands and children were doing other things, or were asleep. The half-moon was high in the sky behind us, so the slope of the mountain was lit, though dimly. The light gleamed, first bright, then dim, then bright again.

"Have you ever seen that before?' Kisil was still staring up at the light.

"I have lived near the Mountain all my life — but that, I have never seen. Never." I knelt and petted Awwa, who licked my hand and whimpered softly. As dogs do, he sensed our change of mood.

The earth whispered again, that same small impact, as one might feel a big man's footstep nearby. "Nor have I ever felt that." We looked at each other, then up at the light, wondering. The whisper came again — and then again. It became a rhythm, a deep throb, very slow, very subtle, but unmistakably there.

As we watched, I felt words rise to my lips again and come out, again almost before I knew what they would be.

"You must go up there."

I hardly knew what I had said. The words surprised me as much as they did my husband — and at that moment, that small throb through the earth grew more pronounced. It had become a drumbeat. A faint one, but growing stronger. The small whispers became a dim, rhythmic pulse, like the slow pounding of a great drum, but very far away. It was, as always, very like a sound, but too low to hear. I have no word for it. We had both felt it before — but not for a long, long time, and never like this.

Kisil turned toward me. "No one may go on the Mountain." His voice, still, was thicker and more impaired when he spoke softly.

I looked up at him and said, "I have." I had never told anyone that.

Kisil blinked, then grinned and cocked his head. "You still have secrets," he said. "That is a good thing to know." He looked up at the Mountain again, and I saw in his face that he felt nothing. He shrugged. "Very well," he said. "As you say — it is only a mountain, after all."

I had not said that, but I did not correct him.

The Mountain continued its deep, faint pulse. Ael Shadu was speaking, quietly, in the only voice I had ever heard Him use — and in a way I had never heard nor felt before.

Kisil's face was solemn — but he was looking at me again. He had been somewhere else, for days, perhaps for weeks, wrestling with something; but now he was with me once more. He was not fearful, nor even resigned. He seemed — *relieved.*

"I would take you with me — but —" He patted my belly, swollen with his second child, if only a little. He smiled, his eyes crinkling with good humor. The earth pulsed, and the light glowed and dimmed, glowed and dimmed.

It was strange how relaxed he was. His eyes, his mouth, showed no hint of fear or trepidation — but his mood of brooding anger was gone. I wondered if he even realized that himself.

I smiled back easily, then laughed. There was no fear in my heart, either, nor did I know why. "And I would go." I went into his arms, and we held each other. "You are meant to go alone, Kisil," I murmured against his chest. "You must go. I know it."

He nodded and turned, looking back up at the light. We both felt the heartbeat of the Mountain through the ground. "Can you feel Him, Kisil?" I whispered.

He shook his head without looking at me. "I never do. You know that, my sweet bird. I think on Him. I wonder about Him. I doubt Him. But I have never felt Him." Then he did look at me. "Do you?"

I nodded, then nodded again. "Yes." Then, "Yes, Kisil. More than I ever have. He is there, Kisil. He is —"

I hesitated. I looked up at the Mountain from his arms, and as we felt that unheard rhythm continue to pound in the earth, that Presence seemed heavy to me, pressing, expectant. This time, I knew what the words were before I spoke them.

"He is *waiting*." I felt it like a storm coming — but still, I felt no fear. It was a storm that we needed, both of us.

Kisil smiled again, his face easy — and then, to my surprise, he shrugged again, and laughed. "Then I should go to Him." He said it lightly, no more fearful than if I had told him that it was my father waiting for him, or some desert merchant. But he was not complacent, not uncaring.

He was *certain*. He was filled with some sort of assurance, some confidence, of which he hardly seemed aware himself. I could only wonder at his equanimity — and love him for it.

He held me for a moment more; then he kissed me, taking his time. He squeezed me again for another heartbeat — and then, without another word, he let me go and started toward the pulsing light.

He had not even troubled to refill his water-skin. I held Awwa back, or he would have followed. "I love you," I said to Kisil's back. He paused then, and as I knew he would, he turned and looked back at me, his eyes warm.

"And I love you," his mouth said, but without sound. Then he turned back to the Mountain and strode on. He did not look back again.

I sat down where I was, far from our tent, to watch as his figure — so dear to me, my very life — grew smaller and smaller as he made his way up the lower slopes. Our camp was near the Mountain, at its foot, but it was still far to the light. A long climb, though not a hard one. And the pulse continued, drumming through the ground.

I scratched behind Awwa's ear and wondered idly, as if it were someone else, if he would come back. It was said that none who had climbed the Mountain ever had. I knew differently — but even so, I wondered. My restlessness was gone, and I felt no fear. There was still that looming, silent Presence, but I felt no unease, no trepidation, none at all. I felt at peace. Assured, like Kisil did. This was meant to happen. I would see my husband again, I knew.

And then I realized something. If Kisil had been able to feel the Presence, as I did — in his heart, and not in his mind alone — he would never have been able to climb the Mountain. He would have been overwhelmed by it.

I looked up at that looming mass of stone, and I shuddered. I could not have done it. In spite of what I had told my husband, in spite of the fact that I had done so before, I could never have gone up that slope, not a single step. Not that night. I was not afraid, but I could not have faced The One, on His Mountain.

Things began to fall into place that night, in many ways, and I began to understand, a little. All these things had happened for a reason, in Kisil's life and in mine. He had been separated from his people all his life, without sharing their customs and heritage, nor their beliefs; and that, too, made it possible for him to go to confront The One that night. He did not really believe that The One was there, before he climbed His Mountain. And afterward —

Well. Afterward was afterward.

35

I watched all night. The light on the mountain remained; brighter, then dimmer, then bright again. The rhythmic pounding in the earth continued as well, steady and unchanging, throughout the night.

Our fire, behind me among the tents, had burned down to dim red embers, and the Moon had set behind the Mountain. It was very dark. Our camp was lit only by the stars that turned silently above. A faint, barely perceptible breeze blew from the Empty Quarter, and there was no sound of bird or beast, even from our dozing sheep. Awwa, too, was asleep at my side. The night was silent, waiting with me. I watched the light and hoped.

The sky behind us began to lighten with a hint of the coming dawn. The vague gray shapes around me in the dark changed back into our tents, and details became visible as light returned to the world. As the sun neared the horizon, the breeze from the desert freshened, as it often did at that time of day. I could hear the others stirring, low voices and sounds of movement from their tents.

For some reason I could never explain, I turned back toward the east — and my mouth and my eyes opened wide. There was a single bright ray of green light there, rising straight from the Earth into the sky, and then it vanished and was replaced by a brilliant flash of blue, as blue as Rivkah's eyes, at the spot on the horizon where it had been. The flash lasted for only an eyeblink, and then the edge of the Sun appeared and filled the world with light and shadow.

I turned back to the Mountain just in time to see the strange point of light on its slope dim and disappear. In the space of a single heartbeat, the light grew faint and was gone. In two more, the pulsing in the earth faded, and then it was gone as well.

My sisters, and the rest of my family, began to emerge from their tents and begin the work of the day; building up the fire, hanging cooking-skins filled with water over it, emptying their night vessels into the privy pit and covering their contents with earth.

Charah first saw me sitting on the slope. She and Walid came to me and asked me what I was doing there, and where Kisil was. I told them what we had seen, and where he had gone.

At their urging, I returned to the camp, sat down by the fire, and told the others. Gershom came out of our tent, rubbing his eyes, and I told him too.

My son had heard the stories of the Mountain — he had seven years by then, I think, or perhaps eight — but he was no more afraid than I. He smiled and sat down beside me, and we waited together.

My mothers tended the fire, and put grain and meal into the boiling skins to make a pottage for breakfast. Malkah and Tharah took the dough that they had set to leaven the night before and kneaded loaves. Soon they placed them in the earthenware vessels we used for baking, and set those on the hot stones. Someone offered me a cup of water, and I drank it.

Soon we were all watching and waiting. There was little talk; whispers only, often behind cupped hands. The others were all frightened and worried — even my father. He may have been the most worried of all.

But I was not afraid, and neither was my son. The rest did not understand this, and I could not explain it to them because I understood it no more than they. All I could do was tell them, "It will be all right. I know it." Gershom smiled, his face untroubled, and I wondered. *How can he, so young, know too?*

The sheep found grass nearby. We had learned to leave the pastures near our camp untouched, to graze the sheep in case there was ever a need to stay close to our tents. We let Awwa mind them, and gathered around the fire and waited.

My father sat next to Gershom, and he was watching me, not the Mountain. Soon he seemed to grow calmer.

When his gaze did return to the Mountain, he seemed almost as calm as I. His familiar hand took mine behind my son, and I squeezed it.

As the time passed, I began to think: *How will I raise my son, if Kisil never comes back?* I looked at Gershom as I was thinking it. It was as if it were something in a tale; I knew it would never really come to pass. I did not feel troubled. I knew that all would be well.

Soon the food was ready. I had no interest in eating, though the others pressed me to, and I drank little. I made sure that Gershom ate, though, and at the urging of my sisters, I took a little milk and bread for the baby that was coming. I watched the Mountain. We all did.

And we waited. The sun grew high, but no one wanted to go back to the tents. Walid and Yusuf made a shelter, a canopy open on all sides, and we waited in its shade. As the sun sank toward the horizon, Rivkah began to cry, and I saw the eyes of my mother Sabah begin to fill as well. My father simply sat, head hanging low. I went back to our tent for my flute.

When I returned, I said to them, "It will be all right. You will see. Kisil will come back to me — to us." I laughed then, and they looked up as one, their eyes wide. I laughed again. "Do not be so sad! You will see!" Then I sat down again and played, and they seemed comforted.

Gershom, as silent as his father, only smiled wryly and nodded. He looked very much like his father when he smiled.

"Look! There he is!"

The sharp eyes of Nazirah found Kisil first. The Sun was well down by then, and the near side of the Mountain was in deep shadow when we finally saw him working his way down the slope. Some of my sisters had returned to despair when I stopped playing, and they clapped their hands and wiped their eyes when they saw him.

We all stood and watched him approach. The girls began to chatter excitedly, and even their husbands and my mothers — and I myself — joined in. "I told you," I said. "He is all right, just as I said."

"But how did you —"

My father frowned and lifted his hand, and we all grew silent. "Kisil has climbed the Mountain and returned," he intoned, his voice deep and grave. "Do none of you understand what he has done? He has gone to the dwelling-place of Ael Shadu Himself — when He is *there* —" He looked at me for a moment, his eyes warm. I realized then that he had known of my explorations when I was small, though he had never mentioned them.

Father went on. "Kisil has stood in the very presence of The One. And yet, he lives."

After that, no one spoke. Even Awwa, who usually ran to greet Kisil, stood still and watched him approach.

Gershom squeezed my hand. "I knew you were right, Mamma," he whispered.

By the time Kisil reached our tents, it was full dark. It had been almost an entire day since he had gone up. The tales say that his face was changed, but he looked no different at a distance, nor when he drew closer. When he finally reached the plain, I saw that he did stand straighter. More importantly, that haunted look — the look that he had borne since I first met him — that look was gone. His eyes were clear and direct, and no longer sad. When he looked at me, I saw a peace, and yet a strength, and a determination, that I had never seen before.

Only then — then, after he had come safely back — only then did I begin to feel afraid. This was still my husband, still the man I knew; but something about him had changed. I could not name that fear, not then, but I felt it.

He was silent as he approached, as I knew he would be. My sisters, their husbands, my mothers, even my father, cried out to him:

"Are you all right?"

"Where have you been?"

"Where did you go?"

"What did you see up there?"

Kisil ignored them as if he had not heard. He looked only at me, and came closer without speaking. Finally, they all fell silent and waited.

When he stood before me, I said, "Tell us."

Kisil looked around as if seeing the others for the first time. He gave my father a respectful nod. Then he hugged me, and Gershom, giving our son a kiss by his ear, and only then did he speak. The others, including Gershom, listened. He knew that they were listening, but he spoke to me only.

"There is —" He stopped, then began again. "There is something that I must do, Tzipporah. Something that —" He stopped again, closed his eyes, and thought. Then he opened them and looked at me, his soft eyes on mine. "Something that I know I must do. That I've always known."

He spoke hesitantly at first. His voice was still thick and impaired, his lisp still prominent, but his words seemed to flow more easily, the hesitation coming from his thoughts and not so much from his injured mouth. I did not sense the effort that it had always taken for him to speak clearly before.

"Did you feel His presence?" I asked hopefully.

He shook his head with that crooked smile I had come to love so much, the same that I had seen on my son's face, and I was comforted. He was, indeed, still my Kisil. "No, Tzipporah." He spoke sadly, as if he knew I would be disappointed. "I felt nothing. It is what I *know*."

"What do you know, Kisil? What happened up there?"

He looked around at the others, and then back at me. He shook himself. "Let us sit down."

We all moved back to the fire, and one of my sisters brought Kisil a cup of water. He gave his staff to Gershom, took the cup gratefully, and drank. I had not noticed till then that his waterskin was missing. He must have left it on the Mountain. He sat down, and Awwa settled himself next to him, as his sire Kadin had always done. He scratched the dog's head, and Awwa nuzzled his side affectionately. We all sat down to listen.

Kisil asked for another cup of water. When he received it, he lifted his face and poured the water over it, letting it run down over his robe. He rubbed his cheeks and head vigorously.

"It took me a long time to find it, Tzipporah," he finally said. "The light." He looked beyond me for a heartbeat, up at the darkening Mountain, then back at my eyes. "It was in a hollow, a place set back from the slope." His hands gestured, trying to show us. "I saw the glow before I reached it. When I peeked around a corner of the rock, I saw the light."

He blinked. His eyes were far away, for a breath perhaps, still seeing it. Then he was looking at me again. "It was only a little distance away, as far as we are from — that spotted ewe." He pointed, and we all looked. We were perhaps ten long strides from the sheep he indicated.

His eyes grew distant again. "I thought it was a shrub, or a bush, at first. One that was on fire, somehow, burning, but that did not burn up. I could not understand...."

His voice was surer, less hesitant, than I had ever heard it. It was still my Kisil's voice, thick and clumsy, but somehow it was stronger, more certain. He was no longer fighting his lisp. He was *ignoring* it.

"Then I saw what it was. It was a fountain — a fountain of fire."

"What?" I thought I had misunderstood what he had said. I did not know what a fountain was. I had never heard the word.

"It was a *fountain*, Tzipporah. A spray, but a spray of fire. Fire, spraying up from the ground, like — like —" He blinked, then smiled. "No, you do not have fountain-springs in this land." He thought. "It sprayed like — like water sprays from a filled waterskin, when it is pierced. You have seen this?"

I blinked at him, trying to understand, to see it in my mind. "Yes..."

"It was like that, Tzipporah, but it kept spraying, and it was made of fire. It was so bright I could hardly look at it."

He shook his head, his eyes filled with wonder. "It came from a crack in the earth. And the fire — it splattered on the ground, all around. It lay there in glowing drops and pools, and it cooled, and it turned black, where it fell."

Something crossed his face then. "Wait—" He pulled something from his sash and held it out. "Here. This is a piece of it."

I took it from his hand. It was a small stone, no bigger than the tip of my thumb. It was black, and smooth and rounded on one side; the other side was flat and rough, with sand and bits of rock imbedded in it. "This is fire?" The dog sniffed at it curiously, and I let him.

"That is what I saw. Liquid fire, that cools and turns to stone." He waved a hand and shook his head, not trying to explain. I handed the stone to my son, who examined it closely. He handed it carefully it to my father, and the others passed it around.

"And then He called me, Tzipporah." His eyes glittered. "I heard it. I heard — Him. I was sure of it. It was my name — *'Kisssssillll.'*" His voice hissed, making the sounds long and sibilant. "Over and over. *'Kisssillll....'* It was not a human voice — but it was a voice. He was speaking to me." He looked back at the Mountain. "He called my name. I thought, He *knows* my name..."

I looked at my father. He was listening, fascinated, his mouth open. We were all listening like that, I think. Kisil's eyes shone in the light of our fire. I had never seen him like that, nor heard him speak so easily. None of us had. Even Nazirah was listening, rapt, the cynical, sour look that was her usual expression absent.

"I answered. 'I am here.'" Kisil glanced up at me. "That is something that others have said, when He spoke to them. According to the tales. 'I am here.'"

I understood, now, that time long before when he had frozen for a heartbeat when I spoke those words.

He held out his cup to be refilled. One of my sisters — it was Malkah — filled it from a skin she had brought.

"I did not know what to do, Tzipporah. I was — awed — overwhelmed — I was — I did not know what to do. I did not know what to *do!* I was trembling, I had to do *something* —

"So I took off my sandals. I cannot even say why. I stood barefoot on the ground in front of the fire, and the ground was hot, hotter than it is in the heat of the day. Holy ground. I remember thinking that.

"I fell to my knees. I hid my head in my arms, waiting. When I heard my name again, I lifted my head and saw the fire, rising and falling, and I sat up. And then —"

Kisil stopped, then went on, and his voice, though still indistinct, grew even surer, even more confident. "Then I saw what the sound was. It was the sound of the fire as it came from the rock. The fire pulsed, and shone brighter, then dimmer — it sprayed high, then low — and the sound changed with it. It made the sound of my name. *'Kisil, Kisil,'* hissing as it came from the earth." He gave a short laugh, shaking his head at his own foolishness.

"I sat back. I was relieved, though I was still trembling and my heart was still pounding. It was only the sound of the fire-fountain. It was a natural thing, if a strange one. I sat back and looked at the fire again." He paused, then blinked and frowned. "I looked at the fire.... And I could not look away."

He gazed at the fire before him now, the familiar fire in front of our tent. In the silence, the small, soft crackle and tick of the burning sticks seemed loud. Kisil's eyes were fixed on it, as they must have been on the fire in the Mountain.

"There was nothing but the fire in the whole world," he said, his voice low. "There was no me, no Mountain — nothing but the fire. No time; no past, no present, no future. No words, only thoughts, thoughts without words. Only that moment, only the fire. There was no — *Him*. There was no *me*." He looked at me and shook his head. "Was He there? I do not know, Tzipporah.

"But beneath all that — behind it — I knew this: that time was like no other. That this would only happen once." He lifted a hand, gesturing his frustration at trying to make his meaning clear. "All times are like that, but this one..." He shook his head. "I cannot explain."

I took his hand. "I understand."

And I did, somehow. Our eyes met, and I could see that he knew. The others were silent, watching and listening. Gershom, especially, was listening closely. I wondered what my son was making of this.

Kisil went on. "All I could do was stare, on my knees, watching the fire as it rose and fell."

He looked around at the entranced faces, and smiled at us. "You look like I must have looked," he said with another laugh, a lighter one, in his voice. We all blinked, then smiled, the spell broken for an instant. My father shook his head as if to clear it, and then he looked back at Kisil and grinned. He made a circling motion with his hand, *Tell us more.* Kisil imitated the gesture, then grinned back at him and went on.

"Then —" He put his hands on his head, as if it hurt, and squeezed his eyes shut. "I saw nothing in the fire but fire. I heard no voice, not even in my mind. But — I thought something. I *knew* something." He dropped his hands and looked at us.

We waited. Gershom shifted next to me, and some of the others took water themselves, but no one spoke.

"I cannot say I *realized* it," he went on. "I think it is something that I always knew." He took my hand, and I thought, *here it comes.*

"What?" I braced myself, afraid of what I was about to hear.

Kisil looked into my eyes and said, "I must return to Egypt."

"I will go with you," I said instantly, and firmly. I cannot say what I had been afraid to hear, but it was not that. I felt relieved, almost grateful.

He smiled gently. "Thank you, my love," he said. His soft gray eyes were still on mine.

"Will you take me? And our sons?" Nothing was more important at that moment. I had to know. Was this the end of Kisil — and me? Of our family?

He saw the fear in my eyes — and he laughed. "Oh, my wild bird — how could I not? You are my life. But this is something I must do."

"But why must you go?" I asked. Even as I spoke, I knew the answer, and Kisil's reply confirmed it.

"I must tell the king, to his face, that he must let the Avru go free."

There was a gasp from one or two of my sisters, then silence for a moment. "Ael Shadu told you this," my father said quietly.

Kisil shook his head. "No, Yisro. I told you: I think I have always known this. I have spent my life running from it, working hard not to face it, nor even think about it. But it is the truth. I must do this."

My father spoke again. "Even so, Kisil, it was Ael Shadu Who revealed this truth to you."

My husband stared at him for a time — four or five heartbeats — then shrugged and looked away. "Perhaps." He thought, then nodded and repeated the word. "Perhaps. I admit that it is strange that I could never take this knowledge from wherever I had hidden it, and look at it directly, until I knelt before the fire. There is that. But I heard no Voice, felt no Presence." He glanced at me. "I never do. I never have."

My father began, "But —"

Kisil lifted a hand and cut him off. "I do not say that this Ael Shadu of yours, this One, had nothing to do with it, Yisro. I do not know that. Perhaps He did. What I do know is that I looked at the truth, and acknowledged it. If it was He Who led me to that place, so be it.

"But if — *if* — The One spoke to me, Yisro, all He said was this: *'I am truly here. And I know you.'* This, and no more. The rest came from inside myself, from my own heart."

I gasped and stared at my father, as all my sisters did. He had spoken those very words to all of us, when he told us of the voice of the Mountain.

Kisil went on, oblivious of the looks that passed between us. " Even so —" He paused again. "Even so — *something happened* to me up there, and *I have been changed."* He smiled at me then. "You know this, my sweet bird. I saw it in your eyes when I returned."

"I do," I said. Then, after a moment: "So you believe in Him? You think He is real?"

To my surprise — to everyone's — Kisil stared at me, wide-eyed, then burst out laughing. It was a rich, full-throated laugh, a laugh like none I had never heard from him before.

"Think He is real?" He threw his head back and laughed again. "He is more real than anything! He is more real than the world!" He laughed again, so hard he was wiping his eyes. "Oh, yes, Tzipporah, He is real. *I* may not be real — *you* may not be real — but *He is*." He leaned forward then, and spoke in an urgent hiss. *"But what He is, is Truth. Truth,* Tzipporah. I felt no Presence, heard no voice. But I know this: God is *Truth.* Perhaps there is nothing else. Only *Truth."*

We all watched Kisil and listened, rapt, but he still looked only at me, his gray eyes on mine. They glittered with purpose, with conviction — and with something else. I could see that he had no idea of the power of his words.

He was silent, his eyes burning into mine, and I felt that fear again. This was the Kisil I knew — but there was something new behind those gray eyes.

I caught the thought clearly now. I knew what I feared.

Was I going to lose my husband to The One?

36

Kisil turned to look at the Mountain, and was silent for a time. I waited. We all waited. We all sensed that there was more.

He came to himself and looked around at us. Then he smiled. "Perhaps He is there; perhaps He is not. No one can really know, I think. But I know — I think I know — His Name. It came to me when I was kneeling before the fire. I heard it there. It is in the language of the Avru."

"He did speak to you!" I cried out.

He shook his head. "No. Not in that way. You will understand when I tell you. But I thought of it, and then I heard it, and it was not in my mind. It was a sound, like a breath, again, like a whisper. I heard it, over and over."

"The word was — is — *'Ehyeh.'* At least that is the first part of it." He looked around at us all, and saw that we were puzzled.

"This is what that means: *'I AM.'* He *is*, but in His own way. He *is* — but not as anything else is. He *is* — but we are not to know What He is, nor guess, nor wonder. He simply *is*."

He shrugged. "I do not think that we *can* know what He is. Our minds could not hold it. If we knew what He is—" He lifted the waterskin and hefted it in his hand. "Our minds would burst like this waterskin, left too near the fire. He is *real*, as Truth itself is real. But like the Truth, He cannot be touched nor seen, and He does not force Himself upon any man.

"That Name seems right to me. I thought of it as I thought of all this. Whether it was *given* to me — I cannot say. But then I *heard* it."

"I am not sure that I understand you, Kisil," I murmured.

He shook his head. "I am not sure that I understand it myself, or that anyone can." He grinned then, and shrugged, a twinkle in his dear eyes. "And it does not matter. We are not to think of Him directly, but of what we are to *do*."

Kisil spoke of The One with more certainty than even my father ever had — and yet he, Kisil, still did not believe, as my father believed, as I believed. God was not real to Kisil, as He was to us — and yet, He seemed even more real to him, somehow. I did not understand it then, and I do not understand it now. But that is how it was with Kisil, always.

I reminded him: "You said you heard it — the Name."

He nodded. "I heard the sound from the earth: *'Ehh-Yehh.'* The fire had sunk down and disappeared. It was gone, and the Mountain was dark. I heard a soft breath, a whisper, from the place where the fire had been. This time, I knew it was only the sound of the wind, of the Mountain. But still, it sounded like, 'Ehyeh,' the word that I had just thought of, but drawn out, long, quiet. No hard sounds, only soft and low — like a sigh, a cry of the heart. *'Ehhh-Yehhhh'....*

"And then there came an answer, just as soft: *'Huuu-Waah,'* *'Ehyeh,"* then *'Huwah.'* And again. And then, *'Ehyeh... Huwah.'* It was a call and response, a chant, a song: *'Ehyeh... Huwah."*

"'Ehyeh-huwah.'" He looked around at all of us. "It was the Mountain, and then my own voice, that I heard. The Mountain spoke the first word, and I spoke the second. When I said them together, I was speaking the Name." He smiled. "It was if I had always known it. *Ehyehuwah.*

"The sounds I heard — they were sounds made by the Mountain, and by me. Perhaps they were only given meaning by my mind. But when you see Truth..." He gestured, palms down. Finality, certainty. "Truth, as it truly is — you know. You cannot *not* know. Whatever He is — *if* He is — He is Truth, and Truth cannot be denied nor resisted once you have seen it." He paused. "He is the reason anything *can* be true. Without Him, there is no *being true*. No — *being*."

Kisil gestured at my father and looked at him. "It is as you said, Yisro. His voice — is our voice. He has no other." His eyes glittered in the firelight. "And I, and the Mountain, have given Him a Name as well. *Ehyehuwah*, Yisro. *Ehyehuwah* is His Name."

I felt a chill. I looked at my father, and he looked back at me, his mismatched eyes wide. My son looked up at me, his eyes even wider. They had heard it too.

There was a clarity and resonance about that word that I had never sensed in Kisil's voice before. His lisp was still evident, but only a trace of it could be heard. The Name seemed to echo in our minds, ringing there like the lingering sound of a ram's horn.

There was no time to reflect on that, or what it meant. I breathed the Name too.

"Ehyehuwah." And I felt it. That *was* His name. The name of God.

My father was staring at Kisil, and I could see his mouth working, also forming the Name. Then he, too, smiled. *"Ehyehuwah,"* he said softly. Some of the others spoke it, and looked at the Mountain. I heard Gershom whisper it too.

It was as if a breeze, a cool breath of air with the muted power of a coming storm, had swept among us; but there was no breeze. Nothing had happened, nothing at all. Only the Name, hanging in the air somehow, in our minds. Even Awwa seemed subdued, watching us solemnly.

We all looked at the Mountain then, and not at Kisil. "Ehyehuwah," we whispered. I thought the earth would move, but it did not.

"That Name will do," Kisil said, as simply as if he were naming a sheep or a child. "He *is*, and that is all we are to know." He looked up at the stars. "He is, as He chooses to be. He is, *when* He chooses to be. He is — *if* He chooses to be. Anything we say about Him will be less than the Truth — except that He is One." He nodded then, looking up at the dark mass of the Mountain. "He is One. He is alone. There is no other."

We all sat there, absorbing this. I saw the wondering expression on my father's face, and I knew, somehow, what he was thinking. *My student has become my teacher.*

Our teacher, I thought.

Kisil spoke again, once more looking at only me. "We may say His Name — but we may not *use* His Name." His voice was still clumsy and thick, but it seemed no longer to require the effort it had always cost him to speak. "We may speak to Him, but we may not *invoke* Him." He smiled and nodded meaningfully at my father "As the priests do, Yisro. It is as you said: Ehyehuwah does not come when called!" Kisil laughed again, as if at a wonderful joke. "He answers to no one. We may not know What He is, or even how He could be, or in what what way He *is*. He is *Sovereign*. He is The One. He is — He Who *is*. The Truth."

He laughed again and lifted his hands helplessly, then let them fall to his thighs. Then he spoke solemnly, intoning the words rather than speaking them: *"Our work is not to know Him. Our work is not to worship or bow down to Him. Our work is to do what is right."*

Then he waved a hand. "But even the Name was not the most important thing, Tzipporah. What is most important, always, is that which we must *do*." He took my hands into his own again. "I must go to Egypt. I must speak to the king. I must tell him to let my people go." He smiled, though a bit ruefully. "I must speak the truth. That is all."

I noted the change. He had said, "*my* people."

He stopped, blinked, then abruptly said, "Come, let us have some food. I am hungry." He wore a surprised expression, as if he had only then noticed.

I realized that I was hungry, too, and I smiled. "So am I."

The fear was still there, but so was a sense of — *this is as it should be*.

37

Gershom was yawning, so I put him to bed. My sisters went to their tents and came back with wine, cheese, bread and dates for Kisil and me. Then they sat down and waited as we ate. No one spoke, not even my father. The sheep had settled down nearby, with no guidance from us, only from Awwa. The dog watched them as we waited for Kisil to say more.

I remember gazing at the dancing flames and eating a date, tasting the sweetness, feeling the fibrous texture of it in my mouth. I understood what Kisil meant. This time, too — it was unlike any other. It was here, soon to be gone, never to come again. Like a storm moving across the desert, like a falling star, like the sun rising or setting. You see it coming, now it is here, and then it is gone, receding into the past. I would never eat that date again. How many such times came, and passed, and never returned?

All of them, of course. We so rarely think of that.

But that time, the time that Kisil had experienced on the Mountain...

I thought, *Kisil is right.* That time was unlike any other that had ever been. I wondered if others would learn of it, and speak of it in years to come.

I chewed the date and watched my husband. I did not understand what was happening to him, but I knew that I was his, and that he was mine, and that we would face it, and go through it, whatever it was, together. He was my life — and I knew, too, that he needed me, in ways that perhaps even he did not know.

Kisil stuffed three dates at once into his mouth and spoke around them. "I am so hungry. I was only gone a short time..."

We all stared at him, and at each other. Walid and Nazirah stifled their laughter. It broke the stillness, the seriousness, of our listening. Kisil looked up, surprised and puzzled. Some of the others laughed too, this time at his expression.

"Kisil." I touched his hand and leaned close. "You were gone all night, and all the next day."

He blinked at me, confused. "I was? But..." He looked up at the Mountain. "I did not think it was that long."

"Yes, Kisil. All night and all day." I kissed his cheek.

He blinked and frowned, then bowed his head in thought. After a few heartbeats, he looked up and spoke: "How long I was there, before the fire, I do not know. Not long, I thought. It seemed only a short time. After I knew the Name, I was still there, beside the fire fountain — but the fire was gone, and the earth was cold. I should have guessed... But I was neither hungry nor thirsty, nor was I tired."

Kisil sat back. He seemed to visibly relax, his mood to grow lighter. He reached for the waterskin, but Nazirah brought him a cup of beer before he could unplug it. He took a drink, smiled, took another, and then went on:

"I was still there, on my knees. But when I got up, I was not stiff, and my joints did not ache." He shrugged and lifted his cup to my father, and they smiled ruefully at each other. They were close to the same age, I knew.

"I thought about Egypt, and the Name, all the way down the mountain." His face brightened. "Yes! Yes, I remember now. It was still light when I started down. I did not notice. I was thinking of all this, and hardly noticed the light, even as it grew dark again. When I got back here, it seemed still the same night."

He turned to my father, pointing a finger at him in emphasis. "It was as you said, Yisro. I had to look within myself, look at the things I had been afraid to look at, afraid to think about. I had to face — *everything*. And I had to tell the truth, to myself."

He turned to me. "And, Tzipporah?" His eyes met mine. "You asked me what I know, my wild bird, a long time ago. What I know for certain. And now I can answer you.

Here is what I know. What I have always known, I think, but could not face.

"The king knows me. I grew up in his palace, as his brother, almost, and he will listen to me when I go to him." He paused again. "No one else will tell him that he must let the people go. No one. Even those who think that would never dare to say it. He is the *king*. He is a *god*, in Egypt. No one — *no one* — will dispute his word or question his decisions." He took a breath. "But I will. I have to. Someone must —" He smiled at me ruefully — "and I am the one. I am the only one. There is no one else."

"Do you not fear the king?" This was Yusuf, my brother-in-law, speaking again.

Kisil waved a hand. "No. The king is only — my uncle. He is only a man." Yusuf's eyebrows lifted, and then he cocked his head and lifted his hands. *As you say*, the gesture said.

"Will you really go?" asked Malkah.

"I argued against it. With myself, if not with Him. I speak — as I speak. My tongue is slow, it is hard for me. But —" He shrugged and shook his head. "All that does not excuse me from my task. I must speak the truth to the king."

"But will he do it?" This was my father. "Will he let the people go?"

Kisil answered him calmly. "That, I do not know, Yisro. I cannot see why he would, or how my speaking will help. But I know that he will at least hear me when I speak, and that is what I must do. Whether or not I succeed — " He paused, and then cocked his head, a half-shrug. "That is not up to me. But I must do what I can do, what no one else can do. I know this." He smiled again, that same smile of acceptance. "Perhaps this is what that means — to speak for God. To speak the truth is to speak for God, Yisro. That is what I must do."

Kisil took another drink, and then added, "But that is *all* I know."

"And you are not afraid." Nazirah spoke skeptically — but her face did not hold her usual cynical sneer, though her words seemed to carry such a tone. I realized that she wanted Kisil to tell her that no, he was not afraid.

Kisil shook his head, then looked at her frankly, and, with a small smile, lifted a hand. It quivered. "Of course I am afraid. I was frightened when I understood this, when I knew that this was what I must do. I still am. How *can* I do it?"

Then he waved his hand again, dismissively. "But I do not fear the king. He is only a man, as I said, though the Egyptians worship him."

"Then what *do* you fear?"

"I fear —" his eyes went back to the Mountain. "I fear what the people, my people, will say. The king knows me as a princeling, an adopted son of one of his sisters, an orphan boy that she protected and loved. He liked me when I was a boy. I do not think that he will kill me outright." He waved a hand carelessly.

Then his face clouded. "But I am no leader. I can hardly speak so others can understand me. And my people do not even know who I am." He shuddered, then said, "And those who do — I remember how they looked at me. My brother Aron. My father. My brother hated me. My father looked — sad. Disappointed."

Kisil looked up at the Mountain again. "But I know what I know. All those things — they mean nothing. They do not change the truth, and they do not excuse me from this task.

"I argued — but it was like trying to argue that up is down, that sand is water." He shook his head. "I could not escape the truth of it. No one else can do this." He gazed at the Mountain and absently scratched behind Awwa's ear.

Words came to my lips again, unbidden, as if someone else spoke. It seemed, again, that I knew the words only as I spoke them. "The king will listen." I stared at my husband. "Something will happen. And he will. He will let the people go."

Kisil saw the surprise on my face. What I had been thinking was, *there must be a way I can convince my husband not to do this. This is his death, the end for both of us.* But those were not the words that I spoke.

And then I spoke again. I remembered something he had told me, and this time they were my words, my thought.

"You are the Deliverer, Kisil. The one in their legend."

He blinked, surprised, then grinned. Then he laughed. I could see that he had not thought of that old tale of his people, not till now. Neither had I; I only remembered it at that moment.

Kisil laughed again. "The Deliverer!" He shook his head in amusement. "I do not know that either, Tzipporah. I know only what I must do." Then he frowned. "Still, though... That idea might be useful..." I saw him chewing on it for a few breaths.

Then he leaned against the donkey saddle behind him and sighed deeply "We shall talk more. But — tomorrow." He smiled and beckoned. "Play for me, Tzipporah. I need your music. Calm my soul, my sweet bird. Give me your peace."

I took out my flute and played. Kisil and the others sat and stared at the crackling fire, so bright in the night, and listened.

I did not know what the others were thinking. My father was stunned, perhaps worried. My sisters looked puzzled, most of them, perhaps a little fearful. Nazirah was gazing at Kisil, and to my surprise, her face held something like admiration. Rivkah was looking at me. Yusuf, and Tharah's husband Walid, seemed thoughtful.

I closed my eyes and concentrated on my playing. I was hoping to be swept away in the flow of the music, as I had been so often — but I could only think of how I was being swept away in all that was happening. I had no idea what would come, but I knew I would follow Kisil, and that The One — Kisil's Ehyehuwah, Who was more unknown than ever — would guide our steps. Kisil might not have been sure of Who or What He was, and neither was I; but I knew that I trusted Him.

I tried to lose myself in my playing. If I could do that, others would be lost in it too. Before long, I had done it, and there was nothing but the music...

I found that I understood some of what Kisil had said. He had been lost too, deep in his thoughts when he finally faced them, as I was so often lost in my music; and there he, like I, found himself.

My sisters told me that I played better that night than I ever had. As the fire slowly burned down to embers, we all went to our tents, one by one, and finally Kisil and I were alone. I put down my flute at last, and Kisil stood. He held out his hand to me, and I took it and followed him.

I felt that fear again as we entered our own tent. I knew that all would be well, but was this man still — my husband? Was I still his wife? Were we still what we had been from the beginning — friends, and lovers? Would he still need my body, as well as my love and devotion?

We were. And he did. He showed me, with a tenderness that had a new element in it. Perhaps it was an awareness of the preciousness of the present moment, for both of us. In the quiet of the night — my son slept deeply, as children do, but we were always careful not to wake him — my fears were stilled. And of that, I shall say no more.

Afterward, I lay with my cheek in the hollow of his shoulder. That place seemed made for me, and resting there with his arm around me, I felt a peace and contentment that was beyond words.

I loved him so much. I whispered to him: "Kisil — I am glad you came back."

He squeezed me closer. "Do not be afraid, my wild bird," came his soft whisper in the darkness. "I am more yours now than I have ever been."

He always seemed to know what was in my mind, often more than I did.

"I am glad," I breathed. "I was afraid I had lost you. To Him."

"No," he said. "Never." I could feel his smile. "We are all His, whatever that might mean. But beyond that —" He fell silent, and I heard his heart beating, slow and steady. "We belong to who we will, of our own choice. He brings us together, perhaps, but He gives us the choice to give ourselves, or not." He kissed my head. "I am so glad that He has brought me to you, and that we have given ourselves to each other. Tell me of the time you went up the Mountain."

I had almost forgotten that I had told him. "He was not there," I said. "The Mountain was quiet." I went on to tell him of my explorations, of the long, twisting cavern-tunnel and its blind end. "It was my secret place when I was small. After my sisters began to walk, I never went up there again. Well, almost never."

"But you never went up when the Mountain was awake?"

"No. I often wondered what it would be like, but I was afraid."

"So was I," he said, and that surprised me. He had not seemed so.

I think he may have said more. But that night, I snuggled under his arm and was soon asleep, conscious only of his soft voice.

This only now occurred to me; I do not know that he was speaking to me.

38

The next day, we received a rare blessing. It rained.

That did not happen often in our land, two or three times in a year. It rained for much of the morning, though lightly, and we knew that there would be grass aplenty for our sheep for the next few weeks. We danced in the rain, laughing and singing. Not only was it a blessing, it was an omen of great good luck.

Only Kisil thought to cover our store of fuel. A sheet of tightly-woven wool, rubbed with oil to shed water, was prepared for this, and he and I pulled it over the store of wood and dried sheep droppings that would feed our fire.

Then we separated, the men and the women, and took the opportunity to bathe in the rain. It was refreshing beyond hope, to feel clean again, and not dusty. We kept ourselves clean all the time — it was one of our family's customs — but we used water sparingly, and rain was a rare luxury for us. After that, we sat in the rain around our wet firepit and enjoyed the coolness and the wet, laughing at our puzzled sheep — and at Awwa, who kept shaking himself, though he too seemed to enjoy the shower.

That evening, after the rain had stopped, we had built a fire. That was not easy. Even after being covered, the wood and dung were still damp, as was the ground. Fa-ther struck his firestones many times, and Kisil too with his own; and though they got good, strong sparks every time, it was long before the tinder would catch.

When the fire was well started, we feasted. We killed a young ram and roasted it over the fire. Male lambs are for eating; a herd only needs one grown ram. If there are more than one, they will always fight. My mothers prepared a special kind of bread, flavored with herbs and ewe's-milk beer, to go with the roots and greens and other foods that they made. Even the delicious smell of the bread baking was festive. It was a joyful time, and even the air felt cool and clean.

After Kisil went up the Mountain, to my surprise, life went on as before. We watched the sheep, we talked, we ate, we laughed and argued and danced and slept. Kisil and I tried to raise Gershom, and my mothers and sisters and father tried to spoil him. My husband and I walked together often, usually in silence, as we always had. In spite of what I had said, though, I never went up on the Mountain, not till much later — and neither did Kisil.

I gave birth to our second son. We named him Eliezer. Somehow I knew we would have another boy, and we knew the name almost from his conception. Once again, Kisil chose it. I did not know what the name meant, only that it had something to do with God — "El" was a name for The One among Kisil's people, as "Ael" was among my own. Eliezer was a strong boy, too.

Kisil and Yisro both reveled in Gershom and Eliezer. My father, who had never had a son of his own, seemed to treasure them as much as Kisil, who was as proud a father as has ever held a son.

Father and Kisil talked often with Yusuf and Walid, speaking with them both of The One, the God Whom we now knew as Ehyehuwah; and now Gershom joined those discussions. Sometimes I joined them as well, but my sisters and mothers rarely did. Oddly, it was Rivkah who sat with us most often, and she sometimes asked very sharp questions. She was pretty, my youngest sister, but she was smart too.

I never asked Kisil when he would go to Egypt, or if I would go with him. The first he would tell me when he knew, and I knew the answer to the second: where Kisil went, I would go, and our sons with us.

Months passed. There were no more lights on the Mountain. In fact, the Mountain was quiet for a long time.

There were no rumblings, no fire visible at the peak, no rolling thunder in the earth that could be felt but not heard. It was as if Ehyehuwah slept, but we knew that could not be. The Mountain slept, but never He.

Kisil spent many evenings with my father, hidden away in Father's tent or in ours, or sitting by the fire. Sometimes the two other men joined them, and I as well, now and again. Sometimes even Gershom did. Before long, there was another man — Kameel, who married Tharah, my second-oldest sister. That marriage ended a certain friction between Tharah and Charah, since the younger had married first, contrary to custom.

I could join them if I wanted, as any of us could; but I heard few of those conversations, and understood little of what I did hear. I saw a growing certainty in Kisil, a kind of strength that rose up at my father's challenges; I saw my father's eyes, laughing even as he argued with my husband. He had a role to play, my father, and it had something to do with Kisil's growing convictions about what he had to do. Like our firestones, their thoughts struck sparks from each other, and some of them caught fire, I think. They were teaching each other.

One night, as they sat by the fire, the argument ended. I saw it happen.

They had been silent for some time, and my father leaned back and nodded, looking at Kisil with a kind of awe in his eyes. "You speak for Him."

Kisil looked back calmly. "Perhaps," he replied. "I say only that which I know — which I absolutely know — to be true. What He would say if He chose to speak." Then he smiled at me. "Though I do not *feel* Him."

It did not seem to occur to Kisil that what he was saying was outrageously arrogant. I knew Kisil, and I knew that it was not, though it sounded so. He was not an arrogant man; he had never a thought for himself, for his own pride, his own authority. He was possessed by a hunger for Truth, a fire that consumed everything else inside him. Now that he had found answers to the questions that had plagued him all his life, he was as certain of his way as a river is certain of its course.

There was a pause. Then my father asked, "Do you understand how different you are, my son? How blessed?"

Kisil blinked. "I am like any other man."

"No." Father shook his head. "He — Ehyehuwah — He has spoken to you directly. Not in sound," he added quickly, as Kisil opened his mouth to deny it. "But He has. You and He — you sit together, like two friends, and you have no need for words." My father reached into his robe then. "Here."

He held out a handful of stones, and Kisil took them. "What are —" began Kisil, and then he saw. "You went up there, too."

My father looked up at the Mountain. "Yes. I found the place. I found your waterskin — and I saw the crack in the earth, the layers of black stone around it, the smaller black stones scattered farther away." He pointed at the stones in Kisil's hand. "Those are Ehyehuwah's words, Kisil. God's words." He paused. "You should keep them. They were spoken by Him, to you."

Kisil clasped the stones in both his hands. "How many are there?" I asked.

Kisil looked. "With the one I brought down myself — there are ten."

"Ten words..."

Kisil and my father looked at me curiously. Why I had asked, and why I had said that, I did not know.

39

The scratching of Zev's reed pen stopped. "I know why," he said.

"Perhaps you do," I said with a laugh, wishing I could see his face. "But there is much more that you do not know. Have you heard what you expected to hear?"

He was silent for a moment. "There was no burning bush," he said at last. "And — and God did not speak from it."

My laugh sounded rusty, but it was there. "What Kisil saw was something far stranger than a burning bush, Zev, and far deadlier. He could have been killed by it as easily as my sister Nazirah could have killed a coney ten paces in front of her. One great burst of fire from that fountain, and Kisil would have been burned alive."

I lifted a hand and shook a finger in Zev's direction. "And God did speak to him, Zev — in the only way He has ever spoken."

"In our minds?"

I smiled. "No. Not in that way either."

"But—"

"Come, Zev. Get the fire going again, and I shall make you some of the bread that my mothers used to make. Well, you will make it, but I will tell you how."

I heard him put the pen down, and the sound of the parchment being moved aside. "Can you tell me some of the stories that Kisil told Gershom?"

I shook my head. "I could," I said, "but I will not. Those do not matter."

Silence again. Then, “Very well. This is your story. You should tell it as you choose.”

“No,” I said sharply. “I shall tell it as it *happened*.”

“Yes, Grandmother. Forgive me. I meant nothing other than that.” I gave a little snort, but I nodded. “You rest now,” he said. “I shall build the fire up.”

I listened as he went to the woodpile and began gathering fuel. He was a good man, was Zev. Later, he would heat water on the fire and bathe me, help me into fresh garments, and perhaps sing some of the songs of his homeland for me as I went to sleep. I knew some of them, I thought, that I had heard from another man.

It was good to be telling the story at last. I silently thanked Ehyehuwah for sending Zev to me.

And then I smiled. I would have him write all this, too.

Book Two: Egypt

40

The day finally came. One night, as we sat around our fire and shared a meal — there were fresh figs, I remember, and some new wine — Kisil said, "We will leave for Egypt tomorrow."

The Mountain had not spoken; there had been no lights, no fire at the peak, no signs in the heavens. I did not ask Kisil how he knew it was time. Perhaps he was simply ready.

Nor did I object, though I thought it would have been better to wait until Eliezer was older. It had been only a little more than a year since his birth. But the time to leave had come. I sensed that myself.

My husband gave us little notice, but we needed little. Even though it was a long journey, we did not need to carry much with us.

The next afternoon, we put packsaddles on two of our donkeys. On one, we packed a small tent that my sisters and I had made for the journey the year before; then some food, empty waterskins, and a basket for Eliezer. The other was laden with blankets and clothing, things for cooking, and two other donkeys were fitted with saddles for Gershom and for me. We took some of our woolen cloth and a good supply of soft tanned sheepskin, with and without fleece, as well, rolled behind Gershom's and my seats. It would all be good for trading, Kisil said.

It felt good to be making preparations. When something you have both dreaded and anticipated comes at last, it is a feeling of sweet relief to be doing something other than waiting. We would leave that very night, after sunset.

After a subdued farewell feast with my family, with tearful goodbyes from my sisters and mothers, embraces with slaps on the back for Kisil from their husbands, and a long, silent hug for each of us from my father, we started for Egypt. The moon was high above us. It had risen long before sunset.

It was waxing, almost a half-moon, as bright as a lamp among the stars to light our way. That may have been one of the reasons Kisil chose to leave at that time. We would travel by night, and the moon would grow brighter for seven days or more before it began to wane.

Late on that first night, we crossed the plain of hard black stones that I remembered from long before, and soon we came to the well where Kisil and I had first met. We filled our waterskins by the light of the moon and distributed them among our donkeys, and paused to remember all that had happened in that place. It was deep in the night, so no one troubled us — not that the Melikites would dare, I thought with a smile. I told Gershom the story as Kisil watered the donkeys. He had heard it before, but now I could point out where we had been standing and where Kisil had found Kadin and mended his broken leg.

We moved on. It was very dark — the moon had set by then — but the way was unobstructed, and the starlight was enough for us.

It was often cool at night in the desert, but the walking kept us warm. It was better than walking in the heat of the day, and we needed less water. When the sky began to grow light in the east, we would stop and pitch our little tent, where we rested till the sun set. We took another square of cloth and made a shelter for our donkeys, to make sure they were protected from the blazing sun as well.

Before sundown, Kisil might make a small fire, where we would prepare a meal. We would eat our breakfast in the evening, one might say, and would put away some of the food for later in the night. When it was full dark and cool, we set out again. And so it went, for many days.

There was a wadi that led in the general direction we wanted — north and west — and we followed that, keeping the Unmoving Star to our right and ahead. We walked on the bank of the wadi, not in its bed. Even in summer, water could suddenly come rushing down such a channel, and it moved fast and violently and gave little warning. Indeed, it happened twice on our way to Egypt, from rains far to the south.

There were water holes and wells along the way as well, but they were often dry. We made sure to fill our waterskins at every opportunity. There was grass for the donkeys, though never much, and we had brought grain for them too.

It was a peaceful time, that first part of our journey. The creaking of the donkey's gear in the darkness, the steady, plodding gait of their careful hoofs, the breeze from the desert, the night sky turning above us. I watched Kisil's sandals and the foot of his staff as we walked, and I remembered that first time I had walked beside him, on our way back from the well where we had met.

We did not speak of the future, of what would happen when we reached Egypt. My thoughts were filled with fearful things — but I did not feel afraid, even so. I do not think that Kisil felt the same. He had a brooding, worried look on his face, and often.

Our sons behaved well, and were little trouble. They were strong boys from a hard land, and even little Eliezer knew better than to raise a fuss over little things. They slept in the day, and Eliezer for much of the night as well. I held him often when he woke, riding one of the donkeys and listening to Kisil telling Gershom tales of his travels. I enjoyed those tales as well. I had heard few of them.

Sometimes Gershom rode with the baby while Kisil and I walked and talked. Our elder son was always eager to help; he had perhaps ten years by then, and though he rode for the most part, he walked a great deal. Kisil walked, always.

Sometimes all three of us walked, while Eliezer slept in his basket. The rocking motion of the donkeys' gait lulled him to sleep as well as my arms did. I rode when I nursed him, of course, and sometimes I dozed myself.

I had thought the journey would be hard, but at first, at least, it was more peaceful and even restful than I had expected. Even Kisil began to relax and enjoy the experience.

In only a few days, we had gone farther from the Mountain than I had ever been. It was still visible on the horizon behind us for many days after that, but one day I looked back and it was gone. This was a new place, and I did not know it or even know of it, though Kisil seemed certain of the way.

I had never been more than a few days' journey from where I had been born, and every morning brought some new sight when we stopped to pitch our tent. I was very conscious of being, with every step, in a new place where I had never been.

The land where we were traveling then was covered with small, spindly plants, of a kind that I had heard of but never seen. They did not impede our progress, but they did not make it pleasant, either. They could be useful, I knew, but not at that time of year. For now, the scattered dead branches served us only as fuel for our small fires.

For some days, we traveled across a wide swath of plain where the grass was sparse but green, a broad pass between a range of hills to our left — hills that had marked the horizon when I was a child, growing up in the shadow of the Mountain — and another range to our right, that continued on to the north. Kisil said we would find it easier going from there onward, and for the most part, so we did.

One night, as we were passing the last of the hills to the north, we saw something on their slopes in the distance, something I could not identify. A dark thing, covering the foot of the hills there. "What is that?" I asked Kisil.

He looked, and then grinned at me. "That is a *forest*. Come, let us go closer. You should see what it is like." We turned toward it, but before we reached it, Kisil hesitated, and then stopped. "Let us camp here. I shall show you in the morning." It was early, long before dawn, but we set up our tent in the darkness and slept.

When it grew light, I saw that what I had taken for a solid, dark thing was in fact a great many things; trees, growing close together. I had never seen trees that grew like that. I had only seen trees that were isolated, or at most growing in clumps of four or five. I did not know what kind of trees these were, nor do I know now. But I remember the coolness of the shade beneath them, and the peaceful, hushed silence there.

We traveled in the light for a day or two after that, stopping to rest at night. The boys were wide-eyed with astonishment, and delighted. Even the donkeys seemed to be less cranky. I noticed on that first day, though, that Kisil seemed unusually watchful. "What is it, my love?"

He glanced at me as we walked along, but his eyes quickly resumed their scanning of the trees. "Different creatures live in the forest than on the plain. Not all are — friendly." From then on, I began to notice small sounds that were as unfamiliar as the place itself. Each night, before we built our shelter, he made sure to gather some of the plentiful wood and build a good fire before our tent. I sometimes saw eyes in the forest, glowing in the light of the flames. They were not the eyes of jackals; they were too small and too close together. They belonged to some small creatures that I did not know, creatures that did not trouble us.

Other than that, we saw nothing. The forest was a small one, Kisil said, though it seemed large to me. Soon we were traveling by night again.

We never hurried. We ambled along as if we were on a stroll for pleasure, or traveling to see relatives. Kisil pointed out many new sights to me: deer, or goats, or other animals that I had never seen. There were unfamiliar birds, and even a little stream that looked as big as a river to me. We crossed it, wading. It barely came past our knees. Gershom was delighted, and we camped beside it for a whole day and splashed naked in its cool water. It ran all year round, Kisil said. He did not know its name, nor if it had one.

Other passages were not as pleasant. We crossed the trailing end of a ridge that we were obliged to go around, because it would have been too difficult to cross it. The ground was rocky and broken even so, and in places it was a maze of treacherous, tumbled stone. Our donkeys, sure-footed and born to the mountains, had little difficulty, nor did Kisil, nor my older son; but I did, and Kisil often took Eliezer from my arms and carried him himself when I had to use my hands. We could have avoided the place altogether, but the crossing, as hard as it was, cut several days off our journey, and perhaps more.

We moved on. I saw the land beginning to change. It grew still greener, less arid, less stony and sandy. The land was not flat, as Midyan mostly was between its black-rock ridges. It rose and fell, in long, gentle waves. Uphill and downhill became a slow rhythm, complementing the shorter rhythm of the donkey's hooves, and our feet, on the ground. We saw black and red earth as well as yellow and ochre. The grass grew thick, and the donkeys ate well.

The land was becoming more populated. We began to stop at small villages or camps, and I found that the people were usually friendly — but then, we were no longer in Midyan. Their clothes and speech were unfamiliar, but Kisil seemed able to speak to all of them, if not in one language, then another. It was on this journey that I learned how much Kisil knew of the world, and began to sense how far and how long he had traveled.

41

Men traveling alone, or groups of men, could be dangerous. Such travelers were always treated with suspicion. But a man with his family were welcome everywhere, and the tradition of hospitality common to all the peoples in that part of the world was an old one. We seldom had to pay for food or shelter or fodder for our animals. Occasionally, a man would be grumpy and miserly with us, but if he was married, his wife would overrule him as she played with our young ones. Gershom, and especially little Eliezer, made the way smoother for us in many places.

I began to pick up Kisil's way with languages. Though it was unfamiliar and strange to my ear at first hearing, the language that people spoke in most of the places we passed was very much the same tongue that I knew from childhood, but with strange accents and rhythms and some altered sounds. At first they had seemed unintelligible to me, but I was learning to listen closely and speak carefully.

Few people asked us our business. When they did, our story was that we were on our way to join Kisil's family in a land to the West, which was true enough in its way. We saw no need to tell anyone more than that.

I had wondered why Kisil always took care to inquire about local affairs, but I soon learned. Though few were interested in us, most people were interested in any news we had to offer from other villages. We told of a new headman here, the death of an elder there, births, marriages, fights, feuds, even a murder in one nomad camp. That story was good for wide eyes and gasps for many days. I, too, began to take care to listen to the local gossip wherever we went. It was better than gold when it came to finding food and lodging. My husband had learned this during his years of wandering.

In one large village, as we were walking among the huts, a short, plump man happened to be walking beside us. He was carrying a basket of bread and figs and other foodstuffs. Eliezer was staring at him, but instead of being annoyed, the man began making funny faces at the child. Eliezer was soon laughing merrily, and Kisil, Gershom, the man, and I all laughed too.

When Kisil asked the man where we could find lodging, he laughed. "Come with me and stay at my house, friend! I am sure my wife will welcome you." He looked wistfully at my sons. "We have no children, and she enjoys the company of little ones as much as I."

We accompanied the man to his little house. It was behind a much larger building, made of brick. "My name is Hanif," he said. "I am a priest of Asira." He said this last proudly, then gestured at the larger building. "This is our temple."

"A priest?" said Kisil with interest. "We must talk. I am most interested in the religions of others."

The man's wife, as short and plump as he, did indeed welcome us. Her name was Rana, and she showed us a room we would have to ourselves. Apparently the priest was used to visitors. Perhaps priests from other villages, or perhaps he sometimes had an acolyte.

It was a pleasant change from our tent, to stay within walls. The couple served us a fine dinner, with meat and fresh bread. We contributed a little from our small store of food, and the boys were delighted with the honey cakes the woman had made only that morning.

After our meal, Rana and I walked to the well together, she carrying two large pottery bottle-things on a yoke, I with four all-but-empty waterskins over my shoulders. "You have fine boys," she told me with an approving smile.

"Thank you. Your husband said that you have no children?"

She nodded sadly, then smiled. "We are happy even so. It was not the will of Asira. Perhaps he wanted Hanif to concentrate on his work." She gazed at me for a heartbeat, perhaps two. "You have very remarkable eyes. Do men fear you?"

I laughed. "Some do. It can be useful." She giggled. Her eyes were a pale blue, like my sister Rivkah's, and I wondered if she used them, too.

"Do you have nephews or nieces? They can be a comfort, and good company as well."

"Oh, yes," she said brightly. "My sister Lina has four, two boys, two girls. We keep them often."

I smiled. "I am the oldest of seven girls myself."

"Seven! How many mothers?"

"Three. My birth mother died when I was small, though. I do not remember her."

"That is sad." We walked on a few more paces. "Do you worship a god?"

"Yes, though we have no temple or priests. We call Him Ael Shadu — God of the Mountain."

"I have not heard of him." She did not seem particularly concerned by that, and was as friendly as ever.

I smiled. "I have never heard of Asira before this day, but then I have never been this far from my home."

"Where are you going? To Egypt?"

"Yes. My husband has family there. I have never met them."

We talked a bit more, about small things, but then she asked, "Your husband, Kisil — has he been here before?"

I blinked. "I do not know. He may have been. He was something of a wanderer before we met, and he is older than he looks. Why not ask him when we return?"

"I will. I am almost certain I have met him before — it is the way he talks. That man had no beard, though."

I said nothing. Later that night, she did ask Kisil if he had been to their village before, and he smiled and admitted that he had. "I passed through here once, long ago."

Rana smiled in satisfaction. "You had no beard then."

"That is true," Kisil said. "I shaved, Egyptian fashion, and did for many years. If I may ask — how is it that you remember me?"

The woman smiled, remembering. "I was at the well, struggling to get a yoke on my shoulders. You stopped and helped me. You spoke little, but I remember that —" She stopped, suddenly embarrassed.

"That I could not speak clearly." said Kisil in his lisping, labored voice. "Yes." He waved a hand. "I am not offended. It is — distinctive." He grinned. His lisp made the word almost unintelligible. The woman laughed, and her embarrassment passed.

Hanif and Rana made us feel welcome, and our boys too, so we stopped to rest there for several days. Kisil spent the evenings talking with Hanif, and with the other men who served the local god, learning of the religion of that people.

One night, the head priest of the district — a wizened old fellow with a withered arm — took us, with Hanif, into their temple. It was a hut very like the others in that village, but perhaps twice as big and built of bricks. At the far end of the long single room was a wooden statue, a very old — and very ugly, to my eyes — image of a man standing stiffly with his arms at his sides. He wore a crude crown and a rude frown. This was Asira, I supposed.

I had never seen an idol before, and now that I had, worshiping one made even less sense to me.

Nothing more happened there, in the temple. As foreigners, we would not be allowed to witness their ceremonies, whatever they were. They killed nothing before the idol, at least. Hanif told us that their offerings were of grain and oil only, and sometimes wine.

After being allowed to see their god, we went back to Hanif's hut, where he shared a meal, after a fashion, with the head priest and his acolytes. Kisil and I, and our sons, and even Rana, ate separately from the priests for some ritual reason or other. Afterward, we gathered in the small open space in front of their temple, and the priests spoke of their beliefs while I nursed Eliezer and chatted with Rana. Gershom played a game with knucklebones that one of the village boys was teaching him.

Kisil pressed them a bit on what the idol could actually do, but never to the point where they became angry; he was very skilled in that way. He listened to their tales and (to my ears) their excuses, and he nodded patiently, saying nothing of Ehyehuwah.

After a few days of this, we said our goodbyes and moved on. They were good people, those idol-worshippers.

They gave us much in the way of supplies for our journey, and even replaced two of our waterskins.

42

Not long after leaving Hanif's village, we entered a land where there were no towns or camps, only a few wandering nomads with their tents and goats and camels. They were not hostile, but neither were they friendly. They went their way and left us alone, and it was clear that they preferred to be left alone as well. We did so, and had no trouble with them.

It was in that land that Kisil became ill. We had been traveling for many days, and we were all growing tired and footsore. Eliezer was cranky, Gershom was too, and I noticed that Kisil was silent. He was always silent, but this silence was different. He often did not answer at all when I spoke to him, and that was not his way.

We settled down one morning near a small stream, and as he finished pitching our little tent, I touched his forehead. It was hot — and worse, it was dry.

"Kisil, you are sick." I insisted that we stop and rest for a time. Kisil was annoyed and said that it would pass, but that night we did not move on. I made sure that he rested all that day, and that night I built a small fire, made him some barley broth, and told him to go back to sleep. He did, though fitfully, and he slept off and on throughout the next day. The next evening after that, he wanted to resume our journey; but when he made to get up, he fell back against the blankets. He was too weak to stand.

We rested another night, and another. He grew more and more feverish, and I grew more and more worried. If we had been near a village, I would have taken him there for help, but there were none near in that desolate land. I cared for him myself, trying to keep my boys calm as I did. It was a very bad time.

By the fourth day, Kisil's fever was raging, his brow the hottest I have ever felt, even on a child. He was raving, out of his head, talking nonsense. He woke me one night, crying out. Ehyehuwah was trying to kill him, he said, and he struggled as if fighting with a man. I could only hold his arms and try to keep him from hurting himself.

Over and over, he cried out, always the same thing, but his voice was slurred and blurred by his illness as well as his wounded mouth. He grew weaker and weaker. Our boys were frightened, and cried, which made my job even harder.

On the fifth day, I finally understood what he was saying: "No, I did not cut them — I did not cut them!" Not long after, I understood what he meant. He had never cut off the foreskins of our sons, as his own had been cut.

Even as he grew weaker, he grew more and more agitated. The fever would not break, and I was very worried. I had never seen anyone so sick. He was not even taking water by then. I did everything I knew to do, but Kisil only grew sicker. Finally, not knowing if it would help, I did it. I cut our sons' foreskins away.

Kisil was quiet, exhausted, so I gave the boys some watered wine with a little poppy in it to make them sleepy, and then I cut them. They did not cry much, only whined a little, then went back to sleep. They were grumpy for a few days, and sore, but I used some of my father's salve on them, and they healed cleanly.

After I did it, when Kisil began to struggle again, I put the foreskins in his hand. "Show him, Kisil! I cut your sons, like you. Show him!"

He struggled, smearing a little of the drying blood on his legs, his face — and finally he understood, and he held them up. "See? See? Look at the blood! I have done it!"

He fell back on the blankets then, as if clubbed. His struggling stopped, and he lay still. It worried me at first, but when I saw that he was breathing easily at last, I knew it would be all right. He rested, really rested, for the first time in days — and so did I.

The fever broke the next day, and he slept for a day and a night. When he woke, he thought clearly again and knew me, though he was still too weak to get up or speak more than a few words at a time.

He had been ill for more than nine days. I made him rest for another day, then two, before he began to really recover. When he did, he remembered everything, even his madness.

"I wrestled with Him, Tzipporah." He was sitting up, drinking a little of the soup I had made for him, and eating a bit of bread and cheese. It was his first solid food in many days, and though he was still weak, he seemed to be whole again. "In my dreams. Ehyehuwah. I knew that it was He, though I never saw His face."

"You fought — God?"

"Yes. It was only a dream, Tzipporah — but in the dream, I fought Ehyehuwah Himself, and He was angry. He would not let me go..." He took another small bite, then another drink. He was eating slowly and carefully. I think his stomach was still unsteady. "He was angry that I had not cut the boys, and He would not let me go.

"Then you did it — and He finally released me. Then He blessed me."

"He blessed you? Did he speak?" I knew the answer.

"No." Kisil shook his head. "He never spoke. But I knew." He paused. "Thank you, Tzipporah. How did you know what to do?"

"I heard you cry out. When I finally understood — "

"Yes. I remember. You were cleaning the blood from my face — I was still breathing hard from the fight, and you were cleaning my face, and I was looking at you. I knew then it would be all right. I knew it was only a dream."

"I love you, Kisil. I love you so much —" I found myself choked with tears, and that was not like me. He took me in his arms, as weak as he was, and held me.

When I could, I went on. "I was trying to reach you. You were somewhere far away. And I do remember that. I remember you looking at me — yes, it was when I was cleaning your face — that you looked at me, really looked at me, and that was when you began to get better. The fever broke not long after that."

His arms around me were warm, but no longer hot. He kissed the top of my head. "I am back, my love," he whispered as he held me. "Thank you for calling me back."

We rested another few days, and then we moved on. I convinced Kisil to ride one of the donkeys for the first few days before I let him continue walking.

43

After we left that barren land, we found more villages than we had seen previously, with more people in them, and more varied kinds of land — larger forests, deeper and wider rivers, and even marshy fens. Much of the land near the rivers was dark and rich, and there were tilled fields, which I had never seen before. What the crops were, I do not know.

More villages, more camps, more nights of travel and days of hiding from the sun. But one day, I began to notice a different feel to the air, and a new scent; and a few days after that, I began to hear a rushing sound, a sound with a deep rhythm, but very slow. I asked Kisil what it was, but he only smiled mysteriously. "You will see."

The next day, we climbed up a low hill — and as we reached the crest, I did see. Water, more water than I had ever imagined could be in the world. We had come to the shore of the ocean. Kisil called it the Middle Sea. I never knew why.

I had never seen an ocean, and it was a revelation to me. I had lived all my life in the desert, and the most water I had ever seen had been a pool no bigger than a large tent. But this water was so wide I could not see the other side. It seemed to go on forever, and the waves, and the sound of them, never stopped. For a woman who had lived in Midyan all her life, it was overwhelming.

We camped there by the shore for several days, and the boys and I enjoyed the water and the waves. Little Eliezer was learning to really walk, and the waves made him laugh. Gershom liked to throw himself into the oncoming waves and let them tumble him about under the surface.

Kisil showed him to be careful of the outgoing waves, so not to be dragged away, and they chased each other and played in the water as if they were both boys.

We all enjoyed our stay there by the sea. There was driftwood, and we kept a fire going easily. We ate fish, and some creatures with shells that Kisil showed me how to find, many different kinds. They were unlike anything I had ever seen, but they tasted good after we roasted or boiled them. The ocean water was salt and could not be drunk, but Kisil showed me how to dig in the sand behind the first row of dunes and find fresh water there.

After we reached the ocean, we walked during the day, following the shore to the west. It was cooler by the water, and beautiful. The sunsets over the sea were grand, the sound of the waves soothing, the breeze refreshing. I even liked the salt smell of the water. Sometimes we walked at the edge of the waves, but when we camped, Kisil always made sure our tent was above the high-tide line. It fascinated me, how the water rose and fell twice in a day. Kisil showed me how it rose with the moon, and then again when the moon was gone.

We passed through fishing villages, saw rocky fortresses over the water, and there were great herds of goats of a kind that I had never seen. And boats, so many boats! I wondered if there were people who lived on the water instead of the land, and Kisil said that there were.

Kisil seemed to know many of the places we passed through, and I wondered if he had passed this way before, as he had passed through the village of our new friends Hanif and Rana.

In one village, Kisil was attacked. We were walking down a narrow lane — it was after sunset, and almost dark — and he was a little ahead of us.

Without warning, two men leapt from the shadows between the small huts. One grasped Kisil's robe near his throat, and my heart leapt into my own — but what Kisil did surprised me, and the men as well. It happened so quickly I hardly had time to gasp; it took a single heartbeat, perhaps less.

Instead of trying to pull the man's hand free, Kisil seized his wrist with both hands — and pulled it *into* him. At the same moment, he spun around, lifting his elbow above the man's arm. The attacker was unexpectedly turned half-way round with his arm twisted behind him, elbow up — and then Kisil simply dropped to the ground. When he landed, his full weight snapped the man's arm, or perhaps his elbow joint, like a twig. I could hear the sound from where I was standing. It was loud, and final. The man cried out, but weakly, and then he lay still. I think perhaps he had fainted. It was all over in an eyeblink of time.

The other man, though confused, was still moving in, arms up, one hand holding a knife. I found the presence of mind to thrust my staff between his feet to trip him, but it was hardly necessary. Before he fell, Kisil sprang up from the ground and drove the heel of his hand into the man's chin, with the full force of his legs as well as his arm behind the blow as he rose. The man's head snapped back and he fell without a sound. Whether he was dead or only stunned, I never knew.

We left them lying there and hurried on. Our boys had slept through the whole thing.

Kisil said nothing till we were a few huts farther along. Then, very quietly, "Have no fear, my love. It is over." We left that village quickly, but without further trouble, and we made camp in a small patch of forest farther down the shore. I was shaken, but Kisil seemed as calm as before. I wondered how many times he had dealt with such things in his wandering past.

Not long after this, we came to the largest town I had seen until that time. It was in a place where a small river reached the sea, and with plentiful water, a small harbor for the boats, and rich soil all around it, a small city had grown up there. There was a market there, one that was there all the time, not just at the full moon. There were temples, and big houses where I supposed wealthy people lived, and even an inn. It was a busy, and friendly, place, but it stank — of animals, and people, and their waste and leavings.

We stayed there for several days even so, while Kisil bargained for more supplies with the woolen fabric that we had brought. We did well in the trades; we had entered a land where cotton was more plentiful than wool, and cloth from Midyan was prized.

The inn was a big house built around a courtyard, with a fire in the middle; the people who had paid for their meals gathered there. Some drank a kind of beer not made from milk. I did not like it, but Kisil had one cup, then another — but that was all. In all our years together, I never saw Kisil drunk.

Gershom and I played our flutes for the crowd one night, and the people seemed to like it. Some seemed disturbed by my eyes, so I kept them downcast and stared at no one. Another night, Kisil told stories, to the young and the old alike. I recognized some of them as my father's stories, and that made me smile. We were well received there, though I could not say we made any friends.

We said nothing of Ehyehuwah or the Mountain. That, Kisil told me, was for his people only. "Later, others may hear of Him. But for now — I am sent only to the children of Avram."

Kisil was watchful at the inn. I saw how he placed his staff at our door, so it would fall and wake us if anyone entered. Once I saw him look a man in the eye, and saw how the man and he stared at each other without speaking — and then how the man moved away.

I looked at Kisil with the question in my eyes. "He had been looking at our donkeys earlier, Tzipporah. I just let him know that I was watching him." We had no more trouble there, nor in any other place where we stayed after that.

We left the town after a few days. It was an interesting place, but I was used to open spaces and few people — and cleaner air. I thought that little town was a huge, crowded city. I laugh at that now; I had not yet seen Egypt.

We traveled on, staying near the shore, moving from village to village. We ate fish, but we ate meat and bread too. Both were plentiful. The land was growing greener, richer, more fertile. Soon we were nearing what Kisil called the Delta — "the land of Goshen," he called it.

That land was in Egypt. I wondered how much farther we had to go.

44

One morning we climbed a long, gentle slope. When we finally came to the top, the ground dropped steeply away, and we were gazing down upon what looked to be the mouth of a broad river that opened into the sea. There were no people visible on the near bank or the far one, which made me wonder. I knew by this time that river mouths were places that settlements appeared, where fishing villages and trading posts could be found. "Why does no one live by this river?" I asked. Kisil shook his head with a smile and explained.

"This is not a river, my sweet bird. The water is salt, and it does not run. It is only an inlet, an arm of the sea. Look at the reeds by the bank. Those are salt-water plants." He gestured to our left, to the south. "Here we turn aside. The water is not deep here, but it is too deep to wade and too far to swim. We must go around." Then he pointed toward the other shore. "Not far beyond this inlet is Goshen. We will not approach it from the south, along the Great River, as the traders do, but from the east, along the shore of the Middle Sea."

Below us, the ground sloped down to the sea. It was not a cliff, but a steep hill that rose from the water. Rather than taking that route, we turned to our left and began to travel down the gentler slope, following the coast. We walked that way for some days, till we finally reached the end of the bay. There were many reeds there, for a long, long way, where the water grew shallow. We probably could have waded across long before we rounded the end, but it would have been unpleasant going.

Soon, after crossing through some soft, salty marshes, we were traveling north again along the opposite shore. "Why do we not cut across the land between? That would be shorter, would it not?"

"Shorter, but drier. I know this country. There is little water that way. There will be wells and even a few springs along the coast. The way is longer, but easier."

After a few more days of walking beside the inlet, we came to the place where it reached the sea. Kisil pointed. Across the water, hardly more than a long stone's throw, was the place where we had been some days before. So many days it took us to travel only that short distance, I thought.

We turned west and went on. The next day, we stopped at a small spring and rested for a day and a night.

The next morning, as we were preparing to break camp, I looked out at the ocean — then looked again at the water along the shore. "Kisil, why is the ocean red?" The water was a pale, ruddy color, as if there were blood in the water.

Kisil looked, and frowned. "I have seen this before. The water turns red like that, and it is poisonous. It makes people ill, no more, but it kills some fish and other creatures. It comes and goes — no one knows why. When it gets into fresh water, it is much worse."

"What is it called?"

"It has no name here. In Greece, they call it the Blood Tide. It does not come often, but it is thought a great plague sent by their gods when it does." He looked out at the water, still frowning. "We are not far from the Delta, where the many mouths of the Great River of Egypt are. That is where the people live, but the Great River flows out-ward strongly there. The water is fresh, even far from shore. I doubt that the red water will trouble them."'

"But you said the plague was worse in fresh water."

He smiled. "Yes, but what I meant was that the flow from the river is very strong. The red water will likely be pushed out to sea."

As we walked along, we passed a pool of water near the shore that stopped us in our tracks. It was not light red, but dark, as red as blood. "There, you see? This is fresh water." He pointed to where the pool was fed by a small stream. “And look there!" He pointed. Above the pool, upwind, the ground was black and gray, covered with ash and charred weeds. A fire had swept through, no more than a day or two before.

"What does it mean?" I asked. I could see no connection.

Kisil shook his head and did not answer at first. He continued to examine the burned patch, his wide brow furrowed with thought. “I think the ash makes the red grow darker, more poisonous. I have only seen this once before, and that too was after a fire.”

“Where, Kisil?”

He smiled. “In the East,” he said.

“In Midyan?” I blinked, confused.

“No. Very far to the east. Very, very far.”

I had not known that there was anything beyond the Empty Land. Once again, I wondered just how far my husband had traveled before we met.

That night, we were snuggling together under the Moon and listening to the waves breaking on the shore. It was a warm night, and we had not bothered with the tent. The boys were sleeping a few steps away, near the glowing embers of our fire.

There was a low murmur through the earth. At first I only smiled at the familiar sensation — but then I remembered how far we were from the Mountain, and I gasped and started.

Kisil looked at me, then nodded as if I had said something true. We lay in silence for a time. The boys had not awakened.

We felt the low rumble through the ground again, softer this time. “Kisil, what is going to happen?”

“I do not know, my wild bird. What will happen, will happen, as it is meant to.”

Then, the earth moved again. It was a shock this time, a blow, as if someone had struck it with a mighty hammer. The impact of it swept past us in an instant.

I looked up at Kisil. “It is far away, my love. Soon we will hear a sound like thunder — do not let it frighten you.“

“You have felt this before? This is not like the thunder from the Mountain. It is sharper, harder.“

"Yes, long ago. In the islands far north of here, when I was a sailor. It is a fire-mountain, like your mountain in Midyan, but much bigger by the feel of it — and much angrier. This is only the beginning. We will feel it again..."

He paused, and I knew he was remembering. "Come, we should move farther up the bank."

We woke the boys — Gershom, at least. Eliezer slept while I carried him, and only stirred a bit when I settled him again, much farther up the bank and well above the shore. Soon we were settled again, and I looked down on the dull red glow of our fire, far below us on the beach, and thought.

I do not remember falling asleep, but sure enough, long before morning, I was awakened by a sound like thunder, as Kisil had said. There was only one clap of it, and louder than I had ever heard before, and sharper. With it came a blast of wind, quick, hard, then gone. Then it was over. Kisil only grunted and squeezed me as I lay against him, and I snuggled closer.

The wind from the north rose, and during the night I arose and peered out of the tent. I saw a cloud of fine gray dust, moving quickly. It seemed to roll along the surface of the water. It swept up the beach and vanished into the ground.

The next morning, our feet burned as we walked on the sand, so we walked in the surf, just at the edge of the water. I told Kisil about the cloud, and he nodded, but said nothing. He was watching, noting everything. We did not use the water sources on our way, till we had passed the gray dust. We relied on our waterskins instead, and dug for water for the donkeys behind the ridge closest to the sea, as we had at first.

The dust was ash, Kisil said later. I wondered from what, then remembered the fire mountain.

Not long after this, we passed some more odd-looking pools near the water. These had an ocean smell, and they were rimmed with white. "What is that white stuff?" I asked. "There are many strange things here. Is that poisonous, too?"

Kisil laughed. "No, my sweet bird. That is salt. The sea water flows into these pools at high tide, and then the sun dries the water, leaving the salt behind. It builds up."

He stopped, staring at the salt pools. “Let us gather some, Tzipporah. Do you still have those skin pouches?”

I had several, bags which we had used to carry food but were now empty. Gershom and I scooped up as much of the stuff as we could, filling six or seven of the skin bags with salt and stowing them among the other burdens on the donkeys. I did not know why, and I am not sure that Kisil did either — though I knew that in some places it was useful for trade. It was lucky that we gathered it, as it turned out; but we need not have done it just then. We passed many more such white-rimmed salt pools before we reached the Avru.

The next day, or perhaps the day after that, we passed through a village; and then another, a surprisingly short distance away. Then another, and another; and soon the villages seemed to be almost continuous. So was the smell; again, the scent of humans and animals crowded together, this time along with the scent of cooking — odors that were unfamiliar to me, but spicy and tantalizing. Kisil would sometimes stop and trade a bit of wool or sheepskin for a meal, and the boys and I enjoyed the exotic flavors.

When we came to the top of a hill one day, I saw that there were houses, small and large, in every direction beside the sea. The houses and barns had begun to change as well. No longer were they hovels, built of straw and mud, but more and more often were real buildings, made of wood and stone and brick, some painted in bright colors. There were pillars and gateways and walls, statues of strange humanlike beings with bird and animal heads, and other things for which I had no name.

We were in Egypt.

45

The people here dressed differently from our own people. No more dark wool and goat hair, but most often cotton, thin and light, dyed in colors I had never seen before. Men wore no beards, and shorter tunics than our long desert robes, tunics which only reached their knees. I recognized their clothes as the kind that Kisil wore when I first saw him, though his had been of a slightly different fashion, with a band of dark thread around the hem and a differently shaped opening at the neck...

I smiled. I remembered that day so clearly, even after so long.

Many men went bare-chested — and some of the women, too, which made me blush. There were people dressed like us, in long woolen robes, the men with long hair and beards and headcloths, and people dressed in ways different from both, in different styles of clothing that I had never seen before. Some wore gold around their necks and wrists and even ankles, and sometimes the gold held stones so bright and sparkling that our eyes were dazzled.

Even the people themselves were different colors — some with skin the dun color of the earth, like us; some darker, some very pale, and some as black as burnt sticks. I even saw a woman with golden hair the color of sunlight, and a pale man with speckled skin and hair as red as flame, much brighter than my sister Rivka's. I tried not to stare.

Kisil sold three of our donkeys, trading them for a small cart that could be pulled by our one remaining animal.

It could hold our few belongings, Eliezer, and me. I felt like a queen, riding in our donkey-cart, but after a short time, I felt sorry for the poor beast and walked instead. Gershom took my place, and thought it a wonderful game, much better than riding the jouncing donkey's back.

We began to hear a noise. It was dim and distant at first, then louder as we traveled on. It was not like the sound of the ocean, rhythmic and peaceful, but raucous, rough, a cacophonous noise, made up of sounds I could not identify at first. Before long I could pick out human voices, shouting, the cries of animals — donkeys and camels, dogs and cattle — and other sounds that I did not know.

We were walking along streets now, between rows of buildings. When we came to another high place, I stopped and stared, like the naive desert-dweller I suppose I was. Gershom, too, looked in open-mouthed wonder, and even little Eliezer seemed fascinated, his big eyes wide. We were looking down upon a real city.

It was the largest city I had ever seen, and I have still never seen one bigger. I realized that we had been inside its borders for some time. It was not a walled city, as were the ones I had heard of in Midyan. These people must be very powerful, I thought, to live without walls.

There were buildings, large and small, as far as my eyes could see. Houses, temples, even towers, all of brick or stone, most painted with fantastic scenes or mysterious symbols, in every color I had ever heard of and some that were new to me. The air was filled with dust, and with both awful stenches and tempting scents that changed as we moved along — the foreign air of cities, to which I had begun to grow accustomed. It was also filled with the same noise that we had been hearing for some time — the racket of myriads of living creatures. The streets were crowded, filled with people, animals, and even — I looked twice, and then stared — a man who seemed more animal than human.

He was dressed, if you could call it that, in rags. He was missing a leg, and hopped along on a makeshift crutch. A filthy rag was bound around his head, covering his eyes. The poor man was blind as well as crippled. I stared at him, as did our older son, but Kisil urged us on. "A beggar," he whispered, "and a fraud. Look closely at his back."

I looked more closely as we passed, and saw that the man's leg was not gone. It was bound high up behind him, with the foot across his behind beneath his rags. It was skillfully done; he really appeared as if the leg were missing, though it was not. Nor was he blind. I saw him peek out from under the rag across his eyes before hopping around a wagon in the road.

A little farther on, we passed another man, sitting in the gap between two buildings. He, too, had a rag bound around his eyes. "Another fraud?" I asked my husband.

"No." As I watched, he gave the man a piece of bread and a handful of dates from our donkey's pack. The man grinned toothlessly and spoke a hoarse blessing. We moved on.

We worked our way down the street, careful of our little cart and our one remaining donkey. People stared at us — some curiously, some appraisingly; some as if we were enemies, some as if we were prey. A few seemed friendly, as the people in the villages through which we had passed had been, but there were few of those. I felt very conscious of being a stranger, and I kept my boys close. I checked my own dagger in my sash and made sure it was loose.

As we moved deeper into the streets, I was more and more entranced and filled with wonder. The city was overwhelming, a dizzying display of wealth and poverty, beauty and ugliness, of — of everything that could be seen in all the world, I supposed.

There were places where people were eating while others brought food and wine to their tables. There were places where there was music, and I could see women and sometimes boys dancing before people sitting and drinking wine. And there were other places, where men sat around things like great smoking bottles, and they sucked smoke from ropelike things and then blew the smoke out of their mouths. I had never seen anything like that in my life, and decided to ask Kisil about it later. I do not remember that I ever did.

We saw slaves carrying great burdens on their backs — at least I thought they were slaves — and rich people being carried in curtained chairs by gangs of sweating men. There were wagons, and carts like ours, and even pushcarts moved by men and not beasts. There were even a few chariots, drawn by pairs of horses. The people gave those a wide berth, and I decided they must be dangerous.

People were playing flutes and drums and other musical instruments, strangely shaped things with strings on them, in the street. I soon saw that they were hoping for alms or payment of some kind. Other people were hawking goods of all description, from cooked meat on sticks to clothing to sandals — some new, some old. We passed shops and stalls and tents, more people selling more things than I had ever dreamed of: leather goods, glass, wine, pottery, animals alive and dead, sweets, jewelry, fish, clothing, bread, birds, rugs, swords, tools, meat cooked and raw, and even plain sticks — to be used as staffs, or walking sticks, or whatever one chose.

There were even children for sale. We passed a small square which must have been a slave market. There were little boys and girls being sold there, as servants or apprentices or anything else one might want. Grown men and women, too, some with skills, some merely pretty.

Farther along, near the many temples — grand buildings, though dirty and ill-favored to my eyes — we saw priests, easy to recognize by their shaved heads, their white robes, and their retinues of acolytes. Many of them were very fat, though not all. Their eyes were heavily painted; many of the people, especially the women, wore some dark stuff on their eyelids and color on their lips, but the priests' face-paint was especially noticeable because of their bald heads. It occurred to me that most of the men were clean-shaven. Few seemed to wear beards, as my husband did — he and all the men that I had ever known.

"Where are we going, Kisil?" He was leading the donkey, his back to us as I walked beside the cart.

He turned and spoke softly, but he did not stop. "To find my people."

"But how —.

"There," He lifted his chin. "There they are."

I looked ahead. I saw a building, apparently another temple, that was in the process of being built. Its walls were half finished, its columns holding up nothing. There were some priests, supervising a gang of slaves putting bricks in place and carrying containers of mud to hold them in place — and beyond, another group pulling at something large and heavy. More bricks, I thought. Then I noticed the slaves pulling it.

They were yoked, or collared, or harnessed, and they pulled or pushed at a thing that Kisil told me later was called a *sledge*. It was a kind of moving platform, piled high with bricks, that scraped along the gritty streets with agonizing slowness. Some of the people were behind it, and pushed with beams of wood that were studded with cross-timbers. Lines of men drove the sledge forward. Others, in front, drew on ropes. Other men poured water from bags in front of the moving timbers that scraped the ground.

Many wore cotton, like the Egyptians, but ragged and threadbare. A few, mostly women — some women worked alongside the men — wore long robes like ours, but those were ragged and filthy too. Some of the men wore only loincloths. Some had sandals, but most were barefoot.

The men wore beards, all of them, and their hair was uncut and shaggy. A pair of guards, also bearded, walked beside them, bearing whips and rods. I saw no one beaten, though. I suppose the people worked hard so they would not be. I looked at Kisil.

"Those are my people. The Avru."

46

We did not stop then. We moved on, going back the way the slaves with the sledge had come. Before long, we passed another such group. Some of the guards watched us curiously, but none of the sweating slaves did. They were too occupied with moving the heavy load of bricks, and did not look up from the ground or their push beams to take notice of us.

As we made our way along, we passed several places where the Avru were hauling and unloading the bricks, buildings that were in various stages of construction. When the sledges were empty, the slaves would throw the pushing timbers onto them and drag them back the way they had come.

I noticed that there were only two overseers, or even one, with each sledge-gang. The people were too tired and dispirited to resist or rebel. Even though the empty sledges were much lighter, the Avru dragged them at the same slow pace they had used when they were piled high with bricks. We began to follow one such group down the dusty street, and kept pace with them, staying some distance behind.

On the way, Kisil pointed out an enormous building in the distance, placed on the highest ground in the neighborhood. It seemed to be all pillars, brightly painted, and with many people coming and going. "That is the king's palace."

I stared at it. "That is a grand building. Is that where you lived as a child?"

"Yes. This was the palace of this king's father. My uncle had a new palace built for himself, in the capital." He gave me a sour smile. "That is their way. I have never seen it, but I know the style." He pointed. "It will have many pillars, and many open doorways to catch the breeze. They like it cool."

"That is why it is on the top of a hill," said Gershom. He was riding the donkey, having grown tired of the cart, and was staring up at the big building.

Kisil grinned approvingly. "That is right, Gershom. High up, where the winds can blow through."

We moved on, following the slaves with the empty sledge, and soon we passed another, a full one, being pushed and pulled by ragged, exhausted Avru. We moved to the side to let them pass.

The houses grew smaller and more widely spaced, and before long we were at the edge of the city. The ocean was in sight again, and farther away, a river. It seemed to me a wide river, but Kisil told me it was only one of many branches of the Great River of Egypt as it flowed into the sea. I wondered how wide the main course of the river was. The hill where the king's palace stood was above it, with other large houses and buildings along its banks.

We had stopped often, and the empty sledge with its gang of slaves was out of sight ahead of us. We followed the track where it had gone. It was not difficult; the ruts were worn deep. I wondered how many trips those sledges had made along this road.

Soon the tracks were running along the bed of a broad wadi, a dry watercourse. There was evidently water in it from time to time, because the center of the depression was muddy. Kisil guided us onto higher ground, and we were soon walking along the bank above.

The wadi spread out and became much wider, and soon we were looking down on what I knew was the Avru camp or village. It was a sort of compound; a wide, long area, all in the dry bed of the wadi, surrounded on three sides by a kind of rough wall, or mound.

The barrier was no more than a long pile of rubble — broken bricks, dried mud, and rough stones of all sizes, mixed with scraps of wood, the remains of discarded sledges and chariots, other castoffs and leavings. There were even broken clay pots, animal bones, rinds and scraps of fruit and other such garbage. The place stank of rotten food and human waste.

Directly below us there was an opening in the wall, or mound, through which the tracks of the sledges went. A couple of bored guards stood or leaned on either side. Inside the space, we could see that there were rows of rough brick huts along the near and far sides of the depression, with low walls and steep roofs of thatching that almost reached the ground. We saw a few women, mostly old, sitting in doorways. Some were surrounded by children that they were evidently watching. There were a few old men, too, but most of the people were in the bottom of the wadi, below and between the rows of huts.

There were the brick pits, filled with thick mud where people were wearily treading straw into the muck. Others, along the sides of the pits, slapped the mud into molds, and still others dropped partially dried bricks onto racks. Between the pits were long stacks of mud bricks, curing and hardening in the sun. Farther on were more people loading the finished blocks onto sledges, and still more waiting to drag them to the temples in the distance, having dragged their empty sledges back for more.

There were overseers watching them as they worked. Some were Egyptian, but most of the overseers seemed to be Avru, though better dressed and fed. Both men and women labored. I saw women working at the bricks, but others were minding dirty children. All were the same color — the gray-brown of the mud. I did not see a single smiling face.

"This is how my people live. It looks just as it did when I was young." The expression on his face was unreadable. It could have been carved from stone.

"How many Avru live here?"

He shook his head. "I cannot say, Tzipporah. I saw the tallies of the the people once, when I was young. I was not much interested then." He made a face as if he tasted something bitter. "There were two or three hundred grown men to work the bricks, counting the old ones who could only tread the straw into the mud. Then there were a hundred or so who serve the Egyptians in other ways, and then women and children." He paused, thinking. "Perhaps a thousand in all, or a few more. That was long ago, but I doubt that there are many more now." His brows drew downward. "There may be fewer. The people here do not live long."

"Are there more places like this?"

He shook his head. "No. The king keeps us together, and nearby, so we can be watched. There are other slaves, though, from other places." He looked at me, still with that same unreadable expression. "There are not many Avru, Tzipporah. We are few, a small people, perhaps the smallest, and we are weak."

"What are we going to do?" Some of the people were staring up at us as we stood there above the compound.

He pointed. "First I must find my family, if I can." He paused. "I must tell them that I have come back, and tell them of my mission. I had a brother somewhere here. Perhaps I can find him, if he still lives."

"Your brother?" I remember he had alluded to him once or twice.

"Yes. Aron was his name. A sister, too, Miryam. My parents — my real parents — are dead, I am sure."

"How will we get into the camp?"

He shrugged. "Walk in. They are not well guarded during the day, and not at all at night. The overseers only watch them to make sure they make their tally of bricks." He gestured, *look around*. "There are no real walls, no gates."

I realized that the mound was not to keep the Avru confined, but only to mark the boundary between the slaves' quarters, with the brick pits, and the rest of the city. It did not extend all the way around the Avru's huts. The far end of the compound was open, and not far beyond was the ocean.

Some upheaval, long ago, had raised the shoreline here. The wadi no longer sloped down to the sea, but rose up and widened, ending in a high ridge between the compound and the water. The slaves were far from the river and its abundant fresh water — that privilege was reserved for the Egyptians — but near the sea. I saw some of the Avru, with yokes bearing pots, climbing up and down the ridge. They were carrying salt water for the brick pits, going back and forth from the camp.

"Look, there are their sheep." On either side of the wadi, beyond the wall, there was a broad swath of grassy land. I could see a few small flocks of sheep, grazing quietly. "The Avru are a herding people, like yours. The children watch the sheep, the older children shear them and milk them. This is the Delta of the Great River. The grass is rich and deep. This must have been a fine place to live at one time."

He pointed to some ruined walls and exposed foundations, on the far sides of the fields. "Those were the Avru's homes. The people were forced to abandon them and move into this — camp, where they make bricks. And there they have stayed. The Egyptians despise sheep as accursed animals, but they allow us to keep them, to help feed ourselves." He smiled bitterly. "The women spin a little wool and make a bit of cloth here, but the quality is poor. Those arts have mostly been forgotten."

I looked at the crude wall, the few guards. "Why do they not just leave?"

He laughed, but without mirth. "The Avru are on foot, with flocks and herds. The Egyptians have chariots and spears and swords. How far could they go?" Then he frowned. "I heard, I think, that a group of them tried to leave, once. I do not remember what happened, but they did not come to a good end."

We began working our way down the slope. It was nearing sunset. Soon, Kisil said, the people's workday would end — not because the Egyptians were merciful, but because it was too hard to make and stack the bricks in the dark. I wondered if they worked into the night when the moon was full.

The slaves' district was a sort of village of its own, separate and distinct. There were no villages so big in my part of the world, though we had passed through a few larger towns on our way. A thousand people, at most, I thought. It was as Kisil had said.

We went down the slope, our donkey struggling with the steep descent. Sure enough, the guards at the open gate, or entrance, took little note of us as we passed, looking over our donkey-cart in a cursory way. The cart marked us as free people, I learned later. The Avru owned only sheep, and not many of those.

Some looked at us curiously as we entered the compound, but most were too tired to give us much attention as they trudged back to their huts. The overseers were moving toward their huts as well.

"Look, Father." Gershom pointed. "Who are they?"

More Avru were entering through the rough gate behind us. They were cleaner, better-dressed and plainly better-fed than the rest. I noticed that their homes, and those of the overseers, were on the other side of the wadi, farther from the brick pits, more widely spaced, and a bit larger than the ordinary Avru's hovels.

Kisil followed our gaze. "Those are the house-slaves, Gershom. There are two classes of slaves here. Some work in the Egyptians' homes and shops, or in the king's palaces and public buildings, cleaning or assisting or entertaining his officials and nobles.

"The rest —" He gestured at the brick pits and the rows of sledges, where the sledge-gangs were dropping their burdens — "Work harder. The house-slaves are better treated. And better housed." He lifted his chin again to indicate the huts on the near side. "Come, let us find someone we can talk to."

"Kisil," I said. My tone must have drawn his attention. He looked at me curiously. "What are you going to tell them?"

He blinked. "That I am here to tell the king to set them free."

"I think you should announce yourself as the Deliverer."

"But —"

"You do not know that to be true. Yes." I nodded at his doubtful look. "But *I do,* Kisil. Do you not see? Everything that has happened to you has been to bring you back to this time and place. It is as my father said, my love. Ael Shadu — Ehyehuwah — has chosen *you* for this task."

He considered that. Before he could speak, I went on: "You know much more of the world than I, Kisil. But I do know this; if you do not speak with assurance and authority, they will not listen. They have to have a *reason* to follow you. This is the reason."

He slowly nodded. "And the only reason," he said thoughtfully. "You are right, my wise, wild bird." He took a fresh grip on his staff, squared his shoulders — and winked at me. He started for the nearest hut, which was lit with a single lamp. I followed.

Kisil called out as we approached the door. "Shelter!" he called. "Shelter for a family of your kin!"

47

A tall, lean man came to the door and looked out suspiciously. He saw us; a man, a boy, a woman holding a small child. We were a dusty and bedraggled little group, but clean and clothed very well compared to himself. He stepped back, gesturing that we should enter, but with a grim expression.

"Come in, then. Though why you would come here, I do not know." He beckoned to two boys, his sons, I supposed. "Jehu. Zadok. Care for their animal." The boys unhitched and led our donkey away, and as we entered the hut, the man said, "My name is Boaz. How are you kin?"

"My father's name was Amram," said Kisil. "Did you know him?"

The man stood still and stared at Kisil. After a moment, he spoke again, his voice as grim as his face. "I know you." He frowned. "You are Moses."

That was the first time I had ever heard that name.

Kisil nodded. "I was called that."

A few others began to gather around the door of the hut. "Send for Aron," said Boaz, without addressing anyone in particular. "Tell him his brother Moses has returned." A girl left on the run, and we heard whispers all around us.

"Moses…"

"Moses has come back…"

"Why would he?"

Boaz indicated a low table. "Come, sit. This is my wife. Her name is Deenah." The woman, small and dark, was bringing cups of water and black bread, plain food, the fare of poor people and slaves.

I rose to help. "We have dates and honey in the donkey cart. We will share."

The man nodded grudgingly, and the faces of the children in the room lit up. I sent Gershom out to the cart to bring the small bag of sweets, and though he scowled at having to share them, he went.

"Are any more of my family still living?" asked Kisil.

"Your father and mother are dead. Besides your brother, your sister also still lives. Why have you come back?" he asked.

"Let me wait for my brother and sister. I will tell then."

Boaz nodded yet again and let us eat, though he watched Kisil closely. Gershom came back with the dates and honey, dodging through the watchers at the door, and I gave the treats to Deenah, the man's wife. She began to hand out the dates to the eager children, one date to a child — and I was pleased that she did not leave out my sons. She gave me a shy smile as I watched.

I wondered what Kisil had looked like when this man, Boaz, last saw him. I wondered, too, why no more was being made of Kisil's return. Only a few people were gathered at the door. Then I realized that these people were tired, tired to the point of exhaustion. Their faces were haggard, their backs bent — and they were dirty, their feet and legs and bodies stained with drying mud.

They see no reason to keep clean, I thought, if they are just going to go back to the mud tomorrow. Even so, the few who were there stood or sat around and stared at us, some in fascination, some with hostility, most with curiosity. And some, with an open, eager expression. Only later did I realize what it was.

Before long, the girl returned. She was accompanied by a man who looked much like Kisil, but older and taller. The people at the door made room for him as he entered. His eyes were the same gray color as Kisil's, but they blazed with hatred as they stared at my husband. We stood as he entered.

Behind him came a woman, as tall as he, also gray-eyed, with an air of quiet authority. I noticed that the people, all of them, bowed to her as she entered, which she acknowledged with a raised hand — a gesture indicating "Not now."

I wondered what her importance could be that she was treated with such great respect.

Aron — I knew this was Aron — was hardly inside the door before he blurted out, "Why have you come back? The king's daughter took you and raised you, you were a prince. Then you saw how we live, and you ran away!" Kisil said nothing, waiting for his brother to have his say. "After you left," Aron went on with an angry gesture, "you were free, you could go where you liked! You could even have gone back to the palace! Why have you come back, after so long? Why are you here?"

I wondered how much I did not know.

The woman behind Aron was staring at Kisil with wide eyes. Wide eyes — and then they narrowed. "Yekusiel," she whispered. "Is it really you?"

She stood very straight, her air of command evident. Kisil moved toward her, brushed by his brother, and embraced her. She was taller than he, with the same penetrating gray eyes, but her curling hair was as white as clouds and her face lined. She was older than Kisil, I knew. Her arms went round him, but I saw a kind of reserve in her posture. "Miryam," said my husband softly.

"Why have you come back?" Aron growled again. His voice was softer, but his eyes still glittered with hatred.

Kisil stepped back, then turned and looked at him — or so it seemed at first.

His eyes were distant, as if looking far beyond the man before him. His expression betrayed no emotion at all — no guilt, no doubt, no arrogance, nothing. Then he looked directly at Aron and spoke — quietly, but with unmistakable authority.

"Let us speak together, Aron. You, and Miryam, and I. My words are for all of the Avru —" He looked around at the others who were watching, taking in those by the door as well — "but the three of us, we shall speak first. Take us —" he indicated Gershom, and Eliezer, and me — "to a place where we can rest, and we shall talk. We have traveled far to come here."

Aron opened his mouth as if to speak angrily again — but then he closed it. Kisil had spoken softly, but as if he expected to be obeyed. My husband waited, looking at Aron impassively, one hand still on his sister's back. She continued to look at him with cool, appraising eyes.

Aron looked at Miryam. Their eyes met; she frowned, then nodded her assent.

I took note of that. It was as if Aron needed his sister's permission, or perhaps only her agreement. I remembered the deference paid to the woman when she had entered. This was more than a woman and her older brother meeting long-lost kin.

Aron made a shooing motion with his hands at the others in the hut and by the door. They all looked up at Miryam. She tilted and tossed her head slightly, confirming Aron's gesture. They bowed and left. Aron beckoned that we should follow him, and we began filing out of the hut.

I went to Miryam, intending to greet her. She looked at me as if from a distance, and lifted one eyebrow, up and down. She asked, "You are his wife?"

"I am." I indicated the small boy standing nearby who held his much smaller brother's hand. "And these are your nephews." She turned and looked — and then finally smiled, her eyes warming as she looked at the children.

"They look like fine boys." She held out her hands. Gershom smiled back and approached her, and little Eliezer blessed her with one of his own beatific smiles and toddled unsteadily forward too.

Before long, the old woman was holding my younger son in her arms, laughing as he reached for the wooden pendant that hung from a thong round her neck. Miryam smiled at me then, and the awkwardness seemed to have passed.

We left the hut, Gershom's hand in Miryam's, and followed Aron and Kisil who were some distance ahead. The two men were walking side by side, but neither spoke. Some people nearby took notice of Miryam and bowed in her direction again. She ignored them, occupied with Eliezer's giggles and smiles.

We were led to a hut nearby. It was not empty; a low, rude bed and table stood in it, with some fairly clean blankets, and a stool or two. A few pots and other utensils were there as well. "Whose home is this?" I asked as I entered.

Aron heard me and turned. "He died. His wife and child went to live with his kin."

"I am sorry. I did not know."

He made a dismissing gesture, a bit sheepishly. I thought, *He knows he is being discourteous.* "This hut is yours, if you want it," he said, in a softer tone.

Kisil leaned his staff in a corner. "It will serve very well." He sat down on an upturned tub, and gestured for the rest of us to sit as well, as perfectly at home as if he were in our camp by the Mountain and Aron and Miryam were the visitors. Aron sat on a nearby stool, with a slightly belligerent air, and looked at Kisil expectantly. Miryam sat on the bed beside me, with Eliezer on her lap. I was watching her eyes.

She knows what Kisil is about to say, I thought. There was a short silence, then Kisil spoke.

"I am the Deliverer."

At that, Aron lifted his hands as if to ward off an attack and rose from his seat. Miryam bowed her head and nodded, as if to herself.

Aron walked around the floor of the hut, eyes shut tight, hands still raised, gesturing, no, no, get away; but after only a few steps, he opened his eyes and sought his sister's. No words passed between them, only a look. He dropped his hands.

Aron turned and looked at his brother frankly. "We knew that long ago. Yes."

Miryam dandled Eliezer on her knee, and he giggled. She smiled at the boy. "When you were a baby," she said. Her eyes rose to Kisil's. "When Mother put you in the Great River, and the king's daughter pulled you out. We knew, even then." She looked down for a heartbeat, then up at him again. "I was told you were the Deliverer before you were born, Yekusiel. A Messenger came to me. In a dream."

Aron sat down again. "It is true. She told me."

Kisil closed his eyes, then opened them. "Let me tell you what happened after I left, and why I ran."

48

As Kisil and his siblings spoke, I began trying to make the one room comfortable. The blankets, as I said, were fairly clean, though worn and threadbare. I spread them on the bed to air, and Gershom and I found places for our things from the cart.

A careworn woman, much older than I, appeared at the door. She turned out to be Elishevah, Aron's wife. We smiled at each other, but did not speak, not then; we did not want to disturb the others, who were deep in talk. We moved outside with the boys and sat down on a small bench there.

"What are their names?" she asked, smiling at the boys. She twisted sideways on the bench and picked up Eliezer, who smiled back happily.

"My name is Gershom," said my eldest. "This is Eliezer, my brother."

"You look like a big, strong boy." Gershom beamed.

Eliezer reached for me. I took him from Elishevah, covered him with my shawl, and fed him a bit more dinner. He had not been eating solid food long, and I was still nursing him from time to time. Elishevah had four sons, and we chatted a bit about our boys. When Eliezer was finished, we went back inside and listened as I got the boys ready for bed.

"I hated you when you left," Aron was saying. His fingers were playing with a small stick. He did not look at Kisil as he spoke.

Kisil laughed, and Aron jumped a little and stared at him. "You hated me when you first saw me, brother," said my husband with an easy grin. "Long ago, when I first came to the camp. And little wonder. I can only imagine how I looked —"

Aron shrugged, then smiled, and then laughed a bit too. "Yes," he said, then laughed a little more. "You were a fine young prince, you were. In your ivory-white cotton, with your golden necklace and your shaved head."

"And painted eyes," put in Miryam, and they all laughed. I felt better. Miryam had seemed withdrawn, at first, but now seemed to be relaxing with her brothers. Still, there was a reserve about her, a caution, that I found puzzling.

"It is true, I did hate you," said Aron. "But you were not one of us. You were just another Egyptian, as far as I could see. You had only that day found out you were Avru."

Miryam's face darkened. "You looked at us, and you were horrified."

"I was," said Kisil. "But not at my being one of you."

The other two exchanged glances, puzzled. "What, then?" asked his sister.

"I was shocked at how you were treated. Like animals."

"But you knew that," said Aron. "You had seen us before — whipped and starved —"

Kisil's face was bleak. "Yes. Yes, I did. And only then, that day, did I understand — that you were people, like I was. Like my —" He stopped. He was about to say "my people," I knew.

"Like the Egyptians," he went on. "Only that day did I understand that it was wrong to treat people in this way... Only that day had I ever even thought about it. I ask you now to forgive me. I was still a child, an Egyptian child, a pampered child raised by our oppressors. I did not know."

Kisil went on: "I was born that day, Aron. Before then, I was a spoiled little boy, for all that I had twenty years or more. But that day, I learned who I was, and who you were. How long did I stay with you?" he asked suddenly. "I do not remember."

Miryam and Aron looked at each other again. "Two days," said Miryam. "Perhaps three. You spent most of the time with our parents."

"Yes... Yes, I remember Mother. She looked —" He thought. "Sad," he finally said. "And she seemed —" He stopped and thought again.

"Hurried?" asked Miryam, with a knowing look.

Kisil stared at her, surprised. "Yes! Yes, hurried! I never thought of that, but that is what she was. How did you know?"

Miryam smiled, but sadly. "She had so much to tell you, and so little time. She knew you would not be with us long... And..."

"And what?"

"She knew that she would never see you again after you left us.".

My husband's face fell. "And she was right," Kisil said, his voice hoarse.

"Yes."

There was another silence, this time more companionable, if sadder.

Aron spoke hesitantly. "Moses — Kisil — we have heard your story of what happened to you on the Mountain. It was hard to understand —" He looked at Miryam, who gestured, *go on.* "But what we want to know is —"

Kisil waited. He knew what was coming.

Aron hesitated still. Miryam took it up. "What we want to know is — what have you come to *do?"*

Kisil spoke simply. "I have come to tell the king to let the Avru go free, in the Name of The One." He let the words lie there, plain and unadorned.

Miryam's face was set, her eyes narrow. She was examining him. "In the Name — of the One Who has no Name?"

"Yes. But He does have a Name, my sister. And I know the Name."

She gasped, eyes wide, but before she could speak, he went on. "I have not come to replace the king and have the Avru serve me, sister. Nor have I come to replace you."

"Me?" Miryam said, as if puzzled.

"Yes. You. I can see that you have authority here. You are held in reverence. I can only guess that it is because you serve The One and teach others of His ways."

Aron confirmed this. "That is true. She is our High Priestess, you might say. She speaks to the people at the New Moon."

I started. "The New Moon is a special day for my people, too. In Midyan. It is —"

"Too dark to work," said Miryam as she turned to look at me. "Yes. A bit of extra rest for the Avru. We sit round our fires and tell stories. Tonight, or perhaps tomorrow."

New Moon would be the next night, if I knew anything. I smiled inwardly. Once again, things seemed to be happening as if planned. We had arrived at the perfect time.

"Miryam teaches us." Elishevah was speaking from behind me. "Some of the other elders — you will meet them — tell us the tales of our ancestors, which they know by rote. And we have songs and chants."

Kisil's eyes were avid. "I want to hear them all." He turned back to his sister. "Miryam, I am still a child in the ways of my people. I have been sent to set them — you — *us* — to set *us* free. But I know so little, so very little of my ancestors, of The One who called me, and of the ways of our people and our heritage. Will you teach me?"

His sister's eyes seemed to lose that appraising look, and she nodded, then nodded again.

"I will." She seemed to relax, for the first time since I had seen her, but I could not have told you how I knew that. Her upright posture did not change, nor did her air of authority.

"Good." My husband pressed his hands together and gave a sort of seated bow. "Good. I thank you."

She looked at him closely, then spoke again. "You know His Name, you say?" Kisil only nodded, but solemnly. "I hope you speak truly. The One has no name that I have ever heard."

"I do. And there is much, much more."

"Shall we gather the people now?" asked Aron.

"No," said my husband. He sighed, and to everyone's surprise, stood and stretched. "Tomorrow is the new moon, is it not?" He looked at me, and I nodded. "I have much to say, and I would prefer to say it only once. I shall speak tomorrow, when the people gather. Give me till then."

I was suddenly aware of how weary he looked. He had been the picture of strength and resolution, and he still was; but he was weary. Then I realized that I was, too. My sons were already asleep on the bed.

Aron looked at us, and I suppose he saw the same thing. He stood, and after a few more words of welcome, he and Miryam left. Kisil saw the bread and cheese, and smiled. “Are there any dates left?”

49

Later that night, Kisil and I settled down together on a pallet we made on the floor. I left the bed for the boys, who were wearier than either of us from our traveling. My head found its favorite spot on his shoulder, and I snuggled close. I said nothing. I knew that if Kisil wanted to talk, he would.

And, as always, he seemed to know what I was thinking. "This is not my home, Tzipporah," he whispered. "My home is our tent by the Mountain, with you and your sisters and your father and mothers. You are my family. Remember that. These are my people, yes; but they are my people because I have returned to them, to do what I must do. I have never really been one of them, welcomed by them, as I have been one with your people and embraced by your family." He held me close, and kissed me. "Our people. Our family."

I nodded into his chest, and then replied further with a little nuzzle. He squeezed me, and in only a few heartbeats, it seemed, we slept.

The next morning, to my surprise, Kisil took off his robe and donned a loincloth like the ones worn by the men in the brick pits. "What are you doing?" I asked.

"I am one of these people. I must take my place among them."

"Shall I go, too?"

"No. Stay here and care for our sons. This is a new place for them, and they need you. Make sure they do not offend."

He went to the brick pit nearest our hut, and I saw him asking his neighbor there what to do.

The man, aged and thin, showed him; take some straw, scatter it on the mud, and mix it in by stamping it. The mud was perhaps knee-deep, and very thick. The work was hard. Kisil joined in with a will, and the others around him, hesitant at first, seemed to accept him as he worked. Before long, I saw them laughing together at some joke Kisil had made. Few of the others, farther away, were laughing. I thought it might have been a long time since anyone laughed here at all.

That was Kisil's way. I had seen it before, but never so dramatically. He could fit in anywhere, make anyone comfortable with him, make anyone smile and laugh.

Our son was watching beside me. "Your father brings more to these people than the words of The One, Gershom. He brings the gift of himself."

"Is Father going to free them, Mother?"

"No. The One will free them. Kisil is only here to tell them that He will."

"Eyehu-" my son began, but I clapped my hand over his mouth, then smiled at him before he could be shocked or fearful.

"Do not say the Name yet, my son," I told him. "It is not known here. It is for your father to reveal it, not us."

He whispered, "All right," though he looked confused. "All right, Mother." He watched his father tramping the mud for a few heartbeats. "May I go down to the mud, too?"

There were, indeed, boys as young as he working in the brick pit. "Go and ask your father," I said, and he ran down the slope. I saw Kisil listen, consider, then nod. Gershom ran back to me, gave me a kiss, then into the hut to change into a loincloth of his own. He was as excited as if he had been told that he and his father were going to the market to buy sweets.

I took Eliezer and went to join some other women to help prepare the evening meal for that night's gathering. It would be a feast, of a kind, though poor stuff; some wilted greens, some lentils and some other vegetables, with a bit of meat added for flavor. Rough bread and a little hard cheese. There was no wine. I brought the rest of the dates from our small store, and they were gratefully accepted.

We worked together, and I showed them how to stretch the dates, using them with a bit of ewe's milk to make a kind of pudding with the hard bread — a recipe that my mother Sabah had once shown me.

I was surprised to find that they had slaughtered some lambs in honor of Kisil's return. We prepared cooking-pits, covering the skinned carcasses with stones and coals and setting them to bake in the ground.

As I got to know the other women and worked with them — they all fawned over Eliezer, who gloried in it — I thought of little but what lay before us that night, wondering what Kisil would say and what would happen.

I could feel the presence of The One, somehow. I felt him in the air, in the sky, in the ground. Once again, I had that familiar feeling, the one I had on the day I met Kisil and on the day when he went up the Mountain.

Something was coming.

50

The night finally came. Kisil and Gershom had managed to cleanse themselves of the mud, and had changed back into their Midyanite robes. Kisil seemed outwardly calm, but I saw his trembling hands.

"Do you know what you will say, my love?"

"I have not planned a speech, if that is your meaning. I intend to speak as plainly and simply as I can, then answer their questions in the same way. It does not seem right to — calculate it, to plan it out."

I was doubtful of the wisdom of that, but held my peace.

The sun had long since set. The time had arrived. We knew that that evening would determine the course of all that would follow, and perhaps the rest of our lives. We stood together in the hut that had become ours, and he held me close.

"My knees feel like water."

"You do not look afraid, Kisil."

"I am not afraid," he said, but uncertainly. "Not exactly. I am only wondering what will happen."

"Something will," I said. "I feel it. I feel Him."

He shook his head with that wry grin I loved so much. "I feel nothing, Tzipporah. I *hope* that something will happen. I hope they will listen."

"But what will you say, Kisil? If you do not believe—"

"I believe in *truth*, Tzipporah. And I will speak truth in language that they understand, as your father did." He smiled. "Perhaps Ehyehuwah *did* speak to me. Whether it was on the Mountain, or in my mind when I first learned that I was Avru — it does not matter." He smiled wryly and cocked his head. "You said it yourself, my wild bird. All truth is His truth, and He has no voice but ours. Is that not so?"

Before I could answer, Aron and Miryam appeared at the door. They said nothing. There was no need. It was time.

Kisil hugged Gershom, gave Eliezer a kiss, took his staff, and left the hut with his brother and sister. I followed with our sons, one in my arms, the other at my side.

Darkness had fallen quickly. It had not taken long for the people to gather. When the word went out that Kisil was about to speak, they came. Even from the other side of the wadi, from the larger huts of the overseers and house servants, they came. By the time we left our hut, there was a large crowd waiting.

Aron and Kisil climbed to the top of a great stack of dried bricks, apparently the place from which Miryam had spoken before. It was the last in the row, and there was an open space before it where the people could stand and listen.

Aron spoke simply. "This is my brother, Kisil, whom many of us knew as Moses." He paused. "Hear him."

Miryam echoed him from beside me, her voice ringing: "Hear him!" Many of the people looked at her at that. Some bowed.

Aron climbed down from the bricks and left Kisil there alone. My husband stood there and waited as more of the Avru came and joined the throng. The people who had already gathered looked up at him, and I saw that more and more of them had that open and wondering look on their faces. I still did not understand it. It was not reverence, or worship, or anything of the kind. What was it?

The places near the front, where one could sit, were reserved, it seemed, for the tribe's elders. Miryam was one of them; the people treated her with great deference, as before, and had brought benches for her and the others. Some women helped her to a seat, and when she gestured that I should sit beside her, no one protested.

I sat, with Gershom and little Eliezer between us. Others joined us there, some very old, others rather more well-dressed and cleaner than the rest — house-slaves and overseers, again. These last received some sour looks and glares, but when they took their privileged places as if by right, no one protested. It was not hard to guess why. A few carried the same whips they used during the workday.

The laborers were still coming from their huts, gathering around, looking up and examining the stranger, my husband, who seemed to be examining them in return. Miryam, too, looked up at Kisil, even as she dandled Eliezer on her knee. She still had that expression of caution, of reserve, on her face. I knew why, and hoped.

The crowd was silent, for the most part, with only a low murmur audible. They seemed to be watching the stranger expectantly — though very many of them frowned at him, their hostility evident, and not only the privileged ones. Evidently Kisil was still well known as the Moses who had escaped slavery and was raised as a prince, at least among the adults. The children and young people merely stared at him curiously.

With a chill, I realized that Kisil stood before an audience that was largely hostile, even hateful. To the Avru, Kisil had never been one of them. He had been one of the enemy, an oppressor, as he had said himself. To the rest, he was a stranger.

Besides their hostility, I had another worry. How will he be able to speak to them at all? I wondered. I had heard Kisil speak with assurance and authority, but never loudly. How could his impaired speech carry to the edges of this multitude? How would his lisp not attract their ridicule?

But then Kisil began. To my surprise, his words boomed out as if from a trumpet, resonating powerfully in the air. "Children of Avram! Hearken to me! I bring news for you all!" His words, though still made indistinct by his injury, seemed somehow magnified, amplified, louder and deeper than I had ever heard it. Kisil told me later that it was a trick he had learned from an actor in Greece. Speaking from the belly, he called it, but I never learned how it was done.

"Our God has sent me here!" He paused and looked out over the gathering. "He has sent me to set you free — to set us all free! I, Moses — I am the Deliverer who was promised!"

For a man who had once been unwilling to speak to a few girls, he spoke now with confidence and authority, as well as with surprising volume.

Many mouths dropped open. Some smiled, some looked to the heavens, some closed their eyes and began to murmur thanks. In the short pause between Kisil's words, a man in the front began to speak. His face was flushed with anger. Many others began to grumble as well. "How dare y—"

Kisil ignored them and went on relentlessly. "The God of Avram, of Yitzhak, and of Yaacov has sent me. He has sent me to speak His words to you and to the king of Egypt!" He lifted his hands, palms up, arms spread wide. "I was spared from death when I was born, as you know. But not to be a princeling in the king's palace, as you thought — and as I thought. I was spared for *this*. Our God — *our God* — has sent me to you. And soon you will all be free. *We* will all be free."

There was an excited murmur running through the crowd, but many eyes were suspicious and hostile. "What is His name?" came a voice, a suspicious voice that held a hint of a sneer in it. I looked for the source of the question, and found it. The man was tall and burly, with an air of imperious command. I examined his appearance. He was dark, with close-cropped, bristly hair and prominent ears that protruded like the handles of a wine jar. His beard was trimmed short as well, unusual among the Avru. I knew why, though; Kisil had told me that fighting-men everywhere — in all the lands where he had traveled — kept their hair and beards short, to deny their opponents a handhold in close combat. Well, he cannot trim his ears, I thought wryly.

Miryam saw me watching the mam. "That is Desan," she murmured in my ear. "He was once a chief overseer, but he grew too arrogant even for the Egyptians. They took that office from him and made him a common house-servant. He has never accepted it."

I knew that Desan's was a trick question. The God of the Avru had no name, as Kisil had told me. Well, He has one now, I thought.

Kisil's voice rang among the stacks of bricks and the rows of rude huts. *"EHYEH,"* he said. *I AM.*

I recognized the words. They were the same words he had told us when he came down from the Mountain, two years and more before.

A short, stunned silence, and then the same man, Desan, spoke out again. "That is not a name!" he growled.

Another tall, heavily muscled man beside him repeated his words: "That is not a name!"

Miryam whispered in my ear a second time. "That is Aviram, brother to Desan. The same thing happened to him. He was his brother's subordinate, and an overseer as well, but now he is a groom and cares for some Egyptian lord's horses." Aviram was as burly as his brother, with the same short, bristly hair and beard and jug ears — but he had a weak chin and eyes that constantly flicked to Desan, clearly his master.

"No, that is not a name," Kisil agreed. His voice boomed out over the crowd with a power that I had never heard in it before. "But that is what He says to you: *'I AM.'* It means, 'I will be as I choose to be, and I shall do as I choose to do.' We cannot call His name and expect Him to come at our command, like a child comes to his mother."

He let those words hang in the air. Then he said, "But as you say, that is not His name. It is said that He has no Name — but that is not the truth! I know His Name — and I will teach it to you. Now."

Kisil stood as still as a stone, only his hair stirring slightly in the sea wind. The setting new moon was visible over his shoulder, a thread of light curving round its circle of deep blue in the twilit sky. He seemed to tower over us all, a powerful, commanding figure. I did not know where this aura of authority came from — I had never seen it before — but it was there. Even Desan and Aviram seemed cowed by it, looking up with eyes that were hostile, but uncertain.

"His Name is — *EHYEH-HUWAH,"* Kisil intoned.

His voice, when he said this, was clear and resonant and as loud as a ram's horn, even though it still held a trace of his lisp. There was a curious stillness about the people. The Name seemed to reverberate in the air, as if it were written there in glowing letters, glowing with the fire of the Mountain. After a heartbeat, Kisil went on, speaking words that seemed to hold that same power — and in that same rich, deep voice, with only a trace of thickness and clumsiness:

"Thus says Ehyehuwah, the God of our fathers: *'I have surely heard the cries of my people, the children of Avram. I know of your suffering at the hands of your taskmasters. And I have surely remembered the Covenant I made with your fathers, and My promise to send you a Deliverer, to set you free from your bondage. I shall lead you out of the land of Egypt with My own hand; and I will lead you into the land that I promised your fathers. And you will surely remember, in ages to come, how the God of your fathers chose you from among the nations and set you free.'* So says Ehyehuwah, our God, the God of Avram, the God of Yitzhak, and the God of Yaacov." Kisil spoke in tones that neither I nor anyone else had ever heard. "Your God and my God. *Ehyehuwah.* He Who sent me. He who *Is.*"

The people stood silent, open-mouthed and staring. I knew what was happening. Kisil never felt the Presence of The One, but all those who heard him did. I felt a thrill to my very bones. My husband — my Kisil, my own — spoke with God's voice. He did not know this himself, but he did. He stood with his face lifted to the sky for a moment, and took a deep breath. He seemed to gather himself again — and then another voice spoke, silky and insinuating:

"Do you bring signs? Miracles? Wonders, to prove that you speak for Him?" This time it was neither Desan nor Aviram, but another man, a small fellow with a curiously well-kept, sleek air about him. He wore a sky-blue Egyptian tunic, heavy gold necklaces and wristbands, and his jet-black hair was long and well-oiled, gathered at his nape. His beard, also black, was short and pointed. I looked at Miryam. She smiled crookedly and waved a hand; later, the gesture said.

Kisil observed him with a curious expression, not of contempt exactly, but of a kind of dry amusement. "What would you have me do?" he asked. "Cast this staff down and make it a serpent?" He pointed at the brick pits. "Change that mud into gold?" He lifted a hand. "Turn this hand white with leprosy, then cleanse it in an instant? Can I make The One God, the King of the Universe — the *ONE* — do tricks for you, like a trained dog?"

He shook his head, then lifted a hand again, this time in command and emphasis. "No one commands Ehyehuwah," he said. "But I SPEAK FOR HIM!" His voice, even with his lisp, was thunder, lightning, booming and cracking into the night air like the fire of God Himself. "You may believe, or not! It matters not to Him — but it will matter to *you! You must CHOOSE!"*

And then there came a rumble, a kind of uneasy growl, through the earth — a shaking that one could not hear, but only feel — like those which we had felt in the desert, but deeper, stronger, longer. The crowd fell silent, and their eyes widened. Miryam's calm was finally penetrated. Her mouth too fell open, and she looked at the earth — then back up at Kisil.

The people looked at each other in fear and wonder, then back at my husband, who stood there like a rock, unmoving, looking back at them. Kisil alone, among all of us, showed no surprise.

51

Another voice spoke up then, an ancient voice, cracked and quavering with age. "He IS the Deliverer!" Many turned to face the speaker, who sat on a stool that had been brought for him. He leaned on a stick he held before him in both hands.

"His name is Yonasan," whispered Miryam, her eyes still wide. "He is among the last of the Elders. He is much respected..." She seemed out of breath.

"How do you know, Grandfather?" asked a man nearby with great respect. "Was it the shaking of the earth?"

The ancient shook his head. "Nay," he said. "Not the quaking. He spoke the *words*. *'I have surely heard — I have surely remembered — you will surely remember.'* I have those words from my fathers, and they from their fathers before them. They can only be spoken by the Deliverer, and they are to be a sign to us that he has come."

I glanced up at Kisil. His expression had not changed. I think that only I could see the surprise in his eyes.

The elder turned to a bald man, even older than he, who leaned on the arm of a younger man standing nearby. "Is it not so, Chaninah?" They had both been given places of honor, near the front.

"It is." Chaninah's voice was a high-pitched whisper, but it carried in the silence. His eyes were white with the frost of age, but he smiled and nodded. "Those are the words. I am blind, but I can hear. Praise —" He hesitated, then went on. "Praise *Ehyehuwah*, that I have lived to hear them and to learn His name."

I heard the murmuring, the gasps and exclamations, of the crowd as the word passed among them that the elders had spoken. I wondered what would happen next. To my surprise, Yonasan then turned to the woman sitting beside me. "What say you, Teacher?"

Teacher, I thought. Even the elders deferred to Miryam. Her authority must be great indeed.

Miryam stood, and was silent. There was no sound from the people. She knows how to command a crowd's attention too, I thought.

"I think —" She paused. "That we have a new Teacher." She turned, and with great ceremony, spread her hands wide and bowed deeply to her younger brother.

The people gasped as one, and they looked up at Kisil in wonder. I had the feeling that Miryam had never bowed to anyone.

"What would you have us do — Moses?" asked Aron, more subdued now.

Kisil turned his face toward the palace. "For now, only wait," he said, and he pointed. "I shall go to the king and tell him what Ehyehuwah commands. I shall tell him to his face." Then he turned and pointed at his brother. "And you, Aron — you shall go with me."

"Me?" said Aron, shocked. He was afraid now, not angry. His eyes cut toward his sister, then back again.

"Yes. Ehyehuwah has laid His hand upon me, my brother, and now I lay mine upon you. Will you go?"

Aron's eyes widened. He looked at his sister, than back at his brother. He swallowed, then nodded — a little shakily, I thought. "If The One stands with us, how can I not go? I will go... my brother. My — Deliverer."

Kisil beckoned, and held out his hand. Aron took it and climbed up. A heartbeat later, the two sets of gray eyes met, and a link was formed at that moment that had never been theirs as children. The younger brother was the leader now, and the older would follow.

They both turned then, to Miryam. "Join us, my sister," said Kisil, and held out a hand to her as well. With the assistance of some of the women, and myself, she climbed up and joined them. The three of them stood together. Using a gesture I had never seen before, Aron and Miryam lifted their hands and blessed the people, using words I did not know. The people responded with more words, all together. Then there was a silence.

Kisil stepped forward. "Now go back to your huts. Fear nothing. We shall not leave tomorrow, nor the day after; but the day of liberation is near. Ehyehuwah, our God, commands it, and there is no one on Earth who can stop its coming. Watch and see! He will set His people free with His own mighty Hand!"

The people seemed confused and disoriented, not knowing what to do. But then Miryam clapped her hands and sang out, "Ehyehuwah has remembered us! The Deliverer has come!" She lifted her hands and gestured, a kind of beckoning, circling movement; and out of nowhere, a circle of women formed, smiling and laughing. More of the people began to smile and nod. Miryam climbed down, and the women surrounded her and began to dance. As the people clapped in rhythm, they began circling around her — and she sang again, "Ehyehuwah has remembered us! The Deliverer has come!"

The women dancing around her responded in unison, "Praised is Ehyehuwah, and blessed is his Name!" I saw other circles forming, throughout the crowd, and other women leading the chant. They danced and sang, the call-and-response ringing forth gaily as the people laughed and clapped and cheered. "Ehyehuwah has remembered us! The Deliverer has come!" "Praised is Ehyehuwah, and blessed is His Name!"

We saw Egyptians, some guards, some not, watching from above the compound. None moved to stop us.

52

The feast began, and a merry one it was, for all that the people were tired and muddy and had little to offer. Even the house-slaves and overseers joined in, though some did so reluctantly. Some, the surliest, went back to their huts scoffing.

Desan and Aviram were among those, and so was the other man, the small one who had questioned Kisil. Miryam told me later that his name was Kodah. He was the head entertainer for the king, the chief and the most highly regarded of all the singers, dancers, jugglers and acrobats in the palace. He was one of the most favored of the Avru slaves. It was not strange that he did not welcome the Deliverer. His place and his honor were secure among the Egyptians.

The people ate, and laughed, and talked, till late. The night was dark, without a Moon, and the only light came from the low fires. I wondered how much more festive the night would have been had there been wine.

Finally, Miryam stood and raised her hands. There was a brief silence, and then a murmuring rippled through the people. It was some sort of prayer or chant, I think, but I could not make out the words.

She raised her voice and spoke. "The day of liberation is coming. The day for which we have waited for so long is, at last, at hand. Give thanks, O Children of Yaacov. Give thanks, and praise, and be grateful. And be joyous!"

She lifted her hands again, and repeated the words of blessing she had used earlier with Aron and Kisil. The people responded again, and then they began to go back to their huts, talking quietly, looking back at Kisil, smiling, even waving. He waved back. I beckoned to Gershom, and we began making our way back toward our hut. I carried little Eliezer in my arms. He was fast asleep.

I stopped at the door of the hut and looked around at the people. Some lingered and watched the two gray-eyed men and the woman as they walked toward us, watching with wonder in their faces, and fear, and uncertainty — and that other expression, which I finally recognized.

It was *hope*.

That night we sat together, Kisil and I, in the empty hut that had been given us. Aron had asked us to share his, but Kisil had insisted that we have our own space. I knew why; Kisil needed to be alone with me and our sons. Especially that night.

I was rocking Eliezer in my arms; Gershom was sleeping soundly, as children will even in the most exciting times. Kisil was sitting on the upturned tub again, staring at the earth floor.

His hands were shaking.

"Did you hear, Tzipporah?" he asked, his voice as shaky as his hands. "Did you hear? Did you hear what I said?" He looked up at me, his eyes wide, as if in fear.

"I heard, my love."

"I know nothing of any special words. I said what I thought they would want to hear. They were — only words. *My* words." His gaze returned to the floor, and he shook his head.

"It worked out well. Would you not say so, Kisil? And the earth moving — that did no harm, as well."

He looked up again, his mouth and eyes wide — and then he smiled, and in another heartbeat, he laughed. I joined him; Gershom stirred, and laughed a little with us, not knowing why, but he was soon asleep again. We tried to stifle out laughter to keep from waking him again, but we could not; we laughed, with our robes gathered over our mouths, till our tears ran.

"Truly — truly, my sweet bird," he finally gasped, struggling to catch his breath. "Truly, I know not what I would do without you. You are —" His face twisted, the laughter coming on him again. "You are — a *miracle*," he said, and then we were off, laughing again as if we were mad.

Finally, we regained control of ourselves. As I wiped my eyes, I thought: Kisil was a simple man at heart, and that was the secret of his strength. Kisil's only thought was to speak the truth, and to do what is right. He was like that from the moment I met him, and he was like that till the end. He was an empty vessel in that way — and, I think, that is why Ehyehuwah could fill him. Kisil would go back and forth, from filled with the power and authority of God Himself, to uncertain and doubtful and astonished, all his life.

At least, that is what I believe — that God spoke through him. I have heard it said that only Kisil — only Moses — knew whether God truly spoke to him or not; but I knew my husband, and even he did not know.

I knew what to say that night. That was not always true, but that night it was. "Could you have done anything else, my love?"

He looked at me, startled, the grin still on his face. After a heartbeat, he shook his head, still smiling. "No. No. All the time I was speaking, I was thinking, 'What should I say to them? What do they believe, about this Deliverer?' And I did my best to play that part. But I did not know, not with certainty... How strange that the words came out — so right."

"Not so strange, my husband. Did you not feel the power in your words as you spoke?"

He frowned. "What power?"

"Did you not see how enthralled the people were? Did you not notice their silence?"

He shrugged. "No. I felt nothing. I was too caught up in thinking of what to say."

"The words that the old man recognized — 'I have surely remembered' — did you know those words before?" I watched his face. "Did you feel that you were *remembering* them? From when you were on the Mountain, before the fire, perhaps?"

He blinked, and his face went curiously blank.

Then he shook his head. "No," he said. "No. There were no words, no thoughts, when I was before the fire. When I came down, I knew that I was to go to Egypt, and that only." He shook his head again. "No. No. I remember choosing my words, thinking about what the people wanted to hear. That their God remembered them..."

"The very thing you have carried with you all these years," I said softly. "The anger at Him, because He had not."

A change came over his face then. It grew solemn, then sad. "Yes," he breathed. "Yes."

He looked away then. I saw his mouth trying to find words, but none came. I saw his eyes fill. "Am I the Deliverer, Tzipporah? Me?"

I took his hand, and squeezed. "Yes, Kisil. You are. There is no denying it." I felt my own eyes grow wet again, though not from laughter. "Do you understand what you have to do?"

His face was both bleak and determined. "Yes. I must speak for Ehyehuwah."

"Yes, Kisil. Your voice is His voice."

"But I am only a man!"

"What other voice will He ever have, my love?"

He lifted his right hand, the one I was not holding. It was still quivering. He looked at it, then made a fist — and nodded. Then he rose and walked to the door of the hut and looked out, his eyes seeking the horizon.

I could tell from his posture that he was in that faraway place again, and I knew better than to disturb him.

After a while, he turned and spoke. "My sister is their High Priestess."

"Yes. So Aron said. And the old man, Yonasan, called her Teacher."

"I have to include her. She should not feel her authority threatened." He returned to the bed and sat down.

"You have already asked her to be *your* teacher, and she has agreed."

"That is true."

I lifted a hand, and he looked at me. I pointed at him. "And she can see that Ehyehuwah is with you, Kisil. She is proud of her position, anyone can see that; but she does serve The One. And she can see as well as anyone here that you speak for Him. Whether you believe it or not," I added quickly, seeing his frown. "*She* does. And because of Miryam — they *all* will."

Kisil shivered and sat down. "Why did it have to be me?"

I understood. When he was absorbed in his task, he was the strongest, bravest, and most charismatic man that had ever been. He was — Moses, the Deliverer. But when he was alone, or alone with me — he was just Kisil, the wanderer, the exile. Still unsure, still a little lost, and still very afraid, even as he tried to do right as best he could.

I knelt beside him and took both his hands in mine.

"Because you are Kisil — and because you are *Moses.* Because you are the man you are. Because of the life you have lived. It has prepared you for this." I kissed his trembling hands. "Do you not see, Kisil? You were chosen for this before you were born, just as the legends said, just as your sister dreamed. And everything that has ever happened to you —"

"Was leading to this." He spoke softly, his speech deeply impaired again. His lisp was always prominent when he was tired.

"You told the people not to fear, my love. And I, your wife — I tell you the same. You, too, should have no fear. When you speak, the words will come, as they did tonight. And perhaps the earth will move again."

Kisil blinked, and straightened a bit at that. Then he nodded, and nodded again. He lay back on the pallet and gazed thoughtfully at the thatching above us.

I took out my flute and played, and soon all three of my men were asleep. I watched them, and for a while they all seemed alike. Children, innocent and trusting, and Kisil the most trusting, and most innocent, of all.

53

"When will we go to the king?" asked Aron.

We were sitting round the walls of our hut early the following morning, eating the hard bread that the Egyptians provided their slaves. There was a little cheese too, and some strips of dried mutton. It was still dark, and we ate by the light of a single lamp.

Miryam, who was holding Eliezer on her lap, listened with interest. My husband chewed, swallowed, and then said, "When the time is right. A few days, I think. No more, surely." Kisil spoke as casually as if he had been asked when he would put on his sandals. He had not looked up at Aron. He was smiling at Gershom, who was playing with his little brother.

Aron watched the boys too, and I wondered if it put him in mind of his own childhood with his little brother Kisil; and then I remembered that Aron and Kisil had not grown up in the same house. Miryam was smiling at our children too, but with a melancholy air, and I guessed that she was thinking the same thing.

Aron spoke again. "Will — will Ehyehuwah speak to you and tell you when it is time?"

Kisil looked back at him, then at Miryam, then said, "He will." He did not look at me.

I knew — both Kisil and I knew — that it was not that simple, but it was probably better not to speak of that. Not then, not at that time and place.

"You sound afraid, my brother," said Kisil.

"He is," said Miryam, before Aron could speak. "So are many of the people. And they have reason to be afraid," she added, lifting an admonitory finger, a teacher's gesture. "They remember what happened to the Eframites."

Aron nodded somberly. "I had thought of that."

"Who are the Eframites?" asked Kisil innocently. I had never heard the name.

Miryam frowned. "Who *were* they, you mean. The Eframites were once a large family, descended from one of the sons of Yusuf, the last-but-one of the Twelve Brothers. They decided to go from Egypt, to go home to the Land, without the king's leave. The rest of us tried to make them stay — I speak as if I were there, but this was long before my time — but they refused and left. Or tried to leave."

"What happened?" I asked.

Miryam turned. "They were murdered," she said, her voice flat and expressionless. "A few survivors came back to tell of it. When they had traveled for a few days, the king sent troops, chariot soldiers with swords and spears. The Eframites were slaughtered without mercy, almost all of them. A few escaped, and a few never left. There are few Eframites left among us today."

"I see." Kisil chewed thoughtfully. "Thank you. I had heard of that story, but I did not know the name of the Eframites, nor the details. That is something I should know." He paused, then added, "I am certain that there is much more that I should know."

We sat silent for a few heartbeats, then Aron returned to his question. "When do you think — Ehyehuwah — will tell you to go?" He was still less than comfortable using the Name, as I think they all were.

Kisil's indistinct voice was soft. "I have no way of knowing, brother. But it will be soon. I am certain of that."

"What else has He told you?" asked Miryam, who was sitting on the only stool.

Kisil's face was impassive, and he did not answer. "We must begin our lessons soon, my sister. I have much to learn."

She looked at him for a breath, her face as impassive as his, then she nodded. "Perhaps today. I suggest we sit with Yonasan and Chaninah, and let them share the tales of our fathers with you. They know them better than anyone, and they love to tell them."

"I would like that very much."

"May I come too?" I asked. "And Gershom? Eliezer is not old enough —"

"Bring them both," said Miryam with a warm smile. "I shall go and speak to the elders." She left the hut, her erect bearing and air of authority intact.

Kisil had not answered her question. I wondered what she had made of that.

54

As the sun rose, the hut grew more crowded. We all stood as the elders of the Avru entered. There were not many of them. They came in, one by one, and I realized that this was a sort of council. No one had planned it or called them; they just came.

A few more stools were brought in for the oldest. Yonasan, the ancient who had first declared Kisil the Deliverer, and blind Chaninah who had confirmed it, were given seats of honor.

I gathered that Aron was considered one of the Avru's elders as well. Desan, the tall, heavyset man who had so rudely questioned Kisil, and his brother Aviram were there too, though no one seemed particularly glad to see them. Miryam told me later that they had invited themselves to the informal council, arrogantly claiming their places as former overseers and intermediaries with the Egyptians. The two brought a few of their followers with them, big men all, some still overseers, some workers in the Egyptians' smithies and stables. I thought of the Melikites at the well. No one looked directly at these men, but no one failed to make space for them, either. Some even bowed a bit as they passed.

The early-morning meeting would be short. Kisil had little to say beyond the things he had said the night before. Standing before them, he assured everyone in the room that he would go to the king in a day or two, and advised them to be patient. Some made to leave then, but Desan and

Aviram and their cronies did not move. Desan stepped forward and pointed at Kisil arrogantly.

"Do you think you can come here and order us about as if you are the king yourself?" asked the big man belligerently. He was much taller than Kisil, and heavier, clearly accustomed to using his size to intimidate others. He moved close to Kisil and glared down at him imperiously, and the others he had brought moved in close behind him to reinforce the implied threat.

Kisil ignored this ploy, smiling up at the former overseer. He leaned back on the table and crossed his arms casually. Suddenly the larger man seemed inferior to the smaller, who stood entirely at ease and was clearly not afraid at all. Kisil cocked his head curiously.

"I order no one," he said mildly. "No one but the king." Then he added, "In the name of our God, of course." He grinned easily.

"Why should *we* want to leave Egypt?" the tall man pressed. "Some of us have done very well here!" The men behind him frowned, chins thrust forward. Though his words were spoken in a growl and were intended to be a challenge, they came out sounding oddly like a whine. He brushed a calloused hand over his close-cropped scalp, a gesture somehow both challenging and vain.

Kisil's smile vanished. He faced Desan, his eyes level and hard as flint. I had seen them like that only once before, at a well not far from the Mountain.

He spoke softly in his thick, clumsy voice. "Yes, you have done well." He paused, and his eyes glittered in the lamplight. "By siding with your people's enemies and oppressors, licking their sandals like whipped dogs, and betraying your own kind." His voice was still soft and mild, but with steel beneath it. He had not moved.

There was a muted intake of breath, and eyes widened. Desan, swelling up and turning crimson, sputtered, "No one can speak to me like —"

Kisil cut him off. "I can, Desan. I do. And I speak the truth. You know it to be so. If you and your men there..." He lifted his chin to indicate the men standing behind Desan, "...want to stay in Egypt and remain servile dogs in the Egyptians' privy — then stay! No one here will stop you, or miss you when we go." Kisil's arms were still crossed, his posture still that of a man at ease.

The tall man was outraged, his eyes blazing with fury. He began to move forward, chest out and fists balled at his sides and rising. His brother and the others made as if to follow. It was another intimidation move, intended to cow lesser men. It was clear that they had used it before. The others in the room drew back a step, fearful of what they were about to see.

I can still see that scene, as if it happened only this morning. The tense faces in the light of the lamps, the rising sun only beginning to lighten the doorway, the people watching, wide-eyed and fearful. Their fear of Desan and his gang was clear on their faces, and Desan's confidence and arrogance were clear as well.

The big men began to surround Kisil. He stood away from the table, dropped his arms, and took a stance that suggested readiness, but not aggression. His hands were open and slightly raised, his feet well apart, weight forward, head erect. His eyes bored into Desan's.

I knew that stance; he had taught it to me and my sisters. I knew well what could be done from that posture. I thought about standing with him, but I had the boys in my lap — and I knew, as well, that this was something that Kisil had to do alone.

His eyes were cold, his hands steady. All his attention was on Desan. He faced him squarely, and somehow, even though he was almost a head shorter, Kisil seemed the stronger man. Of all the Avru in the room, only my husband showed no fear.

I saw Kisil's eyes, and I knew what they were saying to Desan: *Whatever happens, you will be first.*

His eyes never left the larger man's. Then, Kisil cocked his head slightly, as if to say, "Well?"

I too watched, as caught up in that confrontation as anyone — but I felt no fear. I knew that Kisil was the Deliverer sent by God —

But then I remembered that Kisil himself had no such assurance. As far as he knew, he was on his own. I looked at him, and I saw that his confidence came from himself only. And indeed, I knew what Kisil could do, even without his staff. I smiled at the thought, and one or two of Desan's men noticed. They stepped back.

Desan sensed that something was wrong. Kisil was older and shorter than he, but he was not afraid, not at all —

and the big man and his followers were not accustomed to that.

The former overseer's eyes betrayed him first. His eyes shifted downward, then to his brother. After another heartbeat of hesitation, during which Kisil's eyes never left his face, he dropped his fists and stepped back. He looked confused, as did Aviram beside him. The others looked at each other, puzzled, unsure of what to do. None of them had ever encountered this kind of man, I thought.

Then I smiled to myself. No one had. There had never before been such a man.

Kisil stepped forward, and this time time Desan and his gang stepped back — retreating before one man, alone. They hardly seemed aware of it.

"Get out." Kisil indicated the door with his chin. His hands did not move, and his eyes stayed on Desan's. "There is nothing for you here. Nothing to say, nothing to learn — *and no one here fears you.*" He turned away and gestured dismissively. "Go, run back to your masters. Tell them that the Deliverer has come."

Then Kisil turned back, and smiled.

It was a smile that I had never seen on his face before — the smile of a jackal that sees helpless prey, a smile of savage delight. Then he hissed, "Perhaps they will *reward* you for bringing them the news..." His grin widened.

Desan and Aviram paled, and without another word, they fled, followed by the other men. There were only six of them in all, though they had seemed more. Six, I thought, smiling to myself. I had seen Kisil face that number before.

They could still be seen through the doorway, almost running across the wadi. Kisil's laughter — and, after an instant of shocked disbelief, everyone's — followed them.

Kisil relaxed then, his air of watchful readiness gone, and he turned to speak to those who were left. He gestured at the door, waving away Desan and the rest as he would have waved away so many gnats. "Do not fear them. They have no power over you. They never had any, but that which you gave them yourselves."

"But the Egyptians —" A man began. His name, I later learned, was Calev. He was another good-looking young man, with flashing black eyes and a great puff of tightly curled black hair, much like my own. I noticed that he had a long scar down his cheek that reminded me of my father's. He has reason to fear the Egyptians, I thought.

Kisil laughed. "The Egyptians would not come to their rescue. Did you think they would? If all of you turned on Desan and his cronies, and beat them, or even killed them — what do you think the Egyptians would do?"

He smiled coldly. "They would watch — and laugh. They have no love for those — creatures. They have more respect for those who stamp the mud." His eyes swept the room, taking in everyone who stood there. "You remain true to your own people. Desan and his thugs cringe and crawl, for all their pretense of strength. You know this to be true," he finished. "And so do the Egyptians."

The people saw the truth of it, and then they blinked at each other, and stood a little straighter. It was astonishing, how my husband's clumsy, lisping words held such authority.

The blind ancient, Chaninah, spoke in his high, raspy voice. "We have teachers, Moses. We have elders, and men and women who are thought wise." The old man paused. "But we have not, until this day, had a *leader*." He lifted a frail hand as if blessing Kisil. "We are glad you have come."

Others began to speak, echoing his words, but Kisil stopped them.

"I have not *come*, Grandfather," said Kisil with great respect. He bent and held the old man's shoulders. "I have been *sent*. Remember that. Do not look to me for your redemption. Look to The One who sent me."

He turned then to the rest. "I must study with your elders and learn the ways and teachings of our people. Ehyehuwah has sent me; but I know so little of my own, so little of those to whom I have been sent." He bowed, hands over his heart, an expression of humility. "Give me time, my brothers, my sisters. Give me time to become one of you. The day of liberation will come soon, I promise you."

It was light outside now. Kisil snuffed the lamp nearest him, then lifted both hands. "Now go back to your homes and your families, before you go to the pits. Tell them to wait, and hope. There is nothing to decide, nothing to discuss, today."

Then he smiled, lifted a cautioning hand, and added, "And when you go to your tasks, do not show the overseers disrespect and give them an excuse to punish you. Desan will expect that. No, smile at them, be more respectful than ever, and do as you are told, and quickly." He grinned broadly. "Do it happily, and do not hide your happiness. The day of liberation is near. You have reason to be happy." Then he inclined his head at the door through which Desan and his gang had fled. "Some of them may wish to join us when they realize that there will soon be no one here for them to — supervise."

There was a little cautious laughter at that, and then more. "And we will have need of housemaids, and cooks, and grooms as well, perhaps," said the young man named Calev, and there was more laughter.

"Yes!" Kisil grinned. "Let them all join us, if they wish! We have all had to find ways to survive here. Their way was no worse and no better than yours, though the way some have treated their brothers — that must change. But still, we are all Avru. Yes, even Desan. Do not forget that."

After a few more words of encouragement, they began to leave in twos and threes. Aron, too, left, saying he must return to his work. He was a master craftsman in metal, in charge of seeing that a bell that he had cast a few days before was properly unmolded.

I had noticed how closely he resembled Kisil and thought little of it. It seemed natural; they were brothers, after all. Only then did I realize that part of the resemblance was that Aron, too, had tiny scars on his face and arms, just as Kisil did. Aron's were from sprays of molten metal, Kisil's from molten stone. I thought on it, but I could make nothing of it but coincidence.

55

Kisil saw the people out, with words of encouragement for a few. Then he returned to the table, where Miryam and the elders were still seated, and put his hand on that of Chaninah, so the old man would know he was addressing him. "Please stay for a while, Grandfather. I have need of your wisdom and your learning. You, too, my elder," he added, turning to Yonasan. "Honor me with your presence and your words, as well. And you, of course, elder sister," he said to Miryam with warmth in his eyes.

Then Kisil sat down before them — humbly, on the floor, at their feet. "I am your student. Please, Grandfathers — teach me. Teach me, my sister. I am but a child in your hands."

Chaninah smiled, and Yonasan nodded. Miryam looked positively beatific.

"Very well, Moses — Kisil..." She paused. "What would you be called?" she asked.

Kisil thought. "I have taken back my Avru birth-name. But the king knows me as Moses, and it is to give him the command of Ehyehuwah that I have come. Let me be called — Moses."

Miryam nodded solemnly. "Moses you shall be."

"Moses," repeated the two ancient ones.

Chaninah thought. "That is the name that will be remembered — Kisil." His blind eyes sparkled as if with a secret joke.

Miryam beckoned, and I sat on the floor beside my husband. Gershom took his place between us. Eliezer was in my arms, still dozing.

Chaninah could not see us, but when the old man heard our movements cease, he lifted a hand, palm out, in a sort of ritual gesture, and began.

"In the beginning, when Ehyehuwah was creating the world, nothing had form. Everything was tumbled together. All was confusion, meaningless chaos.

"And Ehyehuwah moved through the chaos, and brought order to it with only His words. He spoke, and said, 'Let light be"; and light was. The light was divided from the darkness, and they became separate things. There was light, and there was darkness; evening, and morning. The first day..."

He went on, and Kisil, and Gershom, and I, we all listened. The stories were of how The One had made the world and all that was in it, of the making of the first man and the first woman, and of the things that happened after that. Those stories were more tale and song and legend than history, a way of teaching about ideas more than things that really happened. There were hints of this throughout.

At first, it all seemed to follow a formula, like an ancient chant: "...and evening and morning were the second day..." — and the third, and the fourth and fifth and sixth. The first man was named "Mankind." His name meant "Blood," and his wife's "Breath." It was, in some ways, a child's story. God was said to walk in the garden, as a human would; animals spoke, and angels with flaming swords stood guard. It was a tale of a dream-world, but as with ordinary dreams, there was a truth to it and a meaning that went beyond the things that were seen and heard there.

Chaninah's voice was old and cracked with age, but the words were magical. As Eliezer dozed against my side, we were all swept away in the ancient story.

Later, after that morning's time of learning had ended, Kisil put in his time in the brick pits while it was light. We ate together, he and I and our sons, and then we spent the evening with Miryam and the elders once again, learning more. They continued their lessons, telling him the stories of his people, the same stories that have been passed down ever since.

The next night, the stories changed. They began to be about real people, ancestors of the Avru. These were not mystic giants in some unknown dream-time, as some of the men in the earlier tales were. They were not perfect heroes out of legend, but had faults, did wrong, and were foolish like other men.

We learned of that enigmatic, contradictory man, Avram, for whom this people was named; and of his son, Yitzhak, and the shocking story of how Avram had been commanded to kill him, and almost did.

We learned of Avram's grandson, Yaacov, and how Yitzhak and Yaacov met their wives and had children of their own. We learned of the twelve sons of Yaacov, the fathers of the Twelve Families, and all of all that passed between them.

I felt privileged that we were allowed to listen, I and my sons. Though Eliezer often slept, I thought Gershom found the stories fascinating, and both boys behaved well. One day, those words will be written, I was sure. I still am. They will be pored over and studied and argued about through the generations. At least, that is my hope. Such words ought not be forgotten. I thought of my father, and how much he would love hearing them.

Kisil spoke little and asked few questions as the elders taught him, but now and then he would lift a hand to stop them and inquire about something. Once, he stopped them and asked a question with a hint of urgency in his impaired voice that was, I think, apparent only to me.

"When Ehyehuwah called Avram — did He call him in words? Could Avram hear him?"

Yonasan waved a hand, and Chaninah shook his head. "No?" asked Kisil.

"I do not say *no*," said the blind ancient with a surprisingly white-toothed smile. "I am saying — *who can know?* Avram never said. We know that God spoke to him, but we know not how."

Miryam put in, "It is said that at times, God appeared to him in dreams."

"There is a legend, too, that once God appeared to him in person." This was Yonasan. "A real man," he went on. "He ate and drank with him."

Chaninah spoke in his high, aged whisper. "And his grandson Yaacov. He had an encounter with God as a real man, too." The old man shrugged. "It is said that he wrestled with God all night."

"Wrestled with God?" exclaimed Kisil. I could see the shock on his face. "But —"

"God has no form, no. No body. No face. That is our belief." Yonasan, too, shrugged. "We have no story that explains this tradition."

I knew that that was not the reason for Kisil's thunderstruck expression, but the elder did not.

Miryam coughed lightly. "There may be an explanation, even so. There is a story that has been passed down among the women, Grandfather. It is said to have begun with Leah, one of Yaacov's wives. It is said among us that Yaacov was ill, and only wrestled with The One in a fever dream."

Kisil frowned judiciously and nodded. He had regained control of himself and said nothing about what had happened to him.

"That does not mean that it was not God, still," Miryam went on. Kisil did not look at me, but I saw a finger lift on his left hand, the one nearest me, and I knew that small gesture was for me only; *say nothing*. He need not have warned me.

Yonasan spoke. "As I said; God speaks as He chooses to speak. Dream or not, Yaacov had a new name after that night, and now all our people bear it."

"What name?" Kisil asked.

A new name, I thought. Just as Kisil himself had been given a new name. Just as he had learned God's name on the Mountain.

"Yisrael," said Yonasan. "It means, 'Struggles with God.'" He lifted both hands. "It fits us all."

"That may very well be," put in Chaninah thoughtfully. "About the dream. I had not heard that story —"

"We women keep our own traditions," said Miryam solemnly, but with a glitter in her eyes. We looked at each other, and she saw something in mine, I knew.

It occurred to me later that, once again, none of them had asked Kisil the obvious question.

How had God chosen to speak to *him*?

56

The next morning, Kisil surprised me. When I awoke, he had been up for some time — and he was rubbing a bronze razor on a flat stone, a basin of water nearby. He was preparing to shave his beard and cut his hair, I knew. "Kisil, what — ?"

Then I realized that he had also changed his clothes. He was not wearing the long woolen robes of our people, but a short tunic of Egyptian cotton. His head covering, too, lying nearby, was in the Egyptian style— similar to that of Midyan, but again of white cotton.

I watched as he sharpened the razor. "Where did you get that?"

"It was in my bag. I kept it. I suppose I knew I would come back one day."

When Aron came into the hut, his wife Elisheva behind him, he stared at Kisil sharpening the shining blade. "What are you doing? Are we going to kill the king?"

Kisil gave a snort of laughter. "No, my brother. I am shaving my beard and cutting my hair, in the Egyptian manner." He examined the edge of the razor judiciously, then resumed stroking it on the stone. "I go to see the king, but there are many doors between us. I will pass through them much more easily if I look like the man he remembers. After that—" He shrugged. "It is in God's hands."

Aron's mouth worked uncertainly, but then he nodded at the sense of it. "What will you call him?"

"I shall call him 'Uncle.' That was his name to me, when I was a child. He was not king then, his father was. He was another prince — older than I by a few years, but I was still of almost equal rank."

Aron chewed on that, It must taste bitter to him, I thought, but he made no reply. I asked, more to change the subject than anything else, "What is the king's name?"

"The king?" He paused, then grinned. "His name is Tuth-Mose."

I blinked. Now I understood why Kisil had insisted on using his birth name when we met.

As he lifted the razor to inspect its edge again, I asked, "Kisil, are you sure? You speak on behalf of the Avru. Should you not look like one of them?"

"One of *us*," said Aron. He and Elisheva smiled at me, and at the boys, who were still asleep. I smiled back. I understood that we, as well as my husband, were being accepted into the family.

Kisil stopped and thought. He looked up at Aron, so like him, and then he gazed into the small copper mirror he had taken from his bag for a few heartbeats. Then he shrugged.

"Why is it that wives are so often right?" he grumbled, and the three of us laughed. Kisil grinned and put the shaving implements away. He took out his long, woolen robe again — a Midyanite pattern, but similar to the Avru's weave — and changed back into it.

It was not many breaths later when Kisil took his staff, ready to leave. I looked at my husband, and he looked at me. That familiar wry smile twisted his mouth. "Well, my wild bird, are you not coming?"

I laughed and wrapped a shawl around my shoulders. Elishevah would care for our sons.

The three of us set off. Kisil carried his old fabric bag, his waterskin, and his staff — just as he had when I saw him for the first time.

Outside, a strong wind was blowing dust in from the north, and it was thick in the air. We began to cough, and shielded our eyes. I suddenly realized that this should not be. To the north was the ocean, and the air should have been clean and fresh.

It was not. The wind carried a fine pale dust — and when I licked my lips, I knew what it was; it was ash. Not the burning ash that irritated the skin, but it was ash, nonetheless. Kisil, without speaking, tied a corner of his head covering over his mouth and nose, desert fashion. Aron and I did the same.

On our way to the rude opening in the mound of trash that served as a boundary to the Avru compound, Desan, with his brother, stepped from behind a hut and confronted us. He held a short, heavy stick in his fist, thicker at the far end — a bludgeon. Aviram was similarly armed.

"We are not finished, you and I," the big man snarled. With no further word, he raised his club and lunged, his brother attacking at the same time, heedless of the whirling dust in the air. Both of them were attacking Kisil, ignoring Aron and me. Two big men, both with weapons, assaulting a smaller and older one. It could have been bad, but before Aron or I could move to help, it was over.

I could not see how he had done it, but Kisil somehow stepped to the side and spun Desan squarely into his brother. The two collided with some force, but quickly turned and tried again. Once more, Kisil did not oppose them directly, but dodged to the side and let Desan charge forward — only to trip over Kisil's foot, which hooked the big man's ankle and jerked back just as Kisil dealt him a sharp shove between the shoulders. Desan went sprawling, but Kisil plucked the stick from his hand as he fell and whipped it back across Aviram's face as the other man tried to step over his brother and swing his own weapon.

Blood spurted from Aviram's nose, and Kisil drove a knuckle into the other man's chest, low down, just above his stomach. He went down gasping for breath, and Kisil turned and dropped to his knees — on Desan's back, as he was struggling to rise. The short club was suddenly across the big man's throat. Desan was helpless.

By this time a few Avru had gathered to watch. Kisil forced the big man's head back, lifting his chin with the club. He leaned down and spoke, in a low voice that was chillingly cold and controlled:

"Do you understand, now, how easily I can kill you?" When Desan did not answer, Kisil pulled at the stick harder. *"Do you?"*

"Yuh-yes," came the strangled reply.

A further twist of the stick emphasized Kisil's next words: "If you ever attack me or mine again — *I will.* Do not forget that, Desan."

He stood, picked up Aviram's stick, and flung them both into the mound of trash behind the huts with a disgusted air. He bent to retrieve his staff, and I only then realized that he had thrown it down at the start of the attack. He beckoned, and the three of us continued on our way toward the gate.

"What if they had attacked you with knives, brother?" asked Aron. "Would it have ended differently?"

Kisil nodded, though he did not turn to look at him. "Oh, yes. If they had tried to use blades, one or both of them would now be dead."

I looked back at the pair sitting on the ground in the swirling dust. Aviram was getting his breath back, and stared after Kisil with nothing but wide-eyed terror; but Desan was rubbing his throat and watching us with the blackest expression of sheer, poisonous hatred that I have ever seen, before or since.

Kisil did not look back.

At the unmarked boundary of the slaves' encampment, we passed the first guards easily enough. Two bored Egyptians, burly men with whips but with little interest in those whom they watched, were seated under a rude awning. As we approached, they rose together and stepped forward to ask where we were going. They were much occupied with weeping, burning eyes and dry mouths, and hardly seemed interested in the answer — till Kisil spoke.

"We are commanded to appear before the king," he said simply. The guards looked at each other blankly and hesitated, uncertain. Kisil smiled and added, "Perhaps you should send to the king and inform him that he will have to wait."

They waved us on and resumed their seats, coughing in the wind-driven ash.

"Kisil — is it wise to lie to the king's guards?" asked Aron diffidently.

Kisil replied, his eyes twinkling above the cloth covering his face. "I did not lie. I did not say that it was the *king* who commanded us." He lifted a hand. "They can think what they like."

A short time later, Aron spoke, to ask a question I had asked once before: "Where did you learn to fight like that?"

And he got the same answer. "In a land far away, long ago."

"Do you think Desan will try again?" I asked.

"Not like that. But we should be wary. He was right in what he said. We are not finished, he and I."

57

We made our way through the streets, going uphill. They were still busy, though not as crowded as when we had first arrived. People were hiding from the dust, with cloths draped over their doors. Even so, there was some sort of procession moving slowly down the broad main avenue of the town. Priests were carrying idols on platforms held by four men each, others were swinging smoking pots of scented resins, priestesses in white robes dancing before them and playing timbrels and flutes. The smell of the incense was sour and acrid, and the music was cacophonous and unpleasant to my ears. How strange, I thought, that the music of my own harsh land was so much sweeter. We waited as they passed, then went on our way.

The palace of Tuth-Mose stood atop a hill overlooking the river, where Kisil had pointed it out to Gershom and me before. It was not far. The king liked to supervise the building projects himself at times, or at least pretend that he did. According to Kisil, this small residence was nothing like the complex of temples and palaces and houses and stables in the capital. Still, it was bigger and grander than any building that I had ever seen, with its painted pillars the height of many men, each wider than the hut we had slept in the night before.

The square in front of the palace was crowded. There were petitioners waiting to see the king, peddlers selling them food, drink and other goods, courtiers eager for a chance to sell their influence, and, of course, provocatively dressed women — and a few men — with particularly heavy face paint and elaborately styled hair. Those people were there to sell — themselves. There were small, ramshackle shelters where shaven-headed scribes plied their trade, inking sheets of papyrus for their customers, for every reason imaginable. There were other such shacks, where other scribes read the sheets of papyrus which were brought to them by their illiterate customers — all for a fee, of course. And over all hung the sweet stench of the city — roasting meat, exotic perfumes, perspiring flesh, sweating beasts, urine, and manure.

The entrance to the palace was flanked by two especially enormous pillars, each as tall as ten men, richly painted with figures of kings and gods and animals. There were guards there, of course. Large, imposing, and distinctly unfriendly-looking men who wore short bronze swords at their sides and held spears with wide, glittering blades.

One man, the largest of them all, stood squarely in the center. He was a Kushite, with skin as black as charcoal and arms like the branches of trees. He was bare-chested, wearing only a short kilt and sandals. He held no spear, but his belt was hung with a sword to match his size.

That belt was level with my eyes. I had never seen a man so big, and have never seen one since.

He ignored the fine ash in the air, even though it collected on his muscular shoulders and dusted his shaven scalp. His beefy forearms were folded across his broad chest, above the level of my head — and his eyes were not squinting against the wind. They were watchful, constantly moving, observing the people in the square from one side to the other. I doubted that he missed much that happened there.

The frown on his prominent lips as he stared at us was as intimidating as a thunderstorm, but Kisil walked up to him without a trace of fear. Aron and I followed. I know that I felt rather more timid, and Aron's hands were visibly quivering. His eyes looked like plattered eggs.

When we stood before the glowering giant, though, Kisil did not inquire about the king. He bowed respectfully and said, "My companions and I seek an audience with the lady Basia."

The gigantic guard squinted down at Kisil suspiciously, and then examined the man and woman standing behind him. "Why do Avru wish to see the sister of the king?" he asked, in a thick voice as deep as rolling thunder, rich and resonant.

Kisil took the fold of cloth from over his mouth, revealing his face. "I am her son," said Kisil calmly. "My name is Moses."

The guard's eyes widened. He nodded respectfully — then grinned, his teeth bright in his black face, and nodded again, more enthusiastically. He seemed about to speak; but then, incredibly, he bowed low to Kisil. Very low.

Even then, his head was still higher than mine. Then the man left and ran, still grinning, moving with surprising speed on legs like tree trunks.

We were left standing there between the other guards, who looked at least as surprised as Aron and I. They watched us, but in a respectful sort of way. One of them, also without a face covering, even spoke encouragingly: "Wait, please. It will not be long."

Kisil gave no sign that he was either surprised or concerned. He covered his face again, and we waited without speaking.

The giant returned a short time later. This time, he was walking very slowly. There was an aged man leaning heavily on his wrist, which he held low. The ancient one was shorter than I, barely coming up to the big man's hip. He was bald, with only a fringe of hair above his ears, and he held a cotton cloth over his mouth and nose.

Kisil's face lit up with pleasure, and he removed the cloth from his face again. "Hafiz!" The elder blinked at him curiously, then his old eyes crinkled with pleasure.

"Moses!" he said. "The gods be praised!" His voice was surprising; it was soft, but as rich and full as that of a man of forty. He also removed his kerchief, and we saw the bright smile on his birdlike old face. "My mistress always said you would return some day! I am glad to see that she was right. Come, let us go to her." He regarded Aron and me without a hint of curiosity, then beckoned to us, indicating for the benefit of the enormous Kushite that we could come too. Then he waved a skinny arm and said, "You may go back to your post, Gamba. These people are in my charge now." The elder wrapped the cotton kerchief around his face again. The dust was still swirling around us.

The big man hesitated. Dismay — and something else — was evident on his broad black face. He was staring at Kisil.

Hafiz spoke from behind his veil. "I know what you are thinking, Gamba. What if something goes wrong? You will be held responsible." The old man made a gesture of acceptance. "Very well. You may walk with us." The big man beamed and bowed deeply again. He followed a few steps behind us as we began to walk toward the massive doors.

I could not help feeling that the Kushite's concern was not worry, as the old man had said, but had to do with something else — something about my husband. He kept gazing at Kisil in wonder, and with a hint of — what? Affection? Admiration? What could this dark-skinned giant have to do with Kisil?

The old man, Hafiz, took Kisil's arm as we moved down the corridor, which was broad and brightly lit from wide openings on our left. The hallway was not deserted. There were servants hurrying here and there, some carrying trays, some baskets, some only rolls of papyrus. They were clothed in bright colors, many in fabrics that shone and gleamed like water, and others that sparkled with flecks of gold and silver and other colors. I knew nothing but wool and cotton; I wondered how these fabrics were made. Many of the servants had their faces covered against the dust, but not all.

The ash seemed to be subsiding. Though it covered everything in the palace with a fine powder, it was no longer blowing in through the wide doors and windows. I saw why it was still so thick, even here; the palace was built to be open to the winds, no doubt to keep the rooms cool in this hot land.

The palace had its own distinctive scent; exotic perfumes and foods, flowers and incense — much like the more pleasant odors of the streets, but with only a touch of the bitter tang of sweating humanity, and entirely without the heavy reek of garbage and rot with human and animal wastes in the mix.

There were guards at intervals along the corridor, some on watch before imposing doors, some just standing in the hallway. Many were big, heavily muscled men, but none were nearly as big as Gamba.

As we walked through the hallways on floors of finely fitted and polished stone, Aron and I stared at the walls. Between the wide doorways dazzling scenes were painted, of Egyptian life and of the courts of the Egyptians' gods — and there were other scenes, the meaning of which I could not fathom, showing men who wore the heads of animals and birds, and strange creatures doing mysterious things. The opposite wall was hung with rich and colorful fabrics, and between them ornate doors appeared, some open to reveal scenes of even greater grandeur and wealth. The gleam of gold and the bright glitter of precious stones were everywhere. Aron and I were staring open-mouthed in astonishment. A few of the servants and guards smiled at our amazement.

Moses looked unimpressed. I remembered that this was all familiar to him.

Hafiz spoke quietly. "The king comes and goes, occasionally visiting the Royal City, but my mistress has never left this place." He turned to Kisil. "She has been waiting for you, I think."

"How long has it been, old friend?" asked Kisil as we slowly shuffled along.

The old man thought. "Three tens of years, I think. You would have near fifty years now, Moses, or perhaps more. Your mother is — well, she is very old." His eyes crinkled with an unseen smile, and he added, "I have more than eighty years, myself. I credit the king's table. Not his physicians. They know nothing." The old man chuckled.

Kisil chuckled, too, at Aron and me. We walked along, gaping and staring in wonder. "Grand, is it not?" He waved at the painted figures on the walls, at the finely-dressed servants who peeked out of every room. "This is a foreign place to you," he said, "but not to me. I grew up here. Do not be afraid — or too much impressed."

Aron stared at an enormous painting of a jackal-headed god standing before prostrate men. "Why am I here, Kisil?"

My husband did not pause, but kept walking — slowly, with Hafiz still leaning on his arm.

"You are to be a witness. What I tell the king — you will tell our people."

Aron's face was grim. "Not that it will matter."

"We shall see."

The old man, Hafiz, heard all of this, but he said nothing. "Be ready," he whispered to Kisil as we approached an open doorway. "Your mother is very old, and very frail."

"Does she still wear her own hair?" Kisil asked. I wondered what he meant. Later, I learned. Egyptian nobles, by custom, shaved their heads and wore false hairpieces, both men and women.

The old man laughed lightly. "Of course," he said. "She never held with the tradition. Her brother disapproves, but no one — not even he — can tell my mistress what to do."

Hafiz held back a curtain. We took a few steps down into a cool and tastefully decorated chamber, hung with fine fabrics and with more colorful paintings on the walls. On a beautifully cushioned divan under a wide, open window lay an elderly woman, thin and aged, but still with an air of strength as well as gentleness and grace.

Her hair was long and white, and it shone like a river of silver. I could see why she refused to cut it. She had not shielded her face from the ash, or else had just uncovered it. Though aged, with skin as delicate as parchment, it was almost unlined. Basia was very old, as Hafiz had said, but she was still beautiful. Her face held a kind of serenity that I remember hoping mine would hold someday, if I lived so long. Her eyes shone with intelligence.

I was surprised to find that I instantly liked her. I never expected to like an Egyptian, but Basia was different, and I saw that with my first glance at her.

The old woman turned to we four who had entered, and her eyes, still sharp even at her advanced age, immediately fastened on Kisil. They widened, then filled with tears as she rose, smoothly and gracefully, from her couch. Hafiz, though as old as she, ran to help her. She hardly needed it.

No words were spoken at first. Kisil went to her, and Basia embraced her foster son. He held her tenderly and stroked her hair as Hafiz looked on, with tears on his own lined cheeks.

After a time, she murmured, "I see you have taken a wife, my son."

Her face was pressed against his chest, but turned toward me. Her eyes were studying my face, and there was a tiny sparkle there amid the tears, and a smirk on her lips. She liked me, too.

"Yes, Mother. This is Tzipporah. And my brother Aron."

Aron bowed politely, and Basia acknowledged him with a nod. Then she and I smiled at each other, and I saw something else in her eyes. She must have seen the same in mine, because we both smiled even more broadly. We understood each other in that instant, Basia and I.

She closed her eyes in her foster son's arms, and I understood what Basia knew, and that I knew it too.

I think it was then that I really began to understand a little of what Kisil was, when I saw that there was another who felt it as I did. When I looked back at my husband, I sensed the universe turning, changing — and that Kisil was the point upon which it turned.

He does not know, I thought. *He does not know how important he is.*

Basia did not ask why he had come back. When they were done embracing, she leaned back and examined him, without hurry. Then she spoke simply: "You have returned to free your people. You are the Deliverer."

I found myself speaking, again, almost before I knew what the words would be. "That is why you pulled him from the water!"

She only smiled and resumed her seat on her couch. Then she turned back to Kisil, who was gazing at her uncertainly. She smiled indulgently and gestured at the entry. "Go to him. He is in the Great Hall. We can talk later." Then she turned to me again. "But your wife may stay here, with me. Let us talk, you and I. There is much you want to know, I think. And — do I have grandchildren?"

I laughed, but before I could answer — before anyone could move — the servants turned toward the doorway and stiffened. Basia herself looked, and then, again without hurry, she stood.

I turned. The king of Egypt was standing on the steps.

58

Tuth-Mose stood there in the entryway, with a small retinue of courtiers and retainers behind him. I knew him only by the deference paid to him by the rest; the servants, including Gamba, bowed as one, and deeply. Even Basia, sitting again on her couch, inclined her head in respect.

He was a small man, as small as I; but he had that trick of seeming to look down upon others, even from an inferior height. He was old, but not bent with it — he stood straight, as straight as Kisil's staff. He was bald, with his head shaved in the Egyptian royal style, but no fat and indolent nobleman was he. He was thin, and wiry as well. His skin was loose with age, but with strength visible in the muscles beneath it.

He wore a plain white tunic and ordinary sandals. There was no crown or other sign of his rank visible, and he needed none. His erect posture, his scowl, and his glittering eyes all spoke of power and purpose. Those eyes were small, but as bright and sharp as new knives — and they were fixed on Kisil.

No one was allowed to speak before the king spoke, I learned later; but Kisil did.

"Hello, Uncle."

There was a collective gasp from the syncophants behind him, but Tuth-Mose did not move, nor did he speak. He seemed uncertain — and then he looked at me.

His eyes widened and he took a step back. "Who is *she*?" he asked in a sharp whisper. Those were his first words.

"This is my wife, Uncle. Tzipporah is her name. She has borne me two sons."

"Her *eyes*... "

I had not meant to stare, but I suppose I was. When people were disturbed by my eyes, I looked down or away — but not this time. I stared at the king steadily and did not blink. I opened my eyes a little wider, and lifted my chin, just a bit, while continuing to stare directly into his.

I knew what the effect would be. I had learned the trick when I was a child.

The little man shuddered, almost visibly. I knew the reaction well, though I doubt that it was as obvious to others. The courtiers looked from him to me and back again, anxiously, and some of them surreptitiously made the sign against the Evil Eye, hoping I did not see. I smiled, coldly, and continued to stare at the little man before us.

The king's eyes shifted away from me and back to Kisil. He was shaken, but could not afford to show it. He gestured, twirling a careless hand in the air. "Leave us." He spoke without bothering to turn and look at his entourage. They scurried away, Some tried to look important and busy, but most only seemed glad to leave the king's presence when he was displeased.

When all but Basia's servant Hafiz and Gamba were gone, the king spoke again, looking at my husband, his face expressionless. "Why have you come back?" There was just a hint of unsteadiness in his voice, which was high and reedy and came through his nose.

I knew that the king dared not look at me. He would look anywhere else, but not at me. He feared me. Kisil had noted the king's reaction to my gaze as well. He looked at him silently for a time, deliberately taking his time with his reply, as I continued to stare.

I understood this king. I understood him to his center. He was small, and weak, with a voice like a petulant child's. Nothing about him inspired or commanded respect or deference, nothing but his office alone. He stood as straight and as tall as he could manage, and affected an imperious gaze, to compensate for his own sense of weakness and inadequacy. He surrounded himself with toadies and hangers-on, courtiers who would praise him and jump at his every whim and so inflate his sense of worth.

And now he was old, as well. I noted that he stayed on the top step, at the level of the hallway, keeping himself above us.

I knew this man — and I knew that he could not be commanded or compelled to do anything. His pride would not permit it. He could only be moved by his own fears, and perhaps not even then.

"Why have you come back?" the little man asked again.

After another heartbeat or two, Kisil spoke. "I was sent." His voice was distorted by his lisp, but calm. There was no hint of deference there, nor of fear.

The king's face took on a suspicious, guarded expression. "Sent by whom?"

"By the God of the Avru," Kisil replied, as simply as if he had said, "My father-in-law."

The king's eyebrows rose, and he smiled smugly. "Ah. The god without a name."

"His name is *Ehyehuwah*."

The words hung in the air, almost visible, as the tones resonated in the marble chamber. The voice was my own.

The king's eyes slid over to me, though against his will, I think. Though he tried to hide it, I could see the fear in them. They shifted back to Kisil. "And what does this — Heyuwah — have to do with me — or with you?'"

"You must set the Avru free, Uncle. You must let us return to our land. We are herders, not brickmakers."

"You say 'we,' Moses—"

"I am Avru. My name is Yekusiel, Uncle. It always was." Kisil had cut him off.

There was a shocked silence. "Do not interrupt the king, my son," said Basia softly.

The king waved a hand angrily, dismissing it. "So you are the great Deliverer who was prophesied, then? You? The child who could barely speak in my court?" His face took on a sneer. "You still speak like a child, Moses. Not like a man. A child."

"I know the story, Uncle. I know who placed that coal before me, and who let me put it in my mouth." This was a story I had not heard.

The king frowned and opened his mouth to speak — but before he could, I heard my own voice again: "He IS the Deliverer, little man." I let my eyes bore into the king's. "And what is more, you know that to be true. You know it in your heart, even if you dare not speak the truth aloud."

The king's mouth still hung open. He seemed shrunken for a heartbeat or two, his shoulders sagging, his head turned slightly aside as if fearing a blow.

Everyone froze. There was a tense silence. I saw Aron suppressing a smirk. My impertinence, my open disrespect, were things that no one there had ever heard before. The king's mouth, still open, worked silently for a heartbeat, then he shook his head as if to clear it and went on as if I had not spoken.

"I do not know this God of yours, Moses. Nor will I let the Avru go." He straightened, than sneered, recovering his pose of arrogance. "What will happen if I do not release the Avru? Will this great Heyuwah punish me? Will he strike me down? Will this God of yours smite Egypt in his wrath?"

Kisil did not hurry in his answer. "I do not know, Uncle. But it is right to let the Avru go, and wrong to hold them." His eyes were steady, his voice even. "And you know that to be true."

Tuth-Mose snorted. "No threats? No warnings? Hah!" His quick, sharp bark of laughter sounded confident — but the king's eyes would not meet mine.

"Would it matter?" asked Kisil mildly. "If I told you — " He looked around, then looked through the open doorway, across the terraces, and down at the Great River far below. He smiled, then lifted a hand and pointed at it. "What if I told you that the Great River will turn to blood, if you do not set the Avru free? Would that matter, Uncle? Would you believe me? Would you let the people go?"

The king laughed. Kisil stood there, unmoving, his hand still outstretched. I moved a little, and quickly, just enough so that the king would look at me before he could stop himself. I gave him my best Evil Eye stare and my coldest smile — and his grin faded a little. It was enough. I saw the fear in his eyes again. He turned to leave, then stopped and turned back.

A sly grin was spreading across his wrinkled face. "I see that your people do not have enough work. I shall see that they work harder." He gestured at Hafiz. "Fetch me the

Chamberlain," and the old man left the chamber — not hurrying, but not slowly. The king waited, gazing at Kisil with an imperious glare. We all waited.

It was only a short time later that Hafiz returned. With him was an official of the Court who had clearly been lurking nearby; a short, fat, bald man wearing a wide Egyptian necklace and gilded sandals. A few other courtiers accompanied him, not wishing to miss an opportunity to curry the king's favor.

The king pointed at the man, watching Kisil out of the corner of his eye. "Give the overseers these instructions, Taweel. The Avru will no longer be given straw from the stables. They can gather it for themselves. If they have time to listen to this man's nonsense, they have time to gather straw. And their tallies of bricks are to be the same."

The fat man made an obeisance and went off, walking quickly, with a satisfied expression on his corpulent face. Some of the other officials were grinning. Gamba frowned, but I think that I was the only one who saw.

The king turned back to Kisil. "How long will your people listen to you now, Moses, when they see what you have brought upon them?"

Kisil stood silent. I could see by the expression on his face that he had not been prepared for this.

Tuth-Mose grinned broadly and shook his head — and then his eye caught mine. I smiled at him coldly, and his grin faded a little.

I had no knowledge of what was to come. I only knew that my smile made men nervous. The king's eyes left mine and turned back to my husband.

"Thpeak on, Motheth," sneered the king, mocking Kisil's lisp. "I do not know this Heyuwah, nor will I let the Avru go." He waved a hand dismissively again, then remembered that we were in Basia's chambers and not his own. He shook his head as if annoyed, then left without another word. He did not look at me again.

59

Kisil and Aron returned to the Avru camp, but I stayed, at Basia's insistence. Kisil agreed only after Hafiz promised that I would be accompanied back to the camp safely — by Gamba, the dark-skinned giant. When the big man grinned and bowed low to Kisil with his enormous arms spread wide, Kisil nodded. I could see that he was still preoccupied with the king's pronouncement.

After they left, we sat, Basia and I, in comfortable silence for some time. She had sent her other servants out of the chamber, and we were alone. Only Hafiz, who seemed to have her absolute confidence, and Gamba, who had Hafiz's, remained. I nibbled on a bit of fruit, wishing that I had some for Gershom and Eliezer.

As if she could read my thoughts, Basia gestured that I should take more.

"Take the basket, Tzipporah." She indicated the basket in which the fruit had been brought. "Take it with you. What are the names of your sons?" I truly began to wonder if she had some power to see inside my mind.

"Gershom is the older. He has ten years, a strong boy. Eliezer walks a little, but is not yet speaking."

I saw her wistful expression and I knew what she was about to say before she said it.

"Moses is the only son I have." *Perhaps I can read her mind as well,* I thought.

I inclined my head in sympathy. "Did you know that he was the Deliverer when you took him from the water?"

Her eyes were black and sharp, like her brother's, but warmer. I saw them cut quickly toward the door, then back. Then she leaned closer. "You feel it, too," she said quietly. "I can see it when you look at him. You feel the power that flows through him."

I blinked. I had not thought of it in quite that way — but she was right. "Yes. But he does not."

She smiled and sat back. "If he did, it would not be there." Then she gestured at the basket again, and at another bowl of fruit nearby. "Come, Tzipporah, take some more. The other children in the camp will want some, too. What do you want to know about Moses's —" She hesitated. "Kisil's — childhood?"

Once again, she had touched on the very thought in my mind.

"Tell me —" I thought. "Tell me how his mouth was burned."

She frowned. "It was a silly thing, and cruel. When Moses was a baby..."

She used the name she knew as she told the story, and it *was* a silly thing. When Kisil had been Eliezer's age, barely beginning to walk by himself, he had grabbed the old king's crown from its place and thrown it to the ground. The soothsayers and fortunetellers with which the king had surrounded himself all gasped and muttered. An evil omen, they said. Moses would take the king's crown from him, they said. Moses would end the dynasty, they said. Put the boy to death!

"But my father decided to test Kisil instead." Basia frowned. "He offered him a choice, of a glowing-hot coal or a shining nugget of gold."

"I saw his hand reach out for the gold," said Basia. "But it was a windy day, and at the last instant, a gust of air struck the coal and it glowed brightly. Moses' hand swung to it, and he took the coal.

"It burned his fingers, of course, and he put them in his mouth, as children will; but the coal had stuck to them! Before I could stop him, his fingers, his lips, and his tongue were badly burned. From that time on, he could never speak properly."

"Did he cry?"

She looked at me curiously. “No. He did not cry at all. How did you know?” Then her face lightened. “Of course you know. You are his wife.”

A pair of servants appeared with brooms and cloths, and began to dust and sweep, cleaning up the dust from the ashfall. Basia ordered them out — not impatiently, but kindly. “Please do that at another time. I have a guest, and we would rather not be disturbed.” The servants bowed and left quietly, smiling at their mistress warmly. Their loyalty and affection for Basia were easily seen.

We talked more about Kisil’s babyhood. I asked what kind of child he was. She laughed. "A thoughtful one. He often seemed to be somewhere else —"

"Somewhere far away, and yet still here. Yes, I have seen this. Do you know what it means?"

She shook her head — once, then again, thoughtfully. “What is it?” I asked.

“Sometimes I thought he looked like he was — listening.”

“Yes, I have thought that too. Even when I first met him.”

Her eyes twinkled. “You shall have to tell me about that day. But more often I thought, he is *thinking*, and very hard.”

Then she lifted a finger, like a teacher. “Let me tell you about something that happened when Moses was very small. I saw it happen, and I still do not understand it. Your asking if he cried reminded me.” Behind her, I saw Hafiz’s mouth open, and then he smiled and nodded. Whatever it was, he remembered it too.

“Moses was playing on the terrace — right there.” Basia gestured at the stones beyond the doorway, near her couch. “He was not yet a year old. I saw the scorpion, but before I could pick Moses up or step on it — I was barefoot, but I would have done it even so — it stung him. He was only a baby, barely able to stand. He was not yet talking at all.” Her face grew bemused again as she stared at the place she had indicated. Whatever had followed, she was still puzzled by it.

“What happened?” I asked.

She blinked, coming to herself, then went on. “Well, he cried out, of course. He looked up at me, and his face grew distorted, as children’s faces do when they are about to cry." Her expression was bemused. "All that, I expected. But then he — he just — stopped." She shrugged and shook her head, making the river of silver hair ripple. She still wondered at it, even after so long.

"He looked down at his hand." She looked at her own. "That was where the scorpion had stung him. And though his face was still twisted with the pain, he — *studied* it. He watched the lump grow and redden." She looked up. "Have you ever been stung by a scorpion?"

"Of course. All desert people have. It hurts — and then it grows worse as the poison takes hold."

"Yes. And I could see how badly it hurt. But Moses — my little Moses — he studied it, and he closed his eyes tight, and he thought, then studied it again. He ignored the pain, and he thought."

She shook her head. "I still wonder what he thought *with.* He was small, he did not yet have words. But that is what he was doing. He was *thinking.*" She looked thoughtful herself. "I believe that is what he does when he seems distant like that. He is *thinking.* He thinks more deeply and with greater concentration than anyone I ever met. Hafiz!" she suddenly called.

He stepped out from behind her. "Yes, my lady?"

"Do you remember when Moses was stung by the scorpion?"

"Yes, my lady. An odd thing, it was."

"Tell Tzipporah."

The old man turned to me, still standing with his hands primly clasped before him. "The boy did not cry. His little hand was swollen to twice its size, but he did not cry. I put a paste on it, of mud and herbs, to draw out the sting — and he watched me, the whole time, eyes wide and attentive. If he had been only a little older, he would have asked me questions. I saw them in his face. But he never cried." He shrugged. "It was the strangest thing — well, one of the strangest things — I have ever seen."

That last remark piqued my curiosity, so I asked: "Were there other things? About Moses?" The name was foreign in my mouth, but I used it.

The old man looked at the old woman hesitantly. She nodded, and he went on. "I once saw Moses watching two other boys in the square before the palace, street children. One was older than he, one younger. The bigger boy

— a much bigger boy — was beating the smaller, slapping and punching him and pulling on his ear and laughing as the little one cried."

"What happened?"

The old man shook his head in puzzlement. "Moses calmly walked over to them, and he told the older boy, 'Stop.' Just that. Just, 'Stop.'

"The big boy straightened up and asked arrogantly, 'Why should I?' He was much bigger than Moses, and Moses was wearing only a cotton tunic, not his court dress, and was barefoot. The big boy had no way of knowing that he was a prince.

"Moses just looked at him calmly and said, 'Because it is wrong to hurt someone only because you can.' The big boy sneered, and drew back his fists to strike Moses — but he did not.

"Moses stood there, calmly, entirely without fear — or anger, either. The bigger boy stared at him. He seemed confused. Then he lowered his hands and walked away. The smaller boy ran, and Moses calmly went back to where he had been playing.

"He did not know I had been watching, and said nothing of the incident to me, nor to his mother. He seemed to think nothing of it," he concluded.

I chewed on that. "I have seen something very like that since. Did you ever see anything of the kind again?"

The old man shook his head. "No. Not like that. But Moses never liked to see — " he thought — "*injustice*. He seemed to find it personally offensive, even if it had nothing to do with him. I saw him intervene in disputes later, as a prince, even when he was not obligated." He thought. "When we servants had a complaint — it was Moses we went to. He listened to us, and he seemed to have a way of making things right."

"Did you know he was Avru?" The old man nodded, and Basia did as well.

"We all did," said Hafiz.

"But Kisil — I mean Moses — told me that he did not know he was Avru till the day he went to visit his people."

The old man and the old woman exchanged a glance — a guilty one, I thought. Then Basia gave a small shrug. "No one spoke of it in his presence. I gave orders to the servants to that effect. I wanted him to feel that I was his real mother, and that he was Egyptian."

"You succeeded. He never knew, until you told him."

She spoke sadly then. "And that was the last day I saw him, before today."

I saw the regret on her face, and I spoke gently. "But that was as it was meant to be —" I hesitated — "Your Highness."

"Please — call me Basia. We have too much in common to be formal."

I took her hand. "He had to grow up as he did, Basia. You did not do wrong." She squeezed my hand in acknowledgment and thanks.

I looked at Hafiz then. "But something else Moses said does not fit with what you have told me."

"What is that, my lady?" I blinked at the honorific, but he merely waited for me to speak.

"He said that he knew about the way the Avru lived — but that he did not care. He said he was one of their oppressors, like — like all of you." I spoke carefully. "Like all of the Egyptians, I mean. If he did not like injustice —"

"I understand, my lady. And he spoke truly. Moses was mindful of injustice, but only among his own — or the people he thought were his own." He reddened a bit. "The Egyptians do not often think of the Avru as people — and not only the Avru, but any of their slaves. Like the big black man there by the door —" He nodded at Gamba, who was listening impassively — "They think of them as something more like useful animals than as human beings."

His face had grown red. I realized that he was embarrassed. "I am in an awkward position, my lady. I am a slave myself, but I am Egyptian, and a slave to royalty. I have seen this — unawareness — from both sides."

Basia spoke up. "When he was very small, I remember that he did stand wide-eyed and shocked the first time he saw a slave being whipped. When he realized that there was nothing he could do, he turned and ran." She shrugged. "Perhaps that is how we all learn such callousness. As children, we have no power to end cruelty, so we learn to look away."

I nodded, thinking. Kisil was the best, but by far the humblest, man I had ever known. I had often wondered why he had seemed so haunted and so burdened, even before I knew what that burden was; and I had wondered why, when his judgment was so fair and so wise, and when he knew so much about so many things, why he had never displayed a hint of arrogance. He seemed to carry more guilt than pride, and now I knew why.

I was beginning to learn a little of what had made my husband who he was, and I wondered at it. I had told him before that he was being prepared for something...

"Are you all right, Tzipporah?" asked Basia, and then I saw that she and Hafiz were looking at me, concerned. Even Gamba's big eyes were watching me carefully, with one eyebrow cocked high.

"Yes. Forgive me. I was just thinking."

"Like Moses," said Basia, and we laughed.

"Yes. Like Moses."

"Do you mind that I call him by that name?" she asked. I smiled at that.

"No. That is the name you gave him, and you are a good mother. I shall use it too, to honor you."

Her eyes, to my surprise, were suddenly wet. "Thank you." Her voice was husky. "Thank you, Tzipporah. That means much, coming from his wife." She blinked back her tears and took my hand. "And I am glad that he has found such a good wife."

We embraced then, and wept on each other's shoulders. Hafiz stood by, with a hand on his mistress's shoulder. His eyes, again, were wet too.

60

We talked into the evening, Basia and I, and then the Kushite giant, Gamba, took me back to the Avru camp.

The man frightened me. He was truly enormous, and when I had first seen him, he seemed dour and threatening. I suppose my fear showed, because before we reached the great gate of the palace, he stopped in a deserted corridor. He looked around cautiously, then turned toward me — and knelt.

His huge face was level with my own, and his eyes were gentle. "You need not fear me, my lady." His deep voice was soft. "No one dear to Moses has anything to fear from me. I am your servant. If anyone should threaten harm to you in any way," he rumbled, "*that* man should fear me — for I will defend you with my very life."

I suppose I was staring. I know that my mouth was hanging open, because I remember closing it. "Why?" I asked. I could think of nothing else to say.

"Moses is beloved of all the servants of the king. It was as Hafiz said. If they had complaints, they would come to him, and he would listen and treat them fairly. I never knew him, but we slaves have not forgotten." He stood then, and offered his enormous hand. I could not have reached his arm. "Come, let us go on. We should not stay here speaking so."

Another servant appeared. He glanced at us curiously, but did not pause on his errand, whatever it was. I smiled, I hope graciously, but refused Gamba's hand — as big as a platter, it was, with fingers each as big as two of mine, and twice as long. We walked on, out of the palace and across the dimming square, heading toward the camp. He was walking slowly, but I still had to hurry to keep up with his strides. A few people gaped at him, but more waved. The big man was apparently well known, and liked, in the city.

"There is another reason, as well." We made our way through the people in the streets — fewer than there had been earlier in the day — as the big man spoke. "My father knew Moses before I was born."

I looked up at the giant curiously. He was smiling wistfully. "Tell me."

He spoke softly, his voice like muffled thunder. "Moses is well known among my people. In Kush, as the Egyptians call it — my homeland, far to the south. Though under another name. There, he was called Zunach."

I stopped in my tracks. "Zunach? Moses — Kisil — has been to Kush? What did he do there?" And then I got a glimpse of my husband's mysterious past.

There was an open doorway nearby, and Gamba inclined his head toward it. I went in, and he followed. He was obliged to bend very low to clear the lintel, which was chest-high to him, and to turn sideways to allow his shoulders to pass. It was dark inside, but my eyes soon grew accustomed to it. It was a place where men, I thought mostly slaves, came to drink. Dark, with dark wood and an odor of sweat and beer.

Gamba seemed to be well-known there. He was greeted with smiles and waves of welcome. The men glanced at me curiously, but said nothing. I think it was probably unusual for women to be seen there — decent women, at least — but they knew better than to leer at me while I was with Gamba.

Gamba had to bend to avoid striking his head on the roof-beams. It occurred to me that the palace, with its high ceilings, was probably the only building in the city where he could stand erect without concern. We sat down at a table. The owner began to approach us, but Gamba waved him away. The man bowed respectfully and went back to his jars and jugs. He began to light lamps and place them on the tables for his customers.

"Tell me what happened in Kush," I asked eagerly.

The big man grinned broadly and began. "It was

many years ago. The king of Kokenus — a city in my land — had gone to war, and Zunach — Moses — had gone with him as one of his commanders. Moses had lived among my people for some time, and risen from common soldier to a high rank. He was among the commanders who brought our army victory in the war, perhaps more than any other.

"But when the king returned in triumph to Kokenus, he found the city gates barred to him and the walls heavily guarded. His viceroy, a man named Yanus, had taken over the throne." Gamba snorted. "My father said that what Yanus wanted was not the king's throne, but the king's wife. She was a beautiful woman. I do not remember her name." He rubbed his shaved head with his hand and said, "I think I will have a drink after all. Do you mind?" I shook my head, and he beckoned to the man behind the jugs to bring him one. When Gamba reached for his pouch to pay for it, the man shook his head and returned to his place. After a long, deep drink from the jug, Gamba went on. "Moses showed the king how to take the city. He was a brilliant strategist. The battle was won and the city was regained, but the king was killed in the battle.

"The king's son, a boy named Yamarus, was far too young to reign. So, at the people's insistence, Zunach — Moses — ruled in the boy's place until he came of age, and he was a wise and just ruler. Many expected that Zunach would try to remain king, but he abdicated in Yamarus's favor when the boy became a man — a few years before that, to tell the truth of it. Then, to prevent any conflict or suspicion, he left the city."

I was amazed at the story. Gamba finished the jug — it was not lost on me that he had done it in two pulls — and went on to say, "All this was before I was born, of course. My father said that he had always wondered what became of Zunach. He knew, he said, that he would be a great man wherever he went."

The big man frowned. "Years later, long after Zunach had left, my father was captured by Egyptian bandits — slave traders — and was brought here and sold as a slave." Then he smiled again. "Here, he heard of the good prince, Moses, who had mysteriously vanished long before."

"But how did he know that Moses was the same man as this Zunach?"

Gamba smiled. "My father was not only there in Kokenus when Zunach ruled; he was a captain of troops himself and under Zunach's command, and he knew him very well. The tales he heard of the prince Moses's wisdom and character seemed to match what he knew of Zunach's — but it was another thing that made him certain that they were the same man." He cocked an eyebrow at me and grinned. "It was the way, in the tales of the slaves, that Prince Moses spoke."

It took me a heartbeat. "His lisp!" I exclaimed.

Gamba nodded. "Yes. Zunach spoke in that same way, clumsily and with effort. When your husband spoke at the palace gate and said he was Moses, I knew that he spoke the truth from his way of speaking."

I just sat there, trying to take it in. The big man looked around. "Come, we should go. I have been away too long already. My lady —"

"My name is Tzipporah, Gamba," I said as I stood. "Please use it. You and I are friends now." He grinned, his white teeth lighting his whole face. "We are friends," he rumbled in warm agreement, but he did not use my name. He offered his hand again, and this time I took it. I was no longer afraid. Who could be, when guarded by a man as big as a mountain and as faithful as a son?

61

Gamba left me at the gate of the Avru camp. I meant to tell Kisil of all that the big man had told me, but when I entered the compound, I found chaos. There was a crowd gathered in the place where Kisil had spoken two nights before, and Kisil, this time alone, was up on the stack of bricks, trying to bring some order to the angry gathering. The people were outraged at the king's command — at least, the slaves who worked in the brick pits were.

Desan and Aviram, and the other, privileged slaves, were laughing uproariously, egging the crowd on. "This is your Deliverer?" they jeered. "He has delivered you to more work!"

"Is this the day of liberation, Moses?"

"Will your God bring us straw?" Both laughter and shouts of anger filled the air.

I could see that Kisil was shaken, though he was putting a good front on it. He stood there resolutely, looking back at the crowd, his face grim.

"Where we will find straw?" asked a man in the crowd, his weeping wife at his side.

"Where will we find the time to gather it?" shouted another. "We sleep and rest little enough now!"

"What have you done to us?"

Kisil's eyes held an uncertainty that I think only I could see. Then, for just an instant, less than a heartbeat, Kisil's eyes went to the horizon. Even in the midst of all the jeering and shouting, I thought he was going to go into one of his — trances, I suppose one might call them; but that did not happen. He looked at me, and then, abruptly, even as our eyes met, I saw his expression alter. I saw that determined look come into his eyes, and I saw a hint of that ominous jackal's smile. Something had changed.

"Go back where you came from!" came a shout from the crowd.

"Yes! Go back to your palace, prince!" This was Aviram.

Kisil did not react. He gazed down at the angry mob, calmly, and as if from a great height. Then came a curious thing, one of those which I cannot explain. He lifted his hands — only lifted his hands — and the people grew silent.

He had not spoken a word. I stared at him, and saw that his disquiet, his uncertainty, was gone. He stood straight, staring out at the crowd calmly, without a hint of fear or shame. This is the man who spoke to them the night the earth moved, I thought — and they see that man too, all of them. Even Desan and Aviram were silent, and stood watching, though with frowns and narrowed eyes.

"Children of Avram! Do you truly think that Ehyehuwah your God has abandoned you?" Kisil thundered. His voice was clear and resonant, though it still bore a hint of his lisp. It boomed above the crowd with astonishing power, and I knew that even those in the rear, far from where Kisil stood, could hear him clearly.

"Hear now the words of Ehyehuwah!" He lowered his gaze, and, once again, his voice assumed the depth and clarity that we had heard before, his words penetrating to the edges of the crowd.

"I have not abandoned you to bondage! I, Myself, have turned this king against you, so that you will know that it is not by this puny king's will that you shall go free, but by My will! Tuth-Mose has no power over you! All power is Mine! I am Ehyehuwah!"

The people murmured among themselves. I could feel that some were still angry, but some were listening, with hope returning to their faces.

Kisil went on: *"And now you will see what I shall do to this man who calls himself king! I shall send signs and wonders that will strike terror into his heart, and all the world shall see them! I, Ehyehuwah, will deliver you from bondage*

Myself, with My own hand. MY hand — and not that of the king!" He paused and looked out over the silent people, and at that moment he seemed taller and more powerful than Gamba.

Kisil spread his arms wide. "This is the will of Ehyehuwah, the God of Avram, the God of Yitzhak, and the God of Yisrael!"

Kisil paused, then said, "Your day of liberation is at hand. Watch and see!"

Then Kisil — *laughed.* He clapped his hands over his head and laughed, loud and long. Seeing our wide eyes and gaping mouths, he laughed even louder. !"I do not say, 'Have faith,' my people. *You will need no faith!* You will see with your own eyes how the God of our fathers will deliver us from bondage!"

Kisil said no more. He waved the people back to their huts, then climbed down from the stack of bricks, still laughing. I looked around. Desan and his cronies were nowhere to be seen.

Only I saw that Kisil's hands were quivering. He took me in his arms, and after a brief embrace, we returned to our hut.

"I knew what to say, Tzipporah," he whispered as we stopped outside the door. Then he turned to face me. "And I know what is about to happen. I do."

"He told you?"

He shook his head. "No. Look." He inclined his head slightly, to the northwest, toward the Sea.

I looked. At first I saw nothing, but after a heartbeat or two, I saw it. There was a faint line of red and gold, ascending from the horizon. It was a thread, a nail's breadth high, no more. "It flared bright a moment ago, when I was standing on the bricks," he said. "I know what it means."

"What? What is it?"

"It is a fire-mountain, like the one by our home." He paused and smiled. Those words made me feel warm. "But much larger. And it is —" He groped for the word. "It is bursting," he finally said. "Blasting fire and liquid stone into the air. Shaking the ground for many days' journey, all around. And it will keep doing that, with more and more power, more and more force."

"But what does that —"

"Do you remember the Blood Tide? The red water that we saw in the sea?"

I nodded, and Kisil smiled coldly. "It is coming to the Delta — to the Great River. A wave will come, *tonight*. It will carry the red water up the River. The ashfall will make it stronger." He grinned. "The River will turn to blood, my love."

"Is that why you said —"

"When I spoke to the the king? No." He shook his head. "I just spoke those words — by chance, when I looked at the River from the palace." He shrugged. "Perhaps it was in the back of my mind, after we saw it along the shore. But now — *it is going to happen*, Tzipporah." He grinned like a hungry beast again. "And more wonders will follow."

We entered our hut. My mind was reeling. My husband was striding forward into the dark, guessing and hoping — but The One was with him, making his guesses become the truth.

Later, in our hut, he confided other things to me. I was lying in my favorite place, close against him with my cheek in the hollow of his shoulder. Gershom and Eliezer were asleep, and it was quiet. "I was afraid, Tzipporah," he whispered, his voice shaking. "Here, in our hut, when I was preparing to tell the people about the straw. I asked Him — why have You done this to our people, to me? Why have you brought even greater pain upon us? He did not answer. I thought, it has all been a mistake, a foolish dream that I made myself believe, for my own glory. I knew that I had been wrong. I had imagined it all.

"When I went out to speak, I still felt that way. And then..."

"I saw. Your face changed, when you saw the fire in the sky."

He said nothing, but his lips curved upward and he nodded. I went on: "And then we all saw you, and heard your words. And they were true. It is not by the will of this king that they will be freed, but by the will of Ehyehuwah Himself."

"That is what I — thought of, all at once, in an instant, when I saw it. Does it — *feel right*, to you?"

"Yes. Yes, it does, Kisil. You spoke the truth."

There in his arms, I wondered, yet again, at my husband's humility. We who were all around him, we could hear the words of The One coming through him — but he himself, who gave voice to those words, could not. We could feel their power, but he could not. To him, it was still a lucky guess, a wild gamble, an accident of chance. He confirmed my thought a heartbeat after I thought it: "I am lucky. I have seen these things before, and I know what they mean. I doubt if the Egyptians have ever seen what is about to come."

We held each other in silence for a time. Then I asked, "What happens now?"

"We go back," he said. I lifted my head and studied his face. He looked joyful, like a child winning a game. "We go back to the king's palace."

Watching him, I asked, "When?"

Again the quick answer — "Tomorrow. I think the king will send for us."

He pulled me back down onto his shoulder again, and held me tight. "It has begun, Tzipporah. It has begun."

I was growing used to this new life with him, as different as it was. It was like walking in the desert at the dark of the Moon. I could not see what lay before us, nor could Kisil, I thought. But he knew, somehow, what lay ahead. Not in detail, I thought then, and I still think that now; but he knew.

Not long after this, we felt the earth move again. Ever so slightly, a long, low quivering, a deep rumble, too low to hear — and then a sharp impact, like a heavy blow struck somewhere deep beneath the earth. Soon after, I slept, but lightly, and with strange dreams.

Later that night, I heard the ocean rise up and wash onto the land again. Kisil smiled, but he did not wake.

62

The next morning, we were sent for at dawn. The light was still gray and dim, and there was an insistent — and heavy — hammering at the door of our hut.

I peeked out from behind the dusty curtain, and saw that it was Gamba, the huge Kushite, who had come for us. With him were two other guards. Other Avru were staring from their huts, and with good reason. Gamba was half again as tall as any man there, and wide in proportion. The day before, he had left me at the outer perimeter of the Avru camp and few had seen him.

He bowed when I pulled back the curtain, and frowned blackly. When his eyes cut quickly left and right, indicating the two guards with him, I understood and responded with an expression of fear that I did not feel. His eyes twinkled then, and we continued the play-acting as we spoke.

The big man was abrupt, though respectful. "The king will see your husband. He must come now," he intoned.

"What has happened?" asked Kisil, appearing behind me.

"The Great River has turned to blood," came the rumbling reply.

I heard laughter, and realized that it was coming from my own mouth. "Blood!" I cried. "It has happened, Kisil!"

"You must hurry, Zu— Moses," said the big Kushite.

Kisil turned to me. "I will be back —"

"Take me with you, Kisil!" I said. He looked up, and I opened my eyes wide for a heartbeat, giving him a flash of my Evil Eye look. He caught my thought, grinned, and beckoned. We went together, leaving our sons in the charge of Elisheva once more.

On our way to the palace, Kisil and I spoke in low tones in the language of Midyan. "The king is superstitious," I said. "We can use this. He is afraid of my eyes."

"Yes. You will be useful, my wild bird."

"You mentioned turning the Great River to blood yesterday, and I gave him my stare. He surely thinks that you have done it."

"Not I," said Kisil. "It is as I said. I have seen this before — the fast wave from the sea, and the blood tide, though never together. It is a natural thing."

"You and I know that, but the king does not."

"Yes, and I will use that. But it feels like a deception." After a heartbeat, he added, "Just as it did when I spoke for The One."

"But the truth is always from Him, Kisil." He looked at me. "And it has happened *now*," I added, just as quickly. "Just when you — we — needed it. That cannot be an accident."

"Perhaps..." I saw that he was thoughtful. I felt in my heart the battle in his own, between his humility and his mission, between his reluctance, and his eagerness, to claim this as a miracle of God. Not to the king; to himself.

"Do you not understand, Kisil?" I asked. "It is your thought, and your mouth that speaks it — but it is Ehyehuwah, The One, confirming what you say and what you think. Can you not see?"

It was hard for him. He was at bottom a simple man, and a humble one — and he had not asked to be given this task. "You must go forward, Kisil," I said. "Think. Think more. What happens now?"

We walked along for a bit in silence. The guards were behind us, Gamba in front. "What happens now, Kisil?" I asked again.

"What do you mean?"

"You said you have seen this — this red water before. What happens next?"

He thought. "Well, the water..." He fell silent as we walked, but I saw the light in his eyes again.

"What is it? What did you remember?"

"I grew up here. This is the Delta. The Great River splits into hundreds of little streams here, and there are swamps and bogs everywhere."

"Yes...?"

He waved an arm. "There are frogs. Thousands upon thousands of frogs. They kept me awake at night. The noise was deafening."

"And so...?"

"The frogs cannot live in the red water. They will leave the river and move onto the land. I saw a few, in Attica, do this when it happened there — but that is a rocky land, of mountains and swift-running streams. Not many frogs. Here —" he grinned, the same savage grin I saw when he confronted Desan and his thugs. "There are myriads. Egypt will be covered with them. I doubt that the Blood Tide has entered the Great River before. It will seem another miracle — another plague from God."

I pressed him farther. "Then what?"

"Without water, the frogs will die. There will be a terrible stench — and then there will be flies..."

We walked on, whispering.

The king was waiting for us in the Great Hall. There were no courtiers in sight, only servants and guards, who were insignificant in his eyes — and a pale man, whose shaved head bore a single lock of black hair, braided and tied. The king's son and heir, I guessed, and Basia later confirmed it. The man looked ill, I thought, or perhaps only dissolute with wine and excessive pleasures. He was richly dressed, in fine fabrics and much gold jewelry, but his pallor and sunken cheeks did not speak of good health.

He watched his father with a complacent smile. The little king's face was dark and glowering. "What have you done to me?" he hissed as we entered.

To him, I thought. Not to Egypt, not to his people. To *him*.

Kisil spoke mildly. "I? I have done nothing."

"You said you could turn the Great River to blood, and you have!"

Kisil shook his head. "I did not say —"

"SILENCE!" the little man roared. I noticed that the guards and servants in the room did not flinch, nor even blink. Even his son only watched, still smiling. *The king must roar quite a lot*, I thought.

The cold little eyes glared at my husband. "You have turned the Great River to blood." His tone was imperious and icy. "Now change it back!"

"Will you let the Avru go free, Uncle?" Kisil's face was impassive, betraying nothing.

The king's eyes narrowed. "As soon as the Great River is clear, they may go." The sickly young man smiled more broadly. He covered his mouth with his hand, but a bit too late.

Kisil shook his head. "No, Uncle. Let the Avru go, then the water will run clear." Moses spoke simply, his face still and serene.

The old king looked annoyed — and defiant. "I command —" he began.

Kisil interrupted him again, speaking just as calmly. "No one commands me but Ehyehuwah. Beware of defying Him. Worse things will happen if you do." The king's son's eyes widened, and he put a hand on the little man's shoulder. He was taller than the king, I noticed, but I could see no strength in him.

The king shook off his hand. "You threaten me again?" he shouted angrily. "In my own house?"

Kisil lifted empty hands. "Not at all, Uncle. I do nothing, and I predict nothing. But — Ehyehuwah will act. And worse things — much worse things — will come."

"What things?"

There was a sound from the wide doorway onto the terrace. In that hot land, all the rooms of the palace were open to the wind from the sea, even after the dust storm. It kept these privileged Egyptians cool.

There, on the threshold, was a frog. It squatted there, looking at us with its great bulging eyes, and croaked again.

I gazed at the frog intently, and then slowly lifted my eyes to the king. As I expected, he was looking at me. The boy's mouth hung open, but I gave no thought to him. I was gazing steadily at the king, and I gave him my coldest smile, as I had the day before. I opened my eyes wide, and looked at the frog again. I smiled even more broadly as I stared at it.

Kisil, for his part, spoke no word. The king dismissed us again with an angry wave, and we left.

63

On our way back, Gamba, the big Kushite, confided in us. He had become our regular escort, and walked back to the camp with us without the other guards. He leaned close and spoke, his voice a low rumble. "The Dwarf is afraid, Moses. You can see it in his eyes."

"'The Dwarf?'" Kisil laughed. He unslung his waterskin — the king had offered no refreshment — and offered it to me. I took a drink, then passed it to Gamba, I think to his surprise. He gratefully took a drink — a long one. Then he spoke again. "The Dwarf is what we servants — we slaves — call him. He takes no notice of us, and we hear much. Yes, he is very afraid. We have heard him with his soothsayers and priests, asking them what to do. They pretend to know, but they know nothing, and they are as filled with fear as he."

"Has no one ever seen the red tide before?" asked Kisil.

"Yes, but never like this — and never in the Great River." He grinned. "The king is more than afraid, Zunach — he is terrified."

Kisil stopped, stared, and asked him, "What did you call me?"

Gamba looked down sheepishly, an unlikely sight. "Zunach. Forgive me, Moses. My father knew you, in Kush — in Kokenus. He told me of you, and of what you did there." He inclined his head toward me. "I have told your wife of these things."

Kisil waved that away. "That is all right... Tell me, Gamba -- what was your father's name?"

"He was called Nomba, Moses."

Kisil blinked, then grinned broadly. "My captain of spearmen!"

"Yes! You were his commander — and his friend." The big man's eyes were shining with tears. "He told me of things you did and said in Kush —"

Kisil spoke quickly to stop Gamba speaking. "I only did what any man would do." Then he went on: "Your father was big, if I remember, but not as big as you. Were you born in Egypt, then?"

After a heartbeat, Gamba replied, "Yes, Moses. I was born a slave."

"As was I."

It was a strange, awkward moment. At first, I thought that Kisil did not want Gamba speaking of Kisil's goodness and wisdom before me — and then it struck me; Kisil did not want to hear of such things at all.

He was a truly humble man, my husband. Never was he concerned with his own glory.

We turned into an empty street, and Gamba stopped. So did we, and he surprised us both by stepping in front of us and dropping to one knee, as he had for me. "If there is ever anything I can do for you, Moses — you have only to ask. I am your servant, more than the king's."

Kisil clapped a hand on Gamba's massive shoulder. The big man's face was on the same level as his own. "Just listen and watch, Gamba. Be my eyes and ears in the palace."

"That I shall do." Gamba rumbled. He rose at Kisil's touch, and we walked on.

Before we reached the Avru camp, Kisil told Gamba how to dig behind the first rise next to the fouled river and find fresh water. With that knowledge, we knew that Kisil's mother — and her servant Hafiz, of whom we had both grown fond — would not suffer. When we returned to the encampment, he showed the Avru how to do the same. The wells of the Egyptians were not fouled, but there were few of them. Most of Egypt drew its water directly from the River.

Then, Kisil showed the Avru how to spread salt — the same salt we had gathered beside the sea — in a broad band around the camp, and around their huts. We did it at night, and the coarse salt was almost the same color as the sand, so the guards did not notice — or if they did, thought nothing of it. We did not know why we were doing this, but we soon would, Kisil told us.

Desan and Aviram continued their troublemaking, and the house slaves and overseers, most of them, continued in their disdainful sneers and gibes at the brickmakers and sledge-haulers; but I noticed that more of them came to listen when Kisil spoke that night.

"Ehyehuwah has turned the Great River to blood, and all Egypt cries out to the king," he declaimed from the stack of finished bricks. "And there are more wonders to come. You will see, tomorrow or the day after, why I had you scatter salt around your dwellings. And the cry that rises up from the Egyptians will be greater still."

"Will we leave Egypt then?" a woman cried out from the crowd.

"Not yet." Kisil's voice was loud, though indistinct as always. "Wait, and see what Ehyehuwah will do. He has only begun." There was some grumbling, and much doubt, but the people went back to their huts in twos and threes, most of them talking quietly.

When Kisil had climbed down from the bricks, I saw a group of house slaves approaching. I knew them by their clean clothes, which were of better quality than those worn by the rest, and by their better-groomed appearance.

A young man who seemed to be their spokesman came forward. "Moses, we believe in you. We want to leave Egypt, too. It is true we are better treated than those of our people who work in the pits —" he gestured — "But it comes at a cost. We must smile and bow and pretend that we love our masters. We are to them as dogs, as pets."

"What is your name?" asked Kisil.

"Hosheah. My father's name was Nayun." He was a remarkably good-looking boy. His hair was long, black and curly, his chin only beginning to show a man's beard. He was dressed, as the house slaves usually were, in white cotton, and not the dark, ragged wool robes of the Avru. The others nodded as he spoke, and both Kisil and I saw how they followed his words. I remember thinking, *this young fellow is barely grown, but see how the others look up to him*.

Kisil took the young man's hand in both of his own. "I understand, and you are all welcome. I promise you that there will be no punishment for you, if you join with the rest of your people and put on no airs."

"We will not," said the young man firmly, and the people with him agreed. "We do not do so now. We have not been among those who look down on the rest of our people." He hesitated, and his eyes dropped to his sandals. "We have been — ashamed, most of us. I did not choose to become a house-servant," he added. "I was chosen — because I was —" He stopped.

"Because you were pretty," I said softly. "Like her." I lifted an eyebrow at a young woman behind him, with great dark eyes and skin like fresh cream. She blushed.

He followed my gaze. "Yes. Nor was it her choice. That is true of many of us."

There was nothing to say after that. Hosheah lifted his hands. "What should we do, until the day of liberation?"

"Continue to go to your work. Treat your fellow Avru well." He turned to go, then stopped and pointed across the wadi. "Wait. There is a thing that you can do. Move your belongings to the huts on this side, and give your larger huts to men with families." They blinked at each other doubtfully, but Kisil assured them. "No one will stop you. You were given larger huts because of your service, as a privilege. That day has passed."

The people murmured, but happily. This was indeed something that they could do. "And prepare yourselves for whatever comes," added Kisil. "The day will be soon."

Not long after, of all people, Desan appeared at the door of our hut. He glared at Kisil. "I shall not give up my home for any of these mud-stompers," he said without preamble. "And I thought you said that you came not to give orders, liar!"

Kisil did not bother to rise from his stool. "I gave no orders, Desan. Some of the house-slaves came to me and asked what they could do for our people. I told them. You may do as you choose."

He said no more, but Desan was not satisfied. "I still believe that you have come to lord it over others and press your own will upon all the people!"

Kisil was not even looking at him. "It does not surprise me that you think that, Desan. Some people think that the hearts of others carry only the same thoughts and needs and desires that lie in their own."

It took a moment, but Desan finally understood. He looked confused, and for a moment he dropped his guard and spoke without hostility: "But what else is there, but to seek power?"

Kisil finally looked up. "To seek *justice*, Desan. Justice and truth. Justice, and truth, and peace. The power or glory or honor of any man is nothing next to those things. Your power will die with you, but if you leave those things behind — you will be remembered forever."

Desan frowned, and his hatred rose up once more. "I was master of these people once," he growled, "and I will be again. What do I care what remains when I die? I will have my will done while I live, no matter what the cost."

"Were you truly master? Or were you merely the house-dog of the Egyptians?"

Desan snarled and spat and stalked away.

I watched him go. "Beware of that man, Kisil. Beware of him. He is —"

"He is dangerous. I know. I am indeed wary of him." He smiled. "But I do not fear him. His time is past, and he knows it."

I followed the big man as he climbed the slope to his brother's hut, on the other side of the mud pits. I was conscious of another of those strange — premonitions, but this time it was not a good one. "He will try yet again," I said. "And he may succeed."

Kisil looked at me, and slowly nodded. "I hear, my wife. I hear, and I will remember."

64

That day passed, and then another, but no word came from the palace, and our taskmasters called us to the mud pits and the sledges as usual. There were more rumbles and shocks through the earth, more deep thunder from the clear sky, more unease among the people. What is all this salt for? they whispered.

Gamba came to the Avru camp often, by night, to tell Kisil of what he had seen and heard and to ask for advice. The Dwarf, as the big Kushite called the king, was growing more and more worried, he said. There was little water for the palace, and he was reduced — if it could be called that — to bathing in wine.

We gave Gamba two bags of salt to spread around his own dwelling. He looked puzzled, but I knew that he would use it as Kisil directed.

And he was glad. That next day, the frogs came. They came by tens, and then by hundreds, and by the morning of the fifth day after the River turned to blood, they came by the thousands, hopping and croaking miserably in search of water which was nowhere to be found.

It was considered a privilege of the Egyptians to live near the sacred Great River and its branches. We slaves were obliged to live farther away, near the ocean, and frogs do not live in salt water. The frogs troubled the Egyptians much more than us. When the wind blew from the city, the stench was overpowering.

We did see a few frogs, especially in the mud pits; but not many crossed the salt barrier around the Avru camp, and those that did would not cross the salt around the Avru's huts. The salt burned their already dry skin, and they stayed away from our compound. The Egyptians noticed this, but did not know why. We knew that word would be carried back to the king.

The taskmasters still commanded us to work, and we did. We gathered straw from the fields and the stables, stamped it into the mud, and filled the brick molds. I took up my own place with the Avru men and women, and Kisil and Gershom did the same. One of the old Avru women cared for Eliezer, along with some other small ones, while we worked.

The Egyptian guards were no longer friendly with the Avru overseers as before. They were worried about the frogs in their own houses, and it had not been lost on them that the Avru's huts saw very few of them, and only in the brick pits. We joked that the bricks would soon contain as much frog as mud, but only the Avru laughed.

Soon the guards began to leave, one by one. One of the last told us, "No need for more bricks. No one is building." When he left, the Avru overseers thought it prudent to leave as well, and the people went back to their huts, laughing.

Other things were happening. The sun, as always, was fiercely hot, but there was a kind of darkness to the sky in the north, and the wind seemed more capricious than usual, blowing first one way, then another. There were lights in the sky from the north at night, too, and when the wind came from that direction, there was a bitter, acrid scent in the air.

Gamba visited again in the night, bringing news. "The Dwarf is furious. He will summon you tomorrow."

Kisil grinned. "Very well. We will be ready."

Gamba hesitated, a troubled look on his face in the lamplight. "What is it, my friend?" asked my husband.

"Moses, I am grateful for the salt. My family is not plagued by the frogs — and I have passed the secret on to some of our friends...?" He gave Kisil a questioning look, but Kisil nodded his approval. The big man grinned gratefully. "What happens next?" he asked.

"Flies. You will need more salt. Gershom, fetch him some." Our son brought another bag of the salt we had collected. "Here, Gamba. You will need it soon. I am sending the older children to the sea, to gather more. You might do the same."

"Why will we need more salt?"

"To put on the piles of frogs near your home when they die. If you do not, you will have great clouds of flies. You will have flies even so, but with the salt, not so many."

Gamba's face broke into one of his enormous smiles, like the sun rising. He laughed. "Moses, you are a wonder."

As Gamba had predicted, Kisil was summoned to the king's presence again. This time, I did not go. Eliezer was feverish, and I chose to stay with him. Gamba told me of it later as Kisil listened.

"The Dwarf was frantic, standing there with hundreds of hopping, croaking frogs around him, even in the Great Hall of the palace. Moses' mother was there too, but she did not seem to be bothered. She sat there watching and saying nothing, with a small smile on her face. When a frog landed in her lap, she stroked it, as if it were a pet."

I laughed. "I can see Basia doing that. Nothing would shake her composure."

Gamba stood, and assumed a stiffly erect posture. We were sitting on the bench in front of our hut, or he would have struck his head on the roof-timbers. He lifted his huge fists and shook them. "'Take this plague away from me!'"

Gamba imitated the king's high, squeaky voice perfectly, and we laughed. "The Dwarf was trembling with rage," he said, grinning, his mirth as big as he. He reverted to the high, mocking voice. "'You, or your witch wife, you have brought this upon me! Take them away!'"

The big man grinned at me, his eyes sparkling. "Moses replied so calmly." He suppressed a laugh. "He had no fear of the king at all. 'I? I hafe done nothhing... The frogth cannot liffe in the bloody wather."

Kisil gaped at him, eyes wide, and I laughed delightedly. After a heartbeat, Kisil did too. The big man had mimicked his odd way of speaking, and his stiffness of manner with the king, perfectly.

"'I have done nothing,'" Gamba repeated, still in Kisil's voice. "'What would you have ME do?' Then he looked right at the king and said, 'Will you let the Avru go?'"

"'NO!'" Gamba squealed, and imitated the king's impotent shaking of his fists. "'I do not know this *Heyuwah*! I am king here, and god! No one commands but me! It is as you say — the frogs cannot live in the water!'"

"Then Moses said —" The big man's voice grew deeper — "'You will have flies. Flies uncountable, thousands upon thousands of them. In seven days, the ground will be so covered with flies that you will not see the earth — and you will plead to be freed of them, and you will let the people go.'"

Gamba paused, then went on: "The king was so furious, he called for guards to surround Moses with their spears lifted, and he was about to call for Moses to be killed — but then he thought better of it." The big man looked at me then. "Moses was not afraid. Not at all. Moses even smiled at him, and I think that shook him."

The big man's face was grim. "The dwarf is even more afraid, Moses." He frowned down at my husband. "He fears you even more now. And he fears you, too," he said, turning his eyes to me. "When the flies come, he will be still more afraid."

"And what will come next, after the flies?" I asked.

Kisil considered. "I am not sure. But I have a guess. Do you remember the burning dust?" Gamba looked puzzled. "It will come here — but much more of it, much thicker. Soon, I think, but I am not sure when. When it does, we must tell the people to keep themselves covered, and keep the animals out of the fields."

He suddenly stood up. "I must find Aron, and Boaz. And quickly. Explain about the dust to Gamba." And he was gone.

"Burning dust?" asked the big man.

The flies were terrible for the Egyptians, but for us they were little more than a nuisance. We had few dead frogs about, whereas there were great, stinking heaps of them in the city, soon crawling with maggots and black clouds of flies.

The brick pits were forgotten, but Kisil had the people working hard during the respite even so. They were gathering fodder for our animals and food for ourselves. Some grumbled, but not many. His advice had been good so far, and more and more of the Avru trusted him.

The young man Hosheah saw to it that the house slaves helped with the work, as he had seen that they helped with gathering the straw for the brick pits. Desan and Aviram, most of the Avru overseers, and some of the house slaves still held themselves aloof; but it was clear that there was a new fellowship between the two groups that had not been there before.

Kisil had the people gather as much hay as they could and store it in their huts. Grain, too, when they could find it. "When the dust comes," he told them, "keep yourselves covered, and do not let the sheep or goats or donkeys graze in the field. Feed them what you have stored, and try to keep the dust from their hides if you can. Brush it away or keep them under shelter. It will not be for long. Rain will follow, and it will wash the fields clean."

They blinked at that, more than they did at hearing of the dust. Rain? In Egypt? This never happened. Crops were watered by the rising of the Great River, and not by rain.

"When will this dust come?" asked one of the women.

Kisil looked to the north, across the ocean. He pointed.

There was a cloud there, and it was growing larger. That acrid taste and smell were in the air, and the wind was from the north.

Kisil was staring at the cloud. "Tomorrow," he said.

And the next morning, it began just as Kisil had said. The burning ash, which felt to the Egyptians like biting gnats, came and settled on the land in wave after choking wave. The heavy wool robes of our people protected us, and their thick wool protected our sheep; but the light cotton garments of the Egyptians did little to protect their skin, and many did not even bother with those above the waist. Their bare skin was exposed, as were the hides of their thin-coated cattle. With next to no hair at all, their pigs suffered terribly. The dust burned people and animals alike, and running sores began to appear on their skin.

The dust fell more and more thickly, and the Egyptian cattle ate the dust along with the hay in the fields. Soon they fell ill as well, and before long, there were more cattle dead than living in the Egyptians' fields. The kites and jackals feasted, but all other living creatures suffered — and with the dead cattle, the flies returned.

We were summoned back to the king's palace. It was not Gamba who was sent to fetch us, but another man, an Egyptian we had not seen before, dressed in court clothes, accompanied by two guards. He was finely dressed, but his skin was red and spotted with sores. The guards, though dressed more humbly, had the same appearance and scratched at the welts miserably.

Kisil and I looked at each other but said nothing as we prepared to go. We hoped that all was well with the big man.

The guard pointed at me. "She is not to come."

I stared at him, directly into his eyes, then lifted my hands and gestured in a way that I hoped looked mysterious and menacing.

"I shall go where I choose." I made my already deep voice even deeper for the occasion.

The guard — a young man, new to his post, I guessed — swallowed and made the sign against the Evil Eye. When I followed Kisil, he looked back at me, but said nothing more.

When we reached the palace, Gamba was on duty at the front gate. He grinned at our visible relief, then quickly put his "guard scowl" back on and waved us through before the others saw. Then he dismissed our escort, bade the other guards wait by the gate, and conducted us to the king's Great Hall himself.

"Be ready," he whispered as we moved toward the big room. "The Dwarf is in a towering rage today."

"Do you suffer from the dust?" I whispered.

He grinned and shook his head. "I and my family wash often," he said in his low rumble, then added, "Your mother and Hafiz too."

We walked through the halls of the Palace — and I noted that the place was not as magnificent as it had been on our previous visit. The place was untidy, unswept and dusty, and the halls were cluttered with trash — plates of uneaten food, dead flowers still in their vases, fallen hangings, even castoff clothing and sandals. We saw shattered dishes and pottery scattered across the floors and fabric torn from the stained walls, and I wondered what disorders had obtained here in the past few days — and where the servants were who should have been cleaning.

We entered the Great Hall, and sure enough, the king was standing in front of his throne, surrounded by shivering courtiers and servants. He had evidently been taking his fury out on them. Even that grand room was littered with trash and clutter.

When we entered, the king turned on us furiously — but before he could speak, Kisil spoke first, and forcefully: *"Will you let the Avru go?"*

"She was not to be here!" the king cried in his shrill, nasal voice, pointing at me with a shaking finger. The courtiers, most of whom seemed to be affected by the dust, shrank back and stared at me fearfully.

I gazed at the little king — not smiling this time, but frowning — and I began, very slowly, to raise my right hand.

The king's eyes widened, and he quickly flapped a hand in dismissal. "Never mind!" He was clearly afraid of what I might be about to do. I dropped my hand and nodded, watching him narrowly with my chin lifted, as if giving him temporary permission to go on.

My haughtily superior attitude was not lost on him. The king of Egypt's towering fury calmed down considerably in those few seconds. He watched me nervously afterward, though he tried hard not to show it.

The little man rubbed at the sores on his arms and touched the sores on his face. "Will you heal me?" he asked. It was more a plea than a challenge or a demand — and again, I thought, *me*, he says. Not *us* or *my people.*

I looked around. As I had first thought, all the people in the court were covered with sores. Every one of them bore inflamed wounds and reddened skin for all their gaudy finery. Even the young boys that crouched behind the throne, the king's pages and errand boys, were affected. No one was free of them — no one but Gamba.

I did not see Basia in the room, nor Hafiz. Wise of them to stay out of sight, I thought.

"If you let the Avru go, you will be healed."

"I do not believe you! I do not believe you!" shrieked the little man. "I will have you killed if you do not heal me! Killed, and thrown to the crocodiles!"

There could be no more horrible punishment for an Egyptian, I knew.

Kisil did not flinch. He slowly and mournfully shook his head. "There is worse to come, Uncle. If you do not free the Avru, there will be plagues upon Egypt that will make these seem silly and small." The little man opened his mouth to speak, but before he could, Kisil added: "And if you kill me — *they will never end."*

"What? What? What will your Heyuwah send next? Fire from Heaven?" The king laughed bitterly.

"Yes." Kisil's gaze was steady, his voice flat and toneless. "Hail and fire together, in a downpour of rain like none that Egypt has ever seen. But it will not be I Who sends it. It will come from our God." Kisil frowned. "And even that will not be the worst, if you do not let the people go."

Kisil paused for a heartbeat. "*His name is Ehyehuwah,* uncle." he intoned and a deep and portentous voice. "You will have reason to remember that name."

The little man stood there, scratching and shaking, and glaring at Kisil. "Heal me!" he finally shrieked, shaking his little fists in the air. "Do as I command!"

Kisil stood straighter, though I would not have believed it possible. Then his voice — the same voice he used when he spoke to the Avru — rang through the Great Hall, as loud as a ram's horn in spite of his lisp.

"*King of Egypt! Hear the command of Ehyehuwah, the One God, the God of the Avru: LET MY PEOPLE GO!"*

Mouths fell open, but no one moved. There was a silence after that. Even the king was silent. Then he gathered himself, took an unsteady breath, and shouted back, his voice thin and reedy after Kisil's. "I SHALL NOT!" Then he shook himself and fled to some room behind the throne, dismissing us with an angry wave as he ran. The courtiers watched us fearfully, in silence, as we turned and left the Great Hall.

Gamba escorted us back to the gate, where he left us with a wink. We knew he would slip out to the Avru camp that night, to ask about what he had heard.

No one accompanied us back to the camp, and we had no need of guards. No one spoke to us, or even looked at us. It was not only the king who was afraid.

As we walked back to the Avru camp, I asked, "How do you know these things?"

"I have seen them before. In Attica, and farther west, though in a much smaller way. The fire-mountains belch clouds of smoke and dust, and rain follows — heavy rain, mixed with hail and fire from Heaven. The anger of the mountains north of us is very great indeed, from what we have already seen." He shook his head. "It will be terrible."

"What will happen then?"

"I do not know, Tzipporah. I am afraid of what *might* happen, though. A terrible darkness, a cloud of soot so thick that... Wait." He suddenly stopped, and pointed.

Kisil and I were walking near the stinking River, so red it was almost black. He was pointing at an insect there by the path. There was only one.

He picked it up and studied it, and then he began to smile.

"A grasshopper," I said, puzzled.

"Not a grasshopper." He held it up. "This is a *locust*, Tzipporah. And they do not come singly."

I had seen a few, years ago; but in Midyan, they move on quickly. There is little for them to eat in desert land. I began to get a glimpse of what Kisil was thinking.

65

And, indeed, the next day the rain began.

I call it rain, but it was much more than rain. It was a rain like the one of which Chaninah had told us, the one that had made Noach build his great Ark. I had rarely seen rain at all, and had no standard by which to judge — but to me, it appeared that the Heavens had opened and the Earth would soon be flooded to the height of the tallest trees and mountains, as that tale said. The rain was so intense, so violent, so heavy, that it was difficult to go out in it and breathe, or even to keep one's feet. The sheer pounding of the water could drive a man to his knees.

As in Midyan, little rain fell in Egypt at any time. The land was watered by the rising of the Great River, not by the sky — and rain like that had never fallen in Egypt before, never in all its long history, and has never fallen since.

The deluge went on for a day and a night. Rain could be cool and refreshing, and in the desert rain is a blessing; but not this rain. It pounded like fists, and it burned, like the dust motes that the Egyptians took for biting flies. This rain was a plague.

And there was more. A terrible hail began to fall with the rain, with stones the size of hens' eggs, ducks' eggs, the fists of men. The crops were battered to the ground, animals left exposed were hammered to death, and more than one man or woman caught outside in it was killed — stoned to death with stones that fell from the black, boiling sky.

And there was still more. Fire from Heaven struck the earth, great bolts of white fire, with deafening cracks of thunder that sounded like the end of the world. The fire struck anything that stood higher than a man — and sometimes men as well. One could see the bolts strike five times in ten heartbeats, everywhere one looked. The barrage was constant and unceasing, and there was much destruction.

Shops and homes were destroyed all over the city by the hail and the rain, and many Egyptians were killed, battered or burnt to death. None were lost in the Avru camp; the wadi was below the level of the surrounding houses, and our huts were low and covered with thatching which cushioned the force of the hailstones. A few of the huts were struck by the fire from Heaven, but the rain quenched the burning straw quickly, and little harm was done. The brick stacks and pits were struck many times, but no one was there.

The storm was fierce and terrible, beyond anyone's experience, and not like any normal storm. The cracks and booms of the fire from Heaven were deafening, and the fire and the rain and the hail all came down with killing force. Gamba even saw the white fire run along the ground in the city, blindingly bright, and take one man after another. The thunder was more than thunder; it rolled and rumbled constantly, louder than I or anyone had ever heard, and it seemed to come from beyond the sky. The people were terrified.

And in the middle of all this, the king summoned Kisil — and me — to his presence.

We walked through the storm with Gamba beside us. The big man was terribly frightened, cowering at every boom and crack of thunder, shuddering at the bolts of fire falling around us; but Kisil seemed entirely without fear. The rain was heavy, and we were soaked after only a few steps and struggled to keep going; but the hailstones were not falling where we were, and neither was the fire from the sky.

I knew we were safe, somehow. I took my confidence from Kisil, who walked toward the palace as if it were a fine, clear day. Before long, Gamba, too, seemed less fearful, though his great white eyes were still wide, shifting around nervously as we walked. It was cool, at least, in the rain, and I wondered at that later, too. Before, it had burned, but it did not burn us that day.

The city had changed, so completely that it did not appear to be the same place. Buildings made of mud brick had slumped into great heaps of wet earth. Sun-dried mud brick does well where it rains little — but when it rains hard, it becomes mud again. Those made of stone had been washed clean of their bright paintwork and decoration, and many were scarred from fire. The stalls and shelters in the great square were reduced to shards and pieces and unidentifiable debris. We saw no people in the streets — only wide-eyed Egyptians in doorways and openings and beneath heavy abutments, staring at us in astonishment as we walked through the downpour without fear.

The king was more subdued that day, as well he might be. The Palace was a wreck, the halls filled with reefs and piles of trash; broken vessels, whole ones, fabric, even rotted food and stinking, overflowing chamber pots. Not a servant was to be seen. We knew that Basia and Hafiz were being sheltered by Gamba and his people in their own slave village, so we were not concerned about them; and that was good, because the Palace seemed to have become more of a deserted cesspit and midden than a palace.

The Great Hall was lit with flashes of God's fire and echoed with the cracks and crashes of His thunder. There was no one else there but a single servant who knelt in terror at the foot of the throne. I imagined all the preening courtiers cowering in their quarters, under their couches.

The king spoke, but with less anger and outrage this time. He, too, had been cowed by the torrential storm.

"Is this your God's work — what is his name again?" He seemed almost humbled.

"Ehyehuwah. Yes, it is He Who does this. Will you let His people go?"

The king stared at my husband bitterly, trying to sneer, but his eyes were wide with fear. He glanced at me — only glanced. He feared my eyes and now my hands, I knew.

"I will," he finally said. "Take your people and go. Get out of my land. Only ask your God to have mercy on me."

On *him*, I thought again. Not on his people. Always *him*.

"All Egypt suffers, little man," I said in my deepest tones. "Not you alone."

"I AM Egypt!" he tried to roar, but his voice was shaky and weak as well as high and nasal. "Get out! Get out of my house, and get out of my land!" He still would not look at me.

Kisil lifted both hands, somberly. "When the storm passes, we will go."

The rain lasted for a day and a night. On the dawn of the second day, the rain had slackened to a drizzle, and no more hailstones fell. There had been a structure, made of wood, that the Egyptians used for lifting and placing stones. I saw it after the storm, or what was left of it — a few stumps and broken shards of wood, smashed and burnt black.

The stacks of bricks had gone back to mud, and, just as we had seen in the city, we saw that much of the construction that the king had commanded had done the same. Where once were great buildings of brick and mortar, now were mere heaps and mounds of sliding mud. And once again, the very poverty of the Avru protected them; the thick, overhanging thatch of their huts had kept much of the rain from their walls, and though damaged and weakened, their shelters still stood.

The land was still dark. The pall of thick clouds had not lightened, even after the storm, and the wind was still strong, though unsettled. It blew powerfully from the south, but as the day wore on, it slowly moved eastward. The sky grew darker, but Kisil assured us that there would be no more rain.

"Kisil, we have won," I said joyously. "We must tell the people to get ready. Will we leave tomorrow?"

He gave me a sour look. "We will not be leaving tomorrow, nor the day after. Look."

Egyptian guards, a dozen or more, were approaching the camp. "I expected this," Kisil whispered. "The storm has ended, and the king has gone back on his word."

"What will you do?" I whispered back.

"Watch."

The guards entered the camp and began walking through it, some swinging their whips, some brandishing bared swords. "Get back to the brick pits!" cried the chief of the guards in a hoarse shout. "There is much to be rebuilt! You must work even harder now!"

Kisil stepped forward and faced the man as he passed. "The king said —"

He whirled and lifted his whip. "I know what he said!" bellowed the Egyptian. Though he rasped out his commands fiercely, I saw the terror in his eyes as he faced my husband. "He has rescinded his order! You are to go back to the brick pits! And you are to go now!" We saw the other Avru watching, dozens of them.

Kisil took another step forward, lifted both his hands, and intoned, in a voice loud enough for all to hear: "Go back and tell the king the words of Ehyehuwah, God of Yisrael: *Because you have sworn falsely before the God of Yisrael, O King, there will be locusts across all the land of Egypt. There will be locusts such as have never been seen before this day, and will never be seen again. The crops that have survived My hail, I will destroy with My locusts.* So says Ehyehuwah, the God of Yisrael." He frowned. "Now go."

The guard stared, open-mouthed. Kisil smiled, that same jackal's smile that I had seen before. "Hurry now! Tell your mighty master. Perhaps he can command the locusts not to come." Then he made a shooing gesture, as if to a troublesome child, and turned away.

The Egyptian hesitated, then said weakly, "Return to the brick pits," but Kisil did not even turn to acknowledge his words. The man stood, his mouth working, then left in confusion. The other guards followed.

The locusts came before dark on that very day. The wind was still strong from the east, and that same wind brought them, so many that they darkened the sky once more. We had not seen the sun for days, between the dust, the storm, and now the locusts.

The locusts left the Avru alone. There were no crops in the brick pits, nor in the dust of our camp. But all across the land of Egypt, they devastated the few crops that had been left by the burning dust and the rain and the hail and the fire from heaven. We were all but deafened by the buzz of the insects in their millions, and we could hear the wailing of the Egyptians, even inside our huts.

"Ehyehuwah's wrath is terrible," I said to Kisil as we ate our mutton and bread a night or two later.

Kisil nodded, his face thoughtful. "What comes next will be worse," he said.

"The darkness?"

"Yes. The fire-mountain — to the north of us, I think, and west — is pouring it out, even now, and the wind from the north will bring it." He frowned. "It will be terrible. Even for our own people. I have thought of a way to prepare for it, but it must be done at the last moment before the darkness comes."

"How?"

"I will teach you, so you may teach others. It involves water, and blood."

66

The king summoned Kisil back to the palace again, and again gave his word that the Avru could go free. When he and Aron returned, Kisil seemed troubled. "What is it, my love?"

"The king demands that the locusts be gone before the Avru will be released. I knew they were coming, but I do not know when they will leave."

But that night, the wind, which was still strong, shifted again, and began to come from the north. By morning, it was even stronger, coming from the west — and by sunset of that day, there was not a locust to be seen. The winds that had blown them in had blown them back again. It was as if a great circle of winds had passed over the land, and had now moved onward. The sky, though, was still troubled — dark clouds, rolling, wave after wave, coming from the north, contrary to the winds.

But the king, of course, reneged on his word yet again. The guards came and commanded the people to go back to the brick pits, and the house slaves to go back to their work.

Kisil was furious. "He does not know what is to come," he growled. "The darkness will come next — and it will be the worst of all. This foolish little king's pride will be brought down at last. The darkness will kill his people by the thousands."

"But, Kisil — would the darkness not come, even if the king *had* let the people go?"

He stood still and nodded. "I think so," he said after a breath. "I think so. Still, it is beyond understanding that he so adamantly refuses to do what is so clearly right, even as these things happen to his land and his people."

We set off for the palace. Aron and I followed. We did not even pause for a waterskin, but set off as we were. Kisil had only his staff in his hand.

The city was still a scene of devastation, with unpainted walls and collapsed buildings; but the people had returned to the streets and the square, and some even smiled at us as we passed. They seemed to think the worst was over.

We did not enter the palace. There was no need. In the great square at its entrance, there was a grand ceremony of some sort going on.

Evidently, the king and his priests and courtiers were giving thanks to the gods of Egypt for the ending of the plagues. There were the idols on their platforms, and there were the priests and priestesses with their swinging pots of acrid smoke and their drums and flutes and horns.

And there was the king. It was the first and only time I saw the little man in his magnificent crown and regal robes. The crown was a tall and elaborate thing of red and white and gold, with serpents above his brow and long ear-pieces that hung almost to his skinny shoulders. The robe flared out from those shoulders to the ground, richly decorated with gold and precious stones, made from fabrics and in colors that I had never seen. He carried a golden crook and a golden flail, and stared out imperiously at the crowd before him, carried on a high dais borne by a dozen slaves.

We had not been summoned — but that did not matter. Kisil stood in the center of the square before the palace, and the people ran from him, leaving him standing there alone, with me a step behind and to his left. The priests and courtiers began to turn to see what the commotion was, and finally the king himself looked. He smiled, as if he were victorious — but even then, and even at that distance, I could see the doubt in his face

Kisil roared at the king as if he were an errant child, in the loudest voice I had yet heard from him. His anger was visible, and terrible — and more terrifying still, it was a cold anger, without a hint of hatred or of fear. Kisil held the power, and he knew it.

"Listen to me, Uncle! Listen well, little king! Be humble, and be afraid! You stand before Ehyehuwah, little man! You have broken your sworn word to Him, and once again, all Egypt will suffer for it! *The plagues are not ended!"*

The king stood on his dais, surrounded on the ground beneath by his courtiers and soothsayers, some of his women, and his sallow, sneering son. The king, too, tried to sneer, but all could see that he was afraid. He looked up nervously at the roiling sky. The people in the square — and there were many — all stood still, listening. Some of them, too, looked at the sky and wondered what would come next.

Kisil's gentle gray eyes were as hard as stone, and blazed with icy fury. *"There will come a great darkness over the land,"* Kisil boomed, in a voice like thunder with only a hint of his lisp. *"A darkness thicker than the blackest night! A darkness that has never been seen before, nor will ever be seen again! You will live without light for days! The Sun will be gone, and even your lamps and fires will give no light! It will be a darkness so thick that it can be felt, and you will not dare to move from your place!"*

The people in the square watched with wide eyes and open mouths, looking from Kisil to the king and back again. I stood before Kisil with both hands raised, turning them toward the balcony where the king stood. My fingers were spread wide and curved toward him, like claws.

Kisil's voice rose, deep and resonant — and threatening: *"And in this black darkness, O King, the oldest and youngest of your people will die! All Egypt will be sick unto death! You yourself will cough up the darkness, and you will be too weak to rule your dying people!"*

Kisil then lifted his staff and pointed it at the king as his voice boomed forth like a clap of thunder: *"AND THE AVRU WILL GO FREE, AS EHYEHUWAH HAS COMMANDED, WHETHER YOU WILL IT OR NO!"* He set his staff back on the ground with a ringing impact and stood still, glaring at the king.

The little man on the balcony affected a nervous laugh, then pointed a shaking finger. "You lie, Moses," he cried out shakily in his reedy voice. "Nothing like that will happen! The Avru will remain my slaves forever! This darkness will pass with the clouds, and nothing will change!" He lifted his own hands then, in imitation, I thought, of what I had done. "No one commands here but I!" he shrieked.

"Begone! Do not come here again! If I see you again, one of us will die!"

Kisil only gazed back at the king calmly, which we knew only infuriated him all the more. "You have spoken truly, king of Egypt." His voice was just as calm, though it came forth with great volume. "The next time you see me, one of us will die." I smiled my coldest smile, and after a glance, the king would not look at me. I laughed openly — and then, as Kisil raised his right hand, as if in some curse or blessing, the earth moved.

It was a low thunder, too deep to be heard. The people in the square cried out, and some ran, though aimlessly. There was nowhere to run. The king's eyes widened, visible even from where we stood, and I laughed again.

Kisil's hand, still raised, changed suddenly to a fist. He held it there for a heartbeat — then he raised his staff and pointed at one of the idols held high by the king's slaves. At that moment, the platform gave way, and the statue — a seated man with the head of a falcon — fell to the earth and was shattered. It had evidently been made from some sort of pottery. The people gasped and screamed — and then Kisil pointed his staff at another idol, and it too fell and was broken.

This one was a seated man wearing a crown — and I realized that it was an idol made to resemble the king himself as a god.

I suspected that the platforms that bore them had been left out in the rain for days, and had been weakened by it — and the movement of the earth had startled the slaves that carried them, and added to the stress on the wood. Kisil had seen the signs of the impending fall of both and reacted instantly, turning the impending accident to his advantage.

The slaves bearing the other idols began to set them down. The crowd turned as one to look at Kisil.

He pointed his staff at the king himself, who visibly cowered; and then, without a word, we turned and left the square without looking back.

It was already growing darker. More thick clouds were rolling in, blocking out the sun, almost to the horizon. A thin line of gray remained, and even the setting sun seemed dimmer as it filled the world with an eerie light.

Back at the Avru camp, Kisil called the people together. "A great darkness is coming," he told them, standing on the drying mound of mud that had once been finished bricks. "It will come tomorrow. It will not hurt you if you stay indoors — so you must not go outside for as long as it lasts.

"Here is what you must do to prepare. Gather food and water, enough to last for several days. Dig a privy hole inside your hut, and keep it covered. It will smell bad, but it will only be for a while.

"Slaughter a lamb from the flock. Kill it by cutting its throat, with the sharpest knife you can find, and catch all of its blood — *all* of it — in a bowl or a pot. After you gut and skin the lamb, set it aside. You will roast it in the ground, as you have before. You will dig it up and eat it when the days of darkness are over. But you must use the blood first, while it is fresh.

"Take cloths, and dip the hems and edges in the blood. Cover your doors with them. Leave no gaps where the darkness can get in. Press the cloths to the doorposts and the lintel, and the edges to each other. Fix them in place with thorns or stones or pegs or whatever you have. Leave no gap uncovered, and be sure the blood is all around the sides, everywhere. Place wood or bricks at the foot of the door, and stick the cloths to them too.

"Then go inside your huts and wait. And do not delay doing this! The darkness will be here before sunset tomorrow. A little of the darkness will enter — you will see it — but do not remove the cloths or uncover your doors. Wait. When you see light through the cloth again, it will be safe to leave your huts."

"Why the blood?" asked a woman, who was making a disgusted face.

"The darkness is death. The blood will satisfy it, and keep it from you and make it pass over you. Now prepare yourselves. The darkness may come sooner than I think."

And it happened just as Kisil said. All the next day, the sky remained as dim and gray as twilight; but the great darkness came that next evening, not long before sunset. We could see it blotting out even the little light that was left as it moved toward us from the north. It was still far away, but it rolled toward us like a great sandstorm on the desert

— except for its deep blackness, and the way it seemed to hug the ground.

"Look!" cried a woman as it drew closer. We were gathered near the collapsed brick-pile, and the blackness was coming along the ground, creeping, slithering, like some kind of creature from a nightmare. Long tendrils of darkness slid out before it as if reaching, feeling their way, seeking out the low places, as the great mass of it sloped up behind, towering higher and higher, moving like a living thing, black and boiling.

We ran to our huts, ignoring the shouting guards. Soon they were ignoring us and running too, running for their own homes, for their lives.

Again, the open, airy homes of the Egyptians gave them no shelter, while the windowless hovels of the slaves and servants made the plague fall more lightly on the poor than on the wealthy. We only had the one door to block, while they had many windows and wide doorways, and no time to block them.

As we were frantically stuffing the bloody cloths into the door-cracks, I saw it — the darkness. Tendrils and curls of blackness came in, wafting and drifting with the air, curling around my feet even as we worked. I understood; it was as Kisil had said, a fine black powder, soot and ash from the fire-mountain, but smaller and finer than I had ever seen. "Is it harmful, Kisil?" I asked. "Is it truly death?"

He was working beside me, smearing the blood on the cloth where it touched the doorframe. "It is indeed death, for the very old and the very young, but to breathe it is sickness for anyone. The Egyptians, even the young and strong, will be coughing black phlegm for many days after it passes." He waved a hand. "The cloths on our doors will let in a little, too fine to see. But breathing it in full-strength, without the cloths and the blood —" He shook his head. "That is very bad, even for a healthy man."

And I saw the reason for the blood — the real reason. It congealed and stuck the fabric to the doorways, so the darkness could not enter. The blood truly did keep us safe from the soot.

"What about our sheep?"

"Some will die, again the very old and the very young. But it is less harmful to animals. They too will cough and choke for some time, but they will live if they are strong."

I thought about all this. He had seen this before, I knew; but I wondered if Ehyehuwah had told Kisil about the blood, or if he had thought of it himself.

And then I wondered; *did it matter?*

67

Who can say how long that darkness lasted? Some said two days, some said five. We could not see the Sun, and there was no way to mark the passage of time. We could only huddle in our huts and wait. We moved cautiously, in almost total darkness, with no fire in the hut. Perhaps a small lamp at times, when we needed it badly. Kisil had told us that outside, the darkness would be so thick that even fire would give no light.

Sounds were muffled, but even so, we heard wails and cries of fear from the Egyptians, shouted prayers to their animal-headed gods, and lamentations for their dead, even across the distance from where they lived. We ate a little, drank a a little, and we kept our privy holes covered — they did smell bad, but we grew used to it.

We sang songs of home to keep our boys calm, and they were. As well as the singing, Kisil told stories to Gershom, and the boy made up one of his own, about a lost sheep that found its way home. Eliezer slept a little more than he usually did. Like Kisil as a child, he did not cry, nor did Gershom. Nor did I.

And we waited.

Finally, we saw light coming through the cloths over our doors again. Cautiously, we pulled the cloths free and crept out. We saw others, haggard and pale, many coughing, also coming from their huts and looking around them.

The clouds were gone, the sky clear and blue. The sun was high. It was midday, but the land we saw as we looked around in wonder was unrecognizable. Everything was stained with black; everything. It was as if a black cloth had fallen over Egypt, and only let the land peep through here and there, as if through holes in it.

The fields were black, the roads were black, the buildings and the ground were black. Walls were smeared and streaked, but anything flat, anything on the ground, and the ground itself, was covered with blackness. A thick layer of black lay on everything, and when a man walked, the darkness curled and puffed around his feet as if it wanted to rise up and come back.

Kisil turned and spoke to the people in his loudest voice: "Prepare to leave, my people. No one will stop us."

The people began to move — some back toward their huts, some toward the blackened fields where sheep and goats, dusted with black themselves, waited. I saw a few forms lying still on the ground — as Kisil had said, the oldest of the sheep, and the last-born lambs, most of them, were dead. We, too, returned to our hut, to gather our few things and prepare our sons for the journey.

The house slaves tried to go back to their work, but they soon returned. Most did so joyfully, but some resentfully. They had been barred from the homes of the Egyptians, and some even thrown out. To have an Avru servant was now considered a curse and not a blessing.

The Avru overseers were sent packing as well. Some of the people wanted to punish them, but Kisil stood against that. "It was not their choice to be put over you," he proclaimed to the people. "We are all one now. Those who ask you for forgiveness, you must forgive. Leave the past behind, that it may not keep us enslaved. New lives begin today, for all of us."

It helped that many of the house slaves, and indeed the overseers too, brought gold and silver, jewelry, and even vessels of precious metal, richly worked and decorated, and some even with precious stones. The goods were not stolen — they were pressed upon the people by the Egyptians, who begged for mercy from their slaves. Indeed, some Egyptians even came to the Avru camp with more. "Please ask your God to spare us," they begged as they pressed their gifts into our hands. "Please go from among us, and ask Him to lift His hand from our people and our land."

One woman, as she gave a broad Egyptian necklace made of gold and multicolored gems, spoke bitterly. "Your God has taken my firstborn. Here, take this too. I have no more to give." In the years that followed, I heard it said that the curse fell upon the firstborn most of all, though I am not certain that that was true.

They gave us riches unimaginable only a few weeks before — and all the people shared them. Women who had worn rags and mud could now dress in fine fabrics and wear golden bracelets. I saw old men weep at the sight of their daughters' feet in sandals, girls who had gone barefoot all their lives. "Our wages for two centuries of work," some said, "and not nearly enough."

Later that day — that grand and glorious day — we saw the giant, Gamba, approaching the gate into the compound. He carried a small child on his shoulder, as black as he, and a small black woman walked beside him holding another child in her arms. Many others — some black, some brown, like us, and some pale — walked behind him, and as we watched, more came. There were not as many of these strangers as there were Avru in the camp, but there were very many — hundreds, at the least.

We went out to meet them as the sun was setting. The big man came closer, and as he drew near, he made to kneel before Kisil — but Kisil stopped him. "Do not kneel before me, my friend. You need not kneel before any man." He looked at the multitude behind him in surprise. "Who are all these people, Gamba? Why have they come?"

The giant's face was suddenly grave. He shifted the child on his shoulder. "These are the other slaves of the Egyptians — and some are Egyptians themselves. The poor, the despised, the oppressed." Gamba lifted his enormous hand and gestured toward the Avru camp behind us. "The king has commanded you and your people to leave, Moses," Gamba said in his deep, gravelly voice. Then he turned and gestured at the people behind him. "We would like to go with you. All of us. If your God will have us," he added, with a hopeful expression.

There were so many, of so many colors, dressed in so many ways. Young and old, small and large, many with children, some with their old ones carried on litters, some with carts or wagons, some with donkeys, and even a camel or two. All were looking at Kisil hopefully — and fearfully.

Kisil smiled broadly and lifted his hands high. "All are welcome," he cried out in his most penetrating voice. "Ehyehuwah is not only the God of the Avru. He is the God of all men. Come with us to freedom, and be welcome."

Gamba heaved a huge sigh of relief — very huge — and grinned at Kisil. "Thank you, my friend. Their leaders came to me. They knew of our friendship."

Kisil grinned and slapped the big man on his back — not far above his waist, as high as he could comfortably reach. The little boy on his shoulder laughed.

Kisil laughed too, then asked, "Is this your family?"

The big man grinned and swung the child down from his shoulder. He was Gershom's age, it turned out. On the big man's shoulder, he had looked like a toddler. "This is Nomba, named for —"

"Your father." Kisil ruffled the boy's wooly hair. His small grin was like Gamba's huge one.

"And this is Akoko, my wife, and my daughter Enu." The woman stepped forward. She was shy, and a little fearful, I could see.

I approached and asked her, "What does Akoko mean?"

The woman — taller than I, but not by much — said softly, "It means 'Bird,'" with a puzzled expression.

I laughed. "My name, too, means 'Bird!' I am Tzipporah," I embraced her, even as she held the smaller child in her arms. She laughed with me and relaxed, and we were friends from then onward.

Gamba turned and beckoned to a group of men, as black as himself, who were carrying a curtained litter. "We have brought another friend, Moses."

The men set the litter down, and a graceful white hand pulled back the curtain. It was Basia. Kisil ran to her with a cry of joy.

"Mother!" he exclaimed. "I had feared you dead!"

"Gamba took me to his hut," she said, then coughed. A kerchief that she brought to her mouth came away with a few spots of black on it. "I have a cough, but it is not bad. The blood protected me, along with Gamba's family. I am grateful to him."

"As am I! As am I!" said Kisil, turning and taking the giant's big hand in both of his own. "How can I ever thank you, my friend?"

The big man shrugged. "You told me about the blood, Kisil, and I told others. How could I not save the Lady? She was the only person in the palace worth saving."

"What of Hafiz?" I asked hopefully.

Basia answered with a warm smile. "Hafiz is well," she said. "He is back there among the throng, with the few possessions I could bring with me. No gold or silver," she added with a dismissive wave. "All that I have given away. Just some clothing, some things from Kisil's childhood, and other things that are dear to me."

"Hafiz is well," Gamba rumbled. "But the very old among the royal family, and among their servants, are dead." He shook his huge head. "There was no shelter from the darkness in the palace."

"The king allowed you to leave?" Kisil asked his foster mother.

She gave him a wry grin, and I suddenly knew where Kisil had learned his. "The king was not asked," she said, "and of course, where I go, my servant goes with me." Then she frowned. "The king's son — his firstborn and heir — he is dead too." I remembered that the man had not looked healthy when we saw him at the palace.

"But the king himself still lives?"

"He is very ill," said the big man. "But he closed himself in one of the temples of one of his gods, with heavy bronze doors, and he did not suffer as much as most." Gamba scowled, his enormous face like a thunderstorm. "He thought of no one but himself, and left his sister and son to die. If there is justice, he will pay for that."

Kisil frowned. "There is justice. But it belongs to Ehyehuwah."

Miryam was approaching, gazing at the woman on the litter with an unreadable expression. Kisil smiled and beckoned. When she drew near, he spoke to Basia: "Mother," he said, "This is my sister. Miryam — this is the woman who raised me. I call her Mother. I think she deserves that — and your respect. Even your love, if you can give it."

The two women, both strong in their own ways, faced each other. Miryam and Basia looked into one another's eyes for a breath — and then, as I knew she would,

Basia extended both her hands. Miryam took them without hesitation. "I am honored to meet you," said Kisil's sister softly.

"The honor is mine," said the older woman. Then she smiled, that crooked smile very like Kisil's. "We will talk," she said, and I saw her grip Miryam's hands firmly before she dropped them. Miryam laughed.

"That we will," she said.

Kisil laughed and embraced his sister, then his mother again. He turned and spoke to me. "We will celebrate, and then we must go. I will tell the people." He turned and began walking back into the Avru's compound.

Some of the people saw him walking purposefully toward the brick-pile where he had so often spoken to them, and they began to pass the word.

"Moses is about to speak!"

"Come and hear Moses!"

The people began gathering round him, following him, running ahead to tell others. Soon, all were gathered, and no one had even called them together.

68

"I have much more to tell, Zev. But let us stop for a day and rest."

I heard his chair move, and I knew that he had put down his pen and stood up from it. When I heard him grunt, I knew he was stretching.

"Very well, Grandmother. This is a good time. I shall soon need to make more ink." He was tired, and justly so. We had been at this for some days. I was tired as well.

"Has the sun set?"

"No, Grandmother. It is still — three fingers above the horizon."

"Good. We have time to prepare. The Sabbath begins tonight, if my reckoning is right."

"Yes. And I am not to write on that day, as I did not write last time. Nor will I be allowed to start a fire, I know. Let me build up the one we have burning now."

"That is well."

"May I make ink?"

I thought. "If you have time before sunset," I finally said. "But we will not need it till the next day."

"As you say." I heard his steps as he went to the door, and then the small sounds of his movements outside. I was sitting near the doorway, and even from that distance I could feel the increased heat of the fire as he fed it, and the louder hiss and snap of the flames.

I sensed him returning. "Tell me, Zev," I asked, "Had you heard the story of Zunach and his regency in Kokenus, before you came to me?"

He was still, and silent. "Yes," he finally said.

"I thought as much. Your skin is black, is it not?"

He laughed. "Almost. My mother's mother was Avru. How did you know?"

"The way you speak. It is very like Gamba's way of speaking, though your voice is not so deep. Were your fathers among those who left Egypt with us?"

"No, Grandmother. But some of those came back to Kush after they were freed, and brought the story with them. At times, ever since, a few bands of our people have left Kush and journeyed north, to find the Avru and learn more of Ehyehuwah." He was silent for a heartbeat. "I am one of them."

"How did you hear of me?"

He was silent again. I waited. As with Kisil, I knew he would answer when he was ready.

"You are a legend," he finally said, his voice hushed. "Tzipporah, the widow of Moses — the last witness."

"I see."

"The tales are well known among my people — but I did not believe them. I came seeking you, Grandmother, to see if you still lived, or not. I came to seek —" He stopped.

"The truth."

"Yes."

"And have you found it, Zev?"

I could hear the smile in his voice. "Yes. Yes, I have." Another pause, and then he said, "I would ask you to go on, to keep telling me the story even though I cannot write it — but —"

"Yes," I said. "Let us keep going as we have. I will speak as I remember, and you write it down as I speak."

There was a small silence then, and we listened to the crackling of the fire and the bubble and hiss of the vessel of pottage, meat and roots and grain, that Zev had prepared earlier at my instruction. "I would ask this, Grandmother..."

"Yes?"

"When God spoke from the Mountain... Did He — did He really speak? In His own voice? Or was that Moses?"

I felt the smile spreading over my face. "It was not Moses, Zev." He gasped. I went on: "I will tell you what happened. But you may find that you still do not know."

"I do not understand."

I reached out my hand, and I felt Zev's take it. I clasped it with both of my own. "It has been many, many years since that day, Zev, and I have thought on it every day since. Still, I do not think I understand it myself."

"But you were there."

"Oh, yes," I said, with a laugh that Zev, I knew, would find puzzling. "I was there. You will see, and you will decide. Or not. Let us have some of that pottage now, before it is scorched."

I could almost hear the questions, almost see the expression on his face; but he got up and went to serve our meal.

Much more to tell, I thought. I wondered what Zev would make of it.

Book Three: The Mountain

69

As Kisil was preparing to speak, the strangers were still coming in through the rude gate — and the Avru were watching them. Some seemed troubled or suspicious, or even afraid, but when Kisil mounted the mass of drying, black-smeared mud that had once been a stack of bricks, all their attention was on him.

He lifted his hands, and a slow smile spread across his face. When he finally spoke, his voice burst forth like a ram's horn: "The day of liberation has arrived!" he cried. "Today, we leave this land as a free people! From this time forward, we are no one's servants or slaves! Ehyehuwah, the One God — Ehyehuwah, the God of Avram, The God of Yitzhak, and the God of Yaacov — He, and He alone, has redeemed us from bondage! He has done it Himself, with His own outstretched arm and His own mighty hand! And you have all seen His power with your own eyes!" He pointed, and swept his pointing finger from horizon to horizon. The people looked around at the blasted, blackened landscape. "Look on this accursed land of Egypt, at what Ehyehuwah has done! Let this day be remembered throughout our generations!"

Then he spread his hands again, his gesture encompassing all the people gathered around him. "You see strangers among you. These people are our allies, and our friends. They wish to leave Egypt as much as we, and they wish to join us! *Welcome them!* They will make us stronger and safer on our journey!" The mood of the Avru lightened at those words, and they were more welcoming from that moment. It did no harm that the new ones proved willing to share their carts and wagons and pack animals — and their food, and the gifts they brought. They even shared their wine, of which they had much. Kisil nodded in satisfaction as he saw the smiles and open-armed gestures of welcome among the people.

He gestured for silence then, and silence there was. Then Kisil intoned, "*Do not hate or fear the stranger among you, for you were a stranger here! Let them be to you as one born among you!*" He paused for a breath, then lifted a hand and said, "So says Ehyehuwah, the Lord God of Yisrael! Write those words on your hearts and honor them always!"

He dropped his arms. "Now let us celebrate with a feast! Dig up the lambs which you set to roast, and make bread to bake on the coals! There is no time to let it rise — we shall eat it unleavened — and we shall give thanks for it! It is the bread of *freedom!*"

The people, laughing, set to work, and soon there was feasting throughout the camp. Kisil had commanded that the new people should be welcomed, and they were; with what the strangers had brought, there was enough food for all, and more.

It was the most gloriously happy day that I can remember. We feasted and danced, sang and celebrated, and no Egyptian — other than those who were fleeing Egypt with us — came near. There were songs and dances among that multitude that we had never seen nor heard before, and we cheered and clapped along with all of them.

The sight of Gamba dancing with his Kushite brothers, in the style of their native land — a rhythmic, joyous dance that seemed to speak of love and life and freedom and even of the joys of bravery and fighting and war, all at once — was a sight to behold. They bent and stamped and laughed, moving their widespread arms in rhythmic circles. It was strangely familiar to me, and suddenly I realized where I had seen that dance before. Kisil had danced so on the night we were betrothed! I laughed with delight when he joined them — and I was not alone. Gamba's booming laughter rang out, along with that of all his countrymen. We women, Kushite and Avru, clapped in rhythm, and soon more of the Avru men joined in their dance.

There were many such scenes. I would never have guessed that so many, of such diverse and widely separated origins, could become one people in a single day — and yet so it was. We were no longer slaves and refugees. We had become a nation. In all that black and desolate land, there was one spot of joy and merriment — and it was in the camp of those who had been miserable, broken slaves the day before and were now joyous, strong and free. We feasted and danced till the sun went down.

Kisil mounted the bricks and spoke again.

"Go to your huts," he proclaimed. "Gather your possessions." He pointed at the full moon, which was just rising on the horizon, full and golden. "Ehyehuwah has given us light to travel by! We will leave before the Moon is high. And every family of you, take one of our new friends and their families with you as traveling companions.

"You are filled, with food and wine and joy. That is well. We need not hurry. No one will pursue us, not today. We will walk from this place as one people, a free people, all of us together." He lifted his hands high, and the people responded with a wordless cry of joy.

He climbed down, and only then did I notice Desan and Aviram, with the neat little man Kodah and a few others, whispering at the corner of one of the huts across the wadi. They did not look happy, and I admit that that made me smile. Still, it appeared that they would still be with us, and were still prepared to make trouble. I remembered the feeling I had had earlier, after he and Kisil had spoken at the door of our hut.

I saw Gamba, and beckoned. The big man grinned and joined us, his wife and children following. I pointed out the small group across the way and whispered a few words of advice and warning.

Gamba, once again, was good at hiding his watchfulness. He took care to appear to be looking in a different direction as he examined the troublemakers, and he laughed and nodded as if listening to a joke.

Kisil called his council: the elders, his sister and brother, and the assistants he had already appointed. When they had gathered before our hut, he both gave them directions and asked for their advice. This time, Desan and his cronies were not there, but Gamba was, as well as a few others from among the strangers. We met outside the hut for Gamba's benefit; if we had been inside, there would have been room for no one but the Kushite giant, and he would have been bent double.

Kisil and the rest decided to divide the Avru into their twelve families, and have the strangers go with whoever they had befriended during the preparations. The elders, and the trustworthy ones who had already proven their worth, like Hosheah and Calev, were set over the families of which they were members, and Kisil appointed a few new ones at the recommendation of the elders. The strangers were not neglected. They were told to spread the word that they were to choose leaders from their tribes and nations as well. .

After a few more words of instruction, they all set off to their assigned tasks.

It did not take long. The Moon was not much higher before they had finished, and we began our journey that very night. There was more food prepared for the feasts than we could eat, and the tribal leaders had the people take all which would not spoil. We made sure that they also took many skins of water. Kisil said that there were wells on the way that we were going, but even so, we saw that they all took plenty, and fodder for the animals.

As we moved among the people in the moonlight, giving advice and helping, a man asked, "Where are we going, Moses?"

Kisil stopped. He looked at me, his face solemn yet joyful. "We go to the Mountain of Ehyehuwah. The Mountain of God."

I felt my heart leap. We were going home.

70

In an astonishingly short time, we were moving, and at a rapid pace for having had so little time to prepare. The people were eager to leave Egypt.

Kisil strode along at the front of the column, and Aron walked beside him. Gamba walked with us as well, with his son Nomba on one shoulder and Gershom on the other. Both boys were laughing. They had become fast friends already. Eliezer and I, and Akoko and her baby Enu, all rode in a cart drawn by our faithful donkey. Even he seemed in high spirits, and pulled with a will. Miryam was riding in another cart, and Basia rode with her, giving her litter over to transporting Yonasan and Chaninah. The two women were talking, and from their frequent glances at Kisil, I suspected I knew what they were talking about; and from their laughter and smiles, I knew that they too were becoming friends.

There were many of us in that multitude, but not so many as the tales tell. From a high place, one could see the whole column, from beginning to end; and if a man stopped, we would all pass him long before the Sun moved two hands' width across the sky.

As the people left the slaves' compound, I looked to the flat, dark horizon behind us. Far off, far to the northwest, there was still that thread of fire, curling upward from the earth into the sky.

"It is still there, Kisil," I whispered.

He looked back at it, and as we watched, there was a sudden glare of greater brightness from beneath the horizon for a heartbeat.

Kisil frowned. "To see its flames at this distance... The fire must be very great indeed," he murmured, his voice low. Then he turned away. After a breath or two, he added, "The wonders are not ended. Come, we should move the people farther from the water, and find higher ground inland."

We walked beside the sea, but on high ground, as Kisil had said. The rush of the waves was peaceful and comforting to us. I saw some of the slaves staring at the shore, where once they had gone only to fetch salt water for the brick pits. I stared too, for the sea was still a wonder to me. The world seemed made of only three colors; there was blue water and black land, with white beach washed clean by the waves between.

We were not silent. There was much singing and laughter as we walked, and rode, and sometimes danced along in the bright moonlight. And there was much talk, as we began to learn more about each other and our new friends.

We learned that the strangers' families, most of them, also lived in small huts with only a single door. Some had been told of the blood by Gamba and his friends, but some, guided by pure instinct, had used plain wet cloths to keep out the blackness. Damp cotton over the infant's faces seemed to protect them too. Though they suffered more than the Avru, they had come through the curse of darkness fairly well. Many of their elders were consumed with frequent fits of coughing, and a few died over the following days; but that was true of some of our own people as well.

There were so many strangers! We met people with coarse black hair and narrow eyes who told us that they were from the East, very far away. Kisil seemed to know of their land, but he never said whether he had been there on his travels. The most exotic people, though, to my eyes, were the pale ones from lands far to the north. Some had strangely speckled skins and hair as red as hot iron, like the man I had seen on the street before. They were startled, and so was I, when Kisil spoke a few words to them in their own language, and once again I found myself wondering just how far he had wandered in his younger days. The pale ones had to be careful of the sun, poor things. They burned badly if their skin was left uncovered for long.

It was like a celebration on the move. The people were singing and dancing, even in the night, even surrounded by all the blackness around us. It was that blackness, after all, that had set us free. No Egyptian came to watch us leave, to wish us either well or ill. We were a curse now, to be shunned, avoided, and forgotten as soon as possible.

I have never seen sheep and goats with burdens tied to the their backs before, but I did that day; and that was another miracle — they accepted their burdens and walked docilely before us as we left that accursed land.

As we rode along, Gershom suddenly gave a whistle from Gamba's shoulder. When I looked, he tossed his head leftward, then looked away.

I caught the meaning and looked in that direction. Desan, Kodah and Aviram were walking along together, almost alone. A few of their followers were with them, and some tough-looking men from among the new ones. They were talking. About what, I wondered. Then I saw three or four of them leave and spread out to other groups as we walked.

I looked up at Gamba, and he bent down, allowing the boys to hop from his back. Before I could speak, he said, "I have been watching them — and I have friends who are watching them as well." He grinned. "I set them to this task before we left. A court slave learns much about intrigue, Tzipporah. Spies watching spies." He laughed, a great booming sound; people turned to stare. "As if anyone can hope to succeed in a plot against Ehyehuwah!" He laughed again, even more loudly.

He began dropping back. Gamba's height made him a sort of living watchtower, and I saw his eyes moving as he scanned the crowd.

A short time later, Gershom tugged my sleeve. "Look, Mother." He pointed forward in the dim moonlight. "Those people are having trouble keeping their sheep together. Let us go and help." I saw that he was right. An Avru family ahead of us was struggling with their small flock.

I left Eliezer with Akoko and climbed out of the cart — our donkey gave a chuff of appreciation at the lighter weight, which I thought was impolite — and we hurried forward and began moving behind the straggling sheep, nudging them back to their flock. The people smiled their thanks.

"I wish Awwa were here," Gershom sighed. He smiled wistfully. He had loved the dog so when we lived in Midyan.

I laughed and agreed. A dog would have made it easier. "We will see him soon."

Kisil was leading us along the coast, and I wondered why. "Would it not be better to lead the people across country, to the foot of the inlet?" I asked. "That way would be shorter..."

"There is no water that way, remember? There is little along the coast, but there will be enough. This way will be longer, but safer, as long as we keep to the high ground."

I looked out at the sea. It was some distance below us now. We were, indeed, keeping to high ridges, well back from the water. I wondered about that, too. The land near the beach was smoother and would have been easier going, I thought, for the animals as well as the people.

Kisil and I stood on a high point and gazed down at the moving crowd. They made a long, long column, with stragglers and outliers and clumps of people walking together. I saw a few people riding, mostly the very old and the very young. The Avru had no donkeys, other than Kisil's and mine, but the newcomers had brought many, and even some camels and oxen as well. They carried the people's meager possessions and pulled a few wagons. The Avru sheep still carried their small burdens as well. A motley and disparate mob we are, I thought.

The way was hard. We walked all that night, and stopped in the heat of the day — but not for long. We began walking again when the sun was still high, and on into the night. The people complained, but Kisil and Aron and the others urged them to go on. "We need to get as far away as we can," Kisil told them. "The king may still change his mind."

Finally, on the second night, we made camp long after dark. The Moon was still full, so we could travel late, but the people, especially the children, were very tired.

Kisil and I slept in the same small shelter we had used on our way to Egypt, and I noticed that Gamba and some of his Kushite friends had pitched their shelters around us. I understood, and I was pleased. The big man had appointed himself and his friends Kisil's bodyguards.

I snuggled contentedly under my husband's arm, with my head on his dear shoulder. There were things I wanted to ask him — but when I opened my eyes, it was almost light.

"Come, my sweet bird. Let us have a little of this flat bread, and then we must be on our way." He grinned. "We have a multitude to lead."

The leaders of the people soon established themselves, and they were not always the leaders that Kisil had appointed. Aron, of course, was among them, as was Boaz, the first man of the Avru that we had met. Miryam and I were the mainstays of the women, along with Aron's wife Elisheva and a few others. Hosheah, in particular, was very helpful; he was filled with energy, always laughing, always encouraging the rest. The young man named Calev, who it seemed was a friend of Hosheah's, was another.

I shook my head; had we only been gone one day? It seemed like a lifetime.

The people had awakened reluctantly, and were ill-tempered and grumpy. There was a long journey before them, and few had ever traveled even a half-day's walk beyond their homes.

"My feet hurt!" "Who has my waterskin?" "Did you remember the cooking pot?" "This ground is rocky! Why do we not walk on the beach?" And, of course — "How long till we get there?" Kisil and I smiled at each other at that one. We would be hearing it often, we knew.

These people had been slaves too long, I remember thinking. All they knew how to do well was make bricks — and complain.

Three days on, the people had begun to settle down and resign themselves to a long journey. People fall into a rhythm when traveling: Get up, eat a little, set out. Rest at midday; walk again till nightfall, or after. Make camp, have an evening meal, sleep. Then begin again. I knew that when we entered Midyan, we would be sleeping in the day and walking at night. But that was not yet necessary, and would be hard for the people this soon into our journey.

The Avru and the strangers, even the Egyptians, seemed to be getting along well. I smiled at that. Nothing makes friends like having a common oppressor. Still, there was friction and conflict, and not only between the different peoples. Among the Avru themselves, there was still much resentment at the better treatment of the house slaves and servants compared to that of the brickmakers — and, strangely, the reverse as well. When there was work to be done, it seemed that the strangers, and even formerly privileged slaves were more willing to put a hand to it than the others.

"That is not surprising," said Kisil when I asked him about it. We were sitting at our fire in the evening, sharing a meal of unleavened bread and dried meat and fruit. "Slavery does not teach people to work hard. It teaches them to avoid work."

"Why?" asked Gershom, sitting crosslegged beside his father.

"If a slave works hard, what is his reward?"

Our son thought. "He is praised for it?"

"No," said Kisil. "He is expected to work that hard again, and is beaten if he does not. He learns to do as little work as he can." The boy nodded, and so did I. I had never thought of that.

"It will take a long time before the Avru learn to think and live as free people. There is much theft as well, and for the same reason. People who have had nothing for a long time feel justified in taking the things they feel they deserve. There is much to teach them."

"You have already taught them much, Kisil. That law about treating the strangers as if they were their own..." I stopped. Kisil was staring at me. "What is it?"

"Yes," he said, as if he were replying to something else. Then, again, "Yes." He looked forward. "I wish your father were here."

"Why?" He did not answer, and I spoke no more. I saw that clouded, troubled look on his face, and knew to leave him be.

71

On the fifth or sixth day, we had arrived at the inlet that I remembered from our earlier journey. It was midday, and we had just settled down to rest for a time before turning south and moving on.

The place was barren but for the reeds in the salt water at the shore. All round us, there was nothing visible but land, sky, and sea. The slope on that side was gentle, and the people made as if to go down nearer the shore — but Kisil prevented that, telling them to stay on higher ground, well above the water. I wondered why, but Kisil did not say. Still, he seemed to think it important.

As we rested, we heard distant thunder. Few thought much of it at first, though we looked up at the cloudless sky, wondering; but then we saw the dust. It was behind us, back the way we had come, approaching from the west. And the thunder grew louder. We soon realized that it was not thunder.

It was the sound of many chariots and horses. The king had sent his army to pursue us and bring us back — if he was merciful. I remembered the Eframites, and I was sure the Avru did as well.

The people were terrified. We were trapped between the soldiers and the sea. On our left was the great ocean, and before us, the inlet — too deep to wade and too far to swim, as Kisil had said. To our right was the way we would have to take — but behind us was the growing thunder of the king's chariots. They were still far off, but there was no shelter, no place to stand and fight, even if we had had weapons. Few stones, even, were to be found in that barren place. There was nowhere for us to run, and nothing we could do.

Our sheep seemed to sense our fear. They milled about, bleating piteously and shivering. They were hungry, the poor things. There had been little grass for some days.

In the midst of the chaos, as if to emphasize our predicament, there came another of those heavy, sharp blows to the earth — an impact that we felt through our feet, heavier and stronger than any we had felt before. The sound, I knew, would not reach us for a long time.

I turned toward Kisil, and to my surprise, I saw him smiling his jackal's smile. His eyes were distant; he was thinking again — or listening. I had never seen the two together before.

The people were crying out, weeping, shouting in anger and panic. As we might have expected, Desan and his brother Aviram were at the forefront of the complainers: "What are we to do now?" cried the larger man, Desan.

Aviram joined in. "Did you bring us out of Egypt only to die?"

Others echoed them, in the same vein. "They have swords of bronze! We have nothing!" "We are all going to die!" "Remember the Eframites?" "We will die, or be brought back to Egypt!"

"Let us not be slaughtered, like Efram!" shouted Kodah in his trained, powerful voice. "Let us surrender, and go back to the brick pits! At least there we can stay alive!" His voice was clear and smooth, his words persuasive; people began to nod hopefully, almost eagerly.

Desan cried out, "Yes! Let us surrender!"

These three, Desan and his brother and their friend Kodah, were always ready to lead us back to slavery, to Egypt, where once they had been masters and not followers. More of the people began to join in the cry: "Yes, let us surrender! Better to give up than to die!"

Most of the people, though, remained silent and looked to Kisil. They were afraid, but they trusted him. They remembered the plagues, and the joy of walking out of the slaves' camp in freedom only a few days before.

Kisil showed no fear at all. He climbed onto a donkey-cart and turned to face the people. Once again, he raised his hands, and there was silence — except for the drumming of distant hooves and wheels. Such was the power of Kisil's confidence that even the naysayers, Desan and his followers, fell silent and waited.

"We need no swords," Kisil declaimed in the booming voice he used when he needed it. "Ehyehuwah will fight for us. Wait, and watch, and you will see the power of His mighty hand!"

Desan and Aviram and the others with them began to jeer — and then they grew silent once again. Something was happening.

As we stood there between the king's army and the sea, a powerful wind began to blow. It whipped our robes and our hair, blowing out of the north in a sudden gust like none we had ever felt. It grew stronger and stronger, and then, suddenly, as suddenly as a slap from a strong man's hand, the air *struck* us, as if air could strike like a hammer. Some invisible wave of force went by and through us. Some fell to their knees. Some were even knocked to the ground by the force of it. I had never felt anything like it, and I had no idea what it was; but after it passed, the wind died and all was still.

We all looked up at Kisil. As we watched, he lifted his staff to point at the water. He meant the gesture to say, *Look at the sea;* but that is not how it was remembered.

The water began to fall away from the land before our eyes.

I had never seen anything like it before, nor have I since. The sea ran back as if it were afraid, as if the water were being drained from the ocean, pulling back from the shore to our left and from the inlet in front of us, which quickly became a dry valley, a very broad wadi where once there had been water, but where now there was none.

The inlet was drained dry in the time it takes to draw three breaths, and its bottom was sand, not mud. It looked firm. We looked out to the left, to the ocean — and the sea had fallen away so far we could barely see a gleam of it.

Kisil bellowed at the people in his loudest and most penetrating voice. "Come! Ehyehuwah has drained the sea! We shall cross on dry land! Come, bring your flocks and your children! Hurry!"

The people hesitated, stunned by what had happened — then they began to move. They moved out into the sandy valley with some trepidation, and then with more confidence. "Hurry! Hurry!" roared Kisil. Hosheah, Gamba and others who had become leaders joined in his shouts, and the people did hurry. Once they began to move, they moved faster, and then faster still. Soon most who were able were running across the gleaming sand.

The stillness of the air was eerie. It was as if the passage of time itself had stopped to allow us to cross the inlet. The silence of the sea added to the strangeness of that moment; if the waves still broke on the sand, it was happening so far away that we could not hear them.

The seabed was firm enough to walk on, firm enough to bear the weight of our sheep's hooves and those of our donkeys. It was not "dry land," but it was dry enough. The few carts and wagons we had rolled on it easily, and we made good progress. Even the stones were few, and the way was as smooth as the streets of the city, and smoother. The sheep ran across the wet sand as if there were green meadows and fresh water on the other side, bleating as if in celebration.

Soon, our little column was mostly on the other bank, but that was not enough for Kisil. He urged them on, up, up, mounting the steeper slope there toward the high ground beyond. The people needed little urging. The chariots of Egypt were visible in the distance now, and the tips of the soldiers' spears were gleaming in the lowering sun.

There were people, stragglers, who were still fighting to get their carts and wagons up the steep slope. Kisil pointed and shouted, "Help them!" and men who had already climbed up to safety went back down to help pull the wagons and carts and to carry the children who could not keep up. Gamba, the Kushite giant, all but pulled one heavily loaded wagon up the slope by himself.

The wind began to return as we watched their progress. Few noticed, watching the last of our people mount the ridge, but I felt my hair being whipped more and more strongly.

As the last of the column — the Avru and our friends, the other travelers — climbed to the ridge, the king's army came over the last rise on the other side and fully into sight. At their head was a chariot trimmed in gold, with a little man in it. He wore a distinctive helmet, high, rounded and a vivid lapis blue. It was called the War Crown, Kisil told me later. It was the king, and he carried a spear with a golden head. His grin was as feral and fierce as Kisil's had been, and he looked eager for vengeance. His charioteer was driving the magnificent beasts that pulled the royal chariot at top speed. Pennants and standards waved in the wind from the sea as they charged forward.

"What good has this done?" the complainers among the Avru shouted. "The Egyptians will cross as easily as we!" "Look at their weapons! There are hundreds of them!" We could hear Aviram laughing, and Desan called out, "Spare us! We will come back with you!"

Sure enough, the chariots did not slow, but rolled down the slope and onto the damp sand at speed, coming for us — but then we heard something new.

It was a roaring, rushing sound, loud enough to startle the horses drawing the chariots and make them rear and stare frantically around, their eyes showing white in their panic. Other chariots continued to stream into the inlet, and for a few heartbeats all was confusion and chaos below us as the rear of the King's army collided with the troops in front, and the chariots and horses became entangled with one another. We heard the angry cries of men and beasts, the men fighting to control their animals, the beasts fighting to get free. The roaring sound grew louder, and the whole army was stalled in the middle of the inlet, struggling to regain their momentum.

I looked up at my husband. The jackal's grin on his face was gone. Now, he only looked grim. The rushing, roaring noise grew louder and louder, louder than the shouting of confused and angry men and the cries of their horses —

And then we saw what made the noise. It was the sea returning.

A wave, and more than a wave. A wave such has never been seen on the Earth, not before nor since. One gigantic wave, five times as tall as a man and topped with boiling white foam, was bearing down on the shore like another advancing army — but faster and more powerful and more frightening than ten thousand armed men, than a hundred thousand, more. The wall of blue and white roared into the inlet with a deafening sound, moving faster than any wave any man has ever seen, faster than a horse could run, and though some of the Egyptians tried, none outran it. I saw the king, staring at the oncoming wave with open mouth and wide, unbelieving eyes, his spear still held high as if he would fight the mountain of ocean that was about to wash away his power and his life. Then he turned, and for just an instant, his eyes and mine met. And then he was gone.

I have thought long on what I saw in the king's face in that instant. I have had many years to do so, and still, I cannot say for certain. It was not fear, nor was it anger, nor hatred. Perhaps it was disbelief — or, better, *belief*, and the sudden realization that his belief came too late. But those are only guesses. I cannot truly say, and no one will ever know.

Kisil was wise to have urged us on to high ground. Our people watched in awe as the Egyptians were swept away, even the few who were left on the opposite shore. The water rose, and rose, raging and surging fiercely, almost to where we stood — as if it wanted to wash the Egyptians away completely.

And so it did. As suddenly as it came, the water fell again. In the space of a few breaths, the ocean was as it had been when first we saw it. The inlet was there, the water unsettled, roiling and surging as it rebounded from the far end. Soon it was as still as it was before, with a few low breakers rolling in from the greater sea.

And there was not an Egyptian to be seen. Not a horse, not a spear, not a spoke of a chariot wheel. Nothing at all. It was as if they had never been.

"Kisil, what has happened?" I whispered to my husband. "How can this be?"

"This, too, can happen when a fire-mountain bursts," he whispered back. "The sea can fall away, and then come back with furious force. That is why I had the people keep to the high ground." He smiled. "I did not know that it would happen when it did — but I have begun to trust in Ehyehuwah's timing."

The people gaped at each other, at first in shock, and then they began to smile. Soon they began to cheer — and laugh, and weep, and sing. Miryam took a tambourine and began to dance on the hilltop, and as they had once before, a circle of women gathered around her.

Miryam danced in the center of the circle, slapping her tambourine in time, and she began to chant: "Sing to Ehyehuwah, for He is to be praised!" The women dancing around her sang back in answer, "He has swept the horse and rider away into the sea!" They sang their song over and over, dancing in the circle, laughing and clapping and weeping with joy.

Other circles formed, singing the same song, laughing and singing and weaving in and out. In every circle was a woman giving the call, and around her the other women gave the response. Soon, they — we, for I sang with them — were all singing in unison. They might have heard us in Egypt — but no one cared. I joined in the dance as well, clapping and moving my feet to the song, laughing as Miryam sang out, and singing the words back at her.

"Sing to Ehyehuwah, for He is to be praised!"

"He has swept the horse and rider away into the sea!"

I can hear their song, the Song of the Sea, as I sit here today, even though it has been many, many years since I first heard it, there on the shore of the Sea of Reeds. I have never heard a song more joyous, or one sung with such wonder and celebration.

It was truly a great miracle, the Draining of the Sea. No one had ever seen or heard of such a thing before.

Except Kisil. He whispered to me later that night: "I once saw the ocean fall away like that, and come back again in power. When I felt the blow to the earth, I knew it would happen again, here. I knew that Ehyehuwah would deliver us, and He did."

Perhaps, as with the plagues on Egypt, the miracle was not so much that the thing happened — that the sea fell and rose again — but *when* it happened; and that Kisil, alone of all his people, had traveled so far, and learned so much, that he knew that it would, and knew how to take advantage of it.

Kisil had been right. Only he — only Kisil — could have done this. He had been right, but not in the way he had meant. Only he could have demanded the attention of the king, as he had said; but only he, during his wanderings, had seen the things, and understood them, that would set the Avru free.

Still, though, I thought — who could control such forces other than Ehyehuwah, other than God Himself? Who else could have chosen to drain the sea, and fill it again, just at that moment? How did this happen? Was it Kisil's knowledge, or was it a miracle of the God of Yisrael?

Or was it both?

I remembered my father's voice saying, "The One needs us as much as we need Him. Perhaps more."

72

Afterward, the people did not want to leave.

The songs and celebration, the dancing and the feasting, all faded after a time, as they always do; but still, the people lingered there by the sea. Days passed; they would sit on the hill and look out over the inlet toward the other side, marveling at what had happened before their very eyes. They would look around them at their loved ones and friends, grateful for the miracle that allowed them all to be there, alive and safe, and together. And they would look out at the sea again.

Desan and Aviram, and the others who followed them, were nowhere to be seen. Gamba told us later that they had made camp some distance down the inlet, far from Kisil and the rest. I wondered if they understood that they were defeated, that there was nothing for them to return to in Egypt — but somehow, I thought not.

We camped there by the sea for several days. There seemed to be no hurry, and Kisil was patient. He told me, "These people are not the same as they have been, Tzipporah. They have been slaves for a long time. They know nothing else. But they are changing. What they have seen is changing them, but they are only beginning to grasp that they are really free. Let them rest."

And then, one night, there was another blow to the earth.

We all felt it through the ground, and we all blinked at each other, caught between fear and wonder. Later that night, but before the morning, we heard the sound of it — but this time it came from the east and south, from where Kisil and I had come. Gershom laughed when he felt it. It held no terror for him. "It is Ael Shadu, Mamma! He is calling us!" Little Eliezer only looked confused.

It was still black dark, long before dawn. Even so, the people were stirring, getting up, looking to Kisil in the light of their fires. "What does it mean, Moses?" they asked.

"It means that it is time for us to move on. Begin gathering your things. We travel at night from here onward. It will be too hot in the day."

"Where are we going?"

Kisil stood at the top of the hill above the sea. He turned away and pointed. "There."

When the people looked, they saw it. There was another twisting pillar of fire on the horizon, glowing red and yellow and white. It was far away, but bright, brighter than the full moon. They stared at it in wonder.

Kisil stared at it with them, a smile playing about his lips. "That is the flame of Ehyehuwah. Let us go to Him."

It was the fire of the Mountain where I had grown up, I knew. I hoped my father and mothers and sisters were safe.

As before, we traveled by night and slept by day. Our direction was certain. By day, there was a column of smoke from the Mountain, and at night the pillar of fire. The flaring white in the pillar lasted only that one night, but every night, we could still see a red and orange column of flame in the distance as we walked.

Our steps seemed lighter. Not only were we free of Egypt, but it was certain that there would be no pursuit. There was singing in the column of people, and there was laughter. It was hot, even at night, but the Moon, now waning, gave plenty of light to travel by.

In places, an old man or woman would ride in a cart or wagon, facing backwards, and tell stories to the people following behind. It made the walking easier, and some of the elders had large followings, for they told good stories. I heard some of them; some were funny, some frightening, some would make one think. There were even a few such groups where children walked or rode or were carried, and the stories that were told were for them.

I was surprised when Miryam asked me to mount a cart and speak to the children myself. At first I was fearful — what did I know? But then I remembered some of the stories my father had told my sisters and me when we were small, and that I had told Gershom, and was beginning to tell Eliezer; and so I went. I soon found that I was good at it, and I laughed at Miryam's smile as she rode her donkey and listened with the rest.

We had bypassed the villages that Kisil and I had visited on our way to Egypt, between the city and the Sea of Reeds, the inlet where the ocean ran away. He did not want the people to be distracted or delayed. But now, when we came to others that we remembered, we found them abandoned, their wells and springs stopped, their houses deserted.

We were a large band, by the standards of that part of the world, and we were strangers — and strangers in groups, as everyone knows, are dangerous. The villagers had apparently heard of the Draining of the Sea and of the fate of the Egyptians, and they feared us all the more.

When we passed near or even through the villages, Kisil commanded that we take nothing. We did not touch their food, their livestock, or their goods, even though they had left their homes and flocks unguarded and stopped their wells.

It did not take long for the people to begin complaining again. We had not brought much food, and it was running out — but a much more pressing concern was water.

My father had told me of a spring, off the beaten track, that the people thereabouts did not use much. Its water was plentiful, but it was bitter. Father had also told me, though, that there was a spiny flowering plant there that could draw out the bitterness and sweeten it. He had used it when he traveled that way. "Let us go that way, Kisil," I said when I saw the landmarks. I told him of the spring, and he led the people in that direction.

Sure enough, when we reached the spring and pool, the people rushed toward it eagerly — then sprang back, crying out that the water was undrinkable. As I could have predicted, Desan came forward and pointed at the water. "Look at this!" he cried out mockingly. "Moses leads us to water that we cannot drink! We should have stayed in Egypt! Slavery is better than dying of thirst!" Some of the people began to echo him, crying out "Yes!" and "What are we to drink, Deliverer?" and the like.

I wondered how people could still doubt and complain, after all that they had seen with their own eyes, in sight of the very column of Ehyehuwah's fire. But the bitter heart will always seek out bitterness, I suppose, even when sweetness has been poured down upon it.

Kisil said not a word. I had told him about the shrubs nearby, and without so much as acknowledging Desan or the complaints of the people, he cut some of the boughs and threw them in the pool. Then he walked away, still without speaking. Desan and the other complainers mocked and jeered.

I told a few women to wait a little while, then try the water again. They did, and. cried out that it was sweet. "Another miracle!" they shouted, and the people gathered around, drank and filled their skins — even Desan and his brother. Both had sour expressions on their face, but they drank.

Water we continued to find without much trouble. Kisil knew the signs — which plants needed water near the surface, what rock formations might hold it there, which animals stayed near it — and he would direct the men to places where they would dig. They did not always find water, but very often they did. They even found hidden springs more than once.

The finding of one spring in particular was memorable, and what happened there has become part of the tales. Here is the truth of it: Kisil had recognized the signs of underground water, and knew that there was a spring in the neighborhood. Some villagers had stopped it deliberately, which makes what happened even less of a miracle; but still, it was a remarkable thing to see.

Kisil stood before a stone, perhaps as high as his knee. I could see as well as he could that the bottom of the rock was dark with moisture. Even so, there was no gleam of water there. It appeared that something had been used to mortar the rock in place.

Kisil struck the rock with his staff — once, twice, no more — and it cracked and fell away in two pieces. Instantly, water came pouring out of the spring it had been blocking.

The people cried "Miracle!" yet again, and Kisil did not argue with them. He called the place Merivah. I did not know why.

As I have said, Midyan was a dry land, but it was not a desert — and my husband knew many things, and was a wise man. Did God bring us water? In a way. He sent us Kisil, and Kisil knew how to find it.

73

We were running short of food. We had brought little, and though the land offered a bit of grass for our animals, there was nothing for us. Once again, Aviram and Desan, and Kodah, the court singer, worked the people up and egged them on, trying to instigate rebellion. They and their gang still wanted to return to Egypt, though I wondered how welcome even they would be after the slaughter of the Egyptian army at the sea and the death of the king.

"What shall we eat, Moses? Give us food!" was the cry. It was night, of course, long after sunset and long before sunrise. There was a thin crescent-moon, and one walked cautiously; the desert where we were just then was covered with small, spindly trees or shrubs, and they were hard to see in the dim light. They bore no fruit and few leaves. "Are we to eat these dry branches?" shouted Desan.

Kisil kept his silence, though the shouting continued, till the sky behind us began to grow light. When we were about to make camp, he stood on a cart and lifted his hands.

The people grew silent as they always did. "Do you see these trees all around you?" he asked.

"Call these trees?" asked Kodah mockingly, his rich and melodious voice a sharp contrast to Kisil's indistinct lisp. "These are *weeeeds*!"

Kisil ignored him. "Go, look on their branches. Look at the ground beneath them."

The plants were everywhere, and the people began to scatter and look. I, like everyone else, went to one of the small shrubs and examined it.

On its branches and scattered on the ground beneath it were specks and flakes of some yellow-white substance. In places it formed bumps and seedlike lumps as big as sesame seed. In other places, it was as fine as coarse sand.

I tried to suppress a laugh. I had known of this from childhood. It was a treat we always enjoyed at this time of year, and it would be plentiful on the route we traveled. At first it tasted like honey-cake, but the next taste was different — like some fruit, familiar, but one that I could not quite remember. We called it *manhu.*

"It is food!" came a cry.

"It is, and it is sweet!" came another.

Soon, the people were laughing and gathering the *manhu*, and soon the children began to gather it too. The people ate of it and were delighted. The three chief troublemakers, Desan, Aviram and Kodah, seemed to have vanished, as always, off to their separate camp.

As the people settled for the day, Kisil told them, "The *manhu* will be there every morning. Gather only what you need. Do not be greedy. It will come again."

Kisil settled a few arguments, as was usual in the morning, at the end of a night of walking. Some of them, that day, became a cause for laughter. They concerned people rushing to gather the manhu from trees before others could reach them. At the first of those squabbles, Kisil laughed.

"Look around you!" he said, lifting his arms, spreading them wide. The people did, and then they began to smile. Some even laughed. The scrubby little plants covered the land as far as we could see.

Nothing more was said. Shamefaced, the complainers went back to gathering, poking a little fun at each other as they went.

That was not the end of the complaints, of course. Not all were about water and food. Just as he did the morning of the *manhu*, Kisil settled disputes among the the Avru, and among the others who had joined us — and often enough, between them. They would come to Kisil at all times of day and night with their questions, complaints, grievances, and arguments.

"It is his turn to pull the wagon, and he will not do it!"

"She has taken my favorite shawl!"

"Her children are getting a greater share of our water than mine!"

Kisil patiently listened to them all, as was his way, and he never failed to settle their petty bickering, and dispense justice in more serious matters. But it left him little time to think, and I knew he needed that.

"The trouble is, they have no rules, no laws," said Kisil at the fire one night. "Even where they recognize them, they all feel privileged to break whatever rules they like. The former masters and house slaves because they think they are superior to the rabble, and the poor because they have been deprived of so much for so long. They strike when they are angry, they steal when they see something they want."

Miryam and Aron had joined us by the fire. "It is true," she said. "We have tried to teach them of the ways of Avram and Yitzhak and Yaacov, but they have been poor students. They hear the stories, but do not grasp their meaning." Aron and others nodded.

"They need laws," said Aron thoughtfully. "But who will give them?"

"Perhaps Ehyehuwah will, when we reach His Mountain." This came from our son.

Kisil smiled. "Perhaps He will, my son," said Kisil. "Perhaps He will."

We pressed on, night after night. We gathered the *manhu* in the morning — it seemed to appear as the sun rose — ate, slept through the heat of the day, and as the sun set, we rose and prepared to travel on.

Kisil had sent Hosheah and Calev and some others to climb a range of low hills to our right, to the west, and they returned to tell him that they saw water in the near distance. Kisil nodded. "It is as I thought," he said. "That is the Narrow Sea. It is salt and cannot be drunk, but it has other charms." I knew what Kisil meant, and smiled to myself.

The day came when even the *manhu* was not enough to please them. "We want meat!" they said. "We have sheep, but why should we slaughter our sheep for food? They are our livelihood! Why will Ehyehuwah not give us meat?"

They complained louder every day, but Kisil ignored them, saying nothing. I saw a small smile on his face.

I knew what was coming. After all, we were traveling now in the land where I had grown up.

We saw Desan and his cronies moving among the people, once more trying to stir them up. Kisil ignored them too.

One day, the wind changed. It began to come out of the west. The following morning, Kisil called the people together. They gathered around him, complaining loudly of their craving for meat.

"You will have meat," he said. "You will have meat before sunset of this day, more meat than you can eat."

The complainers began to jeer — then slowly fell silent. A faint sound could be heard, indistinct at first, then growing louder. "Do you want meat?" Kisil shouted. "Here is meat!" He turned and pointed his staff to the west — and, even as the people shouted and cried out, "What? What is he saying?" the sound grew louder still.

It was a fluttering sound, the sound of many wings.

And the quail came. Thousands of them. They came, and alighted on the ground, and were so tired that the people could pick them up and slaughter them with their hands. There was meat that night, and for many days thereafter, till the people complained of that too; but that night, Kisil and I and our sons laughed as we ate fresh quail at our fire.

At that time of year, the quail fly across the Narrow Sea, and beyond it. By the time they reach Midyan, they are exhausted, and they land, to rest.

Or to be dinner for wandering Avru.

The Moon had waned and waxed and waned again to a half-disc before we saw the Mountain clearly. Even on the distant horizon, it did not look as it had when we left — a brooding, dark presence, silent and watchful. The Mountain of Ael Shadu, the Mountain of God, was fully awake.

A great pillar of smoke rose from its summit during the day, and we could see the red light of the fire in it shining throughout the night as we made our slow way toward it. The ground shuddered frequently. Sometimes the flames from the Mountain's peak grew brighter, and we saw the red and yellow fire in the great column dancing like a live thing.

We felt the blows to the earth constantly, and sometimes they were more than felt; we heard them, like the crack and boom of distant storms.

Ehyehuwah is impatient, I thought.

The Mountain had grown calmer when we reached the well where the goatherds had harassed me and my sisters, but we still felt the uneasiness in the earth. No one was in sight there; the Melikites were quick to confront a group of women alone, but when they saw a band of more than a thousand people, they had run away and hidden themselves in the distant hills.

I watched Gamba as he strode along in the front of the column. The sight of that dark-skinned giant had probably made them run a little faster.

It was near dawn when we came to that well. The still-distant Mountain grumbled and smoked impatiently, but the people were tired. Kisil thought it time for a rest. He decided that we would rest there for a day, to draw water and perhaps, that evening, kill a few sheep and goats for a feast. The next morning, or the next at the latest, we would reach the Mountain.

"It is time we began to live in the day again, and sleep by night," he said. "The people can have a bit of extra rest to make the change less difficult."

I was eager to see my father and my family, but I could see that Kisil was right. The people made camp and were soon sleeping in the shade of their tents and lean-tos and other rude shelters.

That evening, as we were preparing to enjoy a night without having to travel, I heard a familiar sound. I looked up, laughing, and Gershom laughed with me. It took Kisil a moment longer, but then he recognized the sound as well. It was the ringing call of the ram's horn, the big one that belonged to my father. It sounded again and again, and I quickly found my own horn and sounded the reply.

Before long, Yisro and almost my whole little family arrived to greet us. I wondered how they knew we were coming, but then I realized that a thousand people walking in that dry land raised a great deal of dust. It hung in the air in the day, even after we had stopped.

Kisil greeted them with his arms wide, and he and my father embraced. I embraced him too, and he whispered in my ear, "I have missed you, little bird." I laughed to hear his voice and see his dear face, and I hugged him again.

"And I you, Father. I — we — have often wished for a word from you, for a bit of your wisdom." He smiled, and then I hugged and kissed my mothers and my sisters, those who came.

"Are you all well?" I asked my mothers. "We saw the flame of the Mountain at a great distance."

Sabah laughed, and Qamra waved a hand. "Your father felt the earth speaking long before the Mountain was fully awake," she said. "He told us not to fear, and we did not. No one has been harmed. Yisro will tell you of it later."

Yusuf and Walid were there, the husbands of Malkah and Charah, both of whom came too; and Tharah with her new husband Kameel. But there was another man that I did not know — a tall man, with long, curling hair and laughing eyes. Basimah told me, with shy, downcast eyes, "This is my husband Salih." I laughed and hugged him too.

"We saw the dust of your passage yesterday," said my father. "Will you camp near our tents tomorrow?"

"We will," said Kisil. "We have been traveling by night, but tonight we rest, and tomorrow we will come to the Mountain. There will be much to do." He looked toward it. "What of your sheep, Yisro?"

Father waved a hand. "They are in the care of Nazirah and Rivkah. There is a young man who is —" He smiled — "*fascinated* with Rivkah. She had her choice of several, since you have been gone, and I think she has chosen the best of them. His name is Musa."

Kisil and I laughed. "What is funny?" asked my father.

Kisil said, with a grin, "'Musa,' in the tongue of Kush, is 'Moses,' Yisro."

I explained the joke to my father, who did not know Kisil's other name. He laughed too, than said with a small, mysterious smile, "Nazirah has a friend, too."

"Oh? What is his name?" I asked.

"Nurah," he said.

"But that is a woman's name!" I said.

Then, "Oh."

He smiled warmly. "Nurah and Nazirah. Their names fit, and so do they." He shrugged. "My daughter is happy, and I shall have grandchildren to spare from my other daughters. It is well." Then he turned to Kisil. "What will there be to do, when you reach the Mountain?"

Kisil said, "We shall speak of that, Yisro. But not tonight. Come, join us at the fire. I suspect that we will see some dancing tonight. Qamra, did you bring your flute?"

My father eyed him, his mouth preparing questions that he knew better than to ask. "Very well," he finally said. "Let us talk of other things." He looked around at the multitude that surrounded us. "You must tell me how you managed to succeed in your task."

I saw a familiar figure approaching from behind my father, and I cocked my head in that direction, signing to Kisil to look. He grinned and said, "Yisro, I want you to meet an old friend of mine. This is Gamba. He has traveled with us from Egypt, and was of much help to us there." He gestured — *behind you* — and Father turned.

His mouth fell open and his mismatched eyes went wide. My father was a tall man, and looked up to few; but the top of his head was well below Gamba's shoulders. His head kept tilting back and back till he could tilt it no farther. The big man grinned enormously and held up an equally enormous hand. "Good evening to you," he said in his basso rumble.

"H-hello," said Father, his eyes wide. He lifted his own hand in greeting, gaping.

"This is Yisro, Gamba," said Kisil. "My father-in-law."

I said, "Gamba has never been in a fight in his life, since he reached his full growth." The big man grinned and nodded. "No one has ever challenged him," I added.

My father laughed nervously. "I believe that," he said. "I do not think it is possible for a man to get that drunk!"

We all laughed, and Gamba slapped my father on the back — but gently, so as not to knock him down.

There was dancing that night, and feasting, and songs. My mother Qamra and I played together again, and we played well. Miryam led a circle dance, and, to my surprise, Kodah sang a song of our ancestors to great applause. I wondered at that, but I suppose he was just currying favor with the people. He did have a fine singing voice, I had to grant him that.

Even the Mountain seemed to cooperate — the earth did not move, and the flame at the summit, though brightly visible, seemed serene and calm, somehow. It did not leap and rage as it so often had while we were on our way.

The Mountain had grown more and more quiet as we approached it, and when we finally arrived, it seemed to sleep, as if it were glad we had finally come. Though smoke still rose from its peaks, and the red light could still be seen at its summit in the night, it rumbled and thundered no more, and the ground was still. The column of smoke was still there, but the pillar of fire had dwindled to a glow in the night.

Desan and Aviram were nowhere to be seen.

74

When the next morning dawned, the people were eager to leave. They had been preoccupied with their weariness and complaints throughout our journey, but that day they were thrilled at the prospect of settling for a time, without having to walk and pull carts and carry burdens. We left earlier than I would have thought possible, and we moved quickly. We arrived at my father's encampment long before sunset.

Father told us that the display two moon-cycles before had been stunning. The Mountain had quaked and shuddered like never before, and the light from the flames rising from its peaks had made the night as bright as day. Still, he and my sisters and their husbands had not moved. There had been some flows of liquid rock, too bright to look at, from the summits, but none had come near the camp, and no one had been harmed. Even our sheep had come through unscathed. And then, as our band approached, the Mountain had calmed down.

When we reached the plain before the Mountain, the people gratefully dropped their burdens. Some began to raise their tents. Many had no tents, but had been making what shelter they could from what they had and could find. My sisters came forth with cloth and cords, and before long we were all engaged in making shelters.

Nazirah was genuinely glad to see me. She embraced me warmly, then introduced me to her friend, Nurah. I embraced her, too, and whispered that we were glad to have her in the family. And I was; Nazirah was gentled by her, I think.

Rivkah's man, Musa, was not unlike Kisil in appearance as well as name. He was not tall, but strong, with rugged features burnt dark by the sun. He was older than Rivkah by some years, though not by as many as Kisil was older than I. He seemed a good man, and I liked him.

Kisil, my father, and Aron and Miryam, had gone into Father's tent, and they stayed in there a long time. I busied myself helping the people find places to settle, showing them which way to orient their tents, and how to mind the placement of their fire-pits with the prevailing winds.

When my husband and the others came out, most of the people were settled and ready for whatever Kisil had to tell them. He climbed up onto an overturned cart and lifted his hands. The people grew silent.

He said, in his loudest and most resonant voice, "We have arrived at the Mountain of God. Our journey has ended for a time. He has called us, and we have come.

"We have no tasks, no burdens. For today, and for tomorrow, Ehyehuwah asks and commands nothing of us but to rejoice as we did at the shore of the sea."

He looked around at the sea of faces around him. "Do you not understand, my brothers, my sisters, my friends?" They returned blank looks. "We are free!" he cried. "We have no masters! We have come here because we *chose* to! We have seen the mighty arm of God deliver us from slavery! We have passed through the sea and have seen the king's army swept away! And we have passed through the desert, with water and food provided by our God — and now, it is time to rejoice!"

The people began to comprehend — and smile, and laugh. I and my mother Qamra took out our flutes, my sisters brought tambourines, and we began to play. Some of the women, and even some men, produced harps and pipes, and before long the people were singing and dancing and laughing again. It reminded me of a wedding; much joy, no sorrow, and a feeling of relaxation, of time without things to worry about and fret over.

There were fires; my wise father had set his children and their husbands to gathering wood and fuel since the day we left, and there was plenty for all. We slaughtered some sheep, and the scent of roasting meat and baking bread soon filled the camp. It was a joyous time.

By midafternoon, I was preparing a kid by our own fire, the fire around which my sisters and I had talked and sung and laughed all my life — that one, or one like it. A young woman — a girl, really — came up shyly and watched for a while. I could see that she had something to ask me, so I stopped my preparations and smiled at her. "Is there something I can do for you, my child?"

"You are his wife?" No need to ask who she meant.

"Yes. What is your name?"

"Liat," she said. "I am the daughter of Rakhel and Aviram."

"Ah."

"Please do not judge us by my father," she said quickly. "Desan dominates him. He always has. My mother and I have traveled separately from him since we left Egypt."

"I judge no one, Liat," I said. "Judgment is for God alone. What can I do for you?"

The child hesitated. "What are we to do now? For Ehyehuwah, I mean?"

I smiled at her. "For now, get settled with your mother. My sisters will help you," I said, pointing at Nazirah and Rivkah, who were helping another woman raise a tent made of fabric that Charah had woven. "Have you a man to help you? A brother, perhaps?"

"No," said the girl. "And my father seems more intent on helping Desan get followers than in helping us."

"Well, my sisters and their husbands will. Nazirah!" I called. "Come and meet Liat."

I left the two of them talking, and searched for Kisil. That Desan was still actively trying to collect followers was something worth knowing.

But Kisil was not to be found. He returned to our tent before sunset, though, and before I could ask, he said, "I was on the Mountain, my sweet bird. There was something I needed to find — and I found it."

"What?"

"Something we will soon need. You will see." He gave me one of his enigmatic, crooked smiles, and would say no more.

We had made sure that the people left an open space in the middle of the camp, where they could gather. In that space, Kisil set up a small shelter, where the people came to him to present their arguments and have their disputes settled. He called it the "Tent of Meeting."

One day, when my husband and my father were engaged in a discussion, Yisro looked up to see a group of people waiting. This time they were from among the others, the strangers from Egypt who had joined us — and who were no longer strangers, but friends.

"Here they are again, Kisil," Father said. "Why do you not appoint some men to assist you, to answer their questions so you need not be bothered from the morning till the evening and throughout the night? You have too much to do to stop for their piddling problems a hundred times a day."

"Men to assist me?" said Kisil. "I had not thought of that."

My father smiled. "It is the failing of many great men to think that they are indispensable in all seasons," he said. "You know some trustworthy men by now. Have them listen to the disputes of the people, and let them judge. The more difficult cases they can still bring to you. You cannot carry this whole burden alone, my son."

Kisil considered that. Then he turned and called to Aron, who was standing nearby, talking to his sons. "Aron! Come — and bring Hosheah, and Calev too. And Gamba!"

My father laughed. "Gamba will be a good judge," he said. "Who would dispute his decisions?"

Kisil grinned. "He is big," he said. "But he is wise too, and good. I knew his father."

"Tell me," said my father, but before he could, I spoke up.

"Women should serve as well," I said. "Perhaps you should call Basia — and Miryam. She already has the respect and trust of the Avru." Then I smiled at my father. "And my father might be among the judges besides..."

He rolled his eyes, which was comical to see, and nodded. "I should have known that my advice would return to me. Very well," he said, before a grinning Kisil could even ask him. "But tell me of how you know this black giant."

After Kisil had given instructions to his new assistants, he did. I listened, and it was a revelation to me to hear the story of Kisil's adventures in Kush from his own mouth.

After that, Kisil was troubled less by petitioners. He set up special tents around the encampment, and appointed men — and, as I had advised, some women, including my mothers, Qamra and Sabah, and Kisil's — to settle disputes.

A few days later, the rebellious voices broke out anew: the wadi had dried up, and once again the thirsty people were clamoring for water. Kisil stood on an outcropping of rocks — the very same one where Father had told me and my sisters of his past, and where he and Kisil had so often talked and argued — and spoke to the Avru in that oddly loud and commanding voice. "I shall go up the Mountain," he said, "And I shall return with enough water for all of you."

The scoffers laughed and jeered. "How can one man bring back enough water for all of us?" shouted one. I saw Desan grinning complacently nearby, and Kodah and Aviram not far away. That was not a surprise. Moses said nothing more, and he set off, alone.

It was full daylight. We watched Kisil work slowly up the slope till he was out of sight. The troublemakers continued to jeer and laugh. After a while, the people grew bored and went back to their tents or to whatever they had been doing.

Not long after, there came a sound — a faint, but familiar sound. It was the sound of rushing water.

We all looked up at the Mountain, and there was a glitter in the sunlight. A few heartbeats more, and we heard it more distinctly — yes, the rushing, burbling sound of water — very much water! As we stared up the slope, there, gushing and tumbling and splashing down as if in celebration and greeting, a stream of water was pouring, leaping, and rolling toward us! It reached the wadi before the camp and began to fill it as we all looked on in wonder. There had been a channel there, but we had not noticed it; it looked like just another crease in the earth, but now we could see that water had flowed there once before.

Kisil followed the water down, to shouts of joy and gratitude. Soon, people were gathered up and down the length of the streambed, laughing, filling their skins and pots and watering their flocks. There was a natural barrier at the end of of the channel, and a pool began to fill. There had been such a pool there in the past, I realized, and now there was one again.

"What happened?" I asked Kisil when he came near.

"Do you remember a few days ago, when I went back up the Mountain? I went to the place where I had heard the water before. There was a rock there, dark and gleaming with wetness, like the stone at Merivah. It was the same, a stone plugging a water source. Today, I went back and moved it with my staff, working the end of it against another rock nearby till it came free. The water came gushing out." He gestured at the stream that had not been there a short time before. 'The rock must have been stopping a spring, or an underground stream more likely."

I smiled. "You have learned to save your — miracles — for when the people demand them."

He shrugged, then grinned. "You could see it that way — but I was not certain that the water would come. I think Ehyehuwah has a way of calling me out to the edge, and then having me step off, hoping that He will catch me." His eyes went to the Mountain, and he smiled. "Perhaps it amuses Him."

I blinked. "You did not know there would be water when you promised it to the people?" I asked.

He shook his head. "No, Tzipporah. I had heard it on the Mountain, I thought it would be there, but I did not *know*." He shook his head again. "I *hoped*."

Then he lifted an expressive hand. "Hope. That is all we have. That is all we ever have."

I looked around. Desan, Kodah, and Aviram were nowhere to be seen.

After the birth of the stream, Kisil warned the people not to climb the Mountain, or even set foot on it or touch it. He set the men to building small cairns of stones around its base to serve as boundary markers. They did it with a will, some trembling. The mountain still smoked, and red light shone from its summit at night, but otherwise it remained still.

The people needed something more to keep them busy, so Kisil had them build an altar of unhewn stone, and set up twelve pillars nearby, one for each of the twelve families. He set each family to building its own pillar, and it became a kind of competition. Much laughter and good-natured banter ensued.

It was then that Kisil went up the mountain a third time. He had told Aron and Miryam, and my father, and Hosheah and Gamba and a few others, of his intention, but no one else knew. This may have been a mistake; but things happened as they happened.

"How long will you be gone?" asked Miryam. "What if the people want to see you?"

"I cannot say," said Kisil. "As long as He keeps me, I suppose. If the people grow restless, it will fall to you to calm them. I will return, I promise you."

"What will you do up there?" asked Aron.

"I cannot say. Ehyehuwah calls me. I must go."

That night, as he prepared for his climb, I drew him to our bed, to sit close to me. There, after a time of silent speech — if you understand me — I, too, asked him: "Kisil, will you be gone long?"

He held me. "I truly do not know, my sweet bird. But I must go back to that place where He first showed me His mind — if that is what happened there — and learn what it is that I must do now." He leaned back and looked at me frankly. "This far, I was certain of what to do. I was to speak to the king, and if the people were set free, I was to bring them here. This, I have done." He paused and shook his head. "I can hardly believe what has already happened. I never thought—" He stopped. Then he said, "What comes now — this, I do not know. I have an idea, but I am not certain it is the right thing."

He rose then and took his waterskin and staff. "But I must go. I will not be long, my love. Wait, and have faith. If not in Ehyehuwah, in me." He lifted the tentflap and was gone.

I did not watch him go. I did not think I could bear to see him walk away and climb, once more, up the Mountain — that brooding Mountain from which few had returned, and from which none returned unchanged. The Mountain that had ended our quiet life together, and brought us to this place.

Neither he, nor I, knew how much would be changed, there in the camp, before he came back.

75

Kisil had been gone only a single day when the trouble began. We had known that something of the kind might happen, but neither Kisil, nor I, nor anyone else, could have guessed how far it would go.

Desan and his gang learned quickly that Kisil was not in the camp. I supposed that they had men watching him, just as we had men watching them. That very night, I heard that Desan had called a meeting. "What kind of meeting?" I asked Gamba, who brought us the news. "A meeting of whom?"

"Of all those who wish to return to Egypt," he said in his deep rumble. "There are some."

Miryam and Aron were in our tent, as were my father and a few others. "Why on Earth would any Avru — or any of the other slaves — want to go back?"

My father spoke then. "Because it is easier, for some, to be told what to do than to think for themselves. They were cared for and protected there, some of them. They were treated like pets and children, to be sure, but then pets and children live safe and secure lives. Here, we are responsible for ourselves, and for our families, and must make our own decisions."

The young man Hosheah was there, and he spoke up: "No one brings us food or provides our clothing here. That is true. But no one tells us when to rise up and when to lie down, what to fetch and how quickly, or how deeply to bow and kneel. I like that.

"But some among our people — they ask me those very things. When to rise up, and when to lie down. 'What shall I give my family to eat tonight?' 'Is it all right if I take some cloth and patch our tent?' Things that no one should have to ask."

"They have lived by the command of others for a very long time," said Miryam. "For many generations. They will not think like free people for a long time. They do not know how."

"Gamba, how many are at Desan's — meeting?"

"Not many. Fifty or sixty."

Aron spoke, his voice low and troubled. "Two of my sons are among them," he said quietly.

"Nadav?" asked Miryam, with a start. "*Avihu*?"

"Yes, both of them." He sighed and sat down on a cushion. "Eliazar I forbade. He is too young, or he would have gone, too. He admires his older brothers. And of course Ithamar is still only a baby."

"Where are they gathering?" I asked.

"Desan has them meeting at a place he found toward the east. It is a — depression, in the ground — like a bowl, but flat at the bottom. A place where everyone can see and hear him."

I felt a chill, and my father's eyes grew dark. "I know that place," I began — but Father gave me a quick, warning look, and I held my tongue.

"What about it?" asked Gamba, who had not seen the glance that passed between my father and me.

"Nothing. I just know where it is." Gamba studied my face for a heartbeat, then nodded and went on in his basso rumble. "Desan speaks — rants and raves, truly — from the center of the place, and the people gather around and listen. And they listen eagerly." He lifted his enormous hands, gesturing his puzzlement. "Why, I do not know. They all know him, they know what he is." He looked at my father. "Perhaps you are right, Yisro. They need a leader. Who it is matters less than that they have one."

Father nodded his head somberly, and looked at me. Then, to my enormous surprise, his wandering eye — *winked*.

We went to the place to see. And, indeed, there was Desan, surrounded by his followers, declaiming in the middle of the *arena*, as Gamba called it. The people were standing or sitting on the slopes around it and listening. As Gamba had told us, there were not that many, a few score at most. They were all house-slaves, or former overseers, or other privileged servants of the Egyptians — Greek singers, Persian dancers and cooks, and some of the pale ones from the North with red or golden hair.

"Why are we here in this barren desert," shouted Desan, "living like shepherds who follow after their filthy, bleating flocks? Why do we shake sand from our clothes every time we rise, and eat tough meat burned with fire and hard bread baked on it? Where are our soft and sweet foods, baked in the ovens of Egypt and boiled with sweet honey and spices in the flesh-pots? Where are our soft beds, with soft covers made of linen and silk? We sleep on rocks and sand, and who knows how much worse it will be tomorrow?

"Who is this *Ehyehuwah*?" he asked, his voice rising scornfully, making the Name into a mocking sneer. He lifted both hands in mock puzzlement. "Have any of you seen Him? Have any of you heard Him speak? No, no! Only *Moses!* Only mighty Moses, who arrogantly came into our land and commanded us to leave our comfortable homes and our Egyptian friends! And for what? For this barren, stony desert?"

"What about the sea?" asked a voice. "What about the sea, that swallowed the Egyptians?"

"Sorcery!" shouted Desan. "What else could it be? Sorcery, too, brought the frogs and the flies and the darkness!" He shook his fist. "And we were not all protected, as Moses promised! Those of us who lived among the Egyptians, our people died too, in the darkness! Death did not pass over *us*, as Moses promised!"

I remembered no such promise, but I saw some of the people nodding in agreement.

"And now he is gone!" cried Desan. "Where did he go? Why is he not here? Why do his worshippers not tell us where he is?"

We were standing, Aron and Miryam and I, in the hollow of a nearby ridge, where we could not easily be seen; but Desan caught sight of us and pointed.

"See! There is Moses's wife, and there his brother and sister! Why do they not speak? Why do they not tell us where he is? You were not even told he was gone, were you? *Where is Moses, woman?"* he shouted, addressing me. "Where is he? Gone to pretend to speak to the God he pretends has sent him?"

Perhaps I should have kept silent, but this was too much. "After all you have seen — after all Ehyehuwah has done for you, *all* of you — you still listen to this viper, this toady, this parasite upon you? How many times has Moses and his God saved you? From the Egyptians, from thirst, from hunger? Are none of you ashamed?" I am pleased to say that there were many among them who would not look me in the eye. Still, they drew closer to Desan and seemed to gather closer round him and his brother and Kodah. I spat on the ground, and we turned to go.

Desan laughed and shrieked, "He is dead, I tell you! He is dead, his wife is a widow, and they have not told us! We must make our own God, and perhaps he will save us from this hellish place!"

We walked back to our tents in silence with Desan's voice still ringing in our ears. What was there to say?

What would Desan do next?

And where was Kisil?

We crept back to the hollow every night, staying low, and we watched as Desan and his followers worked to raise the anger of the crowd. My father declined to go. He gave the excuse that someone should stay in the camp and watch for Kisil.

I was not glad to see that the gatherings grew larger every night. In my husband's absence, the people craved a leader, as Hosheah had said, and Desan was only too glad to be that man. My father was right. These people did not know how to govern themselves and be free. They needed, they wanted, to be told.

And told they were. They were told that their best course lay in going back to Egypt, back to their soft beds and their certain meals. Their disquiet was slowly turning into anger, and egged on by Desan and his accomplices, their anger grew, night after night. I knew that the anger was a falsehood, promoted by Desan and his gang for their own ends; but it swayed the people nonetheless, and anger is contagious. It began to spread.

The meetings were no longer just Desan ranting; they had become performances, shows, even rituals. Kodah, the master singer, was a wonderful showman. He had to be, having entertained Egyptian nobles, and even the king, for so many years. He used his talents to further Desan's ends. Some of the other entertainers from the Egyptian great houses joined him, and they sang satirical songs and put on short dramatic performances, mocking Kisil and his God, mocking the crude, uncultured, mud-smeared Avru who tramped the muck and dragged the bricks, and mocking the stories of Avram and his family and the rest of the tales of their ancestors. They even mocked us, the desert-dwellers who lived in the shadow of the Mountain — Yisro, my father, and his family.

Other songs and plays were performed praising the kind and wise king of Egypt and his beautiful, gracious court, praising the wonders of that wealthy, dissolute nation and demeaning poor desert nomads like the Avru and all their heritage. It was cruel, and it was false, but the crowd loved it.

I grew more and more angry, and felt more and more helpless.

What could I do?

Where was Kisil?

76

One morning, a woman I did not know came to our tent and asked, "Do you have any gold?"

I was standing outside our tent at the time. I turned to her. "For what?" I asked, but when she saw my face, she turned pale and ran. "What was that about?" I asked my son Gershom, who shook his head; he was as puzzled as I.

"Let me ask," he said, and ran.

Few of the people knew Gershom by sight, and that day he showed himself a good spy. Before much time had passed, he came back with his report. "It is Desan and Aviram who are asking for gold. They are going to make a god."

I ran to get Aron, but he already knew. "They are using my sons," he said sadly. "I taught them the art when we were in Egypt. They were my apprentices."

"What art?" asked my father.

"Casting metal. Shaping it and working it. We made bells, and door-hinges — and statues," he concluded darkly.

"An idol. They are going to make an idol." I remembered the crude, ugly frowning man of wood that I had seen in a little village temple the year before, and I shuddered.

Where was Kisil?

That night, Miryam and I went out to Desan's gathering-place alone. Aron was nowhere to be found. But when we reached the place, we saw him.

He was assisting his sons. They had built a furnace of stones in that accursed place, and Aron, with Nadav and Avihu, were working the fire, melting the gold that others were throwing into a great vessel atop it. Nearby there was a great hole dug, and some sort of form was inside the hole, with a channel prepared running down into it.

We watched for some time, and as we did, we saw Aron and his sons carefully tilt the great vessel toward the channel, and a river of light too bright to look at ran down it and into a hole in the shape that lay in the ground. When the vessel was empty, many men began shoveling the white sand back into the hole, covering the form completely.

We went back to our tents and waited. Before long, Aron appeared.

"Did you see?"

We said nothing, our eyes accusing him without words. "Desan and Aviram forced me."

"We saw no weapons at your back," Miryam hissed, in a cold rage.

He looked back at her bleakly. "Avihu and Nadav did not know how to finish the work. Desan told me that he would throw them into the molten gold alive if I did not help. They were bound and ready."

Miryam's mouth fell open, and so did mine. She rose and embraced him.

"You bear no guilt for what you were forced to do," said my father. "The guilt is Desan's, and his brother's." He placed a comforting hand on Aron's shoulder, and Aron clasped it gratefully. He leaned on my father then and wept a bit, and my father held him as if he were his own.

"At least I have my sons back," said Aron after a time. "After what was done to them, they will have nothing more to do with Desan and his people."

"That is good," Father said.

"What are you making for them?"

"A calf, made of gold. Their new god. In seven days, or ten, or twelve — when it has cooled — they will break the mold and worship it."

That night, my father and I spoke by the fire, as we had done so often in the past. "Do not fear, little bird," he told me. "Ehyehuwah has his hand on Kisil, as I told you. Think of all that has happened. He has not brought you — us — all here to come to a bad end."

"I pray that you are right, Father," I said. "But I miss him, and I do worry. The people need a leader, as you said, and only Desan seems to be willing to take on that task... Not for the people, but for his own power and that alone."

My father considered. "Perhaps I should step forward and speak for Kisil," he finally said. "I have spoken only to him, because I am a stranger to these people. But, as Kisil taught us, when there is no one else, we must try and leave what happens up to the One."

I hugged him, and he left me and returned to his own tent and his wives with a kiss. I slept well for the first time in days. My father would fill the void that Kisil had left.

I weep even now, so many years after, to say it; but he never got the chance. Desan's treachery had grown greater and more malignant since we had left Egypt, but I could never have imagined how far he would go. That next night, my father did not come to our fire.

When I sought him out in his tent, at first I thought he was sleeping. But when I called him, he did not move nor answer. I moved closer, my heart pounding — and when I touched him, I knew. His skin was cold. My father was dead.

Murdered. His face was distorted, his beard crushed to one side. Even as I wept, I realized that I knew how he had been killed from the bruises on his arms. Someone — at least one — had held him down, while another held his nose and mouth shut till he died from want of breath.

I left his tent and looked frantically for my sisters, for Aron, for Gamba, for anyone. When I cried out, Nazirah and Nurah were the first to come running.

I had gathered my wits by the time they reached my side. "Have you seen anyone around Father's tent?" I asked. Others had gathered by that time, and no one answered, except by shaking their heads. They looked puzzled.

"Yisro is dead," I said. My voice sounded curiously flat.

Nazirah and Nurah swept into his tent right away, followed by Aron, who had come with Elisheva. They came back out. Nurah was weeping, Nazirah white with rage. "Who has done this?" she asked, her voice a dangerous hiss.

"You know who," I said, "but do nothing. Not now." She glared at me, but after a breath, she nodded.

"We must prepare him for burial," I said. "And that only. For now."

My other sisters were devastated, as were my mothers. Sabah and Qamra had been helping with the Avru sheep, and whoever had killed my father had known that. He had been alone, and the guilt they felt was terrible. "Not your fault," I told them. "If you had been there, do you not think that they would have murdered you too?"

Gershom was desolate. He had had two fathers, and now he had none at all. We all sat round Yisro's fire in silence, or else weeping together, all of us, as my sister's four husbands and our friends tried to comfort us.

They could not. The hurt was deep, and it still is.

That night, with the rising of the moon, we held council. There was no knowing whose hand had really done it, but we all knew from whom the order had come. Aron and Miryam, and Hosheah, Calev and Gamba, and I, were all agreed on that. The rebels knew that without Kisil in the camp, my father had been the greatest threat to Desan's leadership. Gamba was for wringing Desan's neck on the spot, and he certainly could have done it; but I convinced him to say and do nothing.

"They will say that he was an old man, and it was his time," I told them somberly. "Any accusations or attacks, they will use to further their own power and to further discredit Kisil and his leadership." Gamba fumed, but the big man could see the sense of it. He grudgingly agreed.

"For now, we wait. We wait for Kisil. He will know what to do."

We buried Yisro at the foot of the Mountain, in a place of honor near the palm tree where Kisil and I had talked so often; and — I have to grant this — almost everyone in the camp attended the burial to do him honor. Even Desan and Aviram came, and Kodah, all pretending sorrow for the benefit of the crowd. I saw Gamba's big hands working and flexing, longing to have Desan's neck between them, but he kept his eyes down and did not glare at them. It would be better, we decided, if they did not think that we even suspected that my father had been murdered.

I wished only that Kisil had been there. It was not only that I needed him with me as we laid my father to rest.

It occurred to me that if he had not gone, perhaps my father would have been spared. But no one could have known it would happen, and I could not blame Kisil for Desan's evil and treachery.

And then there was this: If my husband had been in the camp, they might have murdered him instead.

We were all conscious of my father's absence, and ached for it, during the following days. I felt grief, of course, but I also felt a kind of abandonment. The firm foundation of my whole life was gone, and my husband was not there to take his place — as if he ever really could. My sisters felt the same way. I could see the hollowness of their eyes and the slow, listless way that they moved. Even Gamba, who had not known my father long, grieved with us.

One day followed on another, and Desan's gatherings grew bigger and louder and more frenzied, with more and more of the people going to listen to him and to his friends and cronies every night as they disparaged Ehyehuwah, and Kisil, and all they had been given — even their freedom, which they were now taught was a cheat and a swindle. They sang their hateful songs, and gathered round the pit where their god was cooling and sang praises to it. The wide, sloping sides of the theater were almost filled now. Near to half of the people were there, hundreds of them, cheering Desan and Aviram and Kodah as they led the nightly rituals and gave the nightly exhortations. And every night, I thought, *If only my father had been here to speak for Kisil.*

Finally, as we cowered in the shadows and watched, a night came when Desan stood on a little platform that had been made for him, and declaimed to the adoring crowd: "Prepare yourselves, my brothers! Prepare yourselves for tomorrow! Your new god will be revealed, and when the sun sets, we will feast and dance and celebrate before him, in his honor and to his glory! Put on your best finery! Bring your finest food, your best wine, your best gifts for sacrifice and celebration! And —" he paused dramatically — "Prepare your things for travel, for when the dawn comes, we will carry our god to Egypt! We will set out for home, and our new god will protect us and bring us safely back to the land where we belong!"

We made our way back to camp — to our camp that was half deserted — with the cheers and shouts of approval of the crowd echoing from that accursed place.

Something terrible had happened there once, my father had said. And something terrible was happening there again.

And for the hundredth time I wondered — *where was Kisil?*

That next morning, we woke to thunder — but there was no storm. The sky was dark, darker than any storm could make it — but the thunder was in the earth.

The darkness was caused by a pall of smoke, smoke from the Mountain. Ael Shadu — The One — Ehyehuwah — had awakened at last, or His mountain had.

The summit glowed red, and fire was visible there again. The earth grumbled uneasily, and we heard it as well as felt it. The shaking of the earth had arisen along with the smoke and the fire. The people, those who were still faithful, were afraid. I moved among them, reassuring them, telling them that Kisil would be returning soon. I hoped I was right. I longed for my father's comfort, for his steadying influence, for his wise words. But he had been stolen from me and from all of us.

The rest of the people — most of them, Desan's followers — who were packing their belongings for their return to Egypt, and who were putting on their finest clothes and painting their faces Egyptian-fashion for that night's celebration, merely glanced up at the Mountain and smirked. What was there to fear? I heard them say. It is only a mountain, made of stone. Our god is made of gold.

I looked up at the Mountain myself, and wondered. Was Desan right? Was I a widow?

Where was Kisil?

77

That afternoon, I went to the new pool at the base of the Mountain to fill our waterskins. That is what I told myself, but I truly went to see the Mountain and look for some sign of Kisil. As I was nearing the water, I saw a furtive figure moving between the tents, skulking and hiding, as if it wished not to be noticed. There was something familiar about it.

I filled the skins, watching from the corner of my eye — and then I saw it slip into our tent and close the flap.

Our sons were in there. I left the skins where they were and ran, pulling my dagger from my sash as I did.

But when I entered the tent, I threw the dagger aside and ran to the figure shivering there next to our pallet.

It was Kisil. He had his arms over his head, and he was shaking. His whole body was shaking, as a man seized by a chill would shake. My first thought was that he was ill, as he had been ill on our way to Egypt; but when I put my arms around him, I could tell instantly that he had no fever. I held him as he shook, and then heard the ragged intake of breath and the small sob that accompanied it.

Kisil was weeping, weeping piteously, weeping like an abandoned child.

This, I had never seen.

"Kisil, my love — thank God you are safe! What —"

He lifted his head, and his gray eyes were red and swollen, his face gaunt, distorted, his cheeks hollow and his cheekbones blotched with red. "I have failed, Tzipporah. I have failed..." He gritted his teeth in anguish. "It has all been for nothing. It has all —"

He buried his face in my robe and sobbed, his despair evident.

"Kisil — no," I said helplessly. "What happened? Why are you —"

He lifted his head and looked at me desperately. "He would not speak to me, Tzipporah! Ehyehuwah is not there! *He is not there!"*

It took a long time for Kisil to tell me. His days on the Mountain, he said, were the bleakest and hardest of his long life, even after all he had been through.

He had gone to the place where the fire-fountain had called him; but it was cold and dark. He waited there, day after day, but there was no light, no Presence, no thoughts appearing in his mind. "The fire was not there, Tzipporah," he moaned. "There was nothing." After seven days and nights, he had begun to wonder if he had imagined it all, or if he had only dreamed it and drawn all of his people into his dream.

Over the the following days and nights, he had wandered up and down the slopes of the mountain, into the long cavern, and even up to the fiery peak, seeking God. He fell deeper and deeper into despair, and as he stared down into the Mountain's fiery heart, he thought of throwing himself in.

"Only you kept me from letting myself fall into the fire." He was staring at me with starkly staring, empty eyes.

"I?"

"Yes, my sweet bird. You. All else is gone now. Ehyehuwah has abandoned me, if He was ever there at all. I have nothing to give this people, nowhere to lead them, nothing I can do." Then he smiled, a ghost, a shadow of the smiles I had known. "But there is still you. Our sons. Our life here — by the Mountain." Then he laughed a small, bitter laugh. "We will not have to take the sheep so far for water, now."

Kisil had lost weight. He had not eaten since I had last seen him, though he had taken water with him, I knew. His clothes were filthy, he stank, and he was as weak as a newborn lamb. It was no surprise that no one had recognized him as he crept back into the camp.

I could see that he, too, had forgotten all the wonders that he had seen. I reminded him: "Kisil — Ehyehuwah has been with us all along! Do you not remember the water turning to blood, the locusts, the darkness? The king and his men thrown into the sea?"

He waved a hand, a gesture both dismissive and exhausted. "I knew those things were coming, or I guessed." His eyes filled again. "Ehyehuwah told me nothing, before or after. I have been lucky, and that only — if this can be called luck, to end like this. Perhaps Ehyehuwah is only a dream, a wish. A mirage..."

He lay back and closed his eyes. "I went up the Mountain for God to speak to me, but God was silent. I was alone. I am alone." He heaved a great sigh. "For the last two days, or three, perhaps, I lay in the place of the fire-fountain again. The one that I thought was a burning bush. And I wept." Then he added, "I thought that He would have mercy on me — but He was not there. And so I came back. Back to you."

His red eyes opened. "With empty hands."

I knew I had to tell him what was happening in Desan's meetings, and that the people were about to unearth their new god and worship it tonight, and that they would leave for Egypt in the morning. I did not know how to tell him these things, in the state he was. *It will kill him,* I thought. He has had all he can take. *I will say nothing, whatever the cost,* I thought.

Only then did I realize that Gershom had been watching with wide eyes from behind a mound of blankets on his bed. When I beckoned, he came, and Kisil smiled to see him. "My sson," he said softly, his speech as impaired and indistinct as I had ever heard it.

"Father, I am glad you are back! But why are you crying?" Kisil pulled him close and wept into his hair.

"Son, your father is not the man —" I lifted a hand and gave Kisil a stern look, a look I had never given him; the look that I gave to Gershom when he was behaving very badly, the look I gave to Desan when he called me a widow.

Kisil blinked, and he hesitated, then started again. "Your father is not — not well, son. Not happy."

"Is it because Ehyehuwah was not there, Father? Up on the Mountain?" The boy had heard it all.

Kisil nodded; I could see his chin quiver, and knew that he did not trust himself to speak.

Gershom freed himself from his father's arms and stepped back. "But, Father — did you not tell us, that Ehyehuwah said, He would be there when He chooses to be there?"

Kisil's eyes widened, and he stared at his son. "He did not choose to be there, Father. That is all," said Gershom, and shrugged. "He will be there when He chooses! There is nothing to be afraid of." The boy smiled at his father, and then at me, too.

Nothing to be afraid of. I wondered how many times Gershom had heard those words from us, when he had been afraid — of the dark, of a sound, of an animal? And now he was reassuring *us*.

Kisil blinked at me, and I gave him another look — the lifted eyebrow, the proud smile, the mother's look that says, *This is our son. Is he not amazing?*

Kisil stared numbly, and then, abruptly, began to weep again. He hugged the boy to his chest. "My son, my son Gershom... You have more wisdom than I. My son, my teacher." He kissed the boy on his head, then abruptly stood. He swayed a bit on his feet, but he stood.

"I went to the Mountain for clarity. But I had to come back here to find it — and it was my son who gave it me, and not Ehyehuwah. There is a lesson there, but I will think on that later."

He swallowed. "I must carry on, and do what I can do, even now, even though all is lost. I must be his father, and your husband, and the leader of this people. Where is Yisro?"

I lifted a hand to stop Gershom from speaking. "Wait, Kisil. Much has happened since you left. Sit down. Gershom, will you run and find your grandmothers and your aunts? Tell them Kisil has returned." The boy grinned, still glowing from his father's praise, and ran out of the tent.

I checked on Eliezer, who was napping. He had stirred a bit and listened after Kisil laughed, but as little ones do, he grew bored and went back to sleep.

Kisil gazed at me expectantly. He sat down on the cushion again, and I began.

"My father is dead," I said, and when Kisil gasped, I added, "But there is more. It began the day you left. Desan has been very — active..."

When Kisil had heard it all, his face was as bleak and drawn as when I had first found him in the tent. I remembered the first time I had seen him at the well — the defeated look of a man who had reached the end of his road. Compared to the Kisil before me, he had looked strong and eager on that day. Now, he looked like a man who not only sees the end of his road, but is gazing into the darkness beyond it.

He sighed. He had that distant look in his eyes again, thinking, or perhaps listening — but I knew from his eyes that he heard nothing and saw only the wall of the tent. "So it *has* all been for nothing." He shook his head in despair. "The people will return to Egypt, to bondage, to the slavery from which Ehyehuwah freed them, and they will go willingly." His head dropped, and he stared at the earth between his legs. "It was all for nothing. It is over." He sighed, deeply, and I could see that he was about to begin weeping again.

I thought, *If only my father were still here.... What would he have said?*

Then, as often happened, words came from my mouth almost before I knew what they were. I found myself speaking as I would to a despairing child, and in my mind, the voice was Yisro's — my father's.

"Kisil, you *know* what you must do."

"What?" he asked, his voice muffled and twisted. "What must I do? How can I do anything? I do not know what to do. God will not tell me, and your father — my best adviser, my friend, my teacher — Yisro is, is dead..." I could hear his voice breaking.

"*You know what you must do,* Kisil," I said again. "That is why Ehyehuwah did not speak to you." Those words had not appeared in my mouth, as others had at other times; I meant to speak them, and I was speaking words that I understood. I knew what my father would have said, and what Kisil had to do, and what he needed to hear. "You said it yourself, my husband; *you must speak for God.* There is no one else who can. It was true before, when we set off for Egypt; and look what has happened. It is even more true now that we have come so far. Now — *especially* now, Kisil — you really *are* the only one. *You must speak for Him."*

"But I am only me." His head was still drooping, his voice thin and plaintive. "I am only me — I am only Kisil..."

"No," I said, firmly. "You are not only Kisil." I waited.

He looked up, his eyes bleak, but curious.

"You are not only Kisil," I repeated. *"You are Moses.* You are the Deliverer." He blinked, and I pressed on: "Look what you have done — *Moses*. You have confronted the king of Egypt, *to his face*. You led the people — and a contentious and complaining lot they are — through the sea and through the desert. You have led them here, to the Mountain."

"But Ehyehuwah will no longer speak to me!" He lifted his hands helplessly, "If He ever did..."

"He has already told you everything you need to know."

"But I ha—"

Kisil stopped in mid-word, and I saw the light begin in his eyes. "Everything you need," I said again. "*You know what you have to do here,"* I hissed, my eyes on him, and I knew they were as sharp as swords. "God — Ehyehuwah — must speak to the people in this place, and tell them how to live. You know the laws that they need, and you must teach them. All this will happen; but *you* have to *make* it happen — *Moses."*

I used his Egyptian name. That was what the people called him, and that was who he was. In our tent, he could be Kisil; before the people, especially that night, he had to be Moses.

His face was still. He had that same distant look that he wore when he was far away — thinking, or listening — but this time he was looking at me, directly at me, seeing me.

He finally spoke, and his lisping voice was soft. "What must I do? Right now? Tell me, Tzipporah."

I could not tell if he was angry, or defiant, or accepting, or preparing to argue. He seemed beyond any of those. I answered him, as directly as I could:

"You must go to that place, that accursed place, where Desan and his gang are preparing to worship their idol. You must confront them, and denounce them, and speak for Ehyehuwah before all the people. No one else can do that."

His mouth opened — I knew not whether to argue, or to agree. But before he could speak, I said again: "No one else — *Moses*. Only you. They will listen only to you. If you do not speak now — tonight — no one will, and tomorrow it will be too late."

"What will happen then?" he asked weakly, his words again almost unintelligible.

"Do you not remember what you said before we left Midyan? 'That is up to Ehyehuwah,' you said. But you knew what you had to do. And you know what you have to do now. You do not need me to tell you, my love. You knew before I spoke." I lifted a brow. "Did you not?"

He slowly nodded, then, even more slowly, he stood. His head hung low again, and he stared at the earth. I felt a wave of despair. *He is going to give up*, I thought; and then he looked at me with both sadness and resolve.

"I told you once," he said in his soft, broken voice, "to have faith. If not in Ehyehuwah, then in me." Then he smiled bleakly, his gaunt face still sagging with despair. "And you do." He sighed. "It will change nothing. The people will not listen. Desan and his gang are going to win. He will take the Avru back to Egypt, and I will have accomplished nothing."

He shrugged, a resigned, hopeless movement. "But I must honor your faith, my wise bird, even if God has abandoned me. I will go, and I will speak. I will say what I can. And as you say, what happens then is up to The One. If He is there. If He is listening."

He lifted the tentflap. "Come with me, Tzipporah. Show me this place again. Let us go and see what kind of god they have made."

Kisil held up he tentflap, and we went out. Gershom was returning, with Nazirah and Nurah close behind, and Charah and her husband Kameel following them. Nazirah looked delighted, and then puzzled, to see Kisil, but there was no time to explain his condition or where we were going. "Nazirah — Nurah — take Eliezer and Gershom and care for them. We will be back soon."

"All right." She grinned at Kisil, a hunter's grin, and said, "Show them the wrath of Ehyehuwah, Kisil. Show them the fire in the Mountain."

He looked at her. It was as if he heard her say something that I did not hear. And then he gave her a thin smile. “I will, Nazirah. I will.”

She grinned more broadly, then shepherded Gershom into our tent. Nurah followed, as did Kameel and Charah.

And the two of us set out for Desan’s accursed meeting-place.

78

We heard the singing and shouting long before we reached the place. It seemed to me to be the sound of a battle, filled with coarse shouts and impassioned cries. I spoke hopefully: "Perhaps they are fighting among themselves."

Kisil shook his head grimly. "That is not the sound of war."

I could see Kisil preparing himself for the sight when we walked up the rise, squaring his shoulders and lifting his chin. I showed him the hollow where his brother and sister and I had hidden to watch, but he would have none of that. He strode directly to the highest point on the rim of the depression and, with a kind of sigh, mounted a rock that seemed to have been placed there just for him. He held out his staff to me. I took it, then knelt there at the base of the rock.

We gazed down on the celebration going on before us, and when I looked up at him, I saw that his face was troubled and uncertain. His hands trembled. I was reminded of the time he had spoken to the people after the king had decreed that they should make bricks without straw. *Please help him now as You did then*, I prayed silently.

Below, the golden idol had been freed from its clay mold, which lay scattered in rough shards around it. The statue was crudely shaped and angular, but was recognizable as a calf, with broad split hooves and stubby horns protruding from its misshapen skull. Its blind eyes looked at nothing, and it stood there stiffly on the ground, like a thing that had died on its feet and not fallen. There were fires lit around it, and its gleaming sides reflected their red light with a deeper red. The calf-figure was made entirely of gold, but I realized that it could not have been solid gold, else it would have sunk deeper in the earth. It was hollow, and empty.

I almost laughed at the thought. Hollow, and empty, it certainly was.

The people were dancing around it in the light of their fires. As we watched, they began singing one of their blasphemous songs. Desan and Aviram, with their backs to us, were leading the singing from before the calf's face, and Kodah was prancing about, draping rich strings of pearls and other jewels around the idol's neck as he turned and leaped. Others were bowing down before the calf, prostrating themselves at the idol's hooves. Still others were offering baskets of food and skins of wine to the calf, as if the dead thing could eat.

I had seen an idol, in that little village on the plain, but I had never before seen one worshipped. I could only think that the people had gone mad, lost their minds. Bow to a carved idol? Why not bow to a saddle or a stool? At least those were useful for something.

Kisil did not speak or move. He just stood and watched. He looked more saddened than anything else.

Kodah saw him first. He stopped his garlanding of the idol, and stared; then he pointed — and laughed. "Look!" he cried. "Look! Moses is yet alive, and he is back! Perhaps he will join us!" His voice was melodious, but mocking.

Desan and Aviram turned then, and they, too, began to laugh. It was easy to see why. Kisil's robes were filthy, his beard and hair unkempt, his cheeks hollow, his hands empty, and he was barefoot. Still, he did not move. He only stood and watched, his eyes moving over the throng.

"Behold our god, Moses!" shouted Aviram. "Come and join us and worship him!"

"Yes, join us, Moses! This god will lead us back to Egypt, back to our warm huts, our full bellies, and our work! He will —"

Kisil lifted his hands. Desan let out a bark of laughter — but fell silent when no one joined him and the singing stopped. I have never heard or seen a crowd go from raucous laughter and merrymaking to deathly quiet so quickly, and I never shall again.

The power was still there, I thought. They would still listen when my husband spoke.

The people stared up at Kisil, some fearfully, some smiling, some suspiciously. I looked too — and felt a thrill along my spine. The uncertain expression was gone. In its place was an expression of cold anger — and more than anger. His face was as dark as a stormcloud, and as threatening. His eyes were slits that gleamed with imperious rage, and his mouth was set in a hard line of merciless judgment. Even when he had confronted and defeated the goatherds at the well on the day when we first met, he had never looked so angry. This one time, and this one time only, I saw my husband in the fulness of his wrath, and it was terrible.

"If that is your god," intoned Kisil, in the deepest and most resonant voice I ever heard from his mouth, *"Let it come and trample me."*

The people turned and looked at the calf.

Need I say that it did not move?

"Well?" Kisil waited. No one moved. *"Well?"* he said again. And then, my husband gave the ultimate sign of contempt in that part of the world, where moisture was precious. He spat on the ground, as I had.

"That is no god!" Kisil roared. "That is a dead thing, a lump of cold metal! Shaped by the hands of men!"

To my surprise — to everyone's — Kisil *laughed* then, freely, fully, without a hint of fear or doubt. "Where is your god's anger, Desan? Why does it not come for me? Why does it not gore me with its golden horns, Aviram? Why does it not stamp me with its golden hooves, Kodah?" The men he named seemed shocked that he had done so, their eyes wide, their mouths too.

Now it was Kisil's turn to point and laugh. "Look at your toy! Look at the shiny doll that Desan and his *servants* have given you! Do you truly worship this — this *thing?"* He spat again.

I was lost in wonder and confusion. Only a few moments before, Kisil had been as dispirited and despairing as I had ever seen him, convinced that his mission had failed and that he had lost to Desan and his cohorts. But now — now he was once again a towering presence, the very Hand and Mouth of Ehyehuwah, the God that he still doubted.

Kisil had stopped laughing. "Did this *dead thing* that you have made bring the blood, and the frogs, and the locusts to the Egyptians? Did it bring the fiery rain, and the darkness? Did it slay them while sparing you? Did it cause the sea to fall away before your feet, and sweep away the Egyptian host when they were at the very point of slaying us all? Did it provide food and water for you in the desert, and even meat? Did it? *DID IT?"*

Kisil thrust out a hand for his staff, and I gave it to him. He lifted it and pointed at the idol. *"CHOOSE THIS DAY WHOM YOU WILL SERVE,"* he thundered. *"EHYEHUWAH, THE GOD OF YOUR FATHERS — OR THIS ABOMINATION, THIS BLASPHEMY, THIS DEAD LUMP OF COLD METAL!"*

Then he set the foot of his staff on the ground and spoke more softly, more reasonably, as a father does to his child. "If you will serve this *idol* and its masters, then stand by it. But if you will serve Ehyehuwah —"

"...step away."

The last two words were spoken in a hissing, penetrating whisper that slid across the wide, shallow bowl like the hiss of a snake.

"Do it now," he added, in the same sibilant, threatening tone.

There was a shudder of the ground, one of those claps of silent thunder that could be felt, but not heard. It was followed by a quivering, a kind of liquid shudder of the earth, that I had never felt before — and I had lived near the Mountain all my life.

The people began to move away from the idol, at first slowly, then faster — then fleeing as if for their lives.

Some, even many, stayed by it. Desan, Aviram and Kodah, of course, and with them stood the most arrogant and cruel of the former overseers, the most complacent and indolent of the house servants, the mockers and the thieves, the toadies and the schemers. Later, I heard the names of all of them. They had recovered from their shock, and stood defiant around their calf-statue, with arrogant grins on their faces.

Desan, laughed again, loudly, with confidence and arrogance, a braying laugh of defiance. Kisil looked at him as one might look at an insect crawling on his robe. "What will you do, Moses?" Desan asked mockingly. "What will your God do to me — to us? What —"

Kisil lifted his staff and pointed it at the earth at Desan's feet. I did not know why, and Kisil himself had no memory of having done so; but so he did.

The earth quivered again; and then again. I saw Desan's eyes go wide, and then drop to the earth beneath him —

And then, before our eyes, before the eyes of all the people who had fled away from the calf and up the slopes of the bowl above it, that flattened space at the center — that natural stage that Gamba had called the *arena* —

It *fell into the earth*, with everything that stood on it. The calf, the fires, the people who had chosen to stand with it, their offerings. The place where they had been an instant before — firm ground at the bottom of that natural theater — dropped out of sight, and in one heartbeat, there was nothing there but a yawning hole in the earth. Nothing else. Nothing at all.

There were screams and cries from the depths, but only for one more heartbeat. Then there was silence.

As we watched, a glaring red light came from the pit that had been, an instant before, a stage. Glowing liquid, too bright for our eyes, slowly rose to the level where the ground had been only a few breaths before.

For another heartbeat, no more, there were things visible in it, flaming things that were unrecognizable — but in a very short time there was nothing to be seen but an undifferentiated pool of yellow fire. A blazing heat came from it, making the perspiration spring out on every face. And even as we watched, transfixed, that brilliant glowing disk began to dim and cool.

The Calf, Desan, Aviram, Kodah, and all its other worshippers were no more. They were gone as if they had never been.

The fires had vanished with them, but now that natural bowl was filled with a greater light — the light of destruction, the light of Ehyehuwah's judgment. The people dropped to their knees or fell on their faces where they were. They screamed, they pleaded, they begged Kisil for forgiveness, howling and weeping and rending their garments. The heat from the pool of molten stone, for so it was, was fierce, and the crowd crawled and scrambled to get farther away from it, even as they wailed and begged for mercy.

Kisil lifted a hand — just one this time — and once again the crowd stopped and fell silent, even in the blazing oven that the bowl had become,.

He looked out over the crowd — then flicked his hand in a dismissive gesture and turned away. He offered that hand to me, and I took it and stood. As we began to walk back to our tents, many voices cried out.

"Moses! Wait!"

"Moses, what shall we do?"

"We are sorry!"

"Forgive us!"

At that, Kisil turned. *"I cannot forgive you.* It is not I that you have sinned against. God alone can forgive you. Ask Him for forgiveness — not me."

He turned away again, but before we could take another step, a woman cried out, "What shall we do, Moses? Please tell us! Please! Please help us! For my children's sake!"

Kisil stopped and turned, once again. He looked at the woman pleading with him, his eyes cold — and then, distant.

He considered her distorted face again and spoke, his voice clear and ringing. "You have committed a grievous sin, a heinous sin," he proclaimed, his voice heavy. He pointed, back toward the camp. "Go to your tents and pray, and repent, and try to cleanse yourselves."

"But how?" came a plaintive cry.

Kisil spoke again, his words hard and direct. "Bury the jewels that adorn you. Burn the clothes you are wearing. Wash your bodies in water and put on clean garments. Take no food or drink till this time tomorrow. Think on what you have done, and what you have seen." He paused, then added, "Ask forgiveness of each other, as well as of God. You have led each other into this horror. Turn away from it. Blame no one but yourselves. And..."

He paused, and when he spoke again, it was in that same dreadful whisper: ***"...remember."***

The people looked back at him fearfully, but still hopefully. I could see that their hearts had been turned, once again, by the power of Ehyehuwah and of Kisil's words.

Kisil could see it too. I saw his eyes soften, if only a little. He pointed at the Mountain, his voice still hard, but with a note of hope in it. "Ehyehuwah will speak to you in three days' time." Then he pointed at them. "Prepare yourselves, and pray. Repent of what you have done. Renounce it forever — and know that what you *say* is of no importance. *Show* your repentance, in deeds of kindness and love. Perhaps — *perhaps* — Ehyehuwah will have mercy on you."

The people began to cry out their gratitude, but Kisil lifted a hand and stopped them. "I do not know what Ehyehuwah will do. I have no promise of mercy from Him, and you will receive none from me. Your fate lies in His hands. It will be life for you and your children and your children's children —" He paused — "or it will be death before you leave this Mountain, and He will replace you with those who never turned away, even as few as they are."

The flat center of the bowl, still glowing with blood-red light, radiated heat. Kisil's face was eerily illuminated, and it was as hard as flint. He lifted his staff, and the people cowered in fear. "Ehyehuwah raised up a nation — *this* nation — from one old man and his aged wife, and he can do it again from those left here — *who never bent the knee to a lump of gold,"* he finished with another hiss of contempt. He pointed to the camp again. "Now go, and repent, and cleanse yourselves, and pray."

The people, chastened and frightened, climbed the slopes of the bowl; some slowly and mournfully, some in a panicky, scrambling half-run.

Kisil turned to me then, and took my hand again. "Once more, I was wrong, Tzipporah. I thought nothing would change." He frowned. "Gershom was more right than he knew. Whether or not God is present does not depend on whether or not we can feel Him." Then his frown changed to that familiar crooked smile. "Or even if we believe in Him, it seems."

"Kisil," I asked timidly — I was still overwhelmed at what had happened, though Kisil seemed to have taken it in stride — "Did you know that would happen? That the earth would swallow them up?"

He shook his head, somberly. "No. I knew nothing. This was not like the darkness, or the sea. I spoke what I thought to be true. I had no thought for what would happen. I hoped that some of the people would leave the idol and come back with us. No more than that. That is all I meant when I said, 'step away.'"

He shook his head, and I saw that the wonder of what had happened was just then coming home to him. Another step, and he fell to his knees and covered his head with his arms.

I knelt beside him. “Kisil —”

“I am Moses,” he said from beneath his arms. Then he lifted his head. “I am *Moses*, Tzipporah. Whether I would rather be Kisil —” he shrugged, a bit ruefully — “does not seem to matter. I am Moses, and so will I be remembered.”

And that has proven to be true.

79

We gathered around the fire before our tent that night. Our family, our friends, the faithful ones who had never doubted nor strayed. Others gathered around their own fires, and they were solemn gatherings after all that had happened. There was no singing, no dancing, no celebration. Kisil and I walked among the people, and he spoke to those at every fire — words of comfort, of promise, of peace. There were many that I did not know well, but I remembered seeing none of them at Desan's meetings. They were those who had never left the camp, had never turned away. More and more of them gathered around the fires as the night wore on, and I was pleased to see how many there were. "They have been keeping to their tents," whispered Miryam, who walked with us. No doubt she was right. They had hidden — but they had never worshiped the idol, nor listened to Desan and his gang.

The others, who had, kept their distance. We returned to our own tent, and on the way, we saw people peeking from around the tents, looking fearfully at Kisil. He ignored them. They dared not come near, but they watched and hoped.

Kisil sat silent before the fire, thinking. His arm was around me, his other arm around our eldest son as I held the younger in my arms. My sisters and their husbands, my mothers, and our friends all sat nearby. We sat in silence, all of us. What had happened at the Accursed Place had sobered us. Justice had been rendered for my father's murder. Whoever had ordered it, whoever had done it, they had surely been swallowed up by the earth and the fire that night. It was a time to think, to contemplate, and to be silent. There was little sound or movement in the whole camp that night.

Before the Moon was high, Kisil looked around at our friends — and with a small gesture that somehow spoke of gratitude, and love, and dismissal, all at once, he sent them back to their own tents. Our sons went with Nazirah, who had become a sort of special aunt to the boys. Perhaps it was her own boyishness that appealed to them, or perhaps her knowledge that she would never bear children. Whatever the reason, she was no longer the sour, cruel girl I had known when we were younger.

Gamba and his family and friends bowed to Kisil, hands pressed together, in the way of their people. Miryam and Aron, and the elders, came and wordlessly laid their hands on Kisil's shoulders — whether to give or receive blessing, I do not know — and after more silent farewells, he and I were alone.

We sat before the fire, just the two of us, as we so often had in this very place, where the Mountain loomed over us. We were home.

"What are you thinking, my husband?" I asked quietly after a time.

He frowned. "It has fallen to me to lead this people — my people." He paused and shook his head. "I fear this task, Tzipporah, more than I feared facing Desan. I wish your father were here to help me do it. But it seems that I cannot escape it."

"You are the Deliverer, Kisil. Look what happened, to Desan and his crew. Was that not Ehyehuwah, confirming your leadership, smiting those who turned away?"

He was staring at me, very directly. I wondered what he was about to say, and when he spoke, I understood something of what lay in his mind. "Perhaps."

"Perhaps?" I asked. "Only perhaps?"

"You said that Yisro had told you that something terrible happened in that place. Do you remember? It was long ago."

"Yes — but he never told me what it was."

"Your mother, Qamra, told me, a short while ago." He looked toward the west, toward the *arena* where that circle of stone was still cooling. "*That* is what happened before. A man and his family had made camp there — an ordinary man, not a bad man nor a good one — and the earth fell away, and he, and his wives and children and donkeys and all he had, fell into the fire and were no more." His eyes were fixed on the flames. "I have heard of such collapses of the earth before," he added. "I have even seen the hole one left, once, far to the south. There was no fiery rock there, just a deep hole. But that place was far from any fire-mountain."

"I thought it was something terrible that someone did."

"That happened later, Tzipporah. That happened tonight. What they did *was* terrible. But I think they might have been swallowed by the earth tonight even if they had been praying to Ehyehuwah." He gazed up at the dark mass above us. "I did not know that it would happen. I thought nothing would happen at all."

"So that was — something that was —"

"Natural. Not a miracle, any more than the blood or the locusts or the fall and rise of the sea. Desan was in the wrong place at the wrong time. No more."

"But, Kisil — still — it happened *when it happened.*" I spoke earnestly. "When it *needed* to happen. Like the earth moving, that first night when you spoke to the Avru. That is the miracle — *when* it happened. Do you not see?"

He nodded, though reluctantly. "Yes. Perhaps that is so. But —" He shrugged. "*That*, I did not see coming, like the locusts or the darkness. I was as surprised as — as Desan." He shrugged again. "But, it did happen — and I suppose I am the Deliverer, even though I still feel like an ordinary man, if a very lucky one." He fell silent then, for many breaths.

Then he added, "I am still a wanderer, Tzipporah. I suppose I will always wander. These people cannot stay here." He sat staring at the fire for a long time then. "What happens next — that seems to be up to me, too."

"Yes." I hesitated, then went on. "You have one more role to play, Kisil." He looked at me. "Perhaps the most important of all." He lifted his brows, asking without words, as was his way.

I looked into his soft, gentle eyes. "You are the Lawgiver.... *Moses.*" He looked away, then laughed at that. He actually laughed, though the laughter did not reach those eyes.

"Yes. Deliverer. Lawgiver. Teacher. Me, Moses. Kisil." He shook his head, as if at a bad joke. "And now my chief adviser, the nearest to a father that I ever had, is dead. Well, at least there was justice for his killers."

"Yes," I said, and found I could say no more. I missed my father, too.

"I wonder what he would tell me," said Kisil, thinking aloud.

I looked up sharply at that. I knew what my father would say, and I said it for him: "He would say, 'You know the truth, Kisil. Look inside yourself. You know the truth. *Tell the truth.*'" Kisil gazed at me, his eyes warm. Then he gave a slow, formal nod, and looked back at the fire.

Strange that a man could bear such a burden, and bear it so lightly, I thought as I watched him. Kisil knew the weight that was on him — but his very doubt seemed to make it lighter. He would do what he could, because it had fallen to him, as he said, and not because he believed that he was worthy of the task.

He looked back at the fire. "I know. I know what I must do. And I am thinking on how I shall do it."

"And what is it that you must do?"

Once again, I felt something approaching. This time, it was something bigger than Kisil and me, bigger than the Mountain, bigger than the world.

Kisil sat gazing into the fire. Then he turned to me and asked, "Do you remember a night when you and Yisro and I talked about laws? About the laws that people must have, to live truly, to act truly, to do justice and good and right?"

"I remember many such nights."

"I have been thinking on that. I think — no, I *know* what those laws must be. Their form, at least, and what they must say, or the *kind* of thing they must say."

"Tell me," I said simply.

"They must be few in number, and simple, and right. Other laws, more detailed laws, can be derived from them later; that will be the work of future generations. But the Law of Ehyehuwah — given to these people, in this place — it must be a set of simple principles, the bedrock of all that is to come." He smiled sadly, remembering. "Your father and I spoke of such laws often. He was of much help in this. And so were you."

"I remember," I said again.

He lifted a hand, a gesture of conciliation. "And you were right about another thing, too. The laws must be more than good ideas, from other men or even from themselves. The people must have Commandments, given directly by their God. It will take a generation, at least, before they will be able to think for themselves on such things. Perhaps many generations."

"You said that Ehyehuwah Himself would speak to the Avru," I reminded him.

"Yes. And what He will say — I know that too, or nearly. You were right about that, Tzipporah. I already knew what I had to do, and I already had what I needed, even before I went up the Mountain again. I wanted Him to confirm it." He shook his head. "It seems that I have to carry on with what I have. There will be no more."

"But —" I spoke in a whisper — "will Ehyehuwah really speak to the people, Kisil?"

He whispered back: "The people will hear Him."

"That is not what I asked."

He nodded, with a determined frown. "I know."

I waited, but it was soon apparent that he did not wish to say more. "How will He speak?" I finally asked. "Tell me, Kisil."

He leaned close and whispered, "I must speak for Him, Tzipporah. As your father and I said — if God speaks, He must speak with our voices." He looked at the fire again. "There is a way. A day, or two, after I go up, they will hear His voice, and I will give the people His laws — the laws that I have written." He made a fist and held it up. "And no one else must know this, Tzipporah. I was not even going to tell you. Everyone must think that they are God's laws, and God's voice. They will be mine — but they will be His, too." He lifted a hand. "Or so I think. I can see nothing else to do."

I had feared this, but this was not the time to argue with my husband on the right or wrong of it. I sat up. "You told me for a reason, Kisil. *You cannot do this."*

"Tzipporah, it is the only way. It may be wrong, but I must —"

"That is not what I mean. It is not wrong — well, it *may* be wrong — but *you must be here, among the Avru,* when He speaks. They will say — those who followed Desan and Aviram, and Kodah, those who are left, will say — that it is your voice that comes from the Mountain, and not that of Ehyehuwah. That it is a fake, a deception. *And they will be right."* I shook my head, firmly. "Besides, they will know it is you speaking as soon as they hear you. Your voice is —"

"Distinctive," he said, with a sour smile. "Yes. As silly as it sounds, I had forgotten that."

I nodded. "You must be *here* when Ehyehuwah speaks."

He listened, and after a few heartbeats, he nodded. "You are right. The Voice cannot be mine." He turned and gazed at me. I began to shiver. I knew what was coming.

"You must speak for Ehyehuwah, my sweet bird."

"I?" I felt the chill then, and knew I had been right. "How can I speak for Him?"

"You are the Lawgiver now, my wife. It is the same as it was for me; *there is no one else.* No one else can know."

"But —"

"Do you trust me, Tzipporah?"

I studied his face. He was as solemn and serious as I had ever seen him, and that is saying much. "You know I do."

He looked at the sky. The Moon was almost full, and it was high, nearly at the zenith. "We have only three days. Let us prepare."

80

Over those three days, Kisil taught me his laws, the laws of Ehyehuwah. There were eight; the Eight Words, he called them. He made me say them over and over, till by the evening of the second day I could say them when wakened from sleep. I did, when he awakened me long before dawn on the third day.

I know them still:

Do not worship other gods.

Do not make an image and bow down to it.

Do not speak my Name to no purpose.

Do not forsake your father and mother.

Do not murder.

Do not steal.

Do not swear falsely.

Do not betray your wife or husband.

And that was all. He and my father had worked out most of these eight laws, Kisil said. I had not heard those discussions, and when I said so, Kisil told me that that was not an accident. "We kept them to ourselves. Your father insisted. They must come from God, he said. I did not agree then, but I honored his wishes — and now I see the sense of it."

I thought of my father, and of his wisdom and love. I still missed him — but I could feel his presence in our tent that night. I could almost see his gentle smile, his mis-matched eyes, his silvery hair.

"But how am I to sound like Ehyehuwah? From the Mountain?" It was not the first time I had asked.

He peeked out the tentflap, then closed it. His face was solemn. "That is another secret — but you know it already. You told it to me, long ago."

I blinked at him, puzzled beyond words. "I will show you, Tzipporah." He looked out again, then gestured, circling a hand, *Hurry*. "It is almost time. You must be in place before dawn. Go and put on your darkest robe."

As I dressed, he busied himself filling a bag with bread and other provisions, and then he chose a filled waterskin. He slung both over his shoulder — and then I saw him pick up my ram's horn, the big one. He hefted it, feeling its weight in his hand, and then he turned to me. "Are you ready, my wild bird?"

When I nodded, with a certainty that I did not feel, he smiled. "Then let us go. I will show you the way, though you have been to the place before."

I blinked, and then I understood.

All of it. All at once.

I understood everything, all of what I had to do.

I looked down at the ram's horn in Kisil's hand. "The cavern." I pointed. "It is like the ram's horn."

"Yes."

We peered cautiously out of our tent, then set out. I was wearing my darkest robes, as Kisil had told me, and he was dressed in dark clothing as well. It was the depth of the night, long before dawn. The Moon, almost full, was halfway down the sky, and the people were asleep. There were a few sentries, but we avoided them easily. In our dark clothing we were all but invisible in the dim moonlight.

When we came to the slope of the Mountain, I balked. "Is it safe, Kisil?" The great peak still glowed and smoked, and there were still rumblings from its depths. The One was in residence here.

"Nothing is safe, my sweet bird. But have we come all this way to come to harm now? Have faith, in me if not in Him." I smiled at the words. "Come, follow in my steps."

The Moon sank lower as we climbed, but there was enough light for me to follow my husband as we began to make our way up the Mountain. By the time we actually began climbing on the steeper slopes, the Moon had sunk beyond the Mountain and it was black dark, all but as dark as it had been for those terrible days in Egypt. I could barely see to follow him in the dim starlight, and the glow from the peak was of little worth. We climbed in the shadows. Soon, we reached the ledge, or shelf, of stone that I remembered from my childhood.

I was actually on the Mountain, I realized — but this time it was at night, when the Mountain was awake, and there was another difference as well.

Once again, as I had been when Kisil climbed it for the first time so long ago, I was conscious of an enormous, brooding Presence, of Something watching me, aware of my approach. I shuddered, but Kisil seemed no more concerned than if we had been walking along the plain below in the full light of day.

It was nearing the end of the night when we reached the place where Kisil had seen the fire-fountain. He pointed it out to me, but I saw only a dark nook in the rocks, and that dimly. We went farther on, and soon we came to the cavern — my cavern, the one I had explored in childhood.

I had forgotten how big it was. Many things we see in childhood seem smaller when we see them as adults — but not this time. The cave's mouth was as enormous as I remembered, its ceiling as high as that of the king's palace, or higher. I wondered, once again, that it was not visible from the base of the Mountain.

The most striking thing about the cavern, still, was that it was *round*. Perfectly round, like the ripple of a pebble dropped in still water. Kisil said it was common to see such caves on fire-mountains, but they more often went straight down into the earth. Indeed, he said that the Accursed Place where Desan and Aviram had met their end might have been the mouth of such a one.

Mouth, I thought, thinking how they had been swallowed up. I looked at the cave's *mouth* and shuddered again.

We entered. The Presence seemed almost palpable to me, as if He, the One — Ehyehuwah — dwelt in this cave, and we were intruding into His sanctuary, His home.

The cave wound deep into the Mountain, as I remembered, and before we had made two turns, the darkness was complete. I could not see my hand before me. "What now?" I whispered — though I thought there was no need to whisper. We were very far from the tents.

To my surprise, Kisil responded with "Sh!" After a few seconds, I felt his mouth at my ear. "Do not make a sound," he breathed, ever so lightly. "It is important."

I heard something tapping, then saw a spark. I realized Kisil had made torches and left them here. He had lit one, a small one, with the firestones he had brought. He thrust three more into the sash around his robe, and indicated more that lay on the floor of the cave in a neat pile. I took some and placed them in my own sash. "Come," he breathed into my ear again. "We have a long way to go." He carefully slipped off his sandals, then gestured for me to do the same. Was this holy ground, I wondered? But I could not ask. Then Kisil laid the waterskin on the ground beside our sandals, but kept the ram's horn. He gestured — *come* — and I followed him.

We moved deeper and deeper into the cavern, the rock dusty but smooth beneath our bare feet. Kisil held the torch high, and I could see some way ahead of us. The cave passage wound back and forth, round and round, doubling back on itself again and then again. It sloped downward, then up, but always deeper and deeper into the Mountain.

The torch guttered low, and Kisil lit another. The tunnel — for a tunnel it was, for all that it was natural — grew gradually smaller; but all the way, as I had remembered, it remained perfectly round. Back and forth, up and down, round and round. I could not guess its length, but it seemed very long that night.

Finally, we came to the long, straight passage, and I could see the end of the cavern. It was just as I remembered.

The chamber at the cavern's end was still there, and I still thought it resembled a ripe fig. Neither Kisil nor I was especially tall, and there was no need for us to stoop. We climbed down the small slope into the end of the tunnel, and Kisil gestured for me to look, after placing a finger on his mouth. I could see nothing to look at. He pointed at the roof and floor and the walls. We were at the center of the chamber, and I think I grasped what he was showing me. I nodded.

We climbed the short slope again into the tunnel proper, and he laid the ram's horn on the ground. Then, he nodded with satisfaction, and we started back.

We remained silent till we had returned to the entrance; then Kisil took me a little way farther, and we went into a smaller cave, really only an overhang of the rocks that was sheltered from the sky and hidden from the camp. There, we sat down, and Kisil explained what I was to do.

81

Kisil left me there on the Mountain and returned to the camp. We kissed before he left, more passionately than we had kissed for days, perhaps weeks, and then he was gone. I sat down to wait. Dawn was near. I saw the faintest hint of gray in the blackness at the Eastern horizon.

Not long after Kisil left, I felt the Mountain stir beneath me. It is beginning, I thought. The Mountain stirred again, and then I felt that deep thunder through the earth, a rumble too low to hear. I had felt that thunder many times in my years of living near the Mountain, but it was stronger here, on its very slopes, than I had ever felt it before. And then, a deep thrumming, a throb, a pulse through the earth, began. It felt exactly as it had on the night that we saw the light on the slope, when Kisil climbed it for the first time.

I waited there, in that little niche in the rocks, until it grew light, and then I waited through all the next day. I had plenty of water, and when I opened the bag, I laughed to find that Kisil had put in a generous handful of dates with the bread and cheese.

The earth was never still. It grumbled and shuddered constantly, so constantly that I almost grew accustomed to it, and through it all, there was that deep, deep pulse, like the pounding of an enormous drum, or the beating of a heart as big as the world. I rested, preparing myself for the night. I even slept a little in the heat of the day, a skill I had learned on the way to Egypt.

And when I slept, I dreamed.

I had never had such a dream before, nor have I since. It was as real as waking — no, it was even more real than waking. I was conscious of every sensation, every sight, every sound, even the air on my skin and the scents that air carried, and I do not recall ever noticing smells in any other dream. I knew, even as I was dreaming, that it was a dream. I have heard of such dreams since, but I had not then — nor would it have mattered.

I was a child again, and I was seated before the fire in my family's camp by the Mountain. It was evening. The fire crackled and hissed under the crescent Moon, and I drew my bare toes through the warm earth by the fire, as I had always liked to do. I smelled the bread baking by the fire, and the lentils simmering on it.

I turned, knowing what I would see; and there sat my father as he was when I was younger, his hair was only beginning to show traces of silver. One eye was on the fire, and the other, as always, looked beyond it. I was overwhelmed with love for him.

Before I could move or speak, he said, "Little bird, do you know where you are?" He had not turned to look at me, but had spoken as if to the fire.

"I am home, Father," I said, and I heard my own voice as it had been then — a child's voice, if unnaturally deep for a child. "By our fire. In our camp, by the Mountain."

He turned to look at me, his dear face half lit by the fire and half in shadow. "No, child. Where are you? You know."

I hesitated, but I knew what he meant. "I am on the Mountain, Father. I am waiting outside of the great cavern that I found —" I hesitated — "when I was little. Like I am now." I stopped. I sounded confused, but I was not. I was in two places, and two times, at once. I suppose that can only happen in dreams, but I only ever had one such dream, and that is all I know of such things.

He nodded. "Yes," he said. "And you are about to speak for Ehyehuwah."

A sudden fear gripped me; did my father not approve? But just as the gasp rose to my lips, he finished his thought: "...As you once spoke for me." He paused for a moment. "Do you remember, little bird?"

"The scorpion," I said in my child's voice.

"Yes. And do you remember what I taught you that night? *This* night, Tzipporah. Do you remember?"

I realized that my hand throbbed with a burning pain. I looked down, and it was swollen. "Yes. That I spoke the truth — even though it was not — the truth."

He nodded again and held out his arm for me. I slid next to him, and I am most grateful for this, I think; once more I felt his arm around me, and I snuggled close and leaned my cheek on his chest, and looked at the fire. His arm, and the warm, familiar smell of him, and his love were all around me.

"It *was* the truth, little bird," he said. "I taught you right and wrong, and you taught your sisters, as I taught you. You did not lie. You will not be lying tonight, when you speak for the One."

I nodded, feeling my cheek rub against the rough wool of his robe. *How vivid this dream is,* I thought. And then he squeezed my shoulders fondly.

"I have missed you, Father," I murmured.

"I know, little bird," he said into my hair. "But it is all right. Kisil had to do what he did — *alone*. Do you understand?"

I did not answer at first. I finally said, "No. Why could he not have done it with you there?"

This time it was my father who was silent, and after a breath or two I understood. "There are things we are not given to know," I said quietly.

"You were always the wisest of my children," he said.

He released me, and I sat up and looked at him. He gazed into my eyes and began to speak.

We talked of laws, the laws that Kisil had written with his help. We talked of The One, and of his silence, and of how that silence was perhaps His greatest gift.

"He gave us the gift of our minds, little bird, the gift of reason — and of knowing that there is right and wrong. But then He left it up to us, to work out the rest. How to think and live and understand, how to learn and find the truth and change. That is what makes us truly human. We are not to remain His children, depending on Him for every need and answer. We are to grow up, just as we expect our own children to grow up.

"Kisil was right, little bird. God is *Truth*, and it is our job to follow the truth, and seek the truth — and with it, justice, and peace. That is what the Laws are for. They truly are His laws, for all that we have written them."

I took his hands. "Thank you, Father." He smiled and squeezed my child's fingers in his own.

"Goodbye, little bird." He leaned forward and kissed my forehead, as he had so many times.

"Will I see you again?"

He was silent. I sighed and nodded. "We are not to know."

He smiled. "We are to trust Ehyehuwah on such matters, little bird. Our work is here, in this life, in this world. Do you understand?"

I nodded, and we stood. I stepped forward and hugged him, my face on his chest, and then I stood on tiptoe and kissed his cheek. "Goodbye, Father," I whispered.

I clung to him for a moment longer....

82

When I awoke, I felt a deep gratitude. I had not realized how much I had longed to see and speak to my father once more — and now that gift had been given me. I smiled and thought, *I am like Kisil now. I have everything I need.*

I looked at the horizon. The sun was almost down. The time was approaching. The Mountain was still grumbling, louder now, preparing itself, the thrum and drum of the deep rhythm stronger than ever. I could feel its growing power, like an approaching storm — but I felt no fear. I sat and waited quietly, thinking of my father and his wise words.

The sun set and the full moon rose. The night fell quickly, as it always did in our land. The Mountain began to shake, and the quaking of the earth became audible, a deep thunder. I ate a little more of the bread and drank of the water — and, smiling at the thought of my dear husband and his fondness for them, I ate some dates too. It would not be long now.

When I looked up, I could see flames rising from the summit, brighter and hotter than before. I could feel the heat of them from where I stood, and I saw how they illuminated the pall of smoke that was spreading out from the Mountain — for the smoke had grown thick as well, boiling up from the earth like the smoke of a kiln, far thicker and blacker than the skeins and curls and puffs that had been rising from it for so long. The smoke was spreading wide like a blanket, blotting out the stars, and the red glow of the fire lit them from beneath. That light from the peaks flared and subsided, rose and fell, as the earth moved and shuddered, and the sound of it grew louder. Soon, the fire from the summit became a glaring pillar of light once again, and the roar of the Mountain's wrath grew louder and louder.

I saw threads and streams of light running from between the peaks of the Mountain, and I knew that they were liquid fire, liquid stone, as Kisil had seen that day so long ago. More and more of them began to flow, and the streams grew wider. They were spectacular, but none came near me.

How Kisil knew this would happen on the third day, if he did know, he never told me. Whether he had seen such things before in his travels, or whether my father had taught him from his long experience with this Mountain, or whether Ehyehuwah Himself somehow told him — I never knew, he never told me, and it did not matter. Once again, Ehyehuwah chose to be there when He would be there.

I took another drink of the water, and on an impulse, ate a few more dates. Then I slipped off my sandals and left them with the food in the rock shelter. I approached the great cavern taking only my waterskin and the firestones. My ram's horn was already in place.

I said I felt no fear, and when I awoke I did not — but now, fear rose in my throat with a bitter taste of copper. The Mountain of God was moving beneath my feet, belching smoke and flame, and I was going deep inside it. I felt very small and very alone as I entered the yawning circle of its gigantic mouth.

I struck a spark and lit one of the torches that Kisil had prepared. Trembling, I took a few more with me and began making my way into the cave.

I thought that the way would seem shorter on this journey, but it seemed much longer now that I was alone. Deeper and deeper into the earth I crept, and the rock under my bare feet grew uncomfortably warm long before I reached the end of the cavern. I glanced upward from time to time; the ceiling of the cavern had been so very high that I could not see it near the entrance. The light from my little torch did not reach it. Farther on, it grew nearer.

As I went on, I could still hear the rumblings of the Mountain, but the sound was muffled, as if the tunnel were somehow separate from the outside world. It occurred to me that I hardly felt the shaking of the earth as well. Perhaps the inside of the Mountain was more stable than the surrounding land.

Or perhaps I had been right, and this really was Ehyehuwah's sanctuary, the center of the world...

And I was entering it.

I shook my head, clearing it of questions I could not answer, and went on.

I walked and walked, carefully, trying always to make no sound. After what seemed like miles, the tunnel had grown small enough that I could almost walk with one hand on the wall as I ascended and descended the slope. I lit another torch, and on I went. Not far now.

I began to see a light from ahead of me, around the turns of the tunnel. It was not the red of fire, not the golden light of the sun, nor the silver light of the moon.

I remembered. I knew what it was, and though I went on, I was trembling.

Finally, I crept cautiously round the last turn, and found that I had finally come to the long straight passage.

There, at the end of that long, strangely round tunnel, was the fire of Ehyehuwah.

It was the same fire that Kisil had seen on the Mountain so long before, and now with my own eyes I saw it for myself, waiting in the very place where I intended to go.

It was, as my husband had said, a fountain, but a fountain of fire. I could see why he had at first thought it a bush, ablaze with ordinary fire — the spray of light was low and evenly spread, making a sort of round shape itself. It was small, half my height, and I wondered if the fire Kisil had seen had been so small. I realized that he had never said. It was issuing from the earth a few paces from the end of the passage. The orange of flame was mixed with bright white light like that of the Sun, and other colors I had never seen and could not name. The heat was intense. In the small cavern, it was very hard to bear. I fell to my knees, and when I knelt, it was easier to breathe — perhaps because of another narrow crack in the floor of the cavern, from which cool air, and not fire, seemed to be rising. I had not noticed it before. As I watched, I saw that the liquid fire that issued from the rock drained back into it and did not accumulate. If I took care, it would not burn my feet.

I began to think of what I was about to do. I was seized with doubt, doubt that I had suppressed for my husband's sake. Was the fire placed here to stop me? Was it a warning?

How did I *dare* do this? Was it right? Would I be struck dead for it? Would the fire of the Mountain itself, *this* fire, stop me before I was done? I had told Gershom how easily the fire could have killed Kisil on the mountain — this mountain...

I realized that I was shaking, quivering with fear, and for a moment I felt that I would not be able to do as my husband had asked, no matter how important it was. I had to give up, leave, flee even.

But before I could move — I found myself staring at the fire. It compelled my gaze somehow. I could not look away. I remembered that Kisil had said the same.

I cannot do this, I thought. *It is wrong. I am not God. Can I speak for Him?*

And then I remembered my dream. As dreams do, it had already faded in my mind — but as I gazed into the fire of Ehyehuwah, it came rushing back.

I felt one strong throb of pain in my hand — and I remembered a day when I had been stung by a scorpion, and what had happened after. I remembered what my father had told me, that very night — my father, yes, that very night, at our family's fire, and here on the Mountain, a few moments ago when I had been a little girl....

The fire-fountain grew smaller, till it was only a handsbreadth high, or perhaps two. That did not seem like a warning, or a threat.

My eyes were fixed on the fire. I remember trying to look away, but I could not.

There was a powerful scent in the cavern, one that I had never smelled before. It was sharply penetrating, strong, yet sweet, almost fragrant. I grew lightheaded. I thought for a heartbeat that I was about to faint, but I had felt that before, and this was different.

I did not faint, but *something* happened as I knelt there gazing into the fire of God. Like Kisil, I cannot find the words to describe or explain it. I was still myself, but I was no longer Tzipporah...

Always I have thought in words, always. Even as a child, even when I was alone, there was always an inner voice, inside my mind, talking, describing, reasoning, arguing, even rejoicing. The only times it had ever been silent, I realized, were at the most intense and immediate and powerful moments of my life — when Kisil and I were touching each other, together, in our tent; when I was giving birth to my sons; when the sea roared in and swept away the king of Egypt and his army. The times when my mind was filled with other thoughts and feelings, and there was no room for words.

And, as at those times, at that moment before the fire — my mind was silent; but it was more than silent. It was filled with a stillness, a watchfulness, that I had never experienced before. There were no words there, no thoughts at all. It was just as my husband had said. There was no time, no past and no future — no Mountain, no Tzipporah. There was only that moment, and my naked awareness of it as being unlike any moment that had ever been or would ever be again.

I saw the cavern, the fire before me, the ram's horn at my side — but I saw them all as if they were living things, as real and present and *alive* as I was myself. I felt that I had been asleep all my life, and was finally awake. I understood, somehow, that all things were One, as Ehyehuwah was One...

I can no longer remember it all, but in that moment, and for that moment, I understood everything — all that was and all that would ever be. As Kisil had said, there was no Voice, no Message, no Presence. There was only Truth.

My fear was gone, entirely gone. I knew what to do; everything around me — the cave, the fire, the air, the Universe, everything — was all part of what I was about to do. Everything that I had ever done, everything that had ever been, was preparation for this moment in my life, in the life of the world. It was as inevitable, as right, as the rising of the Moon.

I picked up the ram's horn and moved behind the fire, to the very end of the tunnel. I was aware of the heat, but it did not touch me. I stood in the very center of the round chamber and lifted the horn to my lips.

I took a breath, and began to blow.

I had always been good at blowing the ram's horn, and it was a familiar, warm feeling to make the sounds. The notes came easily. I was meant to do this, in this place, at this time.

I blew gently at first, sounding the sweet, haunting notes of "Come home, dinner is ready" — and then the louder tones of "Where are you? Sound the reply and tell me where you are" — and then the even louder notes of "Here I am!"

I blew the horn for I know not how long, blowing notes and calls I had never heard. Finally, I blew the shuddering blast of the High Alarm — the quavering, shocking blare that spoke of fire, bandits, wild animals, mortal danger. I blew my best, louder and louder, and my own ears rang in the cavern — and I understood what was happening. I had gotten a glimpse of the idea in our tent, and Kisil had explained it to me later; but now I truly understood.

The cavern itself was a ram's horn made large. The sounds echoed and grew along the curving, round passages, growing more and more powerful, louder and louder, and finally exploded over the camp with deafening force. Kisil told me later that the people were hiding their faces and covering their ears with their hands, trembling at the power of the sounds I made — I and the Mountain.

I knew that the cavern had been created for this purpose. I knew it as surely as I knew that my eyes were created to see, my ears to hear, my breasts to feed my sons. This place had been made for this from the beginning of the world, awaiting this moment.

I blew the ram's horn as I had never blown it, as no one had ever blown it. Beyond the High Alarm, and farther beyond, I blew tones that no one had ever heard, nor ever would again.

And there were answering blasts from the Mountain. Vents on the slopes sounded alarms of their own. Whether shaken to life by my own blasts, or from some pressure beneath the ground that would have sounded even if I had done nothing, I did not know; but we had the same purpose, the Mountain and I, and we trumpeted the notes together, louder and louder. Where my breath came from, I do not know, but I felt I could blast the Mountain to rubble, and I gave it my best to do it.

Something happened to me then — something I cannot tell in words, something that has never happened to anyone else in all the world, but only to Kisil and to me.

The cavern disappeared, and I along with it. For a time — for how long, I cannot say, but for a time — I was in some other Place, a place that was void and without form. There was nothing there — nothing at all.

And out of that void, through no will of my own, I saw and heard myself begin to speak; and the words I spoke were the only things in the world, the only things that existed. I was both speaking and hearing, and I spoke the words as if they were the only words I had ever spoken, or would ever speak again. The only words that could ever be.

I felt like a ram's horn myself — a passage, a vessel, an instrument, for the words of Ehyehuwah. I did not exist. There were only the words.

I began to see again. I saw the cavern, and I saw myself — but I saw as if I watched from a distance, from far above, inside the rock, from the Void where I had become the words. I saw myself floating in the air at the end of the passage, my face turned upward, my arms and legs and hair hanging loosely, turning slowly round and round — behind the fountain of fire, which had grown large, filling the passage from top to bottom, from one side to the other. I *was* the fire, the Fire in the Rock, burning and yet not consumed, the fire of God filling my mind and blazing forth from my mouth, and the Words were the flame. All this could not be, I know; but this is what I saw, and what I remember.

The words I spoke were not the words that Kisil had taught me. They were, many of them, very much the same, and others were words that reflected much that we had thought and said — but they were different.

There was no hesitation, no uncertainty. My voice blared like a ram's horn, even deep in the cavern, from inside the fire:

"I AM EHYEHUWAH, YOUR GOD. THERE IS NO OTHER. I, EHYEHUWAH, BROUGHT YOU OUT OF THE LAND OF EGYPT, OUT OF THE HOUSE OF SLAVERY, WITH MY OWN HAND. YOU SHALL HAVE NO OTHER GODS BEFORE ME..."

Kisil told me later that my voice — which had always been deeper than other women's voices — had boomed from the Mountain with deafening power, in a profoundly deep register beyond any that a human voice could reach. He thought it was indeed Ehyehuwah himself speaking — especially when he realized that the voice was not speaking the words he had written for me.

This had happened to me before, though in a much smaller way. There had been times, beginning on the day I first met Kisil, that words came from my mouth before I knew what I was saying. But this time, the words came with a power and conviction that I had never felt — indeed, I did not feel them even then; the words were separate from me, from anyone and anything, as if the words lived and spoke of themselves. I understood them before I spoke them; but still... It was hard to believe they they came from me.

"YOU SHALL MAKE NO CARVED IMAGES, NOT OF ANY THING THAT IS IN THE HEAVENS OR ON THE EARTH OR IN THE WATERS OF THE EARTH. YOU SHALL NOT BOW DOWN TO THEM NOR SERVE THEM, FOR I, EHYEHUWAH, AM A JEALOUS GOD."

"YOU SHALL NOT SPEAK MY NAME, EHYEHUWAH, WITHOUT PURPOSE."

The next words were new. Kisil and my father and I had spoken of such a thing long before, but it had not been included in the list he had made for me. But they came from my lips with the same certainty and clarity as all the rest:

"FOR SIX DAYS YOU SHALL DO ALL YOUR WORK; BUT THE SEVENTH DAY IS THE SABBATH OF EHYEHUWAH, YOUR GOD, AND ON THE SABBATH DAY YOU SHALL DO NO WORK. NOT YOU, NOR YOUR SON, NOR YOUR DAUGHTER, NOR YOUR SERVANT, NOR YOUR BEAST, NOR THE STRANGER THAT STAYS IN YOUR HOUSE. THE SEVENTH DAY IS HOLY TO YOU, AND SHALL BE HOLY THROUGH ALL YOUR GENERATIONS."

I was not conscious of effort, of shouting. Indeed, I was not conscious of speaking at all, in that other place. But my voice seemed to come from me with a power and a volume that I had never heard before. I went on, with the same laws that I and Kisil and my father had written, though phrased differently:

"HONOR YOUR FATHER AND YOUR MOTHER, SO THAT YOU MAY LIVE LONG ON THE EARTH THAT YOUR GOD, EHYEHUWAH, HAS GIVEN YOU.

"YOU SHALL NOT MURDER.

"YOU SHALL NOT COMMIT ADULTERY.

"YOU SHALL NOT STEAL.

"YOU SHALL NOT GIVE FALSE TESTIMONY."

And then came more unfamiliar words, words which I had never heard nor thought:

"YOU ARE NOT TO CRAVE THAT WHICH BELONGS TO YOUR NEIGHBOR; YOU ARE NOT TO CRAVE HIS HOUSE, NOR HIS LAND, NOR HIS WIFE, NOR HIS SERVANT, NOR HIS BEAST, NOR ANYTHING THAT IS YOUR NEIGHBOR'S."

I was done with the words that Kisil had taught me, and with the words that had been added. I knew that the list of words — now Ten Words — was complete.

But I went on. More words were flowing into my mouth from the void, and I spoke them. I had become the words. There was nothing in the world but the words.

"THESE ARE YOUR LAWS. YOU SHALL FOLLOW THEM FAITHFULLY, AND TEACH THEM TO YOUR CHILDREN, AND THINK ON THEM, AND SPEAK OF THEM, AND REMEMBER THEM, IN THE DAY AND IN THE NIGHT, WHEN YOU ARE AT HOME AND WHEN YOU ARE AWAY, WHEN YOU WORK AND WHEN YOU REST. YOU SHALL HOLD THEM CLOSE AND KEEP THEM, AND PASS THEM DOWN THROUGHOUT YOUR GENERATIONS; AND YOU WILL BE MY PEOPLE, AND I WILL BE YOUR GOD."

There was more, I think; but I remember only the void — and then only blackness.

83

Then I was back in the cavern, standing before the fire, myself again.

Thc cavc was warm, even hot. I was dizzy, but that strong, sweet scent was gone. My torch had gone out, but the fire fountain was higher, and there was plenty of light. As I climbed from that round chamber back into the passage and crept carefully around the fire, I felt the rock heave beneath me, stronger than ever — and as I lit my remaining torch at the fire fountain, I wondered if I had imagined or dreamed it all. But then, all my doubts vanished.

Once more, the cavern disappeared — for an instant only, for the tenth part of a heartbeat — and the Void surrounded me again. In that instant I found one more word in my mouth; but I knew that that single word was not given me in order that I should speak it.

The word was, ***"RUN!"***

I ran. I ran down the tunnel as if my life depended on it, and it was not long before I knew that, in truth, it did. I could hear the rocks cracking and breaking behind me, the bubble and hiss of liquid stone, and I ran harder and harder. I had dropped my torch, but I needed none; the light behind grew brighter and brighter as I ran, and I dared not look back. I could only run.

I had no promise that I would live, I knew, but somehow I ran to the entrance and out, a heartbeat only before the cavern collapsed.

As I lay on the ground, without breath or strength, I saw and felt the mountain shaking all around me. There were fountains of fire from the summit and from a score of places on the slopes — rivers of liquid fire flowed and cooled and turned black. Smoke rose up from the Mountain like the smoke of a furnace, and the earth shook as if it were being pounded by a mighty Hand — as perhaps it was. It was the deepest part of the night, but the light from the Mountain made it as bright as day.

I was still barefoot. I never saw my sandals, or my waterskin, or my father's ram's horn, again. Indeed, that horn is buried somewhere in the heart of the Mountain, and no one will ever see it again, not till the world ends.

Somehow I made my way down from the Mountain through all this flame and tumult. In fact, as mad as it sounds, I walked down the mountain as if I were walking by a still stream on a calm spring morning. I knew that I would not be hurt, and I knew that no one would see me. Indeed, when those who did see me remembered it afterward, they remembered seeing me walking from Kisil's and my tent, and not from the Mountain.

I found Gershom and Eliezer with Nazirah, and I found Miryam and Aron, and they seemed to have no memory of my being gone for a day and a night. I saw Kisil, standing on a high place, arms outstretched, speaking to the people who were answering him in chorus, on their knees. But suddenly I was too tired to listen.

All the strength and serenity that I had been given vanished. I was conscious only of my thirst, my bruised and dirty feet, and my exhaustion. I left my sons with Nazirah again — she acted as if I had only then done so, as if they had been with me — and I went back to our tent, drank till I was satisfied, and then I slept.

I slept the rest of that night and all that next day. Kisil came to me in the evening and woke me. He bathed me, washed my feet, and held me close, but spoke no word till I was dressed again and eating. I had not realized how hungry I was till Kisil brought me food.

"You were to blow the ram's horn, and speak the words I taught you." He was gazing at me with the question in his eyes.

"I did blow it." My voice was hoarse, as if I had been shouting for days. "And I did speak." Kisil smiled and offered me more water.

As I drank it, one of Kisil's eyebrows rose in familiar inquiry. "But you spoke other words as well."

"That was not me speaking," I rasped. "It was my voice — but those were not my words."

His eyes widened. "The — nothing?" he whispered. "The place where there was nothing?"

"Yes."

I told him what I have told you. Then I whispered, because I could barely speak: "Now I know."

He stroked my hair. "You know more than I, my love. He has touched my mind, and more than once. Perhaps."

"Perhaps?"

He shrugged. "You know, my sweet bird. I never —"

"You never feel Him," I breathed.

"No. And so I do not know, still, if it was His thought, or my own." He smiled. "But he never used my voice." When I opened my mouth, he added quickly, "Not like that."

I lifted my hands. It was an effort. "That was the only time," I croaked. "It will not happen again, not for me. Not for anyone."

"Did He tell you that?"

"No. But I know. I think that one last word — 'Run!' — I think that was for you, Kisil, more than for me. He used me once, and will not use me again; but He wanted to return me to you." I touched his hand. "Now it is all up to you, Kisil," I rasped out in my rusty voice. "You must be His voice now."

And then, one more time, the last time, I felt words rising to my lips and coming from my mouth before I knew what they would be.

"There is no Nothing." I blinked, but I went on. "There is no Void. No one will ever go to that place again."

Kisil saw the surprise in my eyes that he had seen so many times before. Then he looked back at the Mountain and nodded solemnly. "Yes... I understand. No more. This will never happen again. Not to anyone." He looked back at me and gave me that crooked smile I loved so much. "If it ever happened at all."

I sighed and moved into his arms. I croaked, "It did, Kisil. But it will not happen again, and it need not. They will not forget."

He clasped me to him, and I nuzzled his chest as he whispered. "No. They will not forget. Through all their generations — they will remember." He looked down at my face. "Do you know what you have done, my darling? What Ehyehuwah has done?" I shook my head weakly. "You have made another Covenant with this people, the Avru. I had not thought of that." His eyes grew distant. "Perhaps it was something like this when He spoke to Avram..."

I listened, or tried to; but soon I was asleep again.

I rested for the next few days, and my voice returned to normal. I had never been so tired. My sisters thought me ill, and we let them think so as I recovered.

I never told anyone about the dream of my father, not till this day, not even Kisil. I am not certain why; but I felt that that was for me only, between me and my father. Only now, when I am telling this story, do I reveal it. The story should be complete, and my father should be honored as he deserves.

Kisil went up on the Mountain again, but when he returned with the Tablets, they bore the words I had spoken, and not those he had written. Those tablets, I saw later; he had prepared them while I waited on the Mountain, but after the people heard the Voice, he had smashed them.

I examined the tablets closely. They were unlike any others that have ever been, I am sure. The letters were *raised* from the surface, and were not carved or drawn by any tool. The stone of the tablets was black, and rough and sandy on the front surface, while the back was smooth and almost polished.

I saw the tiny blisters on Kisil's arms, but I said nothing. I think I know how the tablets were made — and they were, indeed made by the fire of God Himself.

All who wished to could come and see the stones, and they did, and wondered. I asked Kisil why there were two. He showed me that the name of God, Ehyehuwah, was included in the first five of the Laws, but not in the last five. The first tablet was holier than the second, though both came from God through Kisil's hand. "And your mouth," he would whisper with a smile.

The new law, the law of the Sabbath, was a great gift. I think we all realized that, even at the time. A day to do no work, to be with our families, to love them and be thankful

— I wondered why Kisil and my father had not made more of the idea. And the last, about craving that which belongs to our neighbors — well, that was a puzzle to me, but Kisil told us all that it was to remind us that evil begins in our thoughts, long before we act on them.

The people made a golden box to carry the stones, for no one dared to touch them but Kisil. When they made the new Tent of Meeting to hold the box, where Kisil would commune with Ehyehuwah, a cloud of black smoke rose from the ground where they placed it, then went away again. The people said that Ehyehuwah had come to his new dwelling — and Kisil never told anyone that he had set a lamb to roast there, in the earth beneath it, not thinking of any such effect. But, indeed, after that day the Mountain spoke no more, nor ever did again that I have ever heard. The fire in the rock had gone out.

That was the last of the miracles, as people called them — or so we thought at the time. There had been one more, but we only learned of it afterward.

One day, Gamba and Akoko were at our tent, and we were laughing at some antic of our boys. I noticed that Gamba was not laughing, but gazing thoughtfully at the Mountain. "What is it, Gamba?" I asked. "Do you see something?"

He turned to me and shook his head with a small smile, not the enormous grin of which we had grown so fond. "No," he said. "I was wondering something about what I heard — that day."

Kisil cocked his head. "What is that, my friend?"

"How anyone understood it."

Kisil and I looked at each other. "What do you mean?" he asked.

"It was in the language of Kush," said the big man. "We understood it, of course, over where we are camped. But we wondered how others did. Our tongue is not well known here."

"But —" Kisil began.

I saw Miryam walking nearby. "Wait a moment," I said. "Miryam!"

She approached us, her dignified air intact as always.

Kisil had caught my thought. "In what language did Ehyehuwah speak from the Mountain, my sister?"

She blinked. "Why, in the tongue of the Avru, of course." We all stared at each other, mouths open.

Gamba laughed, then nodded and grinned. He pointed. "Ask him," he rumbled. A red-haired fellow with a great red beard was leading a donkey through the tents not far away.

"He spoke in my own tongue," the man said. Then he blinked. "I did not think of it at the time — but He spoke the language of the rocky hills where I was born, far to the North."

We rose and walked through the camp. Everywhere we asked, it was the same: Greek, barbarian, desert tongues, Egyptian, even the strange singing languages spoken by the ones with almond eyes from the East. All heard the Words in their own tongue.

"What language did you hear, Kisil?" I asked.

He thought. "I do not remember," he finally said. "I know many. It seemed to be —" He gave up and shook his head. "I cannot say."

Of all the things I saw and heard in my years with Kisil, I think that was the strangest. I did not understand it then, and I do not understand it now. A true miracle, perhaps? Or just a trick of human minds, which are and always have been the greatest miracles of all? I do not know.

We began to keep the Sabbath. On the seventh day after the Ten Words were given, we rested. Miryam and the elders had kept the tradition of which day was the seventh from long ages past, and the day was the same. Kisil, and Miryam, and the elders would teach the people, and we would feast and sing and tell stories.

We stayed there, in the shadow of the Mountain, for almost a year. Indeed, we celebrated the Deliverance from Egypt there, before the Mountain, at that same full moon of spring. We roasted lambs in the ground, ate unleavened bread, drank wine, and told the story. Fifty days after that celebration — seven Sabbaths — we celebrated again, this time for the giving of the Laws, still in the shadow of the Mountain where they were given.

And one Sabbath after that, we were striking our tents and preparing for our journeys through the Wilderness. No one knew, then, how long they would last.

84

There was much that happened after that, but you have heard the tales; and those tales are true, for the most part. There were battles, and plagues, and snakes, and enemies, and suffering, and wanderings. There were more rebellions, and more complaining, and opportunities gained and lost.

We stayed at one place so long, our children grew up and became adults there, and some thought it would be our home always. It was a lovely place, an oasis of palm trees and springs of water that never ran dry. We called it Kadesh, a name which means something like 'Holy.' We buried Aron there, and later Basia and Miryam. But finally the day came when we moved on, even from there.

After many more travels, and many more trials, the glorious day came when our journeying was over. The Avru — and the strangers who had joined us and became Avru themselves — finally entered into the Land that had been promised to the Father of the Avru, to Avram himself. The earth shook on that day, and the river there at the border of the Land stopped flowing. The people crossed over on dry land, just as they did at the Sea. The people called that a miracle too — but I have seen the river go dry since.

They settled there with little trouble. For the most part, I am told, the people simply found places to live, and lived there peacefully with their neighbors — some of whom were kin from long before the Twelve Sons went down to Egypt.

Still, there were some battles. Gamba fell in one of them, pierced by a spear beneath the walls of Jericho before they fell in the earthquake. His son Nomba grew up to be as big as his father, or nearly, and was as faithful a friend. Kisil gave Hosheah a new name, Yehoshuah, and named him as his successor to lead the Avru when they entered the Land, for Kisil did not go with them.

Nor did I. Here, in the very place where my friend Zev writes this, I watched my husband set off up Mount Nevo, this hill that they call a mountain.

My husband was very, very old by that time, but still vital, still as strong and virile as men half his age or even younger. His eyes were clear, his voice strong, his grip firm. When he set out, he wore a simple white robe, without pockets or sash, and his dear feet were bare. He carried no staff and no waterskin, and wore nothing on his head. I remember I held him close, and I wept a little.

"Now, Tzipporah. Our time was long, and it was good."

"Every day of it, my love," I whispered into his chest. His beard was white by then, and long. I felt it on my cheek, and I wanted to feel it forever.

"But it is time for me to go, my sweet wild bird. You know why."

And I did. He had felt the pain in his chest growing stronger. Every day it was harder for him to breathe. The blessing had been given him, he said, of knowing when his end was near.

"And I must die alone. I must have no grave, no tomb, no resting place known to anyone. I must have no shrine. No memorial. It is not me they must remember, my wild bird. It is the Law of Ehyehuwah." The wisest of our people, in their councils, had already begun to add to the Law by then — but then that was what Kisil had intended.

I do not betray him when I tell of these things. The last words he spoke to me were these:

"A day will come when you must tell the story, Tzipporah. It should not be concealed forever. When that day comes, my sweet, wise, lovely bird — and you will know when it does — tell the truth." I promised him that I would, and now I have kept my promise.

We knew it was time. No one else was there with us, on that day. We were alone, as he had planned. He kissed me, one last time, long and sweetly — and then, with one last squeeze of my hand, he left my side and began walking toward the lower slopes.

"I love you," I called after him. And as I knew he would, he stopped and looked back. His mouth formed the words, "I love you," but without sound. We smiled at each other then, both of us remembering. Then he turned and walked toward the gentle slope before him.

That was the last time I saw my Kisil. I went back inside our tent, as he had told me — we had a tent then; this little house was built for me long after — so I would not have to watch him struggling to climb the rocks. I longed for one more sight of him, but I did what he told me, as I always had.

Almost always. There was that one time, before the fire in the rock, when I did not and spoke words that were not the same I had been given, though that was not my own choice.

But that day, I went inside, and I wept, and I prayed, and I thanked Ehyehuwah for sending him to me, and for the long years we had together. I missed him already, and I have missed him ever since.

Mount Nevo, this mountain is called. It is no fire-mountain, no Mountain of God. It is just a high place, near the river. Kisil wanted to see the Land before he died, and I hope he did. He went up of his own will, and alone. If he was buried, Ehyehuwah Himself buried him.

The rest of Avram's children, and those who traveled with them, went on across the river to their Promised Land. May Ehyehuwah bless them, always; but I chose to stay here. When my time comes, I will go up the mountain too. I believe, I hope, that I will know when that day comes. Will I see my Kisil again, and look into those gray eyes that were always so gentle when they looked into mine? I do not know. But I hope that too.

85

And that is where my story ends. Some will read this and sneer, "So! God never spoke from the Mountain. It was only the voice of a woman, magnified by a cavern." They may think as they wish. That has always been so. But I was there, and the words that I spoke were not the words that we had prepared. Some had never been thought nor written by any man or woman, not even me, before I spoke them. I know that — but that is all I know.

They say now that of all the Prophets of Ehyehuwah, only Kisil ever spoke to Him face to face, as a man does to his friend. I think that Kisil would have laughed at that; but perhaps it was true, even so. No one but Kisil ever knew, or could know, what it was like for him, and he himself seemed doubtful to the very end.

He once told me, "I am a man like any other man, my sweet bird. I have only done what I knew I had to do, and things happened as they happened. If The One made them happen, that is well; but even if it was all coincidence, and even if He is — only *us*, only we ourselves, our dreams and hopes and highest, best thoughts and desires — and even if we ourselves have *imagined* the Good and the True and the Holy — they are still Good, and True, and even Holy, all the same. And if He is — He is *Truth."*

And I think that all that is so. What is God like? What kind of Being is He? Is he truly There — or is He something Other, something that no one has ever guessed at? I do not know; but once, long ago, for just a moment —

for one blazing moment that I shall never, ever, forget — I knew, and had no doubts. None at all. But that moment was long, long ago, and shall not come again.

As Kisil said himself: *I* may not be real — *you* may not be real — but *He is.*

And what He is — is *Truth.*

86

"And that is all, Zev."

His reed scratched on the parchment for a few more heartbeats, and then it stopped. "Surely there is more," he said softly.

"Oh, there is. But what I have told you — those were the things that you wanted to hear, were they not? The truth of what happened?"

He sat in silence for a few heartbeats. "I suppose they were... But I still do not have the answers I sought."

"I know. But those, I cannot give. It is as I told you when we began. Those things happened, but they did not happen in the way of the tales. What these things mean — that, you must work out for yourself."

"But —" He hesitated, in confusion, though not in anger. "Was it you who spoke from the Mountain, or was it — Ehyehuwah?"

I smiled. "I was there, Zev. And even I do not know. At the time, I was sure it was He. But that was many years ago, more than I can count. Now, looking back..."

I bowed my head, then lifted it and turned my face toward his voice again. "Was it truly He, or was I overcome by heat and fumes and the moment? Did I speak words given by Him, or did they well up from my mind like the fire welled up from the rock? Did I truly see the Void, and the Fire of God — or was it all a dream, like the dream of my father?" I shook my head. "I was there, Zev," I said again, "and even I do not know." I shrugged, and felt that catch in my shoulder once more. I will not feel it for much longer, I thought.

I went on: "Were any of the things that happened — the Plagues, the Draining of the Sea, the food and water and meat in the desert, the earth opening to swallow Desan and his rebels — was any of that a miracle of Ehyehuwah? Or were they — accidents? Things that happened at the right time and the right place? Even Kisil did not know, not even on the day that he went up this mountain."

I waited for a few breaths, but Zev said nothing. I could almost feel his confusion. "I can tell you what Kisil said, Zev, if it will help."

"What? Tell me," he asked quickly.

He said, *"It does not matter."*

A breath passed, then another. "What?"

"It does not matter, Zev. The Avru were freed, and they live in their own land now. The Laws stand on their own. Whatever happened — those things are true. All truth is God's truth, and those things are true.

"Kisil learned it on the Mountain, Zev. We are not to know Him. That knowledge is more than we can understand, and more than we need. We are to do what we know to be right — and when we do not know, we are to do our best to find what is right, together, as best we can. The rest, we leave to Him.

"What else can there be?"

There was silence for a few more breaths. Then: "What now?" he asked.

"It is time for me to follow my husband, and go up the Mountain."

I expected some argument, but perhaps he understood me better than I thought. "I will miss you," he said.

I smiled. "And there, let this book end."

87

Thc words of Zev, Tzipporah's friend:

Tzipporah, the mother of my heart, went up Mount Nevo that very afternoon. She went barefoot, in a plain white garment, with only her stick. I watched her for a time, but she climbed as if she could see.

I leave her to the One who lives and acts, but remains hidden.

May her memory be a blessing. I know it was a blessing to me.

The End

Afterword

Afterword

On August 26, 1883, Krakatoa, a volcanic island in the Java Strait, exploded in a massive eruption. The sound of that eruption was heard at a distance of six hundred miles. The waves resulting from it circled the globe seven times. Tens of thousands of people in neighboring areas were killed.

In subsequent days the disaster produced phenomena remarkably similar to the Ten Plagues in the Book of Exodus. Most obvious, perhaps, would be the pillar of fire by night and of smoke by day; but there were also massive rains, enormous dust storms, fiery stones falling from the sky, fouled water, ecological disruptions, widespread disease of humans and domestic animals, and so on. There was also a *tsunami*, wherein the sea falls away, then returns in a massive wave. But perhaps most strikingly, it was also reported that there was *darkness* for several days after the Krakatoa event. The air was so filled with soot and smoke that fires and torches cast no light. It was a darkness that could be *felt*. The similarities to the Plague narratives are very striking indeed.

And with good reason. A volcanic island in the eastern Mediterranean exploded in a similar manner *circa* 1600 BCE, with a force four to six times that of the Krakatoa eruption. This is a matter of geophysical history, verified by copious physical and archaeological evidence. The remnants of that island form a small archipelago which is today called Santorin, the largest island of which is called Thera. Besides its obvious relevance to the Exodus narrative, the Thera explosion is thought to be the origin of the legends of Atlantis.

This novel differs from the traditional account of the Exodus in many ways; but the Exodus, as depicted in the Hebrew Bible, simply could not have happened. This fact has been accepted by serious scholars of both history and the Bible for many years, and for many reasons.

For instance: the number of men who left Egypt under the leadership of Moses, according to the Bible, numbered "about six hundred thousand, besides women and children" (Exodus 12:37). That would work out to a total in the neighborhood of three million people — which was, roughly speaking, the entire population of Egypt at the time.

It has also been observed that such a huge migration would inevitably have left traces in the remarkably complete Egyptian records. Perhaps: but those records may not be as reliable as many think. There is no Egyptian record of the Thera eruption, either — and that *happened*.

In any case, it seems clear that if any such migration or relocation took place around this time, it must have involved a much smaller group of refugees than is recorded in the Bible. It is not at all unlikely that a relatively small group of people might have taken advantage of the chaos and confusion following the cataclysmic Thera eruption to flee their bondage in Egypt and return to Canaan, whether they were actual slaves or merely "enslaved" by debt, social isolation, or even poverty. There are, as it happens, archaeological traces of such a mass migration during this time — and in fact, there are traces of more than one.

What we have in the Book of Exodus — and in the entire Torah, the first five books of the Hebrew Bible — is, according to most scholars, a compilation of multiple *oral traditions,* tales which were handed down from one generation to the next for centuries before finally being combined and then written down by some unknown editor. Many of these traditional oral tales appear to come from other, and earlier, cultures. This may explain why the Flood narratives bear a remarkable resemblance to, among others, the epic account of *Gilgamesh*.

But the Bible is not the only collection of such tales, even in Jewish tradition. The *Midrashim* are collections of Jewish traditional stories intended to explain or expand some of the stories in the Hebrew Bible. They are often acknowledged to be apocryphal — teaching stories or fables

— but some are thought to represent or hint at real memories which are thus preserved in the tradition.

In the *Midrash,* Moses is said to have had *ten* names. The Torah is said to have recorded only the name "Moses" as a tribute to Moses's Egyptian foster mother, who is said to have been a good woman who refused to worship idols, as well as being a good mother to him. Of the other nine names, most appear to have been given to Moses long after the fact as honorifics recognizing his achievements. Only one, *Yekusiel* or *Yekuthiel*, meaning "Hope," seems appropriate for a newborn infant, and in some of the documents, that is said to have been Moses's true birth name. The nickname for Yekusiel is "Kisil."

In Jewish tradition, Moses was a young man when he fled Egypt as a fugitive, and was eighty years old when he came to Midian and met and married Tzipporah. The Bible does not say where he went or what he did in the intervening years; but the story of Kisil's adventures as a military leader and royal regent in Kush is drawn from the Midrash as well, though the story there is much longer and more detailed.

The pronunciation of the Name, "Ehyehuwah," is admittedly a guess, though I think it a fair one. Some scholars of Kabbalah — a mystical tradition not actually part of the Jewish religion, but long associated with it — believe that the Name was a four-syllable word, and have come up with a similar guess which I have declined to use in this book.

Besides telling the story of the Exodus in a more realistic manner, without the usual spectacular "special effects" and obviously supernatural miracles, it will have been noticed that God is "offstage," so to speak, in this book, in much the same way that He is "offstage" in our own real lives. That is, among other things, the point of this novel. Perhaps God was no more present to Moses than He is to ordinary people of the present day. Perhaps God spoke to the "Avru" – the Hebrews – in the same way that He speaks to us, in perhaps the only way that He has ever spoken: through the words of good and thoughtful people who are consumed, not by supernatural visions and ecstasies, but by an overwhelming hunger for *justice*, for *peace*, and above all, for *truth*. According to the Talmud, these are the three things by which the world is sustained.

Now, no one can say that there are no such things as "miracles." We have all seen things that cannot be explained, mysterious healings and the like. Few, though, have ever seen anything like the wholesale abrogations of the laws of physics and Nature like those we see in the Bible. Far more common in most people's lives, I think, are experiences that Carl Jung called *synchronicities:* apparently ordinary and natural, if perhaps unusual, events that occur at precisely the right *time*. The perception of these events rather depends on the belief one brings to them. A "believer" will likely see them as divine intervention, while a nonbeliever will dismiss them as coincidences. Neither perception, of course, can be either proven or disproven. That judgment must be a subjective one, and must remain so.

Given the unquestionable historicity of the eruption/explosion of Thera, I have long suspected that the man we call Moses — if there was such a man — experienced those phenomena as synchronicities, natural. though *apparently* miraculous, events that occurred at the most opportune *times*. Perhaps God never spoke directly to him, any more than God speaks directly to us; perhaps the voice of God, for Moses, just as it is (or can be) for us, was his own conscience — or his own reason, when he applied it with humility and wisdom.

Did God give the Ten Commandments — or are they a list of laws formulated and drawn up by ancient people, or perhaps Moses himself?

Does it matter? What difference would it make if we knew? Do the laws not stand on their own, as the first of many efforts to define justice and give a name to good and evil?

Does God exist? Who, or what, exactly, is God?

Again I ask: *Does it matter?* What difference would it make if we knew? And perhaps even more to the point – how could that information ever be proven or verified?

Perhaps we are not *meant* to know. The rabbis and sages of old taught that trying to define God – formulating a list of God's powers and attributes and thoughts and intentions – is itself a kind of *idolatry*: constructing a mental image of God, then bowing down to that human-made *mental con-struction* as if it were God Himself.

In Jewish tradition, the nature of God – Who He is, or what kind of being He is, if He is a "being" at all, cannot be known. God is the *Ein Sof*, the *totally Other*, different from anything in this Universe or anything that we know. As Arthur C. Clarke once said of the Universe – God is not only stranger than we think; He is stranger than we *can* think.

It is not our business, nor our job, to think about God. God can take care of Himself.

Our business is this world, and our job is to make it a better one, for our brothers and sisters and children and grandchildren, and for ourselves; to seek out and work for the three pillars of the Universe — Truth, and Justice, and Peace. In *this* world, in *this* life. If there is another – and I, for one, hope that there is – that is God's concern, and not our own.

I thank you for reading. May you know Truth, and Justice – and Peace.

Charles Henderson Norman
September 12, 2015